DEADLY LIAISONS

OTHER BOOKS BY JEFF LENBURG

Peekaboo: The Story of Veronica Lake, Revised and Expanded Edition

The Book of Duh!

How to Make a Million Dollars With Your Voice (Or Lose Your Tonsils Trying), Second Edition with Gary Owens

Walk to Freedom: Kriegsgefangenen #6410: Prisoner of War by John L. Lenburg (Edited by)

Renegade at Heart: An Autobiography with Lorenzo Lamas

The Three Stooges Scrapbook, Updated Edition

Career Opportunities in Animation

Genndy Tartakovsky: From Russia to Coming-of-Age Animator

Hayao Miyazaki: Japan's Premier Anime Storyteller

John Lasseter: The Whiz Who Made Pixar King

Walter Lantz: Made Famous By a Woodpecker

Matt Groening: From Spitballs to Springfield

William Hanna and Joseph Barbera: The Sultans of Saturday Morning

Walt Disney: The Mouse That Roared

Tex Avery: Hollywood's Master of Screwball Cartoons

The Facts on File Guide to Research, Second Edition

The Encyclopedia of Animated Cartoons, Third Edition

Who's Who in Animated Cartoons: An International Guide to Film and Television's Award-Winning and Legendary Animators

The Facts on File Guide to Research

Scared to Death: A Lori Matrix Hollywood Mystery

How to Make a Million Dollars With Your Voice (Or Lose Your Voice Trying) with Gary Owens

The Encyclopedia of Animated Cartoons, Second Edition

All the Gold in California and Other People, Places & Things with Larry Gatlin

The Encyclopedia of Animated Cartoons

Once a Stooge, Always a Stooge with Joe Besser and Greg Lenburg

Baseball's All-Star Game: A Game-By-Game Guide

Peekaboo: The Story of Veronica Lake

The Great Cartoon Directors

Dudley Moore: An Informal Biography

Dustin Hoffman: Hollywood's Antihero

The Three Stooges Scrapbook with Joan Howard Maurer and Greg Lenburg

The Encyclopedia of Animated Cartoon Series

Steve Martin: An Unauthorized Biography with Randy Skretvedt and Greg Lenburg

DEADLY LIAISONS

JEFF LENBURG

MOONWATER PRESS

DEADLY LIAISONS
Copyright © 2021 Jeff Lenburg
All rights reserved.

MOONWATER PRESS
P.O. Box 2061
Litchfield Park, AZ 85340

Library of Congress Control Number: 2021922790

Publisher's Cataloging-in-Publication Data
Lenburg, Jeff.
    Deadly liaisons / Jeff Lenburg.
    ISBN 9780996320665 (pbk.)
    ISBN 9780996320672 (ebook)
Subjects: LCSH: Murder -- Investigation -- Fiction. |
    Organized crime -- Fiction. | Prostitutes -- Fiction. |
    Hollywood (Los Angeles, Calif.) -- Fiction. | Palm
    Springs (Calif.) -- Fiction. | BISAC: FICTION /
    Mystery & Detective / Hard-Boiled. | FICTION /
    Mystery & Detective / Police Procedural. | FICTION /
    Thrillers / Crime.
Classification: LCC PS3612.E53 D43 2021 | DDC 813 L46--dc23
LC record available at https://lccn.loc.gov/2021922790

Front cover illustration credit: courtesy of Elegant Accents, Inc.

PRINTED IN THE UNITED STATES OF AMERICA

To Lynn Heise, forever in our hearts.

CONTENTS

1

Luke Beckett remembered only too well under what circumstances brought him to this god-forsaken place, Palm Springs. Lilly was her name, the beautiful seventeen-year-old hooker who looked like a young Scarlett Johansson. It was Lilly screaming her lungs out as her black pimp, Candycane, kept terrorizing her with a lighted cigarette, repeatedly burning her back where it wouldn't show when she was flat on her back with a john.

That night, Candycane was giving it to Lilly good when a tough-as-nails Hollywood vice squad cop busted through the door. Later, investigators would find eleven cigarette burns on Lilly's back. But not before they found Candycane lying draped over a broken coffee table, his jaw broken, one eye staring at the dirty ceiling of Lilly's trick room off Hollywood Boulevard, the other almost punched out of his head, two of his front teeth almost five feet away, an arm-twisted underneath his long, lean body, and, of course, quite dead.

Even Lilly, in her semi-drugged and hysterical state, could tell that. She knew the moment Luke Beckett came bursting on the scene that Candycane was a dead man. Always too quick with those strong hands, many a hard-working pimp had been punished illegally by his rock-hard fists.

Everyone knew Beckett hated pimps. The pimps knew it best of all. They gave him a wide berth as he patrolled his beat. He was a cop who didn't play the game. Hell, play the game? He wasn't even in the game. They could buy this one or rent him. They could con that one, maybe let him have that special girl for the weekend, or pay him off to look the other way. Their kind, for the most part, were reasonable, flexible. Not this one, not Beckett.

Carol Six had bedded almost everyone in Hollywood Vice. But as much as she liked to brag—and maybe even lie a little—she couldn't get next to Beckett. She wanted him more than anyone else. She would have paid him, but no dice. He had busted her at least six times in the last two years. He was terrifying Hollywood Boulevard and the Strip, and no one could hand him as much as a cigar.

Everyone on the street in Hollywood knew they couldn't do business with him. He was like some damned Avenging Angel. They couldn't buy him, lease him, or throw themselves on his mercy. He didn't have any.

Beckett knew before he opened his eyes on Monday morning that it had happened again. The accumulated sweat on his forehead from the hottest July day on record confirmed it. So did the sticky feeling in the lower part of his broad back. He had forgotten to turn down his air conditioner to a cool 75 degrees again last night, and his mobile home was like a goddamned hothouse with the already hot morning desert sun streaming through his small bedroom window.

With a groan, the Palm Springs police lieutenant swung his five-foot, ten-inch frame around the bed and winced as his feet hit the floor encountering something that felt like broken glass. Nothing more than broken peanut shells. Partial evidence of a long, boring Sunday night of quiet, solitary drinking, of waking and sleeping, of munching on peanuts in between drinks, and snapping the TV on and off, repelled and fascinated by turns with all-night movies on the classic movie channel that shows so many commercials during each broadcast it should be called American More Commercials network.

Beckett had survived another restless night haunted by images of his sordid past on the Hollywood vice squad beat. That was after falling asleep for the third or fourth time after watching What's-His-Name, the "King of Used Car Dealers," waltz across the screen of his wall mounted 32-inch 4K ultra high-definition television no less than seven times in a single hour trying to sell his "Gold Star Buys of the Week."

Seconds after waking, Beckett stretched his arms above his head and tried to shake the sleep from his gray-blue eyes. This morning was no different from any other. That whole bunch of ugly characters, flashbacks from the not-so distant past, had flooded his memory from the time he went to bed and woke up. Like scenes from some bad movie he couldn't forget, they kept playing repeatedly his mind more vivid than before. He kept reminding himself: He wasn't in Hollywood. He was in the sun-drenched, half-baked southern California desert, "God's waiting room," so named because of the high number of seniors that endlessly flocked here to retire and live out their final days in peace and tranquility in this earthly paradise until their number was up.

The sooner Beckett got used to the idea, the better. But for Luke Beckett, accepting change of any kind didn't come easily.

Some little crawly thing suddenly walked over Beckett's big toe—over it, down the side of it and up his next biggest toe as bold as could be. Beckett looked down and half-grinned at the audacity of the little bugger, silently congratulating it for its chutzpah before crushing it with the heel of his right foot. It couldn't do business with him, either.

Picking himself out of bed, Beckett shuffled to his feet and headed straight to the shower and hopped inside. The sudden jolting sensation of the jet spray from the high-pressured large chrome shower head felt like a million tiny needles pricking him in the face as he lathered up and got ready for another boring day in the hot desert community that was setting new records of daily highs that week in the upper 120-degree range.

An ex-big city cop, superbly trained, he was used to the fast action. But here, during the summer months, there wasn't enough action in this tiny burg to keep his blood circulating. If he handled every assignment on every shift, he would still be finishing the crossword puzzle in the *Desert Sun* halfway through the morning.

In Hollywood, Beckett was an authority figure, a power. Here, the superstars of entertainment, sports and business world were about as impressed with his uniform as they were with a bellhop's. On the Hollywood Strip, they used to come up to him quaking, asking if they were clean with him and could they help, could they rat on their mother or perform some other noble deed, anything to please him, to get on his good side.

In downtown Palm Springs, the only time a citizen stopped him was to ask if he would like to guard presents at their daughter's wedding reception on his day off, while the tourists, unbelievably lost in this tight-knit town that has only a few main streets, always wanted to know how to get to the worst restaurants, the ones their friends from Iowa had raved about.

Beckett dressed at a deliberately slow pace. It was somewhere around 7 A.M. and his alarm clock hadn't gone off yet. He stood there, hopelessly remembering better days. They weren't that long ago, either. What was it now, two and a half...three years? Yeah, three years. It wasn't boring then. Not then. It sure as hell wasn't.

Her face flashed through his mind. God, what a face. She had everything he had wanted in a woman: The natural corn silk blonde hair, the impossibly bright blue eyes, and the laughing mouth. Plus, she had a body second to none: beautiful high full breasts with a tiny waist, and long, sensuous legs. She could have been anything. Anything. A model or a movie star, but she had been his wife. It didn't seem possible it could ever have happened. Not now, not three years later. But it did happen, and he lived with the memory of it almost every waking minute of every boring day.

Marcia...Marcia Crane was her name, heir to the Crane fortune of Philadelphia. Only there was no fortune. The old man had become involved with that notorious international cartel. The incident brought scandal to his company and finally financial ruin and social disgrace to himself and his family. Then, one night, he kissed his wife and daughter good night, downed a Vodka martini in a single gulp, went quietly upstairs and blew his brains out.

A sensitive young woman, Marcia was unable to handle all that. She dropped out of her second year at Smith University and, unable to face her friends, fled to the west coast where she met and married a good-looking young Irish cop making a name for himself on the Los Angeles Police Department.

What was it old Capt. Cal Murphy used to say about him? A comer. That was it...a comer. Cal was sure Luke Beckett would be a chief one day, or at the very least, a deputy chief. Marcia had faith in him, too. But she hated their lifestyle. Hated their tiny apartment in West Hollywood. Hated having to count the pennies a young policeman makes as a newly made plainclothes detective. Hated his seemingly permanent assignment on the vice squad, assigned to the rat hole called Hollywood, filled to the gunnels with teenage whores and their black pimps, users and pushers and freaks of every description.

It was all flooding back to Beckett again this morning. Memories of the woman he still loved. Memories of street encounters with every scum of the earth. Memories of his reign as self-made "king" of the Hollywood jungle. If only he could forget. He wanted to, but, as hard as he tried, the images didn't go away easily.

Beckett completed dressing and immediately checked out the slim pickings in the refrigerator. Whipping open the door, he recoiled at what he saw. It was like a small bacterial jungle inside. Low-fat milk four days past its expiration date that poured out in white lumpy chunks so repulsive that not even a stray cat would drink it. A half loaf of wheat bread with an invasion of green and white bumps sprouting from its spongy, pale brown texture that looked like small craters on the planet Uranus. Orange juice so bitter that the acid alone would bore a whole big enough deep enough to the center of the earth.

Beckett slammed the door, sickened by the lethal smell. He thought not. He decided instead he would stop at his usual hangout, Bob's Big Boy, and have their daily "Breakfast Special"—two eggs, sunny-side up, hash browns, two strips of bacon, with a cup of coffee, black with no sugar—before reporting to work at 9 o'clock in the morning. Already, Beckett's mouth was watering.

Stepping outside, Beckett found it wasn't any cooler. Tiny beads of sweat again formed on his brow, and large sweat rings saturated his clean white shirt. Even the soles of his black-oxford shoes had turned into putty from the swells of heat rising beneath his feet from the parched desert floor.

Beckett winced in the direct glare of the sun, shading his eyes with the palm of his hand. He groaned, then cursed himself again, this time for having forgotten to park his black Ford Explorer under the solitary tree next to his mobile home that provided a reasonable amount of shade, something scarce in this desert oasis.

Only ten feet away from the appointed spot, his sport utility vehicle was like an oven inside. It was going to be another one of those days, he told himself, 118 degrees, in the shade. Nothing happening in town. Nothing happening at the station. Nothing happening anywhere.

Beckett turned the key to the ignition and headed straight into town. He paid little attention to scenery: the immaculately manicured lawns, the impeccably clean driveways, the palm tree lined boulevards or the majestic San Jacinto mountains with its incredible tramway ride to the top. He had seen it all a hundred times before. He wasn't some tourist who just hopped off the bus from Kansas. He was here, not by his choice, but by the roll of the dice...Someone else's.

The car radio blared a tear-jerking ballad, the latest Miranda Lambert hit, about a couple rekindling their lost love. In no mood to listen, Beckett flicked the radio off. He needed no reminders of what he once had when he was the cock of the walk and

Hollywood vice was a human zoo, a revolving door of life's walking wounded, all trying to get a piece of the action before the action got a piece of them. They were as fine a collection of vermin as had ever crawled out of the sewer.

Big Mary: The 340-pound pig-in-a-dress who specialized in quickie abortions in her back-room apartment on Argyle Boulevard. Not quite up to American Medical Association standards, Big Mary operated with an ever-present cigarette dangling from the corner of her mouth. She wasn't good, but she was cheap. The girls who needed her often didn't have more than a couple of bucks to rub together, so she took their notes, or whatever else they had. Downtown vice was sure she killed at least three girls, maybe four, but nobody could prove it.

The Hawk: Paternal type, mid-forties, steel gray hair whose headquarters were the Greyhound bus station downtown. The Hawk could spot an arriving runaway or star-struck teenager from Nebraska, hoping to be discovered the minute she got off the bus. He had a thousand routines for winning their confidence. But his most effective was telling them he was waiting for his daughter. She was supposed to be on that bus. She was joining him from Nebraska. He had finally, reluctantly, agreed to let her get into show business at his studio, which was Universal, Warner Bros., or Sony Pictures.

"Such a nice, fatherly man, such a good teacher," Beckett thought to himself. The low-down scum had turned out hundreds of underage hookers and was the pimps' "Man of the Year" every year.

"Fatherly type. Good teacher, my ass," Beckett snarled aloud.

Then there was Trumpet, so-called because she specialized in giving motorists and truck drivers what they desired on the spot. Curb service, they called it.

Finally, Godzilla, the ape-man: He used to be a professional wrestler and was now a professional mugger who preyed upon drugged out kids and elderly men and women living in Hollywood on slender pensions.

The tourists drove up and down Hollywood and cruised Sunset Boulevard, saying how colorful it all was. It was colorful, all right. A never-ending passing parade of predators and victims, except for the scum who made child-porn movies in the backs of stores. The hookers worked hard for what they got. Then they turned it over to the pimp and, if he was in a good mood, he gave them a few bucks or told them he loved them. Business was almost always good. But when it slacked off, he would beat a girl or two, just to set an example and inspire the others to greater efforts on his behalf.

Heading north on Indian Avenue to the station, an ear-piercing squeal of metal jamming against metal suddenly jarred Beckett back to reality. Traffic unexpectedly slowed to a screeching halt. Emerging from his daydream, Beckett slammed on the brakes and left a trail of burning rubber behind. The Ford Explorer momentarily swerved and buckled until he quickly regained control and stopped a mere centimeter short of the first painted white line in the crosswalk ahead.

A kindly, gangly senior citizen, unaware of the near calamity that he caused, had entered the cobble-stoned walkway where he shouldn't have been. He was pushing a small cart of groceries in front of him. Walking slowly and deliberately, with a noticeable limp, the man made the long trek across to the other side.

Beckett watched with great curiosity and concern as the elderly man passed in front of the dust-bitten hood of his Ford Explorer. The man looked every bit of his eighty years of age, dressed in clothes that looked like Goodwill specials and so badly wrinkled Beckett wondered if they had been washed.

The wrinkled-faced pedestrian happened to look up and caught Beckett's curious stare. Smiling sweetly, he waved.

For the first time that morning, Beckett smiled. He waved back. It was a knee-jerk reaction on his part, but he was sincere about it. Despite his rough exterior, deep inside Beckett was compassionate when it came to the elderly, knowing someday he, too, would grow old. Should he be so lucky.

The man, despite obvious health challenges, made it to the other side as traffic motored ahead. Beckett proceeded with extreme caution, keeping a watchful eye on the frail gentleman, mindful of his safety. The man limped slowly to a bus bench and instantly collapsed, overcome by the sweltering heat. Removing the straw hat from his balding head, he repeatedly fanned himself, providing little comfort under the scorching desert sun, as he waited for the next bus to arrive to take him home.

Immediately, Beckett's smile faded from his chiseled features as thoughts about his past returned, picking up where he had left. He was working the beat in Hollywood. After only six months, he was already a legend. After a year and a half, Hollywood was his town. People were calling it, Beckettville. He couldn't stop the hooking or doping or anything else. Who could? But he sure as hell could make it tough on everybody and he did.

Suddenly feeling jittery, Beckett popped open a new pack of cigarettes. He barely started the morning without smoking at least one pack before breakfast. It was the only thing that seemed to wake him up.

Holding the wheel with one hand and the cigarette lighter with the other, Beckett instantly lit up. He inhaled and exhaled all his anxiety in one puff.

"What's done is done," he thought to himself. If so, then why couldn't he forget? When would he ever be freed from his past?

Beckett took a few short puffs and quickly mashed out the cigarette in the ashtray full of remnants from the day before. He was trying to quit, on his own, but considering he had tried at least a half a dozen times before, he knew the odds of him succeeding were not strongly in his favor.

Beckett couldn't shake the idea from his head. The one man who could have saved him was Capt. Terry Bowman, who was in charge when Beckett was on Hollywood Vice. A shit-kicker from Alabama, he had the brains of a gnat in Beckett's opinion but clout that wouldn't quit. Bowman never knew what was going on in the street and didn't want to know.

Years before, when he was a young patrolman on vice, Bowman fell in love with a hooker he had busted and decided to reform her. So, Bowman and Lucy Mae Swope were married, and she stopped selling her body. She went to the barter system. Ambitious for her young husband, Lucy Mae worked all her feminine wiles on Bowman's superiors, which accounted for Bowman's fast rise through the ranks of the department to captain.

The real boss of the district, Beckett remembered, was Maybelle Craper, also behind his sudden fall from grace. Craper was tops in her profession. She earned a six-figure income from running girls to the swells in Beverly Hills and Bel Air, as well as serving the Valley husbands-on-the-make who cruised up and down Hollywood Boulevard looking for the underage hookers who bore no earthly resemblance to their dumpy wives.

Beckett could thank Craper for his problems, he thought, and that smart attorney she hired. "What was his name? Teller...Bob Teller...that was it." That night on the Hollywood Strip, Teller walked up to Beckett and asked him if he had ever read anyone his rights. Beckett had answered quietly that, of course, he had. He had even given him a demonstration.

That was the night Sweets, the Argyle Street pimp, was feeling good and decided to treat two of his best girls to a nice dinner at Diamond Jack's near Highland Boulevard. They happened to be coming out of the rear of the restaurant on their way to the parking lot as Beckett and Teller were coming in. Beckett walked up to Sweets and drove a hard right into his stomach. Sweets almost left the ground. He sat down hard, his eyes bulging out of their sockets and his hands clutching the pit of his stomach. Beckett leaned down and looked the terrified man straight in the eyes.

"You have the right to remain silent," he said, quietly.

Sweets exercised his right to remain silent for almost four hours. He was unable to talk, and some people said Beckett didn't have a sense of humor.

Teller was visibly shocked and, for a moment, thought he might throw up.

When he recovered his composure, he said angrily, "That was a disgusting thing to do."

Beckett wasn't in an apologetic mood.

"That's not a man, that's a human leech and a sadist," Beckett shouted, red-faced, with the veins in his neck bulging out. "He's killed two girls so far and he'll probably kill a lot more."

"But you can't prove that he killed two girls," Teller countered, inferring otherwise.

"That's right."

"I see."

Beckett's lips tightened. He wasn't even angry when he hit Sweets. Now he was angry, talking to the incensed young liberal lawyer.

"No, you don't see. No intellectualizing goes on here. The street operates at gut level," Beckett tried to reason. "Sweets runs girls, turns fourteen-year-olds into custom cock suckers. At fifteen, they're junkies and at nineteen they're wishing they were eligible for Social Security. He specialized in virgins and cripples for the freakier freaks who come here to get off on their hang-ups."

"All of which," Teller snapped sharply, "doesn't excuse your un-professional behavior."

Beckett couldn't help himself and sarcastically rolled his eyes.

"Right."

Teller did what any good liberal attorney would do in this case. He turned the whole thing into a race issue.

"You hate blacks, don't you?"

"No," Beckett scoffed. "Only the ones who are into pimping."

Beckett smiled. The anger was leaving him, the veneer of cynicism was laminating its protective layer over his emotions again.

"You really think it's okay, part of your job, morally right, to assault an unarmed man on the street just on sight, just for kicks, just for the fun of it?" Teller asked incredulously.

"No," Beckett replied woodenly. "I was doing exactly what Sweets expected me to do. He does what he does, and I do what I do. Try this for irony: We understand each other."

Teller shook his head and let out a long audible sigh. He could tell Beckett was a handful.

"Oh, I understand something, too," Teller said. "You're the patron saint of the hookers and you hold court on the curb. You sentence pimps on hunches and guesses and you punish them on the street."

Beckett's eyes grew hard. He didn't like any attorney telling him how to do his business.

"There's one fella who will tell you he'd rather have it that way than go to court three times a week," Beckett growled.

"And who's that?"

"Sweets."

Teller shook his head again in disbelief.

"You're still dead wrong," he said curtly.

"Tell me that," Beckett retorted defiantly, "after Sweets turns out your daughter."

That's the way it was, then, Beckett pondered, as he kept his eyes straight on the road ahead. He owned the street and all the souls on it in Hollywood, and they thought he did, too. He rarely busted a hooker unless she threatened a john with a knife or a hatpin or razor. If a hooker rolled a john and he complained to Beckett, he could expect a little more understanding from a brick wall.

Beckett's unofficial ruling always sounded the same: "You just bought an education, asshole. Now go home to your wife and I won't bust you for soliciting prostitution."

Hardly any john ever got busted. Even though the johns did the soliciting nine times out of ten, it was the working girl who took the fall, and the john was released. Beckett never saw the equity in that system, and he fought a losing battle to change it. The hookers were the victims of the pimps, and the johns perpetuated the whole system. If there were no johns, there would be no hookers or pimps. That was the way it was.

Beckett lit up another cigarette. He knew quitting was out of the question, at least for the day. He couldn't help himself. Half the time he wasn't sure why he even needed another. It was a compulsive habit he couldn't seem to shake.

One thing Beckett knew for certain what happened in his past was irrelevant now and he needed to make peace with it all instead of letting it beat him up inside. That included the love of his life, his ex-wife, Marcia.

"Oh, god," he groaned, shaking his head to confirm how he felt. "Marcia."

As the nicotine rushed through his veins, Beckett thought hopelessly again about Marcia—the love they shared, why things went wrong. It was all so clear to him: Marcia wanted everything he could never give her. His credit cards had limits, which she reached. But his patience, only with Marcia, had no limits. He went into debt trying to keep her happy with material things. He only wanted the best for her. So did she.

Marcia was used to the best, he thought, long before that business with her father. The best and biggest homes in Philadelphia, the exclusive schools, the fine clothes, the most expensive cars, and highbrow friends.

Beckett understood all that. That was the worst part. He couldn't blame her for her tastes, for wanting what she was used to having. He didn't even blame her for leaving him. "What the hell was she leaving, anyway?" he thought. A struggling young cop with a dirty job and friends who were as coarse in their way as the people he kept scraping out of the gutter and stuffing into cells until their lawyers came to spring them and then tried to make an ass of him in court.

Beckett shook his head again, crushing the cigarette in his ashtray, now overflowing with butts of every size and description. The past was too painful to remember, yet too painful to forget. He had meted out justice the only way he could under the system, he thought. He worked every way around, over, under and near the system, but rarely in it. That was why they feared him so. They played the game, and he didn't. He made up his own game, with his own rules, and made them play it. It was rigged so the pimps and pushers and blood freaks and child porn creeps always lost, at least, temporarily. But everybody knew something else. They knew that one day the system would swallow Beckett and spit him out, and it did. When Beckett beat Candycane to death, celebrations rang out all along the street and from the highest rooftops. Nobody, but nobody, cared what happened to Candycane, one way or the other. He was just another super-pimp with steer horns on his bright white Lincoln Continental and a stable of beautiful young girls. But everybody knew, instinctively, that Beckett had crossed that little boundary that cops weren't supposed to cross. He had let his temper and his righteous indignation get the best of him.

Once Beckett crossed that line from investigation and arrest and began to play judge and jury, he was asking for trouble. He was always asking for trouble and, this time, he got his and got it good.

Beckett remembered the consequences vividly, trying to move to more cheerful subjects but there were one, as he motored on down Indian Avenue to grab breakfast.

There was no trial. Candycane didn't have a friend in the world. Lilly appeared before the coroner's inquest and the special hearing board. To her credit, she told the story as straight as she could remember it. Candycane was torturing her and accusing her of holding out on him, even though she wasn't. Beckett burst into the room and, well, the rest was history, he remembered.

They didn't fire him. They didn't have to. Captain Murphy had called him in after the hearing had determined that he somehow acted in self-defense and told him the facts of life.

"With this on your record, you're shit here for the rest of your working life," Murphy shouted in Beckett's ear. "You know that?"

Beckett quietly nodded in his place.

Captain Murphy continued to his tirade. He wasn't through.

"I can't make you quit. I can only suggest that unless you want to stay at your current pay grade until your hair turns gray and your teeth fall out and be given every shit assignment every commander can find for you, you get out now. Go to a smaller city or town where they don't read about what happens in this one and start over. You're young, man. Don't decide to do the only thing you can do two, three, five years from now. Save it. Do it...now."

Beckett knew what Murphy said was right. He resigned and that became the straw that broke the back of his marriage. Marcia, who hated police work especially the way Beckett performed it, flew into a rage because he was leaving it. But that really wasn't the reason. She knew it, and he did, too. She had just had it. A full year of living lower middle class and worrying every day and every night whether he was going to get a broken bottle stuck in his neck or knocked off his feet by a sawed-off shotgun was more than she could take. The worst never happened, but all the things that had happened during the past year had exhausted her reserve. She filed for divorce and disappeared, taking nothing because they had very little to split anyway.

Beckett sharply turned left at the next light, now a few short blocks from Bob's Big Boy. He desperately searched the cellophaned pack for one more cigarette and found none. He had already smoked the entire pack in his near fifteen-minute drive to the restaurant with that perpetually smiling-faced fat boy out front, holding the large hamburger on an oversized plate.

Disgusted, Beckett crumbled the pack in his right hand, making a hard fist. He was so mad he could explode. The images, all those memories of Marcia, creeped back into his mind. Somehow, he couldn't escape them.

Beckett had yet to recover. Following their divorce, it took him months to get his act together, but not Marcia. She always had a direction to go, and headed south to Palm Springs, where an old school chum, Cindy Lou Mason, was living with her wealthy husband a dozen years her senior. There is a season in Palm Springs, from mid-October to mid-April, when the nights are cool and so are the mornings, and all the eastern, midwestern and northern states money comes back to remind people who cook in the desert when they're here. Cindy Lou had done herself proud, marrying one of the estimated two hundred millionaires who call Palm Springs home on a permanent basis. Cindy Lou was only too happy to invite Marcia into her home for the week, the month, the year, or however long it took for her to adjust to a new life and shake off the blues that followed a busted marriage.

Marcia liked Cindy Lou's lifestyle. It was what she had always wanted for herself. She did not wait long to remarry. Six months after her divorce, Marcia married one of the wealthiest and most influential men in town, where everybody is wealthy and influential. Lionel Van Ander, of Van Ander department store fame, figured he didn't get the short end of the deal. Marcia was his third wife, the youngest yet, and by far the most beautiful. She was thirty years younger than him—well mannered, well-educated, and well spoken. She would make a fine hostess for all his social functions.

What irony that Beckett should follow Marcia to Palm Springs so soon after her marriage? He didn't really follow her; it was the way things worked out. Cal Murphy advised him to go to a smaller town. He went to Riverside where Bill Cairns, a sheriff's lieutenant, told him about the Palm Springs opening. He had hesitated at first, of course. Palm Springs was a famous resort but still relatively small, with close to fifty thousand permanent residents, compared to metropolitan Los Angeles whose population had swelled to nearly four million. The pace was slower, the people friendlier, the action on the streets, to a minimum.

Two things made up Beckett's mind to make the jump. The opening was for a lieutenant, not a patrolman or sergeant, in the Palm Springs police department, his record and experience qualified him for the job, and the pay was surprisingly good. But then, this was one of the wealthiest communities in the nation and why they call it the "Millionaires Playground."

It was Lt. Lester Horgan's vanity that created the opening for Beckett. Horgan was a good-looking, forty-five-year-old stud whom half the middle-aged women of Palm Springs were trying to maneuver into a second marriage at best and a night in the sack at worst. There were many attractive, wealthy young widows and divorcees in Palm Springs, and proper male escorts were always at a premium. There was something about a uniform, any kind of uniform, that attracted them, especially authority figures like Horgan.

Horgan's problem was not the fact that so many women wanted him; his problem was he liked younger women, say from twenty-five to thirty-five, and his mirror told him he wasn't getting any younger himself.

What decided him on getting a facelift was the morning he was walking to his luxury condominium in St. Baristo, a community of thirty-eight attached villas located steps away from Palm Canyon Drive and the vibrant downtown area, and sixty-two-year-old Mrs. Irene Ashley, a widow, invited him to her place for dinner. The coy wink made her intentions abundantly clear. If a woman her age thought Horgan was in her peer group, Horgan reasoned, it was time to get a face lift and lose ten pounds, maybe fifteen.

Following surgery, after the bruises cleared and the lumps went away, Horgan looked in the mirror and instead of a Ferrari face, he found himself staring at a Ford Fiesta. He filed a malpractice suit and never came back to his job with the Palm Springs police force. He was too embarrassed. The Jaguar driving plastic surgeon had done something to his nose—it was difficult to say exactly what even upon close examination—but he looked like one of those incessantly cheerful Munchkins from *The Wizard of Oz*, and he was much too tall for that.

As appealing as it all sounded, Beckett acknowledged a third reason far back in his well-shaped head that he couldn't acknowledge at first for taking the job in Palm Springs: Marcia was here. This was her home now. Married or not, he might see her occasionally, maybe say hello, or even have a drink together. He harbored no illusions about her other than that. It was over between them. He knew how she felt. She finally had what she wanted. Not a man, but a lifestyle. Not a relationship, but security. Real security she could see, touch, and feel every day she woke up in that prince of a place Lionel Van Ander called home in the one of Palm Springs most exclusive residential areas.

Beckett couldn't help wondering if Marcia was happy. He had so many things on his mind that morning that he drove right past Bob's Big Boy. Discovering his mistake, he began to make a quick U-turn before blurting out aloud, "Oh, to hell with it!" Then drove straight to the station instead. He could always get a cup of coffee there.

Entering the police station, after what seemed an interminable drive to get there, Beckett gave a semi-salute and smile to department receptionist, Betty Corcoran, striding towards his office in the back of the building. As she did every time that he passed either direction, Betty looked approvingly at his well-constructed frame and marveled at how gracefully he walked, often wondering if he was ever attracted to her. She would never know. Beckett never displayed any special interest in any woman, although he had been seen in restaurants and cocktail lounges with some pretty women from time to time.

This was, as Beckett had so accurately predicted to himself, another boring day. Chief Batters came into his office and said his usual perfunctory good morning. He told Beckett he would be doing all the routine things an officer in his capacity does in charge of the burglary and robbery detail in a resort town: interview a couple of hotel robbery victims; pick up the prisoner and take him to the airport for transfer up north; and a couple of routine liquor license problems that seemed to offer no complications.

Beckett went out for a while, completing these routine tasks. It wasn't Los Angeles, but at least he was working.

Then the unexpected happened. At ten minutes to eleven in the morning, Chief Batters walked into his office with a sick look on his face. What he said sounded almost mechanical as if someone had pulled a ring in his back and the voice came out somewhere in his head but not out of his mouth.

"I'm sorry, Beckett. It's Marcia. She's dead."

2

Luke Beckett had taken hundreds of hard punches in the solar plexus. He was knocked out that way twice in the ring long before becoming a cop as an amateur boxer, and more than one street brawler, desperate to elude arrest or resisting in panic, had caught him a hard one in the gut. But none ever made his stomach recoil like the news that Marcia was dead. Every muscle in his face tensed and he started to say something, to react, but no words came out.

Shaking his head in disbelief, Batters just stood there, trying to find something else to say. He found it, after a long moment.

"It's not..." Batters was going to say it's not a fatal auto accident, or something like that, but he realized it was silly to say what it was not. Instead, he said what it was. "It's murder, Luke."

Using Beckett's first name was the Chief's way of trying to convey his sympathy to his new young lieutenant. Emotion came hard to this salty veteran officer. He had learned, like every long-time cop had before him, to mask his emotions well. He had gotten too good at it. So good that he didn't know how to play it any other way.

Beckett quietly nodded. The full impact hadn't sunk in yet.

"Murder?"

"Yes, Luke, murder." Do you want to hear what we've got, or...?"

"Please."

Beckett got up from his chair and walked to the window and stared out of it, as if he couldn't bear to look at the notes in Batters' hand. Batters thought, "He's not ready for this." But then, he reassured himself, when the hell is anyone ready for something like this. There is no good time or bad time to talk about tragedy.

"Okay. Uh, strangled..."

It was as if Batters was shocked, too. Beckett turned around slowly, a look of incredulity on his face. The look was the question, it needed no amplification.

"Yeah, I know Luke. Happened sometime between one and one-thirty this morning during a Sunday night party that went into the wee hours," Batters proceeded, reading the police report with no trace of emotion. "The body was discovered around nine o'clock, when one of Van Ander's yard people was pulling a hose through the garden. Uh..."

Batters was struggling with the details. Beckett's nod gave him some reassurance. He understood. Batters went on, haltingly.

"Name's Connor or Connors. Been with Van Ander for years. Just a, you know, handyman." Batters paused and squeezed the top of his bulbous nose to ease the tension in the moment. Then he continued.

"Anyway, this Connors guy, at first, thought she was drunk or didn't know what. He, well, put his hand to her wrist...she was lying on her back...and, well, Connors called the police. The body is at Morgan's."

Beckett nodded and thought, "Morgan's, right, nice funeral home. "He was there just two weeks ago for the Creighton funeral. Nice lady, Mrs. Creighton.

Batters continued stating the facts from the report in the stoic manner to which Beckett had become accustomed.

"No indication that she was raped, and she was wearing some of her best jewelry," he said, pausing momentarily to clear his throat. "Guess she always wore the good stuff at those fancy parties Van Ander throws all the time. They say he loaded her down with jewelry. Well, I guess you knew that."

Beckett did. He knew, too, that Van Ander had bought her a new red Ferrari 812 that cost three times more than his annual salary. Furs that were too hot to wear except on the coldest desert night and God only knows what else.

"I'm putting Garcia on the case," Batters told Beckett firmly, but with a touch of understanding given the delicate nature of the case. "You can have the day off. Take it. Get drunk. Do whatever you have to do."

With that, Batters walked out, briskly. He was no good at these things. He knew what to say to someone; and whatever he did say always sounded tinny, somehow, like he was reading it off some cue card like they do on television.

Beckett nodded but his mind was elsewhere as Batters exited. He was watching a movie in his head. A movie about Marcia— young, bright, very much alive. Marcia jogging along the beach in Santa Monica. Marcia across a cocktail lounge table, laughing. Marcia's face close to his, their eyes only an inch apart, making unintelligible, contented sounds and snuggling close and warm after they had made love. Marcia...Marcia…Marcia…

The movie ended abruptly when Batters parting words suddenly registered.

"Putting Garcia on the case? Putting Garcia…? Tom!"

Beckett didn't mean to shout; it just came out that way. Batters, only a few steps away, turned on his heel and half ran back to Beckett in the tiny office.

"Yeah, Luke."

"You said you were putting Bobby Garcia on the case? You said that?"

"Of course. Bobby's homicide," Batters reasoned. "You wouldn't want…"

"Yeah. Oh, yeah, I would. I do want. She was my wife, Tom. My wife." Beckett's voice suddenly trailed off.

Batters knew only too well. That consideration had played the major role in his decision to have Garcia conduct the investigation. Beckett had more overall experience than the young Hispanic lieutenant, but Garcia had studied Criminology at the University of California, Los Angeles, better known as UCLA, and had read a few dozen books whose titles sounded like *The Psychology of the Criminal Mind* or some variation of the same theme.

Beckett held Batters so firmly just above the elbows that the older police chief almost wanted to protest.

"Tom, I have to do this. Have to," Beckett said with a self-assured look on his face. "Surely as God you can understand that. My own wife. It's got to be mine, Tom."

Batters looked at him hard. Why would a man want to put himself through a ringer like that? The veteran cop's mind raced. Beckett was more than tough. He was smart and street wise. He had ten times more experience in investigations than young Garcia, and if motivation was any consideration—.

Batters hesitated for a moment, and then finally gave in.

"Okay, Luke. Okay. You got it," he said. "*But* right off the top, hear me and hear me good: By the book. No rough stuff."

Beckett began shaking his head.

"I mean it, Luke," the Chief boomed, "and no 'round-the-clock stuff, either. You've got other assignments and other duties. If any of them suffers, off you come. Understood?"

The Chief's points hit home. Beckett nodded his confirmation of the fact.

"Understood. I swear to God, Tom," he said emphatically.

Batters hated to bring it up, but he was legally bound to do so.

"I know how you must feel, but tomorrow, we've got a full-scale hearing on the Ramirez brothers' incident," Batters said in an empathetic tone. "I can't let you out of that. You'll have to be there. The department might be facing one helluva lawsuit and..."

"Okay, Tom. I'll make it."

Batters nodded, turned, and got on with the rest of his day.

Beckett couldn't think of the Ramirez brothers and their hearing now. It was the farthest thing from his mind. The bastards had been tearing up the Central Cafe, turning it into a junk shop, and he happened to be the first cop on the scene after the call hit the air.

Louie Ramirez had made the mistake of trying to resist arrest. Brother Joe had jumped in and the one they call "King Kong" had broken a beer bottle in half and was trying to brush Beckett's teeth with it. The two Ramirez brothers were at local Desert Regional Medical Center in serious condition. Jose was in a wheelchair, charging police brutality and telling his lawyer that underneath his bundle of facial bandages that he would need thousands of dollars' worth of plastic surgery, all because of police brutality, of course.

"Dirty goddamned liars," Beckett thought privately. He never pistol-whipped any of them, as they claimed.

No one looked at Beckett as he and the Chief emerged from his office heads bowed and went their separate ways without uttering another word. There was no need to say more. The Chief understood a few things about Beckett. Even though he could be a hard man to understand at times, he was a straight arrow, honest and fearless. If he had one flaw, someone had just strangled the life out of it. He loved his ex-wife almost pathologically.

After heading for the parking lot, Beckett's normal impulse when he jumped into his Ford Explorer was to light up a cigarette, even though he was fresh out. This time, he didn't. Any such impulse to smoke died that same day Marcia was murdered. He never touched them again, no matter how strong the temptation.

The policeman in Beckett came rushing back as he pulled his sport utility vehicle out of the lot and headed toward the Van Ander home. He was glad he wouldn't be seeing Marcia's body, glad that someone else had been on the scene first and that she was already out of sight. Surely, he would have become unhinged.

Reverting to what he was, a detective, Beckett was not cold and dispassionate, not uninvolved, but professional enough to conduct the investigation better than any he had conducted before. He could never do enough for Marcia in her young life. He could at least do for her in death what almost no one else might be able to do: Find her killer and...

Beckett pushed the thought out of his mind. The words "kill him" first came to mind, but the professional cop that he was, he knew he couldn't think that way.

By the time he reached the security gate at the restricted compound called Mar Vista, Beckett began thinking like a cop again. He had his investigator's I.D. in his hand and was offering it to the uniformed private guard. It was a needless gesture. Old Sam Court knew Beckett well and admired him. Sam was an ex-Los Angeles Police Department officer like a lot of the security people in Palm Springs who had fled to the desert for a better way of life. He knew what Beckett would be here for and just waved him through.

No one had to tell Beckett where the Van Ander home was. He had driven by it a hundred times, late at night, in the pre-dawn hours of the early morning. Sometimes, he was in the area on official business. Many times, he had only hoped to catch a glimpse of Marcia in the yard or inside the house. Strange how seldom that had happened.

Beckett turned the key off in the ignition and swung his tightly compacted bulk frame out of the driver's seat and thrust his fist in mid-air, about to knock, when door swung open. Charles, the Van Ander butler, had observed him driving up and was waiting for him.

"Lieutenant Beckett. Come in, please. Mr. Van Ander is in the study."

Van Ander was not in the study. He was almost at Charles'

elbow even as he got the words out and Charles was startled to discover him there. Looking grim and much like a man with insomnia, Van Ander didn't offer his hand to Beckett and Beckett was glad he didn't. He wasn't sure whether he could take it or not. Instead, he half-waved Beckett into a gigantic living room and he followed.

Van Ander indicated an overstuffed chair and Beckett sat on the edge of it. It looked too comfortable, and he wasn't in the mood to be comfortable.

Van Ander didn't sit down but began to pace slowly and talk at the same time.

"Of course, I know who you are," he said without a hint of jealousy in his voice. "She talked about you often, what a fine fellow you were and all that. What can I say or...do?"

Beckett almost felt sorry for Van Ander for a moment. But the old Beckett was bubbling up inside. How he would like to get up and shake and slap the old man around until he said, "Yes, yes, I did it," or "I swear to God, I don't know anything about it."

Instead, Beckett watched Van Ander like a cat watches a mouse.

"Mr. Van Ander, forget my personal interest in this," Beckett explained. "Know it's there. I'm here in my capacity as a detective in charge of this case...this...murder case."

It was still hard to say the words, and Van Ander was not insensitive to Beckett's apparent state of mind.

"Anything. Anything at all I can do," Van Ander reaffirmed in a soft, well-mannered voice.

"I appreciate that," Beckett replied soberly. "I...really do."

Beckett could not imagine this man in bed with Marcia. She was as passionate as she was beautiful. Deceptively strong, her lust was both a frightening surprise and a happy secret he had learned long before they married.

Beckett realized he wasn't really listening to what Van Ander was saying. But then, like any experienced cop, he knew that the first few minutes of any kind of interview were often useless, except as a warm-up. People just didn't say anything significant off the top, ever.

"Some arguments, sure. Over little things," Van Ander recounted patiently. "Should she spend the next weekend in La Jolla with the girls? Or did she really need a Halston gown she planned to wear only once or twice?"

Van Ander was much too old for Marcia, Beckett could clearly see that. His receding carefully coiffed white hair, heavily veined hands, facial wrinkles—thinly disguised through that deep, deep tan that year-round residents of Palm Springs wear like a badge of honor—slightly arched back. and shuffling walk told him so.

"...and, then, she wanted this party," Van Ander continued. "To celebrate Ellen's coming out of the hospital after her breast surgery. I know it probably sounds silly, but then..."

He was getting to it now ... The party.

Beckett motioned Van Ander to a chair opposite him and was surprised when he took it. Van Ander sensed they were coming to scratch and wanted this over with. It was all too painful. Now came more details, the kind a man gives when he doesn't really know what to say. About how Marcia carefully selected the napkins and what the menu was that night.

"Well, you know how fussy she was when she was planning a party?" Van Ander said with a small laugh.

Van Ander rambled some more. Finally, he ran out of things to say.

"What else can I tell you?"

Trying his best to keep his emotions in check, Beckett kept the investigation strictly to business.

"I'll want to see that guest list, if you've got it," Beckett said as if the thought had just occurred to him. "If not, I want the names and addresses of everyone who was there. Their phone numbers, too, if you've got them. How many were there?"

Van Ander's brows formed a frown, suddenly troubled.

"So strange. I never...I guess I've never counted our guests. Never thought about it. Not...as many as usual." Van Ander chose his words carefully. "Let's see. The Kehoes were there and the Moshers. Candy couldn't make it. Just George. That's right, just George."

George was a golf pro. His wife Candy was a former fashion model and millionaire ten times over from the vast business empire she built.

Van Ander wrinkled his tanned brow as his thoughts drifted back to the guests that night.

"Perry Baker dropped by but only for a drink. He stayed, oh, maybe an hour. The Gainsworths, of course, were here...Old friends of mine."

Old friends of the same classic movie channels, Beckett recalled quietly, he watched. Ronald Gainsworth was the old movie star who made bundles before taxes and had a reputation for never spending any of it.

"Mary Ann Morrison..."

It was the first unfamiliar name to Beckett.

"This Miss Morrison," Beckett asked inquisitively, "or is it Mrs.?"

"Ms., I'm sure," Van Ander responded without any hesitation. "One of those, uh, feminist types."

Van Ander said it like it was a dirty word.

"Yeah," Beckett inquired further. "Who is she?"

Van Ander made one of those fruitless little gestures that former actors sometime make.

"I don't really know much about her," he added. "But I know she's a good friend...was a good friend...of Marcia's. I thought, perhaps, from the, uh, old days."

"The name doesn't strike a bell with me," Beckett noted calmly.

Van Ander nodded frailly and continued after a long pause.

"Anyway, she and Marcia were very close...Best friends."

Van Ander thus handed Beckett the worst suspect list in the

annals of criminal investigation and he quickly scanned the names. A 72-year-old Catholic monsignor. Hardly worth exploring, he thought. The Lieutenant Governor of the state brought to the party by Van Ander's corporate public relations directors. Interesting possibility, but no. A paraplegic Vietnam veteran who never left poolside. He was there to talk about one of Van Ander's many charity drives, be photographed and set up as a symbol of the drive to help paraplegics in veterans' hospitals. Doubtful. But all worth checking.

Beckett suddenly groaned, audibly.

"Something wrong?" Van Ander asked curiously.

The question irritated Beckett. Why did Van Ander have to take notice of everything he did? Can't a guy groan in...in frustration?

"No. Not at all. May I ask a few questions, please?"

"Of course," Van Ander replied, with a slight but unsteady nod.

"Some may be, uh, a bit personal," Beckett explained. "Bear with me. This is a murder investigation. Let's both try to be cool and objective as best we can."

Van Ander eyed Beckett suspiciously.

"As we can," he blurted out, tensely.

Beckett didn't like the way Van Ander said it but plunged ahead.

"Some people think I'm insensitive," Beckett quickly backtracked his statement. "I mean, in...when I'm working."

Van Ander had heard better than that. He had heard Beckett was made of material harder than steel. True, Marcia hadn't said it. But some of his friends had brushed up against Beckett in minor ways, silly little misunderstandings they claimed they were much too embarrassed over to elaborate, after a charity ball.

"Ask whatever questions you must, lieutenant," Van Ander quickly retorted.

"Right." Beckett paused and then plunged ahead. "Your marriage with Marcia. Happy? Very happy? No problems?"

Van Ander eyed his wife's former lover and husband like he was a thing under glass that he didn't touch. Just examine, carefully.

"Very, very happy."

"Were there any other men?"

Van Ander felt his blood pressure rising. He was finding it difficult to separate the jealous ex-husband from the inquiring police lieutenant. Or could they be separated?

"There were no…other…men."

"You're certain about that?"

"Certain."

The word came out from between pursed lips. Beckett was aware of what he was doing. He was good at it.

Beckett's face was a study of speculative curiosity.

"Social life…Okay?"

"More than okay," Van Ander answered quickly. "Marcia always had fun. Always."

Beckett's eyes became suspicious. Van Ander's face flinched for no apparent reason as he answered the question. Could be nothing more than frayed nerves at his age. Nonetheless, Beckett made a mental note to himself for later.

"The party was held entirely in the pool area. No part of it in here?" Beckett asked, moving right along.

"That's right," Van Ander responded, his face suddenly brightening. "Oh, naturally, people would come indoors to freshen a drink or get an hors d'oeuvre or use the bathrooms. But for the most part, we all stayed outdoors most of the time…"

Beckett suddenly interrupted. "What time did the party break up?"

Van Ander had thought all this through. All his answers were without even normal hesitation.

"It all began about eight o'clock," he remembered, "with people dropping in casually until about nine, and it lasted until, oh, about one in the morning."

Beckett seemed unconvinced and resonated in his next question.

"Not one of those all-night bashes?" he asked.

"No. It wasn't that kind of group," Van Ander explained whispery-voiced. "More, sedate, you might say."

"No," Beckett thought, "*you* might say."

Beckett leaned back in his chair and stretched his legs. This was the part of the job, he hated; he preferred the action on the streets.

"As best as you can remember," Beckett continued, "was anyone arguing over anything at all that night?"

Van Ander deliberated over the question for a moment before answering.

"No." It was a long, drawn-out kind of "No," the kind that tells you someone has really thought hard about it.

"Did anything unusual happen?" Beckett persisted. "Anything at all?" Van Ander replied with a bemused smile, "Ronnie Gainsworth fell in the pool."

"Drinking too much?" Beckett asked.

Van Ander ignored the question, but the answer was about to become obvious.

"Come to think of it, that wasn't all that unusual," Van Ander said with a laugh. "Ronnie falls in my pool almost every time he comes over here."

Probably, Beckett wondered, because the old ham wasn't getting much attention at home that he purposely made a spectacle of himself in public.

Suddenly, Beckett jumped to his feet like a man ready to get moving.

"How about we look at the party area and the, uh, garden area?"

Van Ander obliged.

Beckett had braced himself for the walk in the garden where Marcia's body was found. Better to postpone that for as long as possible. The pool area was beautiful, as he knew it would be, a stunning luxurious palm tree-lined Mediterranean pool, with an unobstructed view of the spectacular San Jacinto mountains, overlooking a lush tropical garden that offered a feeling of intimacy despite its breadth and size. Van Ander conducted a grim tour of the area, reconstructing where each person sat, who was facing whom, what they were drinking, even a small joke or observation this one or that one made.

Beckett made a few notes. He knew he wouldn't even keep them, but he wanted to keep his hands occupied. Then they walked into the garden—so vast and dense the pool disappeared—and Van Ander took him to the very spot where Marcia's body was found. Both men remained silent for a full minute or so.

Finally, Beckett began walking back into the house with Van Ander following him. They didn't break their silence until Beckett had returned to the spot where he had sat down.

"Mr. Van Ander, thanks very much for your cooperation," Beckett said with the utmost sincerity and meant it. "I know how unpleasant this must be for you."

Van Ander nodded and began showing Beckett to the door.

Beckett added, "If I have to talk to you again..."

"Of course," Van Ander interrupted, not giving Beckett a chance to even finish. "Feel free to call. I've told my office I won't be back at my desk for at least a week, maybe longer. I've got to sort all this out in my mind. Make some...adjustments. You understand."

Beckett understood and at that moment, Charles, Van Ander's trusted longtime butler, materialized out of nowhere and was holding the door open for him. Beckett started to put out his hand, automatically, to shake. Van Ander wasn't even looking at him.

"Goodbye, and thanks again."

Van Ander still gave no response as Beckett turned on his heel and walked out to his Ford Explorer baking in the hot sun and Charles shut the massive door behind him.

Van Ander listened for the key in the ignition, heard the motor turn over, and then listened some more as the sound of Beckett's Ford Explorer faded in the distance.

Then he walked over without hesitation to a nearby phone and dialed.

"Mayor's office," the shrill voice on the end other answered.

"Mr. Van Ander," Van Ander said firmly. "I want to speak to the mayor... Now."

"Yes, sir."

A pause, then.

"Lionel...how are you? I've been thinking about you ever since..."

Van Ander immediately made it clear he was no mood for idle chat.

"Larry, I'll say this just once," he threatened. "I want this...this Beckett person off the case. Now, before you say one word, let me remind you who headed your fund drives the last two times you ran and who personally...oh, for Christ's sake, Larry, do I have to draw a picture? Beckett! Get him out of my hair and off my back. Don't you ask why, and I won't ask how."

Van Ander's voice was rising to the point of hysteria. On the other end of the line, Larry Parker, mayor of Palm Springs, got the message loud and clear. Money talks. But in Van Ander's case, it always shouted.

"It's done, John. Consider it done."

3

Starting with the murder of Beckett's ex-wife on Monday, Tom Batters knew the following day after news broke of her death and pending police investigation he would be up to his ass in alligators and wouldn't Timmy Farrell pick this very day to come in and confess to the murder of Frank Hermann, the big condominium developer. It was a beautiful confession, too, all well thought out and superbly detailed, the kind of report that would gladden the heart of any district attorney anxious to hand his hat in Sacramento at some future date.

It was such a good confession that the Chief almost found himself wishing it were true. Unfortunately, Hermann wasn't dead and Farrell was nutty as a loon. Batters wished the county budget was big enough to provide for people like Farrell in order to keep him in some safe, comfortable place where he couldn't do any harm to anyone, let alone himself. In a perfect world, that would be on the top of his wish list.

Batters gave Farrell his solemn word that he would send a car around to his small one-bedroom apartment later in the day and arrest him, when they weren't *too* busy, if Farrell would promise to go right home. Farrell was, of course, delighted and

Batters turned his attention to a note in front of him. It was from Lt. Garcia, who had been contacted by Mayor Parker and given him the message that Van Ander wanted Beckett off the murder case.

Batters hated to get a note like that. He had been a cop a long time, and, though he was a good one, he was getting along in years. Too old for much more police work, and too young to curl up and die. His only chance was to keep his nose clean and keep buttering up the moneyed sons-of-bitches that the local newspaper once called "the power elite of Palm Springs," and be handed a handsome cash gift, not to mention a hefty pension, when he retired to thank him for services rendered.

Mayor Parker's message was the kind of thing that gave Batters ulcers. Here he had put his best on the job in Beckett, a man with a very special interest in solving the case, and Van what's-his-name was sticking the mayor's nose into police department business, trying to influence a key personnel decision.

Batters could hear Beckett walking down the hall to his office. Following him, he knocked on the door frame to the lieutenant's office, twice. Beckett turned and looked around, irritated by the interruption. Batters motioned him to stay put while he took a seat and as soon as he did, he broke his silence.

"As an old United States senator used to say: 'I have here in my hand a piece of paper, and it's got some names on it. One of them is yours.'"

Beckett didn't care much for the Chief's attempt at humor and turned angry.

"What the hell does that mean?" he snapped. "Did I forget to pay my taxes or something?"

"No," Batters explained patiently under the conditions. "You forgot to be diplomatic with *our* Mr. Van Ander, like I told you to."

Our Mr. Van Ander. Since when was he was *our* Mr. Ander, Beckett wondered

Beckett stared at Batters, shocked, by the latest development. He had been investigating the case for only one day.

"He complained about something?"

Batters answered, underscoring every word to make his point clear.

"No, about someone…You. He wants you off the case."

Beckett shook his head from side to side in that frustrated way he did when things were not going right for him.

"Well, yeah, he wants me off the case," Beckett said, trying not to let his temper get the best of him. But it was no use. "Christ's sake, Chief, if you were the number-one suspect, right now the only suspect in your wife's murder, wouldn't you want me off the case?"

Batters eyed Beckett carefully, trying to conceal his amusement behind those cold gray eyes the younger men on the force said looked more like the noses of bullets than anything else.

"He's enlisted the good office of the mayor to convince me that your labors might be put to more productive use in the traffic division," Batters continued, "where you can make sure that the tourists' vans and Volkswagens never, never get in the way of the residents' Mercedes, BMWs and Lexus's."

Beckett shook his head in disbelief. He should have known something like this might happen.

"All right, Chief," he said knowingly, "now tell me what you're going to do."

Batters enjoyed moments like this. They didn't come around very often, and that's why he had dragged it out so.

"I am going to inform His Honor that you have turned over a new leaf. I am going to remind him that you used to be an altar boy, you once studied for the priesthood, that you spend your days off bird watching and donating your free time to underprivileged children," Batters said with a touch of good-natured sarcasm. "Sound good, so far?"

"And if that isn't enough?" Beckett growled.

Batters smiled. His smile was wide enough to light a six-room cabin.

"Then I'll tell him to go fuck himself and keep his needle nose out of my police department and get back with his swells up the hill and bullshit his way back into office again."

Batters said it with such authority that Beckett believed him.

Beckett nodded, satisfied, and then rose to leave.

"Thanks, Tom. Is that it?"

Now Batters' mood suddenly changed.

"No, that's not it. This is it."

Batters needled in his finger into Beckett's firm chest.

"Put on the kid gloves, you goddamned Neanderthal," he said, raising his voice with every word. "You're not grinding pimps and pushers any more. You're doing business with some of the richest and most powerful people in this country. Clout is the biggest industry here. Tourism is way back in second place. Understand me?"

It was a clear warning. Maybe even a threat.

"I understand, Chief," Beckett replied, staring vacantly at his feet.

Batters seemed adequately impressed.

"Okay. That's more like it," Batters said, suddenly lowering his voice. "I know you've got to talk to Van Ander, again and again. But do it with a little bit of diplomacy, for Christ's sake. I can fix this. But I can't keep on fixing it. Don't make any job any tougher than it is. Do you read me?"

Beckett nodded his head up and down in agreement.

"I do."

Batters grunted, "Well, before you do anything, you know what happens in less than two hours from now?"

Beckett didn't remember. Now Batters shook his head.

"Jesus, but you're single-minded," Batters bellowed, his voice resonating throughout the office. "Two hours from now is the hearing…Your hearing…The Ramirez brothers and their fancy attorney. You remember them. You met them socially in the Central Cafe, now renamed The Splinters because that's the way you left it."

Beckett couldn't help himself and unwittingly smiled.

"I had help."

"Yes. I'm sure they were fierce," Batters said sarcastically. "But now I understand the American Medical Association is thinking of making them poster boys of the year, as they do, for every injury known to modern man."

"Okay, okay," Beckett tried to reason. "I'll be there. Can I go now?"

Batters blew about ten cubic feet of frustration out of his lungs.

"Go!"

But Beckett never quite made it out the door.

"Oh, one more thing," Batters shouted after him.

Beckett turned. Now he was really irritated.

"Jesus, now what?"

Batters stopped him with a grin.

"This Thursday, in your office, you're going to meet a television documentary producer from Los Angeles," Batters explained patiently like a teacher would to a student. "He'll have a sound man and a cameraman with him, and they want to be taken to view the various homes owned by our illustrious citizens from the East Coast if you catch my drift."

Beckett nodded.

The Chief meant Beckett had to squire these television people around town, pointing out all the mansions occupied, part-time or full-time, by members of the Mafia. They're all there, with the names right on the mailboxes. No secret about it.

The mob long ago turned Palm Springs into a kind of junior Geneva, a haven, a neutral place, a king of king's X, where members of the five families could come and discuss various ecumenical problems indigenous to their respective businesses and territories. Some of the biggest mobsters in the country have been integrated in Palm Springs social life, and if they don't park in front of any fire hydrants or trash any storefronts, they get the full protection of the local law just like anyone else.

"Can't Garcia play tour guide instead of me?" Beckett begged.

Batters smiled again, savoring the moment. It wasn't that often that Beckett begged—for anything.

"No. Remember, I told you I couldn't leave you on this investigation full time," Batters pointed out. "With Simmons out on maternity leave, you're in charge of hand-holding the media until she returns. Take maybe two, three hours and you won't see them again after that."

"Okay," Beckett said irritated. "Now can I go?"

"Blow! You're gone."

Batters waved his arms like a mother shooing her bratty children out of the house on their way to school.

"And detective?" Batters summoned.

Beckett turned and faced the Chief, wanting to explode.

"Yeah?"

Batters smiled like a child playing a mean prank.

"Have a nice day!"

Beckett scoffed at the Chief's sudden sense of humor, storming out of the office, and taking a swirl of papers with him, swept into the air by his whirlwind exit.

Sticking an unlighted cigar in his mouth, Batters just chuckled, finding the whole incident somehow amusing. Shaking his head, he muttered observantly, "That boy really needs a sense of humor."

***

Luke Beckett had an office away from the office. It was well lighted, his desk was three times the size of his desk at police headquarters, and it was a nice place to meet snitches or people who didn't want to be interviewed in their homes or at the station. Best of all, it was rent-free. Officially, it was called Bob's Big Boy. The manager was happy to have a minion of the law on the premises, although there was never any trouble there. The waitresses were all in love with Beckett, too, or so they told him.

It was funny how Beckett could concentrate better in this place, a busy family-friendly restaurant, than he could in his exclusive little cubicle back at headquarters. But that's the way it was. How did the cliché go, alone in the crowd?

Beckett read and re-read his many notes from the interrogation of Van Ander at his Palm Springs estate. They seemed to yield nothing. Pushing them aside, he took out and examined his condensation of the official autopsy report. Van Ander had been reluctant to have an autopsy performed, but had finally relented.

Strangulation is a difficult way to kill. It's a tool of sadists, maniacs driven temporarily insane by the passions. A gun is quicker, a knife equally effective and silent, although few have the stomach for it.

Marcia had been strangled as she faced the killer. Both were on their feet. The attacker had to be standing very close to her. It had to be someone she knew to allow him...or her...to get so close, close enough to reach up and in one lightning-swift gesture, encircle her throat with his hands. Someone with superb reflexes, excellent timing, and tremendous strength.

The angle of the prominent thumb bruises on the front of her neck indicated the attacker was two or three inches taller than his victim. It is not easy, but neither is it impossible, for a short person to strangle a tall person.

The face-to-face strangulation is more effective than strangulation from the rear of the victim, Beckett contemplated. The thumbs are stronger than the fingers. But a face-to-face strangulation carries with it risks from the attacker as well. An intended victim trained in self-defense or the martial arts might quickly lift a knee and drive it into the attacker's groin. Since the attacker must use both hands to strangle, the victim's hands are free to punch or scrape and tear at the attacker's face with her fingernails. However, the pathologist found no flesh under Marcia's fingernails. There was no struggle, no time or opportunity for resistance.

Marcia's clothing was not rumpled, or disarranged; there had been no struggle of any kind. There was no indication of attempted rape as Batters had previously verified. If it was an attempted robbery, how could the attacker know she would be in the garden at that precise moment?

The thought occurred to Beckett that Marcia might have scheduled a rendezvous with the killer, never dreaming of his intentions. Or perhaps he had waited there in the dark: waiting for any victim to come near his hiding place. But if he were a stranger, why wouldn't she have screamed? The spot where her body was found was no more than twenty-five feet from the pool area, the scene of the party. Extremely thick bushes shielded it, but the other guests surely would have heard even the slightest shout or scream.

Not robbery, not rape, and someone she knew well enough, and trusted well enough, to allow them to come extremely close to her. Perhaps they had been whispering so that the others might not hear their conversation.

It must have been a man. Or a very strong man. But why? It was the apparent lack of motive that was reinforcing the dull pain that never seemed to leave Beckett's forehead.

Beckett was so absorbed in his thoughts that it wasn't until the second time that he saw her that it registered on him. She was a middle-aged Hispanic woman. Wasn't she the same woman who worked as a maid at Van Ander's?

Beckett called out to one of the waitresses, who happened to be coming his way. Her name was Rebecca, a wispy, tall blonde from Mississippi and another recent transplant to the desert. She was the best waitress in the restaurant, in his opinion, always wanting to please the customer. Best of all, she was single.

"What you need darlin?" Rebecca asked sweetly.

"Ice tea, with sweet and low," Beckett said with a smirk.

"Wipe that silly grin off your face, detective," she said jokingly. "Don 't you get any ideas now. You hear."

Beckett wanted to laugh, but he couldn't. It was all business with him, for now.

"Say, that older lady in the white uniform." Beckett pointed to the uniformed employee on the other side of the restaurant. "She does the cooking or cleaning up?"

Rebecca smiled and, in that cute southern accent of hers, replied facetiously.

"You got the hots for her, detective? You want to meet her? Or is it her daughter you're after?" she cracked.

"Yeah, sure. All of the above," Beckett said with a laugh, turning serious again. "But what's her name, do you know?"

"Sure," Rebecca said glibly. "Maria Colter."

"Colter?" Beckett repeated to himself. "What the hell kind of Hispanic name is that?"

"Heck, if I know," Rebecca bristled, giving the counter top a once over with a clean damp towel. "You're the detective. Maybe she had a father named Colter."

Beckett smiled. His smile was an admission that Rebecca was a better detective than he was.

"Do me a favor, will you?" he continued. "Ask her to come by here for a moment. Just want to ask her a couple of questions.

You can clear it with the boss but be, you know, discreet, okay? Don't use the loud speaker."

Rebecca smiled sweetly—the kind of smile that made men melt. "You really think I'm a dummy, don't you?"

Beckett retreated. "Hell, no. Not at all."

Rebecca, without any provocation, pressed two fingers against her rose-colored lips and let out a loud whistle.

"Maria," she shouted. "Get over here. You have a visitor."

Beckett laughed. "I like your style."

Rebecca smiled again, this time with something else in mind. Moving closer, she lowered her voice and said seductively, "I've got a few more tricks I know, if you ever have the time."

With that, the young southerner turned on her heel and walked away, leaving Beckett with his mouth still half-open.

Maria Colter didn't have to tell Beckett she distrusted cops. Her face and her manner said it eloquently. But Beckett, like many a good investigator, was practiced at disarming people. He had seen the manager talking to her so she knew by now he was a cop, and the manager obviously had said he was an okay guy and go talk to him.

"Please sit down a moment, Mrs...it is Colter?"

Looking wilted and withered, she flashed a warm smile.

"Yes. Thank you."

Maria quietly took the padded seat directly opposite of Beckett at the side counter. A woman of medium height, Maria was extremely attractive: She had long, flowing dark brown hair, alert brown eyes, an uneasy but irresistible smile when she showed it, and a soft, smooth complexion that made her look at least ten years younger than her age.

Beckett didn't take time for idle conversation. Facing Maria, he got right the point.

"Are you, well, you must be," he stammered, "related to the Van Ander maid?"

Maria smiled brightly. "Yes, she's my sister...my younger sister, Dolores."

Beckett's eyebrows suddenly arched in a way that made them look uneven.

"Are you twins?" he asked curiously.

"No." It was sort of a long-drawn-out no. "I guess we look alike."

Beckett nodded as his eyes drifted away from her for a second.

"Okay. I get it," he said in a way that he still didn't seem sure. "But you two really do look very much alike."

"Yes. Yes," Maria answered, with hardly a trace of an accent. "I didn't mean to be a smart ass. I've worked all night and I'm tired."

Beckett could not help grinning. The remark somehow struck him funny.

"Is it something I said?" Maria asked nervously.

Beckett, who didn't mean to offend her, quickly wiped the grin from his face.

"No. It's nothing you said. It's just."

He leaned closer so only she could hear his comments.

"Pardon me for saying this," he said in a whisper, "but you speak very fluent English."

Maria immediately softened and smiled warmly back at him.

"Thank you. I was born right here...in Palm Springs. My father is American and my mother is Mexican. English was the language that was spoken most often by both of our parents. I know that sounds strange. People just assume..."

Beckett touched on her hand and patted it. It was an impulsive gesture, not something he usually did when questioning a possible suspect or witness, but it felt right. He could tell that Maria was well educated and bright, hardly the type to be associated with a murder.

"That's perfectly all right," Beckett said seriously. "Actually, I'm the one who should be apologizing for bothering you at all. "

"That's okay. I understand," Maria replied warmly.

Beckett returned to the routine line of questioning, never veering too far off course.

"Listen, I have to talk to Dolores, okay? Now I could do it officially," he said. "You know, call the house, and tell Van Ander I have to talk to her, and all that. But it might make her nervous or embarrass her or something. Besides, I don't really want Van Ander to know I'm talking to her. You understand?"

Maria suddenly turned incredulous.

"But why...Dolores?"

Unfazed by her question, Beckett elaborated further.

"I just want to know what she may have seen before the murder of...Mrs. Van Ander."

It was always hard for Beckett to refer to Marcia that way, as if he never could accept the reality of her marriage to the millionaire industrialist.

"All right," Maria offered reluctantly. "I will tell Dolores."

"Good." Beckett quickly rose to his feet. "Here's my card with both the office and my cell phone number on it. Please ask her to call me. Not this afternoon. I'm tied up. Any time after that. Okay?"

Maria simply nodded.

It had to be okay. Within a short time, Beckett was very tied up. That afternoon, he was sitting in the conference room back at the station, facing Jose Ramirez and his attorney Richard Case, who was filling in for the Ramirez brothers' attorney Bob Teller. Around the table were Chief Batters, Lt. Garcia, and Bob Martin, the Palm Springs Police Department attorney. They made up the department's disciplinary board and discipline was part of what this was all about.

Beckett listened quietly with mounting anger as Ramirez's attorney read off the charges against him. It must have taken eight or ten minutes to read the account out loud, and that was just the printed material. The shorthand of it was this, to Beckett's way of thinking: The three Ramirez brothers, celebrating some obscure Mexican festival and, on their best behavior as they always were, were quietly drinking at the bar. This tourist came in, with a washed out blonde and made some deprecating racial remark about Hispanics in general. Jose and his brothers ignored the insult and several others that followed until finally all hell broke loose.

It was a clear case of racial discrimination, as Chief Batters knew from experience it would be. But then when a friend of this tourist called the police, Beckett came charging in and because they were Hispanics, he naturally assumed they were in the wrong and began beating on them. Beckett wouldn't listen to any of their explanations and being white, naturally sided with the white tourist and kept beating them.

That's the way it was.

Batters, nominated for many a departmental academy award for the kind of dignified, objective demeanor he was displaying throughout this hearing, spoke first.

"Mr. Case, is it?"

"Yes."

"Mr. Case. Interesting name for an attorney," Batters noted matter-of-factly. "We seem to have here what is known popularly as a difference of opinion. My officer's version is rather at odds with the version we've just heard."

Batters then read Beckett's account. It was much shorter and, indeed, rather different. It had the three Ramirez brothers stewed to the gills and making rather repugnant remarks about the various parts of the young lady's body, escorted into the establishment by the tourist, a 110-pound weakling dressed in one of those vague brown suits.

Clarence Ramirez, or "King Kong," concentrated on the young lady's beautiful bosom, allowing as how they looked so chewable from his vantage point. "Sugarless gum," he said. Louis thought her well-rounded buttocks offered more interesting possibilities. He suggested a few.

According to Beckett's account, Jose then suggested she could do something more interesting with those luscious full lips than suck on the straw to her strawberry margarita. Even a 110-pound weakling isn't going to put up with that sort of garbage, so, Borden, his name was, called them out on it and promptly got flung through the air for his trouble. He landed on a stack of empty Coke bottles behind the bar, sustaining derriere cuts, and then the brothers Ramirez took turns trying to stuff him into a taco while his lovely young companion, loyal to the last, got the hell out of there, her dress torn from the experience.

When Beckett arrived, as Batters continued, Borden was beginning to resemble a Twinkie sat on one too many times and Beckett took one on the chin and one in the right rib cage as he extricated the bleeding man from his attackers.

As Batters testified, what followed was standard Beckett procedure for dealing with ruffians. He reasoned with them for two, maybe three seconds. Then he proceeded to beat their brains out.

The ambulance driver who was first on the mop up scene said it was the first four-car crash he had ever seen indoors, but, of course, that wasn't in the official report.

So ended the Beckett version.

Then came what always followed, two completely diametrically opposed accounts of everything: lots of angry talk, threats made and softened or retracted entirely, and new charges arising out of new anger. In the middle of this, Lt. Garcia quietly left the room and no one questioned him. It was a rather long session and Beckett was wishing he could also be excused but he didn't dare leave.

When Lt. Garcia returned, he spoke up for the first time.

"Mr. Ramirez."

Because his voice was so soft in contrast to the high decibel discussion taking place, it grabbed everyone's attention.

"I see you drove your Buick today."

Jose Ramirez frowned and looked at Garcia as if he had lost his mind. Ramirez automatically hated any Hispanic who would put on a cop uniform and harass his own people. They were real spics, the sellout kind, and Garcia was a baiter.

"What in shit has that got to do with anything, Garcia?" Batters blurted loudly, staring straight ahead, as if not listening to any of this.

"Well, sir, it has this to do with it."

At that, Garcia threw down a small bag of heroin wrapped in one of those plastic zipper-lock bags.

"What the fuck is that?" Ramirez asked, thunder struck.

"That, I think you will find, is heroin," Garcia said with a penetrating look. "I tasted it. It came right out of your trunk and I opened the trunk with our department photographer shooting pictures and the police matron looking on."

Ramirez, apologetic, screamed into the attorney's ear so hard the men recoiled.

"Do you see what these bastards are up to? They're trying to frame me. What are you going to do about it?"

Case, unaccustomed to handling criminal cases, wasn't going to hold still for this.

"That's illegal search and seizure," he noted. "It won't hold up in any court. Anywhere."

"Right," Garcia said.

"That's very true," Batters added.

"My fucking aunt," Ramirez screamed, "that's not the point. The point is they planted that horseshit in my car, and they're all pretending they got it out of my trunk. Bullshit. It was never in there. Don't you see what I'm talking about?"

Case wasn't so sure. He had heard rumors that the Ramirez brothers moved drugs across the border and serviced many clients in Palm Springs and throughout the valley whose names are in the social register. This seemed to verify his suspicions, but he was a desert lawyer who grabbed what he could, not having quite established himself yet in the area. So, he kept playing the game he was being paid to play.

"Chief Batters, this, uh, incident," Case fumbled, trying to find the right words, "has nothing whatever to do with the purpose of this hearing. I think you'll agree to that."

The Chief smiled a benevolent, reasonable smile.

"You're perfectly right, of course, Mr. Case," Batters said plainly. "I think what Mr. Garcia may be suggesting here is something like this...Correct me if I'm wrong, Mr. Garcia."

The Chief never called any of his officers Mister. Beckett was so fascinated by the Chief's masterful performance he couldn't take his eyes off him.

"The Ramirez brothers have a record four miles long. You possibly didn't know that. The Drug Enforcement Agency people wear out a dozen keyboards a year writing reports on all three brothers," Batters continued confidently. "Only one month ago, we stopped this same gentleman on South Palm Canyon Drive and discovered, too late, that he had thrown an identical amount of heroin from this very same car out the window before we stopped him. "

Batters paused deliberately and then continued.

"An observant conventioneer with the nameplate, 'Hi, I'm Richard,' picked up the heroin and brought it to us. There was no arrest for obvious reasons. The eyewitness did not want to become involved. But we know, and Jose here knows, that it was his heroin and he's a pusher just like his two brothers. That very same packet of heroin is in our property room right now and you may see it if you so desire."

"I don't so desire," Case said acidly, while his client Jose Ramirez began moaning like a wounded bull. "I would like to suspend this meeting for, say, to another time in order to confer at length with my client. If that's convenient to you, gentlemen."

It was convenient to everyone but Ramirez, whose accent was getting progressively more pronounced as he got angrier and angrier. No time was set or even discussed. Case closed.

"Jeez, I'm being fucked again by these guys," Ramirez screamed at the top of his lungs, trying to comprehend the justice in all of it. "You hire a goddamn lawyer and he don't do you no fucking good."

The pair left, and the two lady clerks outside the conference room blushed crimson as Jose found some very fancy names to call his attorney.

Beckett looked at Garcia. It was rare, but his face was wreathed in gratitude.

"Garcia, by Christ, I really owe you one," Beckett smiled. "I really do."

Garcia was no fan of Beckett's. He even resented him and his tactics at times, but this was a special situation, a special circumstance. Garcia had worked on narcotics investigations for the department, and the Ramirez brothers were his special hate.

"Anyway," Beckett started to say as they walked out of the conference room together, "that was a damn fine thing you did for me, for the department. What a coincidence, finding that stuff in his trunk. And it looks just like the stuff he threw out of that same goddamned car last month, the stuff in the property room."

Garcia flashed a sincere grin that soon dissipated.

"It is the stuff in the property room, man. Where the hell do you think I got it?"

Chief Batters, in the blink of an eye, passed them in the hall.

"I didn't hear that," he said, speaking out the side of his mouth. "Let's get on with our work. And Garcia?"

Garcia stopped, turned, and looked at Batters with a hollow stare. The threatening tone of the Chief's remarks had the young, fiery detective worried.

"You'll have to introduce me to our department photographer sometime," Batters said grinning. "I've been trying to fit him into our *budget* for the last three years."

Batters no sooner finished and burst out laughing as he turned the corner. Beckett and Garcia looked at each other oddly and immediately doubled over laughing. Leave it to the Chief to know.

4

A t ten o'clock Wednesday morning, Marcia Beckett Van Ander's funeral was held at Our Lady of Solitude Church, in the heart of Palm Springs, which surprised Beckett. Not only the expediency by which the funeral and burial were scheduled, but also the fact that he never knew she was a Catholic. He couldn't for the life of him remember either one of them ever exchanging thoughts or conversations about God or religion during all the time that they knew each other, so if she was, it was a mystery to him.

The services were both simple and ornate and in good taste, like everything the wealthy do. Father Bernard Clancy once explained why the rich do things better than ordinary people. He said they could "afford to hire ordinary people to do their planning for them." Beckett thought that was pure hogwash but Father Clancy was a nice man and entitled to his own mythology just like anyone else.

Instead of the usual funeral dirge, the unseen choir sang the old 1970s pop hit, "Feelings," and Beckett felt the hair crawling up his neck. If there was anything Marcia was hip about, it was pop music. She had once entertained an ambition to be a singer and wasn't bad, but she hated "Feelings" like Napoleon hated six-foot grooms.

From his pew in the twenty-first row, he was back far enough. This was a duty assignment and he didn't want to be up close, not for this one. Not with his stomach in a knot, his throat dry and the damned desert sun streaming through aside window and engulfing him like a spotlight when he wanted to be as inconspicuous as humanly possible.

Beckett surprised himself by remembering a couple of prayers he hadn't said since he was in grammar school at St. Ignatius's. By the time they got to the eulogy, Beckett was close to nausea. If he couldn't find any words, even inside his head, what could this stranger in robes find to say?

Father Francis Xavier Monahan stepped to the podium and spoke from the heart. It turned out he had come to know Marcia during her short time in Palm Springs. He spoke in kind and loving terms, saying Marcia was "like an open, vulnerable desert flower, loving and kind and compassionate, with a keenness of mind and warmth of spirit far beyond her tender years." The good priest assured one and all, she was nestled in the palm of God and at peace in her final resting place.

Beckett averted his eyes as pallbearers carried the ivory-white casket down the aisle. He didn't have to look to see who the pallbearers were; he had already checked that out with Mr. Hamill, the undertaker. All were close friends of his, not hers.

Beckett never went to funerals of his own family or friends. This was the sole exception to that ironclad rule and doubted that anyone in the tiny sandstone chapel could be hurting as much as he was, but he tried hard not to show it.

By the time they reached Desert Memorial Park cemetery in nearby Cathedral City and the graveside ritual was underway, Beckett was breathing regularly again and beginning to act like a policeman once more. He began noting whom the chief mourners were, who was standing closest to them and who was standing off to the side, trying to look as unobtrusive as he had tried to look in the church.

Front and center of all the mourners was the elder Lionel

Van Ander, looking moved and crushed, ten years older than his reported seventy-five years of age. Even so, Beckett wasn't buying any of it, not yet.

Next to him was an oddly shaped woman of about sixty-five whose elegant dark clothes masked a dozen figure flaws. That would be Van Ander's old maid sister from East Hampton, Maisy. Then a few close friends, among them a few famous faces and other era entertainers, who were frequent guests of Van Ander, as well as some representatives of Van Ander's various business enterprises.

No surprises. Everyone who had attended the last party turned out for the funeral and gravesite ceremony, except Mary Ann Morrison, who was on the guest list that night. Beckett made a mental note to ask her when he got to questioning her why she did not attend.

Finally, after what seemed like a thousand years, Marcia's body was interred underground. The hopeless sobs of mourners pierced the still, quiet landscape as the casket was slowly and respectfully lowered in the grave. Beckett could not bear the sight. Shutting his eyes, he turned away, trying to force the throbbing heartache from his being.

What Beckett wished for, more than anything else, was that he could bring Marcia back. To hold her, to kiss her, to love her, to beg for forgiveness. But it was far too late for that now. Marcia was dead. Nothing he could do would ever change that. Nothing.

As Marcia's casket made its steady decent to the hardened dirt-and-sand soil below, Beckett thoughts once again got the best of him. That peaceful calm that only comes with death suddenly intruded his mind. Brilliant flashes of light, followed by a kaleidoscope of sharp color images, images of the good times he and Marcia once shared: Their first date...Their first kiss...The time he proposed...The day they were married...Their first car...and so on.

It all seemed so real, Beckett felt he could reach out and

touch her, as if Marcia was still very much alive. Everything was just like it was before. They were happy, smiling, laughing, joyful, young newlyweds on the threshold of a new life together. Things couldn't have been more perfect.

As quickly as the images came, they faded from Beckett's memory. Everything suddenly went dark. That cold, shivering feeling penetrated through his bones.

Beckett opened his eyes. Marcia was gone. So was everyone else. Left behind were two gravediggers shoveling clumps of sand and dirt on top of Marcia's soiled casket, filling in the place where her body would remain for eternity.

Somehow finding the courage, Beckett somberly walked up to the gravesite. He asked the gravediggers to kindly give him a few minutes alone.

Kneeling at Marcia's grave, Beckett quietly took his right hand and brushed the soil from the top of Marcia's dirt-splattered casket. Words were not easily forthcoming, so he knelt there silently at first, staring at what would be Marcia's still form inside the long ivory white box. What he said to her was not so much in words but through his thoughts. He told Marcia how much he loved her. That he would always love her...for as long as he lived. He meant every word, of course. He only wished he was man enough to say it aloud to her now.

For a moment, Beckett swore he saw Marcia's face smiling up at him from the grave, mouthing the words, "I love you, too." The image, however real or imagined, eased some of his pain as he stared back for one final look.

Still kneeling, without uttering a word, Beckett pulled a long-stem red rose, shortened at the end, from his black lapel. He laid the vibrant flower over the spot where Marcia's face would be and bade farewell, planting a kiss with his hand on the ivory white lid.

"Goodbye, my love," he whispered softly.

Rising to his feet, Beckett eased away as the gravediggers returned to their task of filling in the grave under the red-hot sun.

The grieving police lieutenant was sure it was the only visit he would ever make.

***

Chief Batters had told Beckett he could go home after the funeral. But the best therapy, Beckett told himself, was to jump right back into his routine, make himself work. Nothing heals faster than that.

When Beckett returned to the office, there were three phone messages waiting for him on his desk. One from Timmy Farrell, probably wanting to confess to another made-up murder he didn't commit. He tore that one up. Another from his local barber, Manny, trying to make a year-round living in a half-year resort community and wanting to set up a hair appointment. The third number he dialed immediately.

"Mrs. Dolores Colter? Yes. Thanks."

Beckett paused while he waited for Mrs. Colter to come to the phone. A delicate sounding voice answered the other end.

"Hello, Mrs. Colter? Lieutenant Beckett."

"Yes, lieutenant, I understand you need to speak to me." "Yes. Yes, very much. How about I meet you at Bob's Big Boy? You name the time."

"That's too public of a place for me," Colter said. She had something there.

"I understand. Of course," Beckett replied in a consolatory tone. "How about Ah Fong's in Cathedral City? Do you know the place?"

"I do."

"Good. You can walk straight back to the booths. As quiet as..."

Beckett almost said "the grave" and caught himself.

"Very private."

"I can you meet there in a half hour," she said firmly.

"Fine, fine. In half an hour. Right. Thanks very much."

Dolores Colter was enough of a lookalike for her sister over at Bob's Big Boy that they could be twins. But she was much younger and quieter than her sister, and more feminine, almost shy. Beckett imagined her moving in and out of rooms in Van Ander's big mansion without ever being heard and hardly ever seen. The perfect servant...There and not there. Things done magically, like the leprechauns are supposed to do them, if they exist.

After the amenities, Beckett quietly, gently, but with his official air of authority emerging, got down to business. He would mourn Marcia on his own free time. On duty, from now on, he was what he was, a cop.

"Thank for you for coming, Mrs. Colter."

"Dolores. Call me Dolores. Everyone calls me Dolores."

Beckett's eyebrows came together as he managed a grin.

"Okay. Dolores it is."

Short, petite and with a shapely figure, Dolores took her seat. She seemed instantly comfortable in the presence of the handsome police detective, no doubt the result of many assurances from her much older sister about his good character.

"You know why I've called you here?" Beckett asked.

"Yes, I do."

The young housemaid smiled when she said it, for no apparent reason. Beckett didn't really notice. He thoughtfully proceeded.

"I want you to know that what you tell me here today will be kept in strictest confidence," he said sincerely. "Your sister gave me every indication that you would be cooperative."

"Fire away," Dolores said lightheartedly.

Beckett had a great ability to cut to the chase on all matters and this time was no different.

"First, what was your relationship like with Mrs. Van Ander?" he asked curiously.

"We got along fine," Dolores answered, smiling. "No problems at all."

"No problems?"

"None."

Dolores went on to tell Beckett what he wanted to hear. That Marcia was "nicer than the other two Mrs. Van Anders." She was the first to allow Dolores some personal dignity, insisting that she be called "Mrs. Colter" instead of Dolores. She was also the first Mrs. Van Ander to slip Dolores a few extra bucks over and above her salary, which was paid by Mr. Van Ander and by check, usually on a Friday night after the banks were closed and when she was dead broke and needed it most.

"She was more down to earth than his other wives," Dolores offered without hesitation as if she was talking to a close friend. "She never treated me like a servant, but like a member of the family."

Beckett found nothing to indicate that Dolores wasn't being totally truthful with him, and moved on.

"What about Marcia's...I mean, Mrs. Van Ander's relationship with Mr. Van Ander?"

Dolores looked puzzled for a moment, uncertain by what he was implying.

"What do you mean?"

"Did they get along?" Beckett wondered. "Could you call them...close?"

The question struck a nerve. Dolores, suddenly looking uncomfortable, squirmed in her seat.

Displaying far more emotion than usual, having just buried his ex-wife, Beckett instinctively reached across the table. He took Dolores' soft gentle hand and tried to calm her.

"It's okay," he assured her. "I'm sure this isn't easy for you, as close as you were with Mrs. Van Ander. But anything you can tell me would be helpful."

Dolores carefully chose her words as she spoke.

"Yeah, you could say they were close," she said. "She never left his side, or so it appeared."

"What do you mean?" Beckett asked inquisitively.

Dolores grew deathly quiet again. Out of her deep loyalty to Mrs. Van Ander, she wasn't sure whether to answer the question.

Beckett leaned forward in his seat. Returning to form, he pressed her for an answer.

"Do you mean they put on a good act in front of others, when secretly it was just the opposite?" Beckett asked firmly. "Or that there was really no love between them?"

Dolores' face reflected a conflict of emotions. Did she, or didn't she tell. Suddenly, she answered.

"Mr. Van Ander is impotent. "

Beckett did a quick double take. His eyes jerked wide and his whole body tensed. Dolores' answer completely took him by surprise. He was expecting her to say anything but that. But he found the news highly significant, nonetheless.

"Are you sure?"

Dolores eyed Beckett straight in the eye with a look of confidence on her face.

"I'm positive. In fact, I was sworn never to tell anyone."

Beckett smiled. He couldn't believe he got so lucky.

"So why me?"

At that moment, Dolores started to cry. Overcome with emotion, she said, "Because I want to help you find whoever killed Mrs. Van Ander and see that they rot in jail."

Now the tears really started to flow. Beckett searched his pockets for a handkerchief but found none. Thinking fast, he handed Dolores his unused napkin, with the Ah Fong's logo imprinted on front, to wipe her tears away.

"It's okay," Beckett said, comforting her. "Take whatever time you need."

While Dolores tried composing herself, Beckett's mind couldn't help but wander. Mr. Van Ander, a man who had everything, was unable to perform his husbandly duty. What cop wouldn't consider that important, especially him.

Here was a strikingly beautiful woman—his beloved Marcia—who he just happened to know liked sex better than eating, sleeping, and sometimes breathing. Suddenly, she marries someone old enough to be her father to get everything she always wanted in life and, if she's to keep her marriage vows, she's facing possibly years of celibacy. What a cruel joke to play on Marcia, or to have Marcia unwittingly play on herself.

But Beckett took no real satisfaction in Van Anders's predicament. He was a cop now, not an ex-lover, not an ex-husband. If Van Ander was incapable, as Dolores said, then it raised the distinct possibility that Marcia was having an affair with someone whose equipment was in better working order.

Beckett wasn't going to let his conscience bother him for thinking it. After all, the only thing he could do for Marcia now was find the animal that killed her.

Dolores blew her nose in the napkin after which she pulled herself together and looked ready to talk some more as Beckett emerged from his deep thought.

"We can continue this another time if you like?" he generously offered.

"No, that won't be necessary," Dolores responded between sniffles. "I'd rather get it over with. If that's okay with you?"

Beckett nodded in a way to indicate he had no objections.

"Fine. If that's how you want it."

Beckett continued his line of questioning and didn't hold back in his interrogation of her as a witness.

"Based on what you just told me, did you ever see Mrs. Van Ander with any other men?"

Dolores quickly shook her head as she drew the napkin closer ready to break into tears any moment.

"There were always good-looking men hanging around—tennis instructors, surfer types, young movie and television actors, the kinds of people Mr. Van Ander thought were part of the 'in' crowd and whose youth and energy might rub off on him," Dolores recalled, pausing a moment to dry her eyes with the tear moistened napkin. "In fact, Mr. Van Ander was not above matching up couples, who sometimes wound-up coupling behind the swimming pool or in one of the seven bedrooms in the house during his famous all-night parties."

Beckett wondered out loud, "But what about Mrs. Van Ander?"

Nervously folding the napkin over twice in her bare hand, Dolores proceeded to weave a good story for the police lieutenant.

"I never knew of Mrs. Van Ander having any liaisons with any other men, if that's what you mean," she said, seeming sincere. "She played tennis on their own court with Mr. Cooper, but so did Van Ander and everyone else. She played golf with Betty Checkers and sometimes her husband came along, but he rode the electric golf cart because he had an artificial leg."

Suddenly, the teary-eyed Hispanic woman, in her early thirties, fell deathly silent. Like a person harboring a deep, dark secret, she groped for the right words without her voice or facial expression giving away the fact that she was being less than forthcoming with him.

"It wasn't that a lot of young men hadn't tried," she continued, "but Mrs. Van Ander gave every indication, like I said, that she was very fond of and very loyal to Mr. Van Ander."

Beckett seemed satisfied with Dolores' thorough account of his ex-wife's relationship with the aging millionaire, for now.

"I have a few more questions," Beckett offered, "if you don't mind?"

Dolores nervously fidgeted again with the tear-soaked Ah Fong's napkin in her hand, doing her best not to bring attention to her actions. She smiled at Beckett convincingly.

"Be my guest," she said.

Beckett finally steered the conversation to that fateful night of Marcia's murder. He uttered the obvious.

"Where were you on the night Mrs. Van Ander was murdered?" he unshakably asked.

Dolores twisted in her chair, her nerves finally breaking.

"Do I have to answer that?" she replied quietly.

"No, you don't," Beckett said seriously. "But, sooner or later you will, when I ask you to testify."

"Testify!" Dolores jumped from her seat as though she were shot from a cannon. "Nobody said anything about me testifying."

Beckett was anything but patient with the hysterical housemaid. He snapped.

"Dolores, calm down!" he shouted.

Beckett's booming voice attracted the curious looks of patrons seated close by. Lowering his voice, he tried to reassure her.

"That's if this case should ever go to trial. It's a big if. First, we have to find substantial evidence..."

Dolores was now standing outside the booth, ready to leave.

"Thank you, lieutenant." She didn't stop to shake his hand. "But I think I'll be going now. If I say anything else in the future, I'll do so with an attorney present."

"But Mrs. Colter...Dolores. Wait!"

Dolores quickly exited the restaurant. She was out the door in no time.

Beckett snapped a twenty-dollar bill from his wallet and tossed it on the table in frustration to cover the bill. He chased after her.

Pushing his way through the swinging glass door, Beckett was instantly blinded by the searing rays of the blistering sun. Squinting uncontrollably, he searched the parking lot for any sign of Dolores. It was no use. There was no trace of her anywhere.

Suddenly, directly in front of Beckett, a woman, fitting her description, drove off in a blue 2003 Ford Fiesta sedan. Beckett managed to catch a quick glimpse of the driver. It was Mrs. Colter. She raced by him at breakneck speed and bolted into the one-way street, in the thick of moving traffic, without even looking and headed south.

Beckett hopped in his Ford Explorer, just a few feet away, and took off after her. He, too, barreled through the intersection and ran the red light as cars from the other lanes converged in his direction, and narrowly missed him as he slipped through.

Dolores stared hopelessly at herself in the rearview mirror. She was in tears, confused and upset. She felt sick to her stomach, like a traitor for betraying the confidence of her employer. She was so full of angst over the situation she wanted to scream as cars unknowingly sped by her in the other lanes.

Carelessly weaving in and out of traffic, Dolores jumped ahead of the long parade of cars on the four-lane road. South Palm Canyon Drive, the main artery through town that connected to Highway 111, was jammed with tourists and other weekenders from Los Angeles streaming into town. It looked like an impossible situation.

Beckett pondered his dilemma. He quickly studied his options.

"Okay, Sherlock. Think."

Dolores was in no waiting mood. She pressed her foot on the gas pedal, increasing her speed. Black eye shadow, mixed with tears, was now streaming down her face.

Suddenly, without warning, Beckett darted through a small opening to the outside lane. Two cars in the adjoining lane, unable to brake in time, instantly collided. The two motorists angrily raised their fists, screaming profanities in Beckett's direction as he passed ahead of them and the logjam behind them.

Beckett wasn't through. He hopped his SUV on the narrow sidewalk and crashed through a brown metal trash receptacle, spraying garbage all over the place, as innocent bystanders scurried out of his way. Racing down the concrete walkway, Beckett kept one eye on Dolores; the other on the tourists ahead.

Spotting Beckett in her rearview mirror, Dolores sped faster. Tears continued to swell in her dark brown eyes. By now, she was over the edge.

Beckett made up the slack, bolting the 3.5-liter, six-cylinder eco boost charged Explorer back on the asphalt road, ahead of the traffic on the outside lane. He found himself neck and neck with Dolores. He screamed out to her to help.

"Dolores! Pull over."

Dolores paid no attention, her eyes peeled ahead, crying, and hysterical.

Beckett tried once again to talk some sense into her. Raising his voice above the din of motorists, he shouted, "Dolores, slow down! Please. Let's talk this over."

Dolores tearfully raced ahead. She wasn't listening.

At that moment, the traffic signal at the next intersection suddenly turned red. Cars unconsciously began to cross the intersection. Dolores never stopped. Panic-stricken, drivers frantically swerved out of her way, many peeling off the side of the road. Others, not so lucky, collided, sending broken glass and metal everywhere.

Remarkably, Dolores roared through the intersection untouched and unscathed as a black Lincoln Continental spun out of her way to avoid a collision and Beckett slammed his brakes stopping short of rear-ending the car in front of him as Dolores sped away.

Beckett slammed his fist in anger. "Damnit!"

Within minutes, police arrived on the scene with sirens blaring. Officer Suarez walked up to Beckett standing outside his Explorer to provide him with an assessment of what had transpired.

"You wouldn't believe me if I told you," Beckett said with a snarl. "In my years on the force, I have never seen anything like it. I'll provide a complete report when I get to the back to the station."

"Any charges?"

Beckett quickly surveyed the surroundings—miraculously, no serious damages, outside a few scratched bumpers.

"Unless somebody comes forward, I would say no."

Later that afternoon, when Beckett submitted his report, he recommended no charges be brought against Dolores Colter and the whole matter was effectively dropped.

***

It was near dusk, the end of a long, horrendous day. Beckett was seated in his usual counter seat at Bob's Big Boy, having a quick cup of coffee. He wasn't there for pleasure. Dolores's sister Maria was expected any moment. She was working the dinner shift. Beckett had tried calling her after the high-speed chase involving Dolores but her cell phone went straight to voicemail, and he knew of no other way of reaching her. Based on the time that had lapsed since Dolores turned hysterical on him driving recklessly away, he doubted Dolores had spoken to her sister yet about the incident. Beckett wanted to break the news to Maria personally.

Maria, in an unusually talkative mood, made her way to the counter, where Beckett seemed preoccupied, poring over a cup of his steaming hot brew.

"I take it you have spoken to my sister," Maria said cheerfully.

Beckett, in his own world, snapped out of it. He looked up and there was Maria smiling in his face.

"Yes, I did," he responded smoothly. "Have you spoken to her this afternoon?"

"No, I haven't. My cell phone keeps going to voicemail, and I can't receive or make calls. I don't know why. I'll have to take it to the local Verizon store and have them look at it."

Maria paused to catch her breath for a second and then continued.

"How did everything go?"

Beckett decided to hold off on telling her the bad news. Eventually, he would get to it.

"Fine. Fine. Your sister was very cooperative."

"I told you she would be."

Maria leaned closer, practically touching Beckett's shoulder, so what she was about to say was heard by only him.

"I must say, it's awfully weird, if you ask me," Maria offered, "how someone so beautiful, so wanted by men, preferred women."

Employing all his will power, Beckett refrained from revealing surprise, disappointment, anger, or any other emotion.

"What did you say?" he asked incredulously.

"Do I have to be more specific?" Maria audibly sighed. "Your ex-wife had a female lover."

Beckett didn't have to ask himself how Maria knew that. No doubt she heard about such gossip from her sister. But why Dolores neglected to mention it to him made him suspicious. She made it very plain how much she liked and respected Marcia, so she was, of course, protecting that little corner of her dead mistress' reputation, attaching no special significance to what appeared to be a flaw in the lady of the manor's character.

"If so, then who?"

Maria whispered the name in Beckett's ear.

"Are you sure?"

Maria smiled but only to make her point.

"Never more positive."

Beckett's mind began spinning with ideas filling his head on what this all meant.

"How positive?"

Maria lowered her voice to a whisper as she filled him in on the dirty details.

"They shopped together, they golfed together, they took jeep rides into the desert together to study dunes formations and the flora and the fauna," Maria explained without sparing any particulars. "They took occasional weekends together shopping in San Francisco, or walking along the cove of La Jolla, or sun bathing in the nude on a private beach in Santa Barbara. They were an item all right."

Beckett still had doubts. This was his now deceased ex-wife she was talking about.

"What makes you so certain?"

Maria shook her head in a manner that was unflappable and convincing.

"Everybody knew. There were the secret little exchanges of meaningful glances...those discreet little touches to the hand," she continued, "and much more. Enough to convince even someone who didn't want to be convinced that some hanky-panky was going on between them. I'm surprised, lieutenant. Didn't Dolores tell you about this?"

Beckett glanced down at his lukewarm coffee and suddenly grew silent. That pit in his stomach returned.

"What's wrong?"

Beckett never looked more serious in his life when he spoke to her next.

"Maria, there's something I came here to tell you."

Beckett stood up, walked around the counter, and faced her so what he said could be heard only by them.

"About your sister Dolores, this afternoon she tried taking her life."

"What?" Maria said, turning emotional. "You can't be serious. My sister? Dolores?"

"Yes, Dolores," Beckett said bluntly. "After speaking with me, she turned hysterical when I told she might have to testify if Marcia's murder ever went to trial. She sped off from the scene. I couldn't catch her. She ran through I don't know how many stop lights and it's lucky she didn't kill herself or others."

Immediately, Maria burst into tears. The mere fact Dolores had tried to end her life pushed her over the edge, and never stopped crying as Beckett stood there motionless. As the rage inside of her built to a crescendo, she began violently beating Beckett's chest with her tiny fists in frustration until finally crumpling in his massive arms.

Beckett didn't know to say, or what to do. Instead, he let Maria cry for as long as was necessary.

5

Thursday morning, Beckett hardly got out of his Ford Explorer after pulling into the parking lot when Lt. Garcia collared him.

"Beck." No one on earth ever called him that, except Garcia, who now imagined they had some personal bond between them since the Ramirez brothers' incident. "That television documentary crew from Los Angeles is in your office, waiting for you."

Beckett smiled tenderly at Garcia as he stepped out on his sport utility vehicle.

"The Chief must be riding you hard for you to meet me out here."

Garcia roared at that and clapped his new pal Beckett hard on the back as they headed inside.

Beckett was not overjoyed at the prospect of conducting a tour for the Los Angeles television documentary team. He would be civil, as always, but he would cut the tour short and nobody would know the difference so he could then get on with the murder investigation, which, admittedly, was moving at a snail's pace.

Beckett's first disappointment came when he saw the producer. If his driver's license said he was twenty-two years old, he must have had it printed by Old Deak, the Sunset Boulevard purveyor of ready-made identifications Beckett knew from his days as a Hollywood vice detective. Deak conducted a brisk business in fake driver's licenses, sold mostly to minors or men who were spending weekends in motels with minors and flashed at bartenders in the area who grudgingly admired Deak's artistry.

Why Beckett was thinking all this through the introductions he would never know. He shook hands with Bill Touhy, the producer, a nice enough fellow who seemed harmless, and his cameraman and soundman who were busy loading their equipment into Beckett's black Explorer.

Beckett climbed behind the wheel, the producer and crew in toe, for a drive through Palm Springs. Touhy sat in the passenger side, the cameraman perched in the right-hand side rear so he could poke his camera out the window and the soundman who seemed to own more wires than AT&T was already recording and assuring everyone he had hours and hours of whatever it was he was supposed to have to do his job.

Beckett usually tried to talk like reporters and producers thought cops talk, the way they did in popular crime shows like *Blue Bloods* and *Law and Order*. He used expressions like, "That's what's going down," he heard Donnie Wahlberg as Detective Danny Reagan say one night. He could see that his little phrases were immediately understood by the documentary crew.

Beckett first took them to the northern part of Palm Springs. They passed a lovely home owned by a top Teamsters official with mob connections, another by a Chicago Mafia chieftain, two more here, four more there.

"They call this area Little Lombardy because there's so many Italian mob guys billeted here in homes ranging in price from a million on up to your guess is as good as mine."

Next, Beckett drove them to, and into, Southridge, the very

posh, gated, and secluded private community in Palm Springs with luxury home enclaves valued up to $10 million and they looked at Tony Accardo's home and the cameraman shot stills of Accardo's name on the garage door. Big Tuna wasn't home, apparently, nor were any of the others and that was just as well. It was off season and they were in colder climes and, if they were home, Beckett would have to explain why he was almost, but not quite, invading their privacy. Technically, legally, there would be no problem while he kept the documentary crew on public roads and off private property. But he knew how these guys operated. He knew they would come back and shoot some more on their own, possibly on private property, and he could not be a party to that. They used up what seemed like miles of digital video shooting the enormous estates and prestigious residences in the Movie Colony previously owned by notable celebrities Cary Grant, Frank Sinatra, and Jack Benny, and lavish mid-century homes in the famous Deepwell Estates neighborhood whose most famous residents included Loretta Young, Jerry Lewis, Eva Gabor, Liberace, and William Holden, and on they went.

When they finished, to Beckett's surprise and chagrin, they rendezvoused back at the Palm Springs airport with a helicopter pilot and he and the producer Touhy and the cameraman went aloft and shot all the areas all over again. This time they got superb aerial views of the estates they couldn't quite see from the ground because that's the way they were designed, for maximum security and privacy. Beckett grudgingly admitted that these guys knew what they were doing. They covered all the bases.

Touhy had an expense account and afterward they all broke for lunch at Paul D'Amico's restaurant. He mentioned there was one in West Hollywood and Beckett said he had eaten there many times. Beckett was welcomed warmly by the maître d' Louis when they walked inside and immediately thought Beckett had to come to see the owner.

"Paul's not here, lieutenant," he confessed, "and he'll sure as hell be disappointed, he missed you."

"It's fine, Louis, I'm not here on police business. Some other time perhaps."

Soaking up the posh surroundings, Beckett and Touhy and his crew chatted awhile after ordering. Touhy picked up the conversation from where they left off before entering the restaurant about his work as a Hollywood documentary producer to impress the good lieutenant, not that it was warranted.

"I enjoy my work," Touhy gushed. "I believe it's my calling to do what I do."

Beckett countered with short smile. "I can't tell."

"As I started to say before, I have produced one thousand four hundred and twelve documentaries on Hollywood, the runaways, the street prostitutes, etc. and so on, including some of names and faces from your old territory when you were a vice squad detective."

Beckett decided this bright young kid was either lying or he was six months older than that fellow who ran Shangri La. Maybe he had one of those pictures in his Glendale apartment that grew old in the closet while he stayed young. Well, no harm in any of it, he thought.

After lunch, Beckett bid Touhy and his crew goodbye, thanked God he wasn't in public relations, and got on with the business at hand…investigating his ex-wife's murder.

Back at the station, Beckett dialed Mary Ann Morrison's number. She wasn't home, or she wasn't answering her phone. Just as well. Right at that moment, Bernie Sandy stuck his head round the corner and announced himself.

"Good afternoon, lieutenant. How's tricks?"

Beckett was glad he chose a time when he had a few minutes to shoot the breeze. Sandy wasn't his favorite private eye. His association with him dated back to his days working as a vice squad detective in Hollywood where Sandy originally got his start as a private investigator—a term he preferred people call him instead of a "private dick." Ordinarily, Beckett didn't have too much use for private investigators. In fact, he didn't.

actually producing

Although it was a dying profession, Sandy apparently never received the memo it was. Beckett couldn't understand it. They spent most of their trying to find out who was patting whose tush and looking under beds and following middle-aged husbands and wives trying to recapture their youth.

After relocating to Palm Springs, Sandy followed Beckett a year later. Occasionally, they would have an interesting case to talk about, but lately that was almost rare. Most of the time, they didn't want to talk about what they were doing unless the situation called for it. This was one of those times.

Beckett could tell Sandy had something on his mind he wanted to spill—fast.

"Bernie, you look like a guy ready to spill his guts."

"You know me too well," Sandy said with a laugh.

"So, what's is it that brings you here?"

Sandy leaned forward within a whisker of Beckett and in a low voice answered.

"I've heard something that might have a bearing on this Van Ander murder case you're working on, but I'm a bit reluctant to spill it because, well, I know how sensitive it's got to be for you and what I've heard is, well, somewhat intimate."

Beckett shot an understanding glance his direction. He respected Sandy, as much as he could a private investigator. He explained that he had asked to be assigned to the case and assured Sandy in so many words, "I can handle any part of it like the professional you hoped I am."

Beckett's comment put Sandy at ease and he was more forthcoming.

"I think I have a suspect for you. I'm not sure. But I just might."

"Give me a name."

"Johnny Robelli."

The vision of Johnny Robelli immediately came into Beckett's head. They had never met, never spoken, but Beckett knew all about him—the ambitious young man anxious to rise in the organization…not just any organization, mind you, but the known Mafia organization.

"I know him too well. The Philadelphia Robelli's. Old man Carlo with one eye, right?"

"The same," Sandy anxiously replied. "Johnny's the kid who made good. The other one's a Protestant minister and so the old man naturally never talks about that."

"He lives on the south side of town."

"Right."

"Dresses like he owns six clothing stores."

"I see I can't pull a fast one over you," Sandy said with a chuckle. "He is one and the same. The same good-lookin' guy."

"If you like the type," Beckett quipped.

Sandy laughed. "Good one, lieutenant."

"What about Robelli? What's the connection?"

Sandy seemed to be apologizing in advance for whatever it was he had and Beckett didn't like that. It made his information more suspect.

"Don't take this as gospel. But Robelli, uh, was seen with Mrs. Van Ander in several places, several times. I mean, like, not fundraisers for the charity of your choice, but intimate cocktail lounges, joints like that. Midafternoon…Late at night…Off hours, like they didn't want to be seen."

"The source of this, this information?" Beckett asked.

"Will you take my word for it? It's good. It's offered without vindictiveness on the part of the source. No ax to grind, take my word for it."

Beckett didn't mince words with Sandy. He went straight at him like he did any prostitute or pimp when he was in vice cleaning up the streets of Hollywood.

"You don't want me to talk to the source?"

"I can't Luke. Give me that. You protect your sources."

Beckett nodded, though deep in his gut he didn't like the conditions under which Sandy was offering the information.

"True. It works both ways. Okay. Any more?

"Just that."

"It's enough for now. Thanks, Bernie. I'll buy you a drink when this is over."

Sandy smiled for the first time since walking into the station.

"Thanks, lieutenant. That's what I like about you. You're a straight shooter who never lets a favor go unpaid. Not that I expected anything in return."

Beckett glanced up at the clock and quickly ushered Sandy out the door. "Thanks, I'll be in touch if I need anything more from you."

As Sandy left, Beckett could feel that knot coming back in his gut. That jumble in his stomach was all because of Marcia. Why in heaven's name had she become involved with another woman and at the same time with the son of a notorious Mafia figure— the same one who tooled around town in a vintage white hardtop Thunderbird probably paid for with a thousand needle tracks up and down a hundred teens' arms—who may have been behind her murder? It was enough to make Beckett sick.

Beckett wanted to immediately jump into investigating Robelli and his alleged connection to Marcia's unexpected death, but Chief Batters had other plans.

"Get over to the Katie Cahill place," Batters told him before he had set foot in his office. "Her maid arrived this morning and thinks the old gal's been kidnapped. Probably just wandered off, and is lurking somewhere among someone's petunias."

That was an optimistic assessment on the Chief's part, as Beckett soon discovered when he stepped foot into the privately gated Cahill estate—a sprawling four bedroom, four-and-a-half bath showplace with upscaled and high-end finishes throughout—on East Alejo Road. It was ultra-modern and contemporary inside and like stepping into a museum: priceless art hung on walls, every stitch of furniture having a place and purpose, and simple and clean appearance throughout, right down to its imported Italian marble flooring, that was striking to the eye. Young police officer Pete Halper was holding the fort until Beckett arrived and fortunately had already dealt with the media to whom someone had leaked the story. They had taken pictures, outside and in, and some closeups, according to police officers at the scene, of the wedding picture on the mantle. It was old Patrick Cahill, looking young and virile beside his radiant new bride Katie.

"I think you'll want to see this right away, lieutenant," Halper said escorting him down a long hallway.

Halper led Beckett into the bathroom. There on the mirror of the vanity was a message made from letters cutout of newspapers and pasted to the glass with white glue. It read: "We'll be in contact."

Beckett examined the design and lettering more closely. It looked like the work of amateurs and not serious hostage takers, but had a police photographer snap a photo of it anyway.

"We'll want to dust the entire place for fingerprints, especially in here," he said pointing to the mystifying message on the wall for which there were no immediate clues. "You didn't touch anything?

"No, sir."

"The reporters and photographers, they didn't handle anything?"

"I wouldn't let them."

"Good. You have any idea which member of the family they're talking about when they say they'll be in touch with someone?"

"Beats me," Halper said with a shrug. "Our background check shows she has no living relative. Maybe a cousin in Dublin, Ireland, but that's another old lady, maybe older than Mrs. Cahill, and she's never been to this country, so no one here would even know she existed."

"Screwy," Beckett said shaking his head in disbelief. "Then the kidnappers simply goofed. They assumed she would have family, and they noted the telephone number and they plan to get in touch on this phone. What else?"

Halper agreed.

The two officers then walked around the house to look for something—anything—that might give them a clue as to who might have taken Mrs. Cahill. The why was easy enough to guess. She was worth billions, loaded in every sense of the word. She would be a good snatch if her kidnappers could pull it off.

"Well, what the hell," Halper said. "She was very old anyway. She must have been seventy-five, did you know that?"

"Seventy-five, eh? Well, Halper, what right did she have to live, right? Sometimes you can be a perfect asshole."

"Hey, don't take it personally. I was just thinking that she's lived most of her life and…You know."

Beckett didn't know and stood there flat-footed without saying a word and let Halper continue to make a fool of himself.

"Was she someone important? Was she somebody?"

"Everybody's somebody," Beckett said, gingerly examining a handmade doily that looked like a museum piece.

"Well, sure, but you know what I mean. Who exactly was she?"

Beckett walked over to the wedding photo and stared into it long and hard.

"Did you ever hear of Patrick J. Cahill?"

Halper shook his head. He had not.

"Okay, if you've played pool or billiards six times in your life, the odds are that at least four of those times you were playing with Pat Cahill's balls. No pun intended. He made billiard balls for a living and a very good living it was, from the looks of this house."

Beckett sighed. He needed to move on. There was more work to do

"I'll order the dusting of fingerprints and then talk to the neighbors and the maid to see if they know anything."

Halper handed Beckett the name and address and phone number of the maid, Conchita, and Beckett wasted no time leaving the scene. Could Mrs. Cahill's disappearance and murder of his ex-wife Marcia be related? To say it hadn't crossed his mind would be an understatement.

6

Thelma Morrison was a loser all her life. It ended at age thirty-nine sprawled in an alley in a pile of garbage where three street thugs had gang-raped her. One of her attackers had panicked at her screams and hit her too hard across the face slamming her head onto the hard pavement and died upon impact.

Thelma's only daughter, Mary Ann, didn't bother to come to her mother's funeral. It was the cheapest plan on record, a private charity case handled by a small fundamentalist church Mrs. Morrison attended a few dozen times either to get out of the rain or to pick up tricks. The pastor, Reverend Hugh Masters, was a kind man and burying Mrs. Morrison was, as he saw it at the time, an act of Christian mercy. Besides, he got a fifty-dollar kickback on every stiff he directed to Greely, Greely and Terrence, the local neighborhood mortuary.

The service, not unexpectedly, was austere. No family or relatives, no flowers except a small clutch of plastic lilies that Reverend Masters placed on each casket during the service, but removed before it was moved. Thelma Morrison's transport to a better life beyond was a plain wooden box half-heartedly covered by the world's thinnest coat of varnish. The same prisoners who attended all church funerals were on hand to mumble a few half-forgotten prayers and to wait in impatient anticipation of the coffee and donuts that would traditionally follow once the business at hand had been completed. Masters gave Thelma what only he knew to be the short sendoff and noted with some satisfaction that poor old Mrs. Dooley's hacking cough seemed to be getting worse.

Thelma Morrison's daughter, her only child, was not among the mourners. She didn't even know, at the time, that her mother had shuffled off this mortal soil and if she had, she might have said, in her own sentimental way: "Tough shit."

On her eleventh birthday, Mary Ann Morrison's father, a one-eyed alcoholic on a disability pension from Amtrak, had raped his pretty young flesh-and-blood daughter for the third time. On this occasion, the terrified youngster finally screwed up enough courage to tell her mother. Thelma was outraged, of course. She slapped Mary Ann as hard as she could, sending her reeling across the room. Thelma screamed at her, telling her she must have provoked the poor man with her young well-developed body for her age, always parading in front of her father, with only half her clothes on. Even at eleven, Mary Ann was about seventeen I.Q. points ahead of her mother and her father, combined, and she decided that this was not the healthiest way for a young girl to live. So, she sought the advice and counsel of that nice Los Angeles social worker, Irene Patton, who had come several times to address her health class at school, and sprung her into another home—a foster home—her own.

Mary Ann was grateful to Mrs. Patton who, when the time was exactly right, showed Mary Ann exactly how to be grateful. Irene was a lesbian and playing on the girl's guile and gratitude turned little pretty Mary Ann into the kind of little pet that made Irene the envy of all the other women in her peer group in the sewer. That's what inspired Mary Ann to go into business for herself, as a lesbian hooker in Hollywood.

But Mary Ann was not working the streets of Hollywood

when Beckett did his nightly raids in the area. They had never set eyes on each other before, but Beckett had set eyes on copies of her long rap sheet, thanks to an old friendship with Sgt. Ray Toohey of Hollywood Vice.

Late Thursday afternoon when Beckett came calling, Mary Ann answered the door of her large and comfortable-looking tract-built home on a quiet cul-de-sac in the heart of Palm Desert.

"Lieutenant Beckett, Palm Springs police," Beckett said quickly flashing his identification.

"Yes, I've been expecting you."

Beckett was immediately dazzled. She was darkly beautiful with luminous brown eyes and dark natural auburn hair. It tumbled to her shoulders and was complimented by a floor-length pink cashmere housecoat that was tied casually in the front in a way that revealed cleavage on top and her firm well-shaped derriere on the bottom.

Beckett followed her into the well-appointed living room with gray-washed wood beamed, vaulted ceiling and a warm and inviting marbled fireplace for added ambience. Mary Ann waved him to a chair and he took it. She stood in front of him with a half-smile on her lips and ice cubes in her eyes.

"Two cold beers. That's what we need."

"Not right now, but thanks," Beckett said fleetingly, and too late for her to hear.

Mary Ann had already disappeared into the kitchen to retrieve their drinks while he looked around the beautifully decorated room. Everything was artfully arranged, impeccably furnished, and looked like it had been purchased retail in Beverly Hills. Some of it, in fact, had. Of special interest to Beckett were the many black-and-white and color photographs on the walls, some of them personally autographed, of former and current movie stars—all of them women, beautiful women. The same went for the glass coffee table, covered with all women's magazines—*Cosmopolitan*, *Vogue*, and a couple he had never heard of before.

Mary Ann soon returned with two cold bottles of Budweiser

beer on a tray and two tall, long-stemmed graceful hand-blown Italian tulip glasses, made from crystal and the shape of which Beckett hadn't seen before. She poured his beer, handed it to him, and then poured her own and sat directly across from him in a straight-backed chair. Her sitting motion caused the housecoat to part just enough to reveal her long, well-tanned and perfectly shaped legs. It was a practiced gesture on her part, one she no doubt had made countless times before, to draw attention away from the real purpose of their conversation. Beckett tried to concentrate on her face, but Mary Ann was aware of his apparent discomfort and she was not about to put him at ease.

Smiling sweetly, Beckett almost forgot who and what she was for a moment.

"Well?" she asked coyly.

Beckett came crashing out of his thoughts.

"Oh, yes. Thanks for the beer. Well, of course, you know why I'm here."

"Of course. What can I tell you?"

Beckett took a second gulp of beer, even though he had a hard fast of rule of never drinking on the job while working a case, and began.

"First, let's start with the nuts and bolts shall we. Van Ander told me that about half an hour before Marcia excused herself and said she had a headache, he had gone to bed, had retired early. Is that right?"

"I'm not sure of the half hour, but, yes, I remember him leaving just before she did."

"Good. All right, Mr. Van Ander leaves, the small talk goes on and then Marcia…Mrs. Van Ander…says she has a headache."

"Lieutenant," Mary Ann snapped testily, "we both know you knew her very well and we both know that I knew her very well. Let's call her Marcia."

"Very well," Beckett responded coolly. "Marcia leaves, saying she has a headache. Where are you at that point and what are you doing?"

Mary Ann looked at him as if she had just caught him going through a dead man's pockets.

"I was sitting in a lounge chair sipping a strawberry daiquiri and listening to one of the world's most boring men, our beloved, as yet un-indicted lieutenant governor, blathering on about some nonsense."

Beckett didn't let on that he, too, wondered why that no-good lieutenant governor hadn't been indicted as he continued with his questioning.

"That's where you were and what you were doing when…Marcia"—still having trouble saying her name in front of this woman— "excused herself and left the area."

"Yes."

"You saw her go into the house, following her husband who had left earlier."

"Yes."

"When she didn't return, weren't you concerned?" Beckett asked.

"No."

"Why?"

"It wasn't unusual for Marcia to cop out on one of those parties," Marcia explained. "I was her only real friend there. All the others were *his* friends."

Beckett momentarily noted how Mary Ann said "his" with obvious disdain for Van Ander as she continued.

"Marcia and I both copped out early to lots of other parties like that," she concluded.

Beckett paused thinking to himself, "Don't tell me where you went and what you did. I don't want to hear about it," before probing her further.

"How much longer did you stay at the party? With Marcia gone?"

"Just a few minutes."

"And then?"

"Then I went into the house without saying goodbye to

anyone," Mary Ann said uneasily, "used the bathroom, and quietly left. The front way."

"You didn't hear any unusual sounds before you left.?"

"No."

Beckett was finding it all too hard to believe that Mary Ann didn't know more and pressed her harder.

"Where did you go...after you left the party?"

"Straight home."

"Here?"

"Yes, here."

Beckett thought he noted a trace of impatience and irritation creeping in Mary Ann's voice. If he could penetrate her defenses and get her guard down, then just maybe he would get what he needed from her.

"Was anyone waiting for you here?"

"No. I live alone."

"You didn't go out. Stay home the rest of the evening?"

"It was pretty damned late. I went straight to bed."

Mary Ann shifted her sitting position slightly. The robe fell open a little farther exposing more of her legs than Beckett bargained for.

"You know, you have the look of a man who's very good at what he does."

"You mean, police work."

"I mean whatever."

Beckett tried not to look at Mary Ann's legs and beyond.

"I'm complimented. I think."

Mary Ann smiled back at him. Beckett thought it was an on-cue smile with no warmth to it.

"Do I make you uncomfortable?"

"Why should you?" Beckett said defensively.

"That's not the question," she persisted. "Do I?"

"Well, if it will help move along this discussion any," Beckett said. "Yes, you do...a little."

"Just a little?"

Beckett took a couple of beats, and then said, "Are you familiar with the expression…bullshit?"

Mary Ann flushed, and there was a short, awkward silence for a moment. He had saved his next question for last in case Mary Ann blew her top and ended the interview.

"I'm sorry to have to ask this of you, but it's strictly in the line of duty and this is a murder investigation."

He could see the muscles in Mary Ann's jaw tighten in anticipation of what he was about to ask next.

"I'm a cop. You know I checked your record in Hollywood. You were busted a couple of times for using heroin."

Surprisingly, Mary Ann wasn't as upset as he expected her to be.

"That was a few years ago."

"Yes, it was. But I've got to know if you're still a user."

"I'm not," Mary Ann responded emphatically.

"Not good enough. I want to see your arms."

Mary Ann's eyes flashed her anger but she obviously was struggling to control her emotions.

"And if I don't care to show you, my arms?"

"There are other ways. Legal ways."

Of course, Mary Ann knew that, having been busting before. She nodded and rose slowly, her eyes riveted on his without blinking hers.

"All right, lieutenant, I'm going to satisfy your curiosity, once and for all."

With that, Mary Ann flipped open the sash of her housecoat, and let it slip off her shoulders onto the floor. She was naked, and Beckett could remember only seeing two other women in his entire life who were so perfectly formed. One was Marcia, the other was a black hooker he had busted and who had tried to entice him into forgetting about taking her to the station.

Mary Ann now seemed to be enjoying what she hoped was Beckett's consternation at her attention-getting move. She inched toward him, sensually, and turning her palms outward, extended both arms for him to examine.

"Take a good look, everywhere you want," she said. She turned her arms again and slowly turned her whole seductive body around and then faced him again.

Beckett remained stony-faced. He would be damned if he would give her the satisfaction of reading anything into his face.

"Thank you. You can dress now."

"Oh, can I?" Her tone turned suddenly sarcastic. "Are you sure you want me to?"

"I think so. You made your point."

"What do you think that point is, lieutenant?"

"How is this? What you see is what you don't get."

Mary Ann smiled sweetly at him as she reached down and picked up her housecoat, slowing drawing it around her once more.

"You get the message. Any more questions?"

"Not for now. But I may want to contact you again. Like they say in the movies, don't leave town without notifying us."

As Beckett turned west on Highway 111 and headed for his mobile home on the outskirts of Palm Springs, he was turning two thoughts over in his head. Mary Ann had to be added to the list of suspects. She and Van Ander were the only two people at the party, not counting the house servants, who were away from the party at the time Marcia was in the garden. Van Ander disappeared into the house before Marcia excused herself and went into the garden. He could have seen her go into the garden from his upstairs bedroom window, just above the garden on the east side of the house, and slipped down and killed her, quickly and noiselessly.

Mary Ann went into the house after Marcia left. She could have slipped outside the side entrance and made her way to the garden where she saw Marcia go there. Marcia would have been visible through either of the two side windows of the living room. So, both had the time, and the opportunity to confront Marcia. Ironically, each might have had the same motive—jealously. Van Ander, maybe aware of Marcia's romantic alliance with Mary

Ann, became furious enough to kill her when she refused to give her up. Or Mary Ann, demanding that Marcia leave her heterosexual husband for a permanent lesbian relationship, killed her when she refused.

But could Mary Ann Morrison strangle Marcia? Beckett remembered looking at Mary Ann's arms as she held them out to allow him to examine them for telltale needle marks. As distracted as he was by her curvaceous naked body, he remembered how surprised he was to see that they were unusually muscular for a woman who otherwise was the epitome of feminine pulchritude. Perhaps Mary Ann engaged in some sport, probably tennis, or lifted weights as had become fetish with some women to give her such well-developed arms. As Beckett surmised, it takes a lot of strength to strangle another human being, and to do it silently, for no one reported an outcry. Mary Ann Morrison might be that strong. On the other hand, she could have hired someone to do it, a strong man, just as Van Ander might have done.

Beckett's summation in his mind over possible suspects as he pulled into the driveway of his mobile home was short lived. The following morning, Lionel Van Ander walked into his massive, oak-paneled study, stared at his collections of .999 silver this and that from the Franklin Mint, removed a collector's Colt .45 from its velvet-lined case, carefully loaded it, and blew off the top of his head. But not before he penned a love poem to the memory of his beloved Marcia.

Scratch one suspect.

7

Fate decreed that Luke Beckett should be the last to learn the jarring news that Lionel Van Ander had committed suicide. It was eight o'clock Friday morning when Dolores Colter heard the roar of the Colt .45 from the vicinity of the study. Indoors, it sounded like a cannon going off.

Colter had dropped a skillet full of eggs she was beginning to turn into an omelet for breakfast and took off on a dead run for Van Ander's study, her hysteria increasing with each step she took. By the time she had reached the study, she was in such a state of high emotion that she collapsed on the floor, almost on top of the dead body that was sprawled on the Indian rug, face down, the revolver still clutched in his right hand. She was crying uncontrollably and screaming repeatedly, "No, no, no!" It was as if she said it long enough and loud enough, she might be able to reverse what had happened.

Without checking the body, she staggered to her feet and lurched out of the study to get to the phone in the living room. In her state of extreme anxiety, she forgot that there was a phone not three feet from where Van Ander's body lay with blood running out of the right temple and top of his head where the bullet emerged and tore into an unimpressive little volume, entitled, *The Family Book of Verse* by Lewis Gannett, on the third shelf of the bookcase where Van Ander stood and fired the shot that took his life.

Frank Connors, who had been with Van Ander for the last four years, ran through the kitchen door as Dolores screamed for help into the phone after calling the Palm Springs police. Patched through to Lt. Garcia, the highly distraught woman was unable to collect her thoughts or say anything intelligible, lapsing into a stream of panicked Spanish and gibberish that confused Garcia on the other end of the line.

Finally, Connors grabbed the phone from Dolores' vice-like grip and asked Garcia to hold on a moment. When he asked Dolores what had happened, her hysteria got the best of her again. The best she could do was scream unintelligibly and point to the study. Connors ran to the room, surveyed the scene before him, and then returned to talking to Garcia on the phone.

"Lieutenant Garcia?" he asked frantically.

"Yes, this is Lt. Garcia. What happened? What's wrong?"

"He's dead," Connors explained, casting the emotions of the moment aside. "It looks like he shot himself."

"Who shot himself?" Garcia queried on the other end. "Who?"

"Mr. Van Ander."

"Is he at home, in his home?"

"Yes, sir," Connors affirmed. "In the study."

"Don't touch anything. Don't move. Don't let anyone leave. We'll be right over and an ambulance is on the way."

Lt. Garcia slammed down the phone as hell broke loose in the station to scramble together a team in the early morning hours to rush to the scene to investigate.

At the Van Ander estate, Connors ended the call and looked at Dolores, who was slowly beginning to regain her composure.

"Is there something we can do for him?" she asked.

"No. I think he's dead. I know he is."

"Did you check?"

"No."

Connors went back to the study. Dolores already had made up her mind that wild horses couldn't drag her back to that room to see for herself.

Connors walked slowly, carefully over to the body. Looking closely at it, he knew he was looking at a dead man. He didn't have to touch the body, not the neck, not the wrist, for any sign of pulse. Lionel Van Ander was gone, and the world, for Connors and a great many other people, would never be the same again.

Van Ander chose eight o'clock that morning as the appointed hour for his death. An hour earlier, Beckett had collected Bruno "Pops" Panke from the station's holding cell, packed him into his personal sports utility vehicle, and began the one-hour drive to Riverside, where he would deliver Pops to the sheriff of Riverside County and what would be, after trial and conviction, Pops' eleventh trip the joint. Pops was sixty-two-years-old and he had spent more than forty of those years in various city jails, county jails, country work farms, and state penitentiaries. Pops was the consummate screwup. He had tried his hand at all the conventional things: burglary, armed robbery, grand theft auto, con games, even bank robbery. But he always got caught. If he didn't get caught in the commission of the crime, he got caught trying to make his getaway, or selling his loot.

Pops insisted that he was the victim of colossal bad luck. That was partially true. But Beckett knew something else. If there is one thread that runs through all consistent lawbreakers, it is stupidity. They are simply too lazy or too dumb to earn an honest living, and Pops was the dumbest of the dumb.

This was Pops' eighty-ninth arrest, and it was typical of the kind of mess he always seemed to get himself into. He had decided to hold up Cassidy's all-night eatery on Indian Avenue at the north end of town and he arrived at the restaurant at seven o'clock in the morning. The manager had just opened the place. What Pops didn't know, and hadn't checked out, was that the restaurant had dropped its "open all night" policy several weeks before. So, when

Pops put his gun on the manager, he explained that Pops was the first customer and there were only a few dollars of change in the cash register. Pops took that but, being Pops, didn't leave. He had a brilliant idea. He would wait until several customers arrived, and maybe he would snatch two or three hundred dollars from their wallets before he roared out of town on the I-10 freeway scot-free.

Pops warned the manager to be cool, not to try and signal anyone that anything was wrong, and always keep in his sight, which the manager did. At 8:20 A.M., the first customer arrived. He took one look at Pops, put him up against the wall, searched him and found Pops' gun and the four dollars in change he had taken from the cash register. Then Deputy Sheriff Bernie Krantz phoned the Palm Springs police and they came and took Pops away.

Now Pops said that was just bad luck and no one could deny that it wasn't the greatest good fortune to have the first customer who came through the door be a deputy sheriff. But if Pops had cased the joint, he would have learned that the local police regularly stopped by this same restaurant. Several of them headquartered there, just as Beckett headquartered at Bob's Big Boy.

Pops naturally told the details of his latest escapade to Beckett, who could never get used to the idea that part of his official duties was chauffeuring prisoners to or from lockups, or to or from airports for extradition to another state. Chief Batters considered it highly important work and refused to assign it to anyone below a sergeant. So, this was Beckett's turn again.

Pops insisted on telling Beckett the story of his life, and Beckett charitably agreed to listen. Pops was a legend around southern California and Beckett had never been in his company before for more than a few moments at a time, so he was genuinely curious to know what made this professional loser tick.

At Pops' request, Beckett turned off the radio and listened as the older man began to weave his tales. It was because he had turned off the radio that Beckett didn't hear the first news bulletin on Van Ander's death. It came when Beckett was still fifteen minutes from the Riverside County lockup.

By the time he reached Riverside, Beckett's sides were aching and his eyes were watering from laughing so much. Pops couldn't figure out what was so funny. He was telling him the tragic story of his wasted life. It was nothing to laugh about. What was so funny was Pops rushing out of the First National Bank and Surety Company of La Jolla and falling into an open manhole? He might have been killed. Or the time that he very expertly looted three rooms in the Desert Palace Hotel and, with his arms loaded, somehow managed to back through the door to the main dining room and stumble in just in time to hear the tail-end of a tribute to the new director of the California Police Officers' Association? Nothing funny at all about that time in Santa Barbara when he went to work despite a heavy cold, and clocked in with a fast side street stickup of a jewelry salesman he had been following. Just as the salesman handed over his sample case, Pops was wracked by gigantic uncontrollable sneeze. That's how he happened to shoot himself in the right toe and was unable to get away before the police came.

So it went with Pops: "Just bad luck. Plus, bad judgment, poor timing," Beckett thought, "and probably the man wasn't playing with a full deck." Otherwise, why would he have spent four grueling hours cracking that giant safe in the Wunderlin Storage and Warehouse building in Bakersfield without realizing the safe was being stored for "future use." Of course, it was as empty as Pops' head, and when in frustration he stuck a little too much explosives in the door, he blew a hole in the wall and lost his eyebrows and another front tooth. He was nailed by the nighttime security guard, of course. Nothing but an explosion that big could have jolted him awake.

At the Riverside County Lockup, Beckett hardly got in the door when he was swamped by deputies who wanted to know everything he knew about Van Ander's suicide. That was the first time he learned of it, and that was the way he learned the unexpected news. He got a quick fill-in on the phone from Chief Batters right after giving Pops a friendly slap on the shoulder, turning his papers over to the desk sergeant, and heading for the parking lot when a booming voice behind stopped him.

"Zorro!"

"Zorro" was Beckett's old Hollywood nickname and the voice was unmistakably that of Captain Matt Tierney of the Riverside sheriff's office. Tierney and Beckett went back to those days. Beckett remembered him as a sergeant, and close to being the most honest cop he had ever met.

"You don't kiss hello, you don't kiss goodbye," Tierney said kiddingly.

"Sorry, Matt, I'm in one helluva hurry."

"I know all about that, and that's okay. But you're forgetting something."

"Like what?"

"Like this."

Captain Tierney pointed to a disconsolate looking man, about thirty-five, who was standing off to the side of the squad room, looking at his own shoes.

Beckett cursed himself. How could he forget his delivery schedule? Take Pops Panke up, bring Willie Tread back. Pops was headed for the slammer again. Willie was scheduled for trial in a week or so for a botched savings and loan stickup in Palm Springs. He reminded Beckett of the man who was followed by a black cloud wherever he went, which summed up Willie perfectly.

"Christ, you're right. I forgot about Weepin' Willie. Well, put a ribbon around him and I'll take him home to mother."

"I've already checked his mittens and fixed his lunch," Tierney quipped playing along. "He's ready to go."

Beckett jerked his thumb toward the door, waved goodbye to Tierney and the others, and motioned Willie toward his unmarked black Ford Explorer in the parking lot.

Willie started up almost as soon as Beckett had cleared the parking lot.

"It was a bum rap, man."

"Yeah, Willie, yeah," Beckett said rolling his eyes. "What's your name now?"

Willie Tread had more names than a wall of fame

"Kerrigan...I like the sound of it."

Beckett looked at Willie, not even trying to mask his displeasure.

"Tony Pignetti. How do like the sound of that?"

"I ain't used that name in, maybe, ten years."

Beckett nodded. Better not give him too many opportunities, he thought. Pops was funny and didn't know it. Willie was morose and didn't know it, a real drag.

The silence lasted only a few minutes. Then, Willie sighed audibly. Here it comes, Beckett said to himself. Brace yourself.

"Jeez, Beckett, I hate to go back. I was trying to put together a few dollars just to get out of town and now I'm headed right back."

Trying to put together a few dollars in Willie's case was shoving a .38 caliber revolver under the nose of a middle-aged lady cashier at the Dependable Savings and Loan and nearly giving her a coronary. A silent alarm brought the Palm Springs police to the door and they were waiting for Willie as he walked out with nearly twelve thousand dollars. He was lucky he didn't get his head blown off, Beckett thought.

As usual, Willie was in a pensive mood. Something about Beckett always made Willie reassess his station in his life, perhaps because they were in the same age group.

"Did you know I was born in the slums, Beckett?"

Beckett stayed silent. He knew what was coming. He had heard all it before from more than his share of con men like him.

"There were times," Willie complained, "when we were hungry."

Willie was off and running, but Beckett wasn't listening.

"You should have seen me when I was kid," Willie continued. "I had the cheapest clothes in Hamilton, Ohio. Threadbare they were."

Finally, Beckett broke his silence. He wasn't in the mood to hear it. He had other things on his mind.

"Look, Willie, blow it out your ass, okay? Lots of people are poor, and they didn't go around sticking up people who are just as poor as they were."

Willie nodded but his silence didn't last long.

"Okay, okay. Who expects a cop to understand the human condition anyway?"

Beckett was busy doing a mental litany of his own. After delivering Willie to his appointed destination, his thoughts were back where they belonged—on the Marcia Van Ander murder case and now unexpected suicide of her husband Lionel Van Ander. How much did that have to do with the other? Soon he hoped to find out.

As he pulled up to the Van Ander residence, the place was sealed off by police cars and crime scene tape preventing any unauthorized intruders on the premises with the investigation into Van Ander's suicide in full swing.

Inside, Chief Batters had taken charge and things had calmed down considerably since the discovery of Van Ander's dead body earlier that morning. Pictures had been taken of the crime scene, officers Kelso and Bayne had questioned Colter and Connors more in-depth about the sequence of events as they remembered it, the coroner was on his way, and Van Ander's personal physician, Dr. Gene Osmond, was emerging from the bathroom as Beckett walked in.

Beckett was introduced to the good doctor by Batters who filled him in on the details. Batters then turned to Beckett and said, "What do you think. Can we wrap this up?"

Beckett was incredulous. He knew how anxious the Chief was to end this case successfully. The news media was all over him seeking answers, and so was the mayor's office.

"Wrap it up?" Beckett responded quizzically. "That wasn't a confession you showed me. It was some of the worst poetry I've ever read. If it had gotten into the hands of a critic, he would have shot the author himself."

Nobody laughed. Beckett really hadn't expected they would. It was his way of ridiculing Batters' suggestion that perhaps Van Ander's suicide was proof that he had killed his wife Marcia and now had taken his own life because he couldn't handle the massive guilt.

Batters motioned Beckett to step to the side of the living room. As they did, two ambulance men emerged from the bedroom, gingerly picking their way through the milling bodies in the living room. Beckett stopped them momentarily to take another look at the corpse. He pulled back the sheet, studied Van Ander's lifeless white face for a moment, and then replaced the sheet. The ambulance driver and attendant carried out the corpse as a television news mobile unit for local KESQ-TV Channel 3, the self-proclaimed "Desert's News Leader" which had just pulled up, began reporting from the scene. Later that night, Beckett would marvel at their timing. They got the entire scene of the body being carried through the front door, down the stairs, across the lawn, onto the driveway, down the driveway and into the waiting ambulance. The doors shut and the ambulance moved off, silently.

Through all that, which took about two minutes, KESQ's top television news personality, Rick Mason, was doing a live stand-up reporting of what he had learned so far about Van Ander's suicide. Mason was speculating that Van Ander may have taken his life because he was despondent over his wife's recent death. That was a safe, non-actionable piece of conjecture. They continued to broadcast live reports from the same scene throughout the afternoon and evening's newscasts, as did their NBC television affiliate rival KMIR-TV, topped off with a live interview with Chief Batters, who merely said an investigation was "in progress."

Dr. Osmond had propitiously walked in the front door on the heels of the police. He was making a social, not house call, and had seen the first police cars arrive in front of Van Ander's house. It was he who officially pronounced Van Ander "dead" at the scene. Osmond was an older man who had seen much in emergency rooms and during riots and at the scene of plane crashes in his storied career, but the sight of his close friend and long-time patient lying dead by his own hand obviously had moved him deeply. Still, he was a professional, and when Beckett asked for a few words with him, he was composed. The two men walked out by the pool area. Beckett spoke first when they halted at the edge of the pool.

"Doctor, would you have any objections to answering a few questions...about Mr. Van Ander?"

"As long as you keep your questions professional," the doctor said, "I have no objections."

"They are, and the answers are very important to the murder investigation of Mrs. Van Ander."

"I see. What can I tell you?"

Right away, Beckett jumped started his questioning in typical no-nonsense fashion.

"I know you're not a psychiatrist or a psychologist, but you know—or knew—the deceased, Van Ander. I mean, both as a patient and as a friend."

Dr. Osmond nodded affirmatively after taking a deep breath in response to Beckett's question.

"Yes. He was a good man," he said, pausing for effect. "Oh, some minor flaws, like any of us. But, overall, a gentleman, a good husband I think, and certainly an ethical businessman."

Beckett thought long and hard about his next line of questioning—he knew he may not get another chance to interview the good doctor and wanted to make it count—before continuing.

"I understand. There may be no one else available to me who can answer this question, so please consider it very carefully.

Do you think Mr. Van Ander took his life because he was despondent over the death of his wife?"

Dr. Osmond took his eyes off Becker and stared into the deep recesses of the pool, ablaze with the late morning sun. It was a long moment before he gave his response.

"How can anyone know?"

"I'm only asking for an educated guess. I'm not writing it down, not quoting you. I really wanted…need…your opinion on this. Some people think his suicide may indicate he murdered his wife, or hired to have it done."

The mere notion that Van Ander could murder his wife, much less anyone, was repulsive to the longtime practicing physician who wasn't known for wearing his emotions on his sleeve.

"Not in a million years," he said. "He loved Marcia very much. He told me on more than one occasion she was the first and only woman he ever loved."

"And you believed him?"

"I had no reason not to."

Beckett momentarily collected his thoughts before probing further.

"Then, knowing him as well as you did—probably better than anyone else—you think he killed himself in a fit of despondency over Mrs. Van Ander's death?"

"No," Dr. Osmond said emphatically.

The answer startled Beckett and few things did.

"No?"

"No. I don't think Marcia's murder was the primary reason," Dr. Osmond offered, "although I'm quite sure he was despondent over her death."

Now Beckett was confused and he wasn't the type of person to become easily confused. Why would Van Ander commit the most heinous act of all by taking his life if Marcia's murder wasn't a motivating factor?

"What's left then…that I don't know about?"

Dr. Osmond looked around to make certain no one was in earshot of them. Then he leaned close to Beckett speaking barely above a whisper.

"He was dying. Cancer of the prostate gland. He might have been able to live for, oh, who can say, many months. But he couldn't face it. At least, that's the only conclusion I have."

Beckett thanked the doctor, promised to keep his counsel private, except for routine confidential police report he had to make out, and the pair went back into the house.

Most of the police officers had been released to other duties, and Batters was leaving with Lt. Garcia who had accompanied him to the scene.

"Right where it was," Beckett said, "except now I've lost my primary suspect."

Batters, whose mood shifted like wind, shot him a stern look.

"If you can't crack this in the new few weeks, we're going to close the book. We haven't got the time and manpower to devote to a continuing, interminable investigation."

"Right," Beckett responded coldly.

"Just so you…understand," Batters said.

"I do."

As Batters and Garcia left, Beckett went looking for Connors, Charles, the butler, and Dolores Colter, the housemaid. He didn't know how to proceed, except by the book. He understood that investigating a murder was like working a jigsaw puzzle. When the pieces didn't fit, keeping looking until he found the right ones that did.

By the book it would be and, even though his previous questioning of Colter went badly, Beckett would interrogate her and other the servants next. After that, he didn't have the slightest idea what to do next.

8

Fear is the one human emotion police offers know best. They learn to recognize it early, and in all its degrees. They learn to deal with other people's anxieties, sometimes using them to their own advantage. But first they learn to deal with their own, for fear can be a frequent and constant companion that can be an asset, that starts adrenaline flowing, or a liability that completely immobilizes.

It was fear, unmistakable fear, that Beckett saw in the eyes of the Van Ander's gardener, part-time chauffeur, and handyman Frank Connors when he interrogated him that Friday morning. It was nothing like the ill-at-ease concern he generated in Charles, the butler, when he questioned him. Or the worry he read in Dolores Colter's eyes the second time he spoke to her. No, Connors was trying desperately to mask a fear that went far beyond normal concern in the middle of a police investigation. Beckett was sure of it. He had spent too many years questioning too many people not to be able to read the symptoms.

Yet, Connors said all the right things. He corroborated the factors given Beckett by Charles and Colter. Collectively, the three servants had accounted for everyone's movements during the crucial hour before Marcia's disappearance and prior to the discovery of her body in the garden.

Charles had seen Van Ander retire to his bedroom and had not seen him emerge. Mrs. Colter, busy making cocktail snacks in the kitchen, had not seen Van Ander enter the house, but she did see Mary Ann Morrison walking in the direction of the bathroom. She got busy, however, and failed to see where Mary Ann went after that.

Could Mary Ann possibly have gone to the garden without Dolores having seen her? After much soul-searching, Dolores confirmed it, "Yes."

From Charles' viewpoint, could Van Ander have gone to the garden without him having seen him? "Yes, but..."

Mrs. Morrison confirmed the same. "Why, of course, yes."

That left Connors, standing there in the garden, his strong, gnarled worker's hands grasping the fan rake so hard his knuckles were white. As Connors told Beckett in step-by-step fashion, "I had turned on the sprinklers after dark, forgetting Mr. Van Ander had told me not to sprinkle that day because he noted that a few of his roses were in danger of decaying from too much watering."

Connors turned off the water just a few minutes after he turned it on.

"When did that take place?" Beckett inquired as he shuffled through some papers he was carrying in his right hand.

"As best I can figure about 12:45 A.M.," Connors said unequivocally.

Beckett stayed on subject continuing to probe further.

"Was it usual for you to be watering at almost one o'clock in the morning?"

"No, it wasn't. But I never could sleep when there was a party," Connor said, brushing a wisp of hair out of his eyes. "I was unofficially on standby alert during any of Mr. and Mrs. Van Ander's social functions. Often, one of Mr. Van Ander's guests would drink too much or snort too much cocaine or smoke too much dope. Mr. Van Ander would insist they either stay overnight or have me drive them home and return their car to them the next morning."

Connors added that he did not sleep very soundly, if at all, on party nights. Sitting around that night in his small room, bored and restless, he decided to turn on the sprinklers and then remembered he had made a mistake and turned them off again.

"Had you seen Mrs. Van Ander in the garden at the time?" Beckett asked.

A significant pause and then.

"No, I hadn't."

"Did you see anyone else nearby?"

"None that I remember," Connors offered. "I could hear the muffled sounds of laughter coming from the party. Some far-off crickets chirping. A car or two passing by on the next street. But, no, Mrs. Van Ander was not in the garden around one o'clock in the morning. Only I was."

Trying not to put him too much on his guard, Beckett told Connors, "We'll talk again," and when he walked away added Connors to his suspect list.

On his way out of the house, Beckett noticed Charles arranging a vase of flowers near the entrance to the living room. He had liked Charles almost from the first moment he saw him. Something about his bearing, his style, his grace. He was tall and his dark hair had grayed at the temples. Beckett first thought upon seeing him was that he looked more like the lord of the manor—right out of Hollywood central casting—than Van Ander did. His natural curiosity got the better of him.

"Charles!" Beckett shouted after him.

"Yes, lieutenant."

"I was thinking," Beckett started, "I suppose you and the others will be looking for new positions now that this household is, uh, so disrupted?"

"Yes, sir."

"Tough spot, I'm sure, for you."

Charles smiled patronizingly at the police lieutenant.

"Not really, sir. I'm rather good at what I do, and on a number of occasions, various of Mr. Van Ander's friends have said, 'If you ever want to let go of Charles, I'll take him.'"

Beckett laughed for first time that day.

"Sounds like the player draft in the National Football League."

Surprisingly, what was meant as a friendly comment was taken as an affront by the stately butler.

"I don't consider myself a piece of baggage, lieutenant," he bristled. "I'm a professional and I happen to be rather good at what I do."

Beckett tried to make amends than let the offense stand.

"Don't misunderstand me, Charles. I just thought, well, you sound well educated and you certainly make an impressive appearance and..."

Beckett's effort to apologize fell flat on its face.

"You would have thought I might have aimed a little higher in life?" Charles quickly countered.

"Well...?"

"Lieutenant, I live in million-dollar houses. What kind of house do you live in? I drive limousines and expensive sports cars. What kind of car do you drive? I eat the finest food, drink the best Scotch, and I'm respected. You don't have to be a millionaire to live like one, you know."

Beckett shook his head and smiled. Charles had backed him into a corner and knew it.

"If there's anything I can't stand," he said, "it's a butler who's five times smarter than I am. I asked for that."

It was the first time Beckett had seen the austere Charles smile.

"Yes, sir," he said, "and the butler did it!"

As Beckett walked out the front door, he thought to himself, "That smart son-of-bitch has probably been waiting all his life to drop a line like that on someone like me."

Half an hour later, Beckett was leaving his office and heading toward the Palm Springs Tramway. Johnny Robelli, tall, attractively built, handsomely tanned Italian mafioso, had consented to talk to him and meet him there.

Robelli's old man father, the legendary Carlo Robelli, got his start in the mafia by brutalizing and extorting money from second-hand clothing merchants in New York City's aptly-named garment district along Seventh Avenue and graduated to some of the fanciest labels in the world. Today, the Robelli fortune was reportedly immense, and the old Italian immigrant could point with pride to the fact he owned several clothing factories in New York, and a national chain of retail clothing outlets headquartered in Chicago. To say nothing of the tribute he was still getting from union officials and management people alike. The senior Robelli extracted legal tributes from both sides, playing the peacemaker. He did it so well. With his people in key union jobs, he always got a "yes" vote on a strike and after the walkout was underway four or five weeks, just enough time to give the managers heartburn, he stepped in and settled the strike, for which he was well rewarded by both sides.

People could say this for Johnny Robelli's old man: He was rough and tough and at times ruthless, but he was a man who had made it on his own. The wrong way, yes, but his way and without help, or apology.

His offspring playboy son Johnny was cut from the same cloth. He carried a gun and, of course, had a permit to go along with it. He had a Mickey Mouse title with one of the local security services and technically was a private guard. That gave him the gun. If Johnny Robelli knew where the offices of his employer were, it would come as big surprise to Beckett.

Johnny Robelli seemed to be employed, full time, playing tennis at the Palm Springs Racquet Club and Thunderbird Country Club and, of course, on many private courts in the area. He was almost good enough to be professional—the same with golf.

At the Palm Springs Tramway, Beckett paid for his ticket and waited in line with the tourists at the loading station. It was always jammed, even off-season. The tram was a major visible tourist attraction in Palm Springs. The Chamber of Commerce liked to call it "the eighth wonder of the world." The breathtakingly beautiful ride took passengers up to the Mountain Station at the top of the San Jacinto Mountains where it was generally forty degrees cooler than the desert floor below. This day, it was near 115 degrees in the Coachella Valley and would be very close to 75 degrees at the tram's top-of-the-world final stop. The ride, as Beckett knew it would, took exactly fifteen minutes. The tourists, as Beckett knew they would, oohed and ahhed from inside the large rotating tram all the way up and feverishly snapped pictures and selfies with their cell phones.

By the time they reached the 8,516-foot mark, Beckett and the rest of the passengers disembarked. The air was clean and, by contrast with that below, remarkably clear, and best of all, cool. Whenever he entertained the thought of returning there, for whatever reason, the memory of the smog quickly brought him back to reality.

Beckett moved with the crowd, his eyes searching for Johnny Robelli. He found him, as he thought he might, at the bar. At his side was a curvy blonde showing a little more cleavage than seemed appropriate in the early afternoon. She was the kind of girl who would look sexy in a nun's habit. But she also looked cheap, and the obviously expensive blouse and skirt she wore somehow looked dime store. Maybe it was her style, or lack of it.

Robelli had been watching Beckett, and first spotted him in the mirror behind the bar. He already had his girlfriend coached in what to say and what not to say, how to act and not to act, and when to split if he should need some privacy.

They couldn't quite classify Johnny Robelli as a gangster, although the area newspapers always did. It was, in fact, a bum rap. His father was a gangster, no doubt about that, and mafia, too. But while Johnny spent mafia money, he didn't earn it. He was part of the second-generation mafioso families that caused their male parents to wring their hands. No guts, no ambition, no nothing. Just play, spend, and play some more.

Young Robelli knew about Beckett. Beckett had always been interested in the structure and administration of organized crime. For a short time, he had been on loan to the Riverside County Sheriff's office as an undercover investigator specializing in the comings and goings of the organized crime figures residing in the county, and Palm Springs was part of the county. In that role and another, as a member of a special mob squad formed by the state attorney general's office for publicity purposes before the last election, Beckett had interviewed most of the known mob figures living in Palm Springs. Law and enforcement had its own version of the welcome wagon. One or two people like Beckett would show up, inform the mobsters that they knew who they were and where they were, and caution them not to drop any corpses within the corporate limits of the city or they would suddenly find they were no longer welcome as taxpayers in Riverside County. It worked because the mafia figures wanted it to work.

Palm Springs was, as Beckett knew, was safe ground, even for the warring mobsters. They did not want war here. It was no man's land. They sunned themselves, drank their vino, ordered up call girls when their wives were not around, and had many jolly get-togethers behind the guarded walls of their restricted compounds. Trouble in Palm Springs? Not to worry. Pity the troublemakers if they should break the truce.

Johnny Robelli knew more about Beckett than he wanted to know. He knew about his reputation in Hollywood, not just from Marcia, who talked to him a lot, but from his father Carlo. Beckett would never learn that on at least two occasions mafia bagmen had requested a hit on him. Nothing overt like a shotgun blast, but maybe an auto accident, or just a permanent disappearance that would raise suspicion but never furnish any proof of what had happened.

The mafia was into Hollywood, mostly in the financing of motion pictures and hard-core pornography. It was in the latter area, plus some organized prostitution, that made them aware of Beckett. But someone high up had overruled any hit on the tough young cop. The media liked him too much. He was a celebrity in blue. Bestselling former Los Angeles Police Department officer-turned novelist Joseph Wambaugh, well-known for such fictional works including *The New Centurions*, *The Onion Field*, and *The Blue Knight*, had never mentioned him once on a late-night talk show. The mafia didn't take out a guy like that, even if he was a bastard. The media would make him a martyr, the heat would never end.

Robelli could guess what Beckett wanted to talk about: Marcia. What else? That such a spectacular woman had once been Beckett's and his former wife, the mere thought unnerved Robelli to no end.

"Robelli?" Beckett asked approaching him at the bar.

Robelli was irritated right off the top. Not Mr. Robelli, just Robelli. The contempt he had for Beckett was written all over him—not even a handshake. Beckett just stood there staring a hole right through the famed mobster's son until he finally spoke.

"Yes, and you're Lt. Beckett. Sit down, have a drink. What will you have, sport?"

Beckett hated anyone who used the term "sport" and Robelli was no exception.

"Scotch and water."

Robelli put up two fingers. "Two"

"Hey, what about me?" the voice on the other side of Robelli asked. Robelli hadn't even bothered to introduce the woman next to him.

"You're taking a walk, babe," Robelli said matter-of-factly.

The blonde setup girlfriend nodded brightly, giving Beckett an up-and-down once-over look, before Robelli gave her his parting shot.

"Go look at the tourists for a while."

Whatever-her-name-was slunk off into the distance and a half-dozen pairs of male roving eyes virtually followed every jiggle in front and every ripple in the rear of her clinging rayon dress.

"Nice chick," Robelli stated. "Not much upstairs, but it's the first floor and the basement that count. Right, sport?"

Beckett tried not to look as irritated as he was.

"I'll try not to waste your time or mine, Robelli," Beckett said plainly. "I want to know when and where you met Marcia Van Ander. What you did? Where you went? Exactly what your relationship was? How it ended, if it ended, before her death? We can talk here or at the station."

"Jesus, hold on there!" Robelli reacted violently. "What kind of a barrage is that? I've got some rights to privacy, haven't I?"

"Not in a murder investigation. Your relationship with Mrs. Van Ander is completely relevant to this investigation."

"Okay, okay," Robelli said in a calmer tone. "I've got nothing to hide."

"But you used to do a little hiding, didn't you? At the Castaway Inn. At Emelio's in Indio. That weekend in La Jolla…I could go on."

"What the fuck is this!" Robelli thundered, his voice rising in anger. "An inquisition? Were you having me tailed?"

"No, just information I've picked up since…the murder. You were close with her. I want to know *how* close."

Robelli gave Beckett a long, cold stare, a bit shell-shocked over the line of questioning and then answered.

"Okay, Marcia and I met at one of those celebrity tennis affairs for charity over at Tamarisk Country Club. We were each paired with a movie actor, and neither of them showed up. Learned later they were both gay and they were billing and cooing down the street at the Moonlight motel. So, we were teamed up and that began our friendship."

"How close a friendship was it?" Beckett countered.

"Very close."

"Were you sleeping together?" Beckett inquired further.

"Yes."

Beckett felt that knot coming back into his stomach. He downed his entire drink in one gulp without realizing it, but the action wasn't lost on Robelli.

"How long did this relationship go on?"

"Maybe six, seven months," Robelli replied.

"It ended?"

"Yeah. About three months ago."

"How did you break up?"

Robelli knew what the good lieutenant was fishing for but didn't take the bait.

"Very civilly, very amicably. Marcia was a married woman. Her husband wasn't, you know, too good with the stick. Prostate trouble, I think she said. We didn't break up, we just sort of agreed to part, to not see each other, except in a very superficial, social way."

Beckett processed it all, but deep down he wasn't buying it.

"I see. No hard feelings. Still pals."

"You might say that, yes."

Beckett, reverting to his Hollywood vice squad style, tried a different tactic with Robelli to put an end to the drips and drabs of information he was eking out of him.

"Try this: A guy gets lucky and latches on to a very beautiful woman. He falls in love with her. But one day she says, that's it. It's over. He pleads with her but her mind is made up. She tells him to take a powder. His ego can't take that, so he decides to get even with her and…"

Robelli bolted to his feet like a missile launched into space and exploded.

"Hold the phone, sport. Jesus, you've got an active imagination! You're sitting there trying to build a case for murder on me, a case made of nothing, except the fact that I was getting it on with this broad for a…"

Beckett clamped a hand on Robelli's shoulder, not realizing he was squeezing hard enough to hurt him. He got the words out through very tight lips.

"Not a broad…a lady."

"All right, all right," Robelli softened as the sting in his shoulder ran down to his fingertips from Beckett's vice-like squeeze. "A lady. It's just an expression. The short of it is this: I didn't kill her and I don't know who did. I don't go around killing for a piece of ass. I can get all I want."

Referring to Marcia as a "piece of ass" was the excuse Beckett now admitted to himself he was hoping for ever since he got Robelli's message to meet up with him.

Beckett smiled back but Robelli could tell something was coming. His father had warned him two days ago, "The man smiles and strikes like a cobra. We could use him in the organization if he wasn't such a crazy."

Robelli instinctively began to move from the stool and quickly glanced around, looking for a friendly face, or a uniformed officer. He sensed that he was dealing with a maniac.

Beckett reached out and caught him by the top of his necktie and slowly drew him close. His voice was now low and very soft.

"Robelli, if I find you killed her, I'll come for you. No flashing red light, no siren, no gun. Think about it."

Robelli started to say something, but thought better of it. He simply nodded. Then Beckett released him and headed back to the tram boarding area. Robelli coughed, loosened his tie, and watched him go. His so-called girlfriend, standing off in the distance watching them, returned. Robelli's face was ashen.

"Geez, you look like you saw a ghost," she said.

"Shut up!"

"You can't talk to me that way. I got a right to talk."

Robelli pushed the forefinger of his right hand so hard against her left breast that she squealed in pain.

"Shut up or I'll break your hand."

She wisely shut up as Robelli watched Beckett vanish from sight with a single thought on his mind: He would be seeing the good detective again. He could bet on it, but in ways Beckett never expected.

9

Beckett knew it wasn't going to be good, knew it the moment he heard the icy tone of Chief Batters' voice as he ordered him into his office late Friday afternoon. Methodically, Batters closed the door behind him while at the same time waving him to a chair opposite his desk. Then, Batters sat down and fixed a stony stare on Beckett, who started to say something and got cut off at the knees.

"No, I'll talk, you listen," Batters started for openers as Beckett sat there quietly. "From the very beginning, I had second thoughts about putting you on this case. You're better trained for it than Garcia, but she was your wife and you haven't been very objective."

Beckett looked as if he was about to say something in his defense but Batters quickly shot him down.

"Just listen. I backed you up with the Ramirez brothers' beef because I know those bastards, and you were right. But you're like a bull in a China shop. I've got complaints from almost everyone you talked to. They think you're a bully, or worse, they think you're determined to pin a murder one on them and, of course, every single one of them is innocent, including the murderer, until proven guilty."

"That greaseball Robelli beefed," Beckett snapped.

"Yes, he did," Batters continued. "Said you implied he was guilty and said when you proved it, you were going to come and kill him without a gun."

"It wasn't quite that way," Beckett explained.

"Which tells me it was almost that way, lieutenant."
Whenever Batters called him "Lieutenant," Beckett knew he was in a heap of trouble.

"Robelli could have done it. He had an affair with Marcia and whatever or whoever broke it up, that could have triggered him," Beckett surmised, stating his case. "Why he'd want to kill her, who knows how that peanut mind of his works. Maybe she rejected him and it was more than his ego could take. As simple as that. You know he thinks he's a modern-day gigolo."

Batters held up his hand, a signal to cut off the conversation and for Beckett to stop.

"This Morrison woman and well-known lesbian...she put a beef in through Murray Eaton's office. Didn't ask that you be put off the case, just that some officer who wasn't a dedicated 'male chauvinist pig,' I think is the way she put, be assigned to look over your shoulder. What's that all about?"

"She's a suspect and knows it," Beckett countered in his defense. "She'd like to change investigators every time she changes her panties."

"This man Frank Connors...whatever you've done to him, he's scared stiff. Garcia talked with him at the house the other day and Garcia says every time Connors looked in your direction, he turned blue," Batters paused and continued. "Then, yesterday, Garcia sees him at the local grocery store and walks up to say 'hello.' This Connors turns around, says Garcia, and looks waist high at him first, seeing only the uniform, and almost shits. Then he tells Garcia he thought for a split-second it was you. What the hell is that about?"

Beckett found all the accusations at the very least unsettling as he was only doing his job the best way he knew how—full bore.

"Now that I don't know," Beckett explained. "I know he's scared of me, or the situation. I don't know which and I don't know why. Maybe he is our man."

Batters shook his head. He had the look of a man growing progressively more impatient.

"And maybe my St. Bernard is a snow leopard," Batters exploded. "This is a murder investigation, yes. But that doesn't give you carte blanche to go storming into these people's lives and scaring the shit out of them, threatening them. The next thing you'll be hitting them with two-by-fours. You've always been effective in the past, but you haven't been the soul of subtlety."

"I'm not the State Department," Beckett quipped in an attempt soften the moment with a little humor, which failed to hit its mark and instead sent the Chief over the edge.

"You won't be with the police department if you don't pull in your horns. Line 'em up and knock 'em down. Like a human bowling alley. Scare 'em, push 'em around, and if they whine, break their heads. Everyone out there is a crook until proven otherwise. Treat 'em like crooks until they prove to you, they're not. The Gospel according to St. Beckett."

Beckett wondered who put the bug in the Chief's ass.

"Chief, for Christ's sake, I'm not all that bad. This is a tough case, with a lot of possibilities. If I've stepped on a few toes…"

"You always do," Batters interrupted, getting his point across quickly.

"…I'm sorry. Look, I must see all of them again, you know that. Suppose I promise to be the epitome of diplomacy, what if I promise to do that?"

At this point, as far as Batters was concerned, it was too late for apologies and more promises he felt Beckett couldn't keep, yet he offered him a chance for reconciliation as small as it was.

"Understand this," he said firmly. "If there are any more major beefs about you, I'll either set you down or throw you out. That's a promise. That's all."

Beckett rose, looked Batters straight in the face, and walked out.

It wasn't enough aggravation trying to solve a murder case. Beckett had to deal with the Palm Springs clout of a whole town of self-important, connected people, every one of which knew someone with influence to back them up, or protect them. Johnny Robelli had the mayor in his hip pocket and Mary Ann Morrison had an ally in state assemblyman Murray Cotton, who had garnered unparalleled power through his unique ability to raise millions of dollars in campaign funds for his political pals. Rumor had it that much of Cotton's money was laundered by the mafia, but prove it.

Chief Batters was a good cop. Whether he was getting heat or not and obviously was, he wasn't about to crack under it and just wanted to protect his flanks while he remained in his position of authority until he retired without anything or anybody screwing up his plans, especially Beckett, the bad boy who had a habit of making too many enemies.

After leaving the Chief's office, Beckett went back to his office to work on the investigation. The whole time his mind kept going back to Frank Connors and his apparent fear. Fear he could sense, fear he could see, fear he could almost smell anytime he talked to him. Why? What was his secret? Who was he trying to protect? And why? Or if he had committed the murder, what would be his motive? Connors had access to Marcia as much as anybody else on Beckett's list of suspects. He was on the inside and trusted. If someone else wanted her killed, for whatever reason, who would have a better crack at her than Connors?

It made great sense to Beckett who kept pacing up and down in his office pondering his next move. Could Marcia's murder have been a muffed-up kidnap attempt? Surely, she was very prominent in Van Ander's will, and he was crazy about her. That much was certain. Van Ander would have provided very well for her in case something happened to him, and especially would have done so when he got the word that his ticket was being punched.

Knowing he was dying of cancer, he would have cleaned up all his business and Marcia was a big part of that business marked, "Personal."

Beckett decided he would concentrate his investigation in Marcia's murder now more on Connors, and the first thing he did was make an exhaustive check of his background by phone and computer. It yielded next to nothing. If anyone had ever led a dull, boring, uneventful middle-class life, give the prize to this one. Connors was now forty-three years old. He was married briefly to a woman named Suzanne Doran—it lasted six months. In her petition to the court to dissolve their marriage, his then wife had complained that she rarely saw him change his shirt, he wanted to spend every waking moment in front of the television set watching reality television shows or football, and he inhaled canned beer like other people do air. He did not beat her. On the other hand, he didn't excite her either and soon, she began playing around their lower middle-class neighborhood in West Covina. Connors had never been pinched, never been terribly poor, never saw a hundred-dollar bill in his life, never won the daily double lottery, never fought in a war, and never fathered a child. The sort who if he called the Suicide Prevention Line, they would put him on hold.

Connors had a high school education and he was the kind of teenager that when he shoved the yearbook into someone's hands to autograph, they always said, "I can't think of a thing to say." He went to one high school class reunion, just three years after graduation, and half the class couldn't remember his name. That was Frank Connors—Mr. Unremarkable. But he was involved some way, and whatever it was Beckett would find out.

Beckett drew up his "In" and "Out" list. Out, for serious consideration as suspects, was the Van Ander's butler, Charles. If Van Ander had been murdered instead of Marcia, Charles would be a long-shot on the basis that he wanted to hurry whatever was in Van Ander's will. The rich and famous, like Van Ander, always leave something for the true and faithful servants, and Charles had been with Van Ander a long time. But Charles was too classy for anything like that. He had more than $38,000 in savings and earned extremely good money, even for a first-class butler. He loved his lifestyle and he had a nice home in Cathedral City that was half paid for, even though rarely stayed there. Charles also genuinely liked Marcia. No motive there, so scratch Charles.

Also out was Dolores Colter. Like Charles, she had nothing to gain, and even more to lose if trouble came to the house. Servants live in constant fear that other servants will steal, or do something they shouldn't, and the aura of suspicion will surround them. Even though Dolores fled the scene scared the first time Beckett questioned her, it was plainly evident she was no criminal, or capable of murder. Dolores also liked Marcia, who gave her gifts and cash because Marcia remembered what being suddenly poor was like. No, scratch Dolores.

"In" at the top position, Connors, because he put himself there. Beckett couldn't think of a motive for him any more than he could for Charles and Dolores. But while the latter were upset, Connors was on the edge of panic, and that meant something. "In" for Connors.

Holding the second "in" spot: Johnny Robelli. Whatever the motive would be, it would have something to do with his hyperkinetic joint. Robelli's primary goal in life seemed to get between as many female legs as he could before he wore that thing out, and he had amassed an impressive score so far. An "in" for that greaseball Robelli.

Also, still "in" was Mary Ann Morrison. Beckett couldn't shake the feeling she was somehow involved. Many a lesbian affair is a desperate one, not because they're toasting the wrong side of the bread but because society places unconscionable pressures on their homosexual lifestyle now more than ever. Mary Ann was a tortured child, and now she was beautiful, cool, and sophisticated when she wanted to be, gutter smart when she needed to be, and a tormented woman capable of murder. In Beckett's eyes, Morrison remained on the "in" list until proven otherwise.

Beckett's head ached. He felt very well-organized writing down his thoughts, but that didn't move the investigation along one inch. He felt a little more optimistic, but didn't know why. He had to come up with something soon. Batters was growing impatient and wasn't about to let up the pressure on him now, especially after all the complaints lodged against him to get him kicked off the case. This wasn't an ordinary murder investigation. It was just what Batters suspected it was...the core of his existence. It was a vendetta, unannounced. Beckett believed in his heart that when he finally discovered the killer, he would kill him, just as he told Johnny Robelli up at the top of the Palm Springs tram. Whoever killed his Marcia wasn't going to go in for a few years, or get off on a temporary insanity wrap, or buy an early parole. No, he or she was going to die. Beckett would see to it that they did. Let Batters add that to the Gospel of St. Beckett. Retribution was his, sayeth St. Beckett. In the words of St. Beckett, "Put that in your book, Batters: Always get even, the golden rule of the streets."

Beckett was the first to recognize his own flaws. He knew that he tended to see things as black and white, and good and evil. In his heart, he knew that life was made up mostly of shades of gray. The result was it made him more cynical. He looked for the flaws in people and always found them. Beneath it all, he understood no one was perfect. Not even his beloved Marcia. She had her flaws, her bad habits, her weaknesses. The difference was, he loved her, blindly. Beckett never pretended to love anyone else. He could count his friends on the fingers of one hand. If he had one, maybe two, he was rich. Most people had a dozen or so acquaintances and no friends. He had three, maybe four. He had had his love. Whenever he wanted it, he had sex. But he never confused the two. Also, he had his work. What else did a man need?

When Beckett was getting ready to go grab a sandwich for dinner at Nate's Deli on South Indian Canyon Drive, a hop, skip and a jump from the station, on his way home, a call came in.

It went straight to voicemail on his cell phone and he retrieved the message instantly. It simply said, "This is Mary Ann Morrison," and then cut off.

Beckett first tried to look up Morrison's telephone number in his contacts but remembered he didn't need to check; he had her number memorized. He called and caught her in the shower.

"No, not here," a dripping wet Mary Ann said when asked by Beckett if he could meet her at her place. "Could we meet somewhere in town?"

"How about the Central Café in twenty minutes?

"Where's that? It sounds like a dive."

Beckett was talking about the place Chief Batters had said his hot-tempered police lieutenant had reduced to kindling wood the night he asked the Ramirez brothers to dance with his fists.

"It's where the elite meet to watch the bartender steal from the owner and cut the whiskey," Beckett offered. "Right on north Palm Drive."

"Fair enough. Let's make half an hour. Okay?"

"Fine. I'm always on time."

Forty minutes later, Mary Ann walked into the Central Café and five guys at the bar that Friday night vowed to never return home to their wives again. She was dressed in the tightest jeans Beckett had ever seen, except on the few hookers on Hollywood Boulevard who had the perfectly shaped cheeks for them. Mary Ann had a super tush, there was no doubt about that, and gorgeous chest always trying to escape their nylon captors in the most tempting way. The wavy auburn hair was tumbling over the white silk blouse, unbuttoned almost to the navel. Beckett used to hate it when Marcia dressed in an attention getting way, especially as a married woman. He even charged her with "advertising," said it was an affront to the man she was with...him. Somehow with Mary Ann he didn't care. He was almost proud of the fact that the casuals at the bar were hot for her body, and here she was giving him the big hello and joining him in the end booth. The outward smile he flashed as she sat down opposite of him was deliberately meant to ingratiate himself with a suspect who had complained to Chief Batters about his attitude.

Mary Ann sat down with the formalities and said, "What are you drinking?"

She made it two...Margaritas. There was a Hispanic bartender, Jose, on duty. They never let him touch the margaritas. He always ruined them. The owner Pat Hogan had the formula down pat, so it was Hogan's margaritas that were delivered and immediately praised.

As Mary Ann raised her glass gingerly to her lips, trying not to spill a drop and losing in the attempt, Beckett wondered about the psychology of a female homosexual like her. He had encountered literally hundreds of homosexuals on the job when working in vice on the streets of Hollywood, but most of them were not typical. They were the overt, aggressive kind, male and female. Mary Ann was far and away prettier than most of the lesbians he had met. Most seemed to him to be trying to be a man. Mary Ann was keenly aware of her obvious womanly attractions, and capitalized on them. Beckett wondered if she dressed the way she did to attract women, or to give the finger to men, attracting them, and then having the special pleasure of blowing them off. That was the ultimate feminine putdown.

"I wanted to bury the hatchet," Mary Ann said between sips.

"In my skull," Beckett snapped back, but not sarcastically.

"No. I pulled a cheap trick on you when you came to my house. You didn't deserve that and I had no right to try to pull your chain. You hadn't pushed me around."

Without showing it to her, Beckett couldn't believe what she was saying. "Is she for a real or trying to butter me up?" he thought.

"Hell, I didn't mind all that much. You satisfied my male chauvinist curiosity. You've got one helluva body there. News to you I know."

It was the first time he heard Mary Ann laugh and it had a kind of music in it.

"Hey, let's start over again, like this: You know what I am, I know what you are, but that doesn't mean we can't be friends."

"That's okay, socially," Beckett said. "But you know you're technically a suspect in a murder case I'm obligated to investigate."

"Sure. I understand that. No problem."

Beckett was beginning to like her. Years of being a cop and long experience as an undercover operator had given him the opportunity to develop his peripheral vision and his hearing to the maximum degree. As Mary Ann talked, he listened not only to her but also to as much of the conversation at the bar as he could manage. Four of the five men killing time there had come in together, and one was close to drooling, unable to take his eyes off Mary Ann.

From the moment she walked in and sat down, the conversation at the bar had switched from the relative merits of the Mercedes and Jaguar and the Saturday night World Federation fights on television to sex. They were taking turns sneaking glances at Mary Ann, who was facing them. Beckett could see the action out of the corner of his eye and he could hear two words out of three. It was the kind of situation that could get worse and make a timid man very insecure.

Mary Ann must have been aware of it, too, because she seemed to be stealing surreptitious glances in the direction of the bar, although she gave no other indication that she was aware or concerned.

"This really is a kind of strange situation, isn't it?" she suddenly asked.

"Strange?"

"I mean, we both loved Marcia and were loved by her," Marcia said with her eyes gazing in his direction. "Look, I know now that must bother you."

Mary Ann seemed to be half-pleading for him to be more understanding, something Beckett wasn't sure he had it in him to give.

"Don't sweat it. Sure, it's kind of bizarre," he said plainly. "But I can handle it. At least, as well as the next guy."

Mary Ann inched forward pushing her Margarita aside to give what she was about to say greater impact and her eyes softened as she spoke from the heart.

"She really cared for you. I mean, *really*. But I guess you know that. You must."

Beckett's eyes met hers as she sat there anxiously waiting for a response.

"She asked for the divorce, I didn't."

"Ah, yes. But not because you weren't a good guy," Mary Ann said flashing a warm and seductive smile. "Not because you weren't sensational in bed."

"She told you that?" Beckett asked, stunned.

Beckett didn't know whether it was a compliment or the need, and he felt resentment that Marcia would discuss something so intimate and deeply personal as their love-making with a lesbian lover such as her.

"Hey, don't let your male ego get ruffled," Mary Ann said defending herself. "She didn't go into detail, I swear. Marcia had too much class for that. She just said you were wonderful. Take the compliment and let it go at that. Nothing else is meant by it."

Mary Ann looked and sounded sincere, and Beckett dropped it.

"Did she want to see me for any special reason?"

Mary Ann stared into her now half empty glass.

"Yes. Uh, this may sound a little foolish."

"I deal in foolishness all the time. What is it?"

Mary Ann fidgeted with her Margarita making rings around the top rim of the glass with her right index finger in answering him.

"Well, Marcia worried about someone, or some situation. Like, she didn't say exactly what, but there were a few times when we were together, she'd talk on her cell phone where I couldn't overhear her, and become involved in an emotional conversation with someone on the other end of the call. Every time she returned, she was irritated, even worried, although she'd always try to mask it from me."

Beckett felt there was a missing piece that either Mary Ann was holding back or didn't know.

"She never told you what it was all about?" he asked suspiciously. "Never gave you a clue who she was talking to?"

"Never."

"Maybe trouble with the husband," Beckett blurted out for no other reason than it was the first thought that came to mind.

"I don't think so. You've got to understand where she was coming from," Mary Ann pointed out. "She didn't love the guy, but she liked him and respected him. He knew that, and he settled for that. He was crazy about, really crazy about her, and he was kind to her."

"I'm glad to know," Beckett said with a pause. "Could the voice on the phone belong to Johnny Robelli?"

Mary Ann screwed up the corner of her mouth in anger.

"That son-of-a-bitch, that phony stud."

Her reaction was much unlike how Beckett perceived Robelli and, like his, maybe out of jealousy.

"Not the kind of guy you bring home to mother," Beckett quipped.

For a moment, the apparently sophisticated Mary Ann reverted to her old rough-and-tumble street persona using the kind of language she felt appropriate for the situation.

"I wouldn't take him to a rat fuck."

Somehow, that didn't sound right, coming out of so beautiful a woman, but then, Beckett told himself, he had heard and seen everything and it's a little late for him to be shocked.

"She toyed with him," Mary Ann continued. "I don't know what the attraction was."

Beckett thought to himself, "I'll bet you don't. He had what you don't have." Instead, he kept his thoughts to himself and said to her, "I'd love to bust him for something, anything. I think I could get him two or ten for overtime parking. But he's a very careful cat."

One of the men at the bar had left his stool and was making his way to the men's room. He made a point of stopping momentarily near their table, drinking in Mary Ann with his deep-set blue eyes. He sighed, deliberately loud enough for them to hear, grinned, and moved on. Mary Ann gave him a look that could freeze molten lava as Beckett said, "An asshole. I'll speak to him on his way back."

From what Marcia had told her about this man, she could imagine how Beckett would "speak to him."

"Don't even bother," Mary Ann said.

Moments later, the man emerged from the restroom but this time looked straight ahead as he walked back to his place at the bar without incident.

Now Mary Ann got up to go to the women's room and Beckett rose as best he could in the booth. She disappeared behind the door, and The Sigher walked over to the cigarette machine next to it and studied it. Beckett studied him. He was a big one, all right. Dressed like a construction worker might dress. He didn't look like he smelled very good, probably stopped off with his buddies on the way home from work.

Mary Ann opened the restroom door and the man took two quick steps and blocked her path. Beckett never overheard what he said. He immediately saw red, and was out of the booth in a split second. But before he could reach the man, he saw his body lurch and he almost fell on top of Mary Ann.

The man fell to his knees as Beckett reached him and Mary Ann had her hands held up in a gesture that meant stop. Beckett looked at the guy, groaning and moaning on the floor, then back at Mary Ann, who weighed in at about 118 pounds, soaking wet.

They walked back to the booth as the other three men jumped off their barstools and went over to help their struggling friend. The bartender Jose was a close second behind them.

They picked up the man, and half carried him outside. The bartender, meanwhile, walked over.

"I'm sorry, lieutenant," the bartender apologized. "They weren't regulars."

"No problem," Beckett replied, staring at Mary Ann with a new kind of admiration in his eyes.

"If it's not a trade secret with you, Samurai," he said turning his attention on her, "what in the hell did you do that slob?"

Mary Ann was the soul of modesty. She gave it to him like a recipe of poundcake.

"You take your right knee and kick him in the groin, then you give him a karate chop across the nose."

"Swell," Beckett said breaking into a wide grin. "I think I'm glad you're on my side. You are, aren't you?"

Finally, Mary Ann's radiant smile appeared.

"That, my friend, was the real purpose of this meeting. To convince you of that. Shall we go?"

They went but to two different places. Mary Ann went to the day spa for a scheduled facial and mud bath body treatment an hour before closing time while Beckett called it a day and headed straight home. And the romantic sigher? His friends escorted him straight to the emergency room of Desert Regional Medical Center with a broken nose and the terrible fear that he would never make love again, at least, not for a very long time.

10

Across town later that same evening, Johnny Robelli was stationed in his special place: Booth number nine at Enrico's. He felt important here and was treated in a special way that made him feel good, like some people do in their reserved pew in church on Sunday morning. It gave him a sense of belonging that nourished his starved ego.

Enrico's Ristorante was a family-owned Italian restaurant on South Palm Canyon Drive with a Mama Mia ambiance managed by Enrico Pasquale's family and corporate enterprise known for its deep ties to the mafia. Booth number nine offered the best overview of the entire restaurant. Robelli could see every seat, and therefore everyone in the restaurant, from where he sat. It was elevated about a foot, a decorating device that made it stand head and shoulders above the other booths in the place. Its exact duplicate, booth number three, was about thirty feet across the room with the same view, but it was too close to the kitchen where the Italian cooks are as famous for screaming as they are for broiling, baking, and basting.

Robelli loved to sit in booth number nine and play out his secret fantasies. His favorite was the classic movie, *Casablanca*. He was Rick, tortured by his lost love, brooding in isolation over

Ilsa while every other woman in the city sought his attention. But Robelli also played another role: He was mafia. His name said so. People knew who his father was and therefore who he was. Johnny liked playing mafia because it got him lots of attention and the kind of respect that's engendered only by fear. Outsiders didn't need to know that he had never committed a real crime in his life. Early on, Carlo Robelli knew he had sired a weakling. His only son was extremely handsome, but it was obvious to the old man that this was not the vehicle with which to establish a family dynasty. The Robelli family would die with the senior Carlo. He was sure of that. Johnny was more interested in women than in sports. His fast mouth kept him from getting into the kind of street fights that better prepare a growing Italian for the future conflicts and clashes that test his manhood.

Old man Robelli never tried to bring Johnny into the family business. What could he do, where could he be placed? Carlo's second man in charge Vito Antonetti didn't want him in the labor racketeering end. Angelino Vitale, the third in command of the Robelli organization, politely suggested that Johnny wasn't the type for the strong-arm work that had to be done in the garment industry. Louis, Armando and Dante Robelli, the sons of Carlo's two deceased brothers and nephews, all suggested that there must be better things for Johnny to do, and there were. He became a playboy, just like any other rich man's son had the opportunity to do.

Carlo Robelli wasn't even all that disappointed. He had seen too much death in his time, and ego didn't dictate that his son had to carry on the family business. The pain in Carlo's chest grew just a little strong with each passing day. With pain like that, everything else, somehow, seemed less important than it once did. All Carlo wanted for his son was for him to stay out of big trouble, and not bring disgrace to his father's name now that he had so little time left. Johnny knew what few rules there were. He was smart enough to abide by them most of the time.

Johnny's real world was one of an assured with certain income each week that enabled him to live in the same style as the rich and influential of Palm Springs, whom he admired so much. He had no responsibilities, except to play by the few rules set down by his father. They did not include getting a woman pregnant and paying them off. Every man understands that sort of thing is part of the maturing process and the drinking was part of being a man. What Carlo didn't like was the drugs, so Johnny soft-pedaled that small division. He wasn't hooked on cocaine, he just enjoyed sniffing it with his friends from the record and movie colonies, and the old man never knew the difference.

Johnny kept his eye fixed on the entrance of Enrico's as he toyed with a flashy diamond crusted ball point pen he carried him just for show, making tiny tic-tac-toe squares in the white space of the red-and-white checkered tablecloth, but making no attempt to fill them in. He was slowly sipping a glass of house red wine. That was a drink his father always approved of.

"Wine never hurts you," old man Robelli once said. "It warms the blood and makes you better in bed."

Johnny smiled as he thought of his aging father, him with his inflated pride and endless prejudices and myths.

Johnny then nodded slightly as J.T. Tracey passed his booth with a friendly wave. J.T. was one of the most influential growers in the Coachella Valley. Carlo's friends from Riverside, members of the family, had aided J.T. many times, beating up organizers from the Farm Workers' Union when they tried to raise their wages above minimum wage. J.T. had been very grateful. There were many people like J.T. in Palm Springs, people who owed the family favors for services rendered. Another one of them was coming through the door now, looking around for Johnny until spotting him at his usual table. It was Dalton Spears, problem solver, with a history of taking care of the unsavory side of the family business.

Problem: Subject borrowed a huge sum of money from family sources when conventional financing for his speculative mail-order insurance scheme was denied him. The longshot paid off, subject is enjoying huge success and a lavish lifestyle, but now he's complaining about crushing interest on his loan and threatening to talk to the local newspaper about it.

Solution: Plant a weight-sensitive bomb in subject's Jaguar F sports coupe. Blow up and kill subject. Problem solved.

Problem: Subject went to a family loan shark to finance a medical education. Now he's a Beverly Hills specialist, coining money. But after making only two payments on his accumulated debt, he had told the people he borrowed it from, "Go to hell," and if they bothered him again, he'll go to local authorities and the FBI and tell them everything.

Solution: Bury subject, alive, bound, and gagged twelve-feet underground in a remote area of the desert where the red fire ants and maggots will take care of the rest after he suffocates to death. Problem solved.

This was the man who joined Johnny Robelli at booth number nine. The only thing on Spears' record was a court appearance seven years back in Dayton, Ohio, when he was picked up for speeding and they learned he had four outstanding traffic warrants, all of them for the same infraction.

For a man who reportedly had a dozen professional hits to his credit, that was a fine record. It proved he was smarter than the police. The good ones always are.

"His name is Beckett," Robelli explained after taking a long sip of vino from his crystal glass. "Lieutenant Luke Beckett."

"I know him, about him." Spears said it like he was impressed. "Where from?"

Spears, who had managed to keep a low profile all these years, lowered his voice so prying ears wouldn't catch wind of what he was about say and laid it all out in black and white for young Robelli.

"Two places…Hollywood. He was a holy fuckin' terror there, a ruthless son-of-a-bitch nobody could do business with. He fucked up Solly Weiss so bad Solly closed his operation and went back east to Philly. He half-killed a dozen of Petey Loomis' pimps and he made a fuckin' hobby of breaking down back doors and smashing movie equipment shuttering the porn movie business single-handedly."

After a short pause, Spears collected his thoughts. He wasn't finished and had more to say about the so-called Avenging Angel of Hollywood vice fame.

"Then, in Riverside, which is where I actually first rubbed shoulders with him in person. He was on that mob squad bullshit thing the A.G. dreamed up to get brownie points with the media. This Beckett bastard, someone didn't clue him in. He took it seriously, like he was supposed to do something. The whole operation in Riverside County took its lumps before they reached the right man and shut off his water. He's crazy that guy. Ask your old man. He met him through that Welcome Wagon thing."

Robelli nodded. His father Carlo had warned Johnny many times about Beckett and his capacity to do what few cops would—wipe the streets clean of every kind of vermin no matter what it took and keep his reputation intact.

"Stay clear of that one," Carlo cautioned his hotheaded son. "Some cops you could buy and others you could scare because they had family. Not this one. This blue-eyed devil has his own set of rules. He is tough, smart and dangerous."

Young Robelli knew Spears was the solution to his problem— a problem by the name of Luke Beckett.

"I want him hit."

Spears sunk back in the booth and whistled under his breath in disbelief over what he just heard roll off the tongue of Carlo's only son.

"You're fuckin' kidding. Right?"

"I'm not kidding."

Spears fixed his grey eyes on Robelli and began drumming the index and middle fingers of his right hand on his lower lip.

"Oh, wow."

Robelli grew irritated wondering if he had made a mistake calling Spears to meet him. Knowing of his reputation in his father's organization, he didn't think he was asking too much. It was what the mafia did and was standard procedure. Take out a guy who was giving them too trouble so they're never heard from again.

"What's the fuckin' big deal? So, what if the guy is dangerous."

"To you, or to the family?"

"What the hell does that mean?" Robelli asked perplexed. "I am family."

"Sure, you are family, Johnny, but is he in the way of the family business, or is this personal?"

Robelli wasn't about to back down, not after that day high atop the Palm Springs Tramway after Beckett publicly humiliated him and got away with it.

"That's none of your goddamned business."

Robelli was right, except Spears always liked to know who he was working for.

"Okay, okay," Spears confessed. "I was a little out of line."

"A whole lot fuckin' out of line," Robelli said fuming, knocking over his half-filled goblet of house red wine across the table and onto the floor with a huge crash from the shattering glass that drew the attention of a busboy who scurried over to clean it up.

"Okay. But this must be a special ticket," Spears said softly. "You understand that?"

Robelli nodded and appeared pleased that Spears was on his side.

"As much as it takes."

Spears smoothly responded, "Within a month, okay?"

"Within a month, fine."

With that, Spears slipped out of the booth and left Enrico's in nothing flat. Robelli noticed he hadn't even touched his drink; a sign that this assignment had penetrated his irritating cool. Robelli wondered if that was something to worry about. But a couple of great looking women had just entered the restaurant and he went back to playing Rick.

11

There were many things that Beckett hated about Palm Springs. Number one was the oppressive mid-summer heat. Weekend refugees from cooler, more humid climates always defended the heat. "But it's dry," they would say.

"To hell with dry, Beckett always said. "It's also hotter than hell off-season."

Residents often pointed out that it was a dry heat, so they could stand it. They withstood it even better than the tourists by fleeing and wintering in Newport Beach, a coastal city one hundred miles in neighboring Orange County, known for its sandy beaches and sundry of waterfront shops and restaurants and more temperate, cooler climate.

Beckett wondered why the year-rounders always pretended to love the desert so much. They always retreated into their homes, turned down their air conditioning, and hibernated during the summer like bears do in the winter. He never found the answer, but kept asking.

Beckett really did love the desert. Unlike most Palm Spring residents, he had seen the sand up close, had bothered to get out of his car and walk into the desert, allow some sand into his shoes, see a sunset that wasn't framed by a picture window, and even knew a few Agua Caliente Indians who still owned a good chunk of downtown Palm Springs.

When he wanted isolation to think, Beckett would drive into the sand dunes as did that Saturday afternoon. Because of his affinity for the desert, he solved the Katie Cahill kidnapping case. The magnificent isolation of the desert allowed him to finally clear his mind, collect his thoughts, and noodle the Cahill kidnapping all the way through to a brilliant deductive conclusion.

Not really. It just sounded like a better story.

What happened was that his throat was crying for a beer and he stopped at a roadside grocery store on the other side of Indio. Inside was this little lady standing in front of the cookies, crackers, and snack shelves, and she looked terribly familiar. Beckett extracted a Lite beer from the beer case, popped open the top and took a long draft, then nodded to the clerk.

"That little old lady looks familiar to me. She a local resident?" the off-duty lieutenant asked.

"Visiting someone around here," the young man replied from behind the counter and waved off Beckett paying him for the beer. "I think that's what she said."

Beckett nodded and walked to the front of the store, positioning himself so that he could see the woman's reflection in the front window. He watched her pay for her purchase and followed her with his roving eyes as she walked out, got into a 1996 Cadillac Fleetwood, and slowly drove down a side road.

There were no trees or tall buildings anywhere in the area. Beckett could follow her progress without leaving the little parking lot behind the grocery. He saw which house she went to, then got in his Ford Explorer and drove to it. No other vehicle was parked within a half a mile and there was no garage.

Beckett didn't remember the license, but he sure as hell remembered that Mrs. Cahill drove a 1996 Cadillac Fleetwood. One of a new age of luxury sedans in its day both spacious and elegant, there weren't that many of them around, even in a community of car buffs and collectors, one of whom dubbed it "an automotive dinosaur on its way to the tar pits." But why in the world would kidnappers allow their victim to go shopping by herself? Something didn't add up.

Beckett knew Mrs. Cahill only from pictures, a wedding photo and another taken about fifteen years ago. Either it was her or this was going to be a terribly embarrassing moment in his long, storied career.

Beckett knocked on the door of what appeared to be one of those big, comfortable prefab homes that had begun proliferating in the outskirts. His hand was casually stuck in the right pocket of his jacket, touching a snub-nosed .38 caliber pistol when the old lady answered the door.

"Hello. I'm Chuck from Rudy's grocery," Beckett offered. "The boss said you dropped this in the parking lot."

He handed the woman a single package of unopened original flavored, golden sponge cake, creamy filled Twinkies.

She took them, looked at them, and immediately handed them back to him.

"I wouldn't eat that junk. It's made of cardboard."

"Oh, then Rudy made a mistake. Say, I'm sorry. Hope I didn't disturb you."

"Not at all," the woman said breaking into a warm smile. "I was just going to have a cup of tea. Would you like to join me?"

Beckett's first thought was maybe someone was crouched in the next room listening and explained why she was trying desperately to keep him there. He decided to chance it.

"Yes, thanks. I was just about to go on my break anyway."

As the woman fussed with the teapot and some packaged tea after entering through the front door, Beckett paused and asked, "I wonder, may I use your bathroom, Mrs...."

"Of course, right in there."

She pointed him toward the hallway leading to the guest bathroom sandwiched between the master bedroom and guest bedroom.

Beckett checked the bathroom, flushed the toilet, then took out his gun and headed for the only room with a door blocking his view. He burst into the guest bedroom, squatting, and sweeping the room with his pistol clutched in both hands.

"Freeze!" he screamed.

"Huh?" came the voice from the kitchen, and the woman joined him in the bedroom.

"What did you say? What's wrong?"

Beckett felt like a fool. How did he explain something like this?

"I, uh, I'm sorry ma'am. It's kind of hard to explain."

The woman looked at the gun, still in Beckett's hand, and he apologized and put it away very quickly.

"Are you a holdup person?" she asked.

Beckett fumbled for his identification in one of his pockets.

"Oh, no ma'am, I'm a police officer… Lt. Beckett."

A look of resignation crossed the woman's face and she sat down on a nearby chair as a feeling of resignation swept over her.

"So, you figured it out," she said with a look of defeat in her eyes. "Well, I was ready to go back. It was even more lonely here than it was back there."

That was it. Dawn finally broke over Beckett. This was Katie Cahill and he smelled a hoax.

"You weren't kidnapped," he said, "were you?"

Cahill admitted that she was not. It wasn't the first time something like this had happened. Someone facing a life of loneliness decides to do something bizarre to attract attention to herself. With Mrs. Cahill, it was staging a fake kidnapping—her own. She would "release" herself from her kidnappers at a future date. As a matter of fact, she was planning to do it tomorrow. Now, the twinkle was gone from her eye. She had been having fun, anticipating the many interviews with reporters, her invisible neighbors materializing and dropping in, anxious to hear all the exciting details. Maybe she would be asked to do a few national television interviews as well to talk about her hair-raising experience. Instead, now, it was all over in a flash.

Beckett finished his tea and broke into a wide grin.

"Kate, you're a devil."

"I guess I'd like to be," she said, sweetly.

There was a long silence, then Beckett smiled before another light bulb went off in his head.

"Tell you what, if you don't tell anyone, I won't either," he said. "If you promise that you will go back to Palm Springs tomorrow, just as you planned, I'll forget I ever saw you."

"You would do that? For me?"

"Why not? Have a ball, Katie my girl. You know that commercial that talks about only going around once?"

Katie Cahill grinned from ear to ear and it showed as her face brightened and eyes sparkled once again.

"And here I am, going around twice. Well, God bless you, sergeant."

Then she stood on her tiptoes and gave him a big kiss. He didn't even mind the demotion.

Driving back to his place, Beckett decided that he was six times a fool. What if the old lady cracked up, or went senile, and told the *true* story. He would be pounding a beat in Calcutta, probably cleaning up after the elephants.

But Mrs. Cahill kept her word. She returned to her home with the most remarkable kidnapping story ever heard. It was a story replete with danger, desperation, raw courage, triumphing over adversity, and a whole lot more that everybody she told fell, hook, line, and sinker.

***

That afternoon, Beckett returned to his mobile home. In his mailbox was an envelope addressed to him. It was from John Drew. No greeting—but that was Johnny—when Beckett opened and read its contents.

"Look at the bottom of this letter, you turkey," he wrote. It was signed Sgt. John Drew, Hollywood police division.

Beckett laughed. It was in-joke between them. He used to tell Drew he didn't stand a chance of making sergeant "even in the Cub Scouts," even though they don't have such a ranking. Emailing would have been a much faster way to communicate, but Drew didn't feel comfortable emailing and using a computer was an ongoing battle for him. When he had something important to communicate, he did the old-fashioned way by sending a handwritten letter. Drew had a good reason for writing Beckett—to bring him up-to-date on how much things had gone south in the Hollywood division since his dismissal. As he wrote:

> Sorry, I took so long to write, but you know me and computers! You needled me enough about it back in the day when you were Zorro and I was just a child in swaddling clothes. :) Hey, tiger, they really miss you back on the boulevard. The hookers are wall-to-wall now that Zorro isn't around to spoil the fun. There are so many "johns" now they must take a number like you do in butcher shops. Everybody's been back in business ever since you left. I heard that Mulligan got mugged the other night while he was reading some drag queen his or her rights, which is it? :)
>
> Beanhead Tierney still doesn't know what's going on, but I'd bet he'd give anything to get you back. No kidding. Every time he turns around one of the television stations is doing another series on vice in Hollywood and it's driving him crazy. He's afraid internal affairs is going to start looking at his operation and wonder how he got to be the richest captain in the United States. Listen, I'm coming down next month. Can you get me a good rate on a room? I'll have Dolly with me. Thought you might introduce her to Palm Springs society.

Dolly was a hooker, but one of the nicest people Beckett ever made. Her street name was "The Tunnel," which doesn't require any explanation. Dolly was a dedicated victim and everybody took advantage of her. They say a john got her off one night and broke into tears because the fifty bucks he'd paid for her services he had taken out of the orthodontist fund and his wife was going to kill him. She gave back the fifty. That was Dolly. Drew knew the story. He probably even loved the girl. She would have a wonderful weekend in Palm Springs. For two days, she'd be treated like a lady. Beckett made a mental note to take the pair to dinner in the poshest restaurant in town if he was available or if he was too busy working a case and couldn't spare the time at least have them drop by the station to say a quick "hello."

Suddenly, a large unmarked black-and-white sedan roared to a stop spewing a cloud of sand and dust behind it. The man bathed in sweat from head to toe jumped out and moved slowly toward Beckett's front door. It was Chief Batters.

Beckett walked outside shielding his eyes with the palm of his right hand in the glaring sun to greet him.

"Chief, what brings you to my neck of the woods?"

"Goddamned air conditioning is busted again. Is that what they mean by police brutality?" Batters muttered with his voice rising in anger. "It's brutal to have to drive in that oven without so much as a poop out of the vents. It'd be a great place to sweat someone out."

It was the same problem every summer: the cooling systems in the Ford sedans conked out under the duress of the intense heat while the air conditioning in Beckett's mobile home, though not icy cold and cooler than it was outside, worked without fail.

Seizing the moment, Beckett got his digs in for good measure.

"Why don't you come inside and cool off? I can assure that it's a pleasant 130 degrees out there in the shade. A little broiled birdie told me."

Batters swung his legs up the front steps and walked inside.

Beckett was certain Batters didn't come in just to bitch about the air conditioning again. He was right.

"Luke, I got to talk to you. I'm sorry to intrude on your private time but what I have to discuss is too sensitive of a subject and I felt this was the safest place we could talk," Batters said as he took a load off in a padded recliner close by and cooled down.

The Chief addressed him as "Luke" this time. Then it must be important. Otherwise, he'd call him Beckett and some choice names not fit to print.

"I've had a pre-arranged, confidential meeting today that wasn't scheduled on purpose so the subject it if wouldn't become public with our beloved mayor and his equally dunderheaded police Commissioner John Le Clerque about my retirement."

Batters had wanted to retire for some time. He could quit whenever he wanted, but he wanted that goodbye testimonial dinner the last chief had. It was worth maybe twenty-five or thirty thousand dollars to him. Not that he needed the extra money, it was a matter of protocol. One thing about Chief Batters: He ate and drank protocol like it was going out of style.

"They won't let me step aside without appointing a replacement," Batters explained, "and I recommended you. But..."

The "but" was no surprise to Beckett; the fact he recommended him was.

"...they won't buy it. They say you're like a coiled snake, a loaded gun, an accident waiting to happen. Oh, yes, that pinhead Le Clerque had an even more dramatic phrase. He said you were a—and I'm quoting him verbatim— 'a time-bomb waiting to go off.'"

Beckett laughed so hard he almost fell over in his chair.

"Le Clerque? Of course, he'd say something like that. I understand there's a city ordinance here gives him the right to pee in the men's room or the ladies room, whichever strikes his fancy."

"I'll take the fifth on that one!" Batters said with a chuckle. "But he's got a vote. Anyway, they decided it's time we had a chief from the ranks of the minorities and they picked..."

"Garcia?"

"Right. What do you think?"

"Hell, yes," Beckett seconded. "He's a good man. Straight and honest as they come. You know that."

"Yeah, I know that. I like him," Batters confessed. "But he wouldn't make a patch on your ass as far as police work is concerned."

"Maybe not. But who gives a shit? How much cop business is there in this town anyway? In the last few weeks, we hit a fifty-year high for action, what with the murder, the suicide and the kidnapping."

"You know, when you put it that way," Batters chuckled again, "you're right. It's like you brought all the business with you."

"I'm glad you mentioned that. I could use a good suspect. I'm getting a little desperate."

Batters was on his feet now, ready to leave. He had come and said all he wanted but got in a parting shot before he did.

"I don't need to tell you that it's important to me that we...you...solve this Van Ander thing. I'd hate to walk off the job with a big one like that still on the books. You know what I mean."

"Sure. I'll give it the old college try, you know that, Chief."

"I know that. Thanks for the cool air."

Batters slipped on his polarized aviator sunglasses, proceeded to leave, stopped short of the front door, and then let out a long audible sigh.

"I pity the next Chief whoever that is."

"Why is that Chief?" Beckett asked.

"I hope the goddamned air conditioning works!"

Batters swung open the door and sucked out all the cold air with him and left.

As soon as he departed, Beckett knew the Chief didn't just come to visit because he was wanted to talk to him about his replacement. He could have done that in a private meeting behind closed doors back at the station. Beckett sensed his real motivation was wanting to wrap up the murder investigation expeditiously since the importance of it was weighing heavily him, not to mention the power elite of Palm Springs who no doubt was pressuring him to put to end to it and spare the names and reputations of many powerful players being bandied about in the press.

Beckett retrieved his cell phone and dialed Frank Connors' phone number. He had tried calling him before to question him again. It rang off the hook but no one picked it up. It was the eighth time in a row he had tried to reach Connors at home that same day. Every time he called him at the Van Ander house, they said they couldn't locate him. Beckett knitted his brows. What was it with Frank Connors?

12

The love making had been exhausting and Beckett wasn't even breathing hard. That irritated his lady love Jo Ann Tracey. She had enjoyed every second of the forty-five minutes she had spent in bed with him. What irritated her, hurt her, was that he seemed to make love mechanically like it was a duty to be performed. Oh, he was good at it, all right and he knew it. What grabbed Jo Ann was that he never seemed to enjoy it as much as she wished he would. That was the maddening thing about this man. She could never quite reach him.

Jo Ann wanted to possess Beckett, consume him. But having worked for so long as a police detective, he was always in control on duty and off and he knew that, too. He rarely called her, she called him. This time that Sunday night when she phoned him at the last minute it was, "Come over for a drink and we'll watch the latest episode of *Roadside Attractions* on Channel 29. It's about popular wood-carved statues in the communities of north central Minnesota."

They never touched the remote, but that was Jo Ann's fault. She wanted to turn on Beckett, not the show about a bunch of wooden people that were of no significance to her. As always, he had given her everything she wanted physically and, as usual, nothing she wanted psychologically. She half sat up in bed, propping two pillows under her long blonde hair, and watched Beckett as he stepped into the shower of her apartment.

"He still loves that dead girl," she murmured to herself. "He can't sleep with a dead girl so he sleeps with me, and God knows how many others."

Jo Ann could do so much for Beckett, for his career, for his psyche, if he would just let her. He needed her but didn't know it yet.

Her wristwatch said midnight on the nose as Beckett dried himself off and began dressing. She loved to watch him dress and undress. She talked about her work in the jewelry department at Macy's at Westfield shopping mall in Palm Desert, a growing suburb in the middle of the Coachella Valley. It didn't interest him and it interested her, but it was something to say to fill in the dead spots. She never asked him about his work and he never volunteered anything. Their relationship was strictly physical. He knew it and she knew it. Each had his needs. The needs were served. She would like to take it further, he would not. Same old story.

"Want a nightcap?" she asked hopefully.

"Thanks, no," Beckett said finished dressing. "Got to be up a little earlier tomorrow. I've got to find someone."

Jo Ann shrugged her shoulders, and her pretty breasts moved up and down and side to side. She was top-heavy for a woman with such a slender frame. Beckett had combed his hair in the mirror and smiled as he saw her watching him.

"Everything okay?" he asked.

"You bet," Jo Ann said. She could complain if you wanted, but the fact he asked was better than good. It was the before and after that always left her insecure and frustrated.

"Will I see you again, soon?"

"Sure," he said.

Beckett came over to the bed, sat down, took her gently by

the shoulders and whispered, "Got to run. It was nice being with you…really."

Jo Ann leaned forward and kissed him, hard. He smiled and squeezed her shoulders as an indication of his love for her.

"I'll give you a call when things calm down a bit, okay?"

Jo Ann drew up her shapely legs and pulled her knees close to her breasts and sat there, like a contortionist.

"I am a goddamned fool," she told the empty room after Beckett left. She thought she heard it agree with her.

Beckett stopped at the liquor store on the corner and picked up the early morning edition of the *Los Angeles Times*, his favorite newspaper back from days on Hollywood vice. He liked to read the morning paper at night and watch the all-news cable networks in the early morning hours. That was about the only news he got, unless his schedule allowed him to intermittently check the latest updates on his smartphone throughout the day.

It was approximately 12:20 A.M. when he got back into his Ford Explorer and headed for home. At 12:31 A.M., he stopped for the signal light at North Indian Canyon Drive and East Tahquitz Canyon Way when suddenly the situation turned violent.

Four pistol shots split the quiet pre-dawn air and Beckett dived for the floor in front of the passenger seat, simultaneously clawing at the revolver in the shoulder holster under his left arm. Before the echo of the last shot had died in the desert air, he heard the roar of a high-powered car. He came up with his gun in his hand and saw a large dark sedan making a fast getaway through the parking lot to Frenchy's of Palm Springs and disappearing out the back way to North Palm Canyon Drive from sight. The assailant already was out of range and Beckett gunned his engine, spinning his Ford Explorer in a half circle in the intersection. In a second, he knew he was screwed.

His left rear tire had been punctured by one of the bullets. Another had torn into the upholstery near the top of the driver's seat. A third went through the rear window and out a side window and the fourth either missed the sport utility vehicle entirely or passed through the open front windows inches from his head and shoulders.

Officer Parker was about a block and a half away in his squad car and had heard the shots and reached the scene as Beckett was still taking inventory. Beckett had no police radio in his Ford Explorer, and there wasn't a store open for blocks. There was no point in calling for a road block. This was a local boy trying to make good and he probably was already safely garaged in a predetermined place.

Not one other Palm Springs citizen had heard the shots, or if one had, he failed to materialize, probably too scared to get involved. People can't tell the difference between shots and backfires anyway. Parker radioed the station and, on Beckett's advice, neglected to tell the dispatcher what really had happened. He asked instead for a tow truck to fix the flat tire on his Ford Explorer.

The truck arrived, and Beckett extracted a promise from Parker not to tell anyone what had happened.

"It's no skin off my nose, either way, lieutenant," he said, unfazed by the hail of gunfire that preceded his arrival on the scene.

Beckett waited until the tire switch was made, showed the tow truck driver his auto insurance card, signed the man's paper, and drove home slowly.

Someone had just tried to blow his head off, and he was almost as physically cool as when he had stepped out of Jo Ann's shower earlier. Beckett wondered if something had died in him, wondered if nothing moved him anymore. It has been said if a person loses one sense, the others are heightened. If that is true, if Beckett had lost some of his emotions, one was still intact and maybe, just maybe enhanced. He felt the rage building up in him. He always had plenty of rage to suit any occasion, and now it was directed at the only person he could possibly think might be frightened enough to want him dead…Frank Connors.

It was one o'clock in the morning when Beckett reached the Van Ander residence. Charles answered the door in his purple and black trimmed velvet robe and silk pajamas startled to see the lieutenant at that hour. Straight shooter that he was, Beckett got right to the point.

"Frank Connors here?"

"No, lieutenant," Charles responded groggily, "he no longer lives here. He was paid off yesterday."

"Do you know what his plans are?"

"No, sir," the bleary-eyed butler answered. "I haven't heard from him since he left."

"Thank you, Charles. Sorry to have awakened you."

Beckett turned on the overhead light in his Ford Explorer and retrieved Connors' home address from his smartphone. He reached the rundown little apartment building in ten minutes. It was a four-flat complex, a throwback to the early days in Palm Springs when people from Los Angeles came down on weekends and built them before lumber became a little more precious than gold. Beckett had to use a small handheld flashlight to read the names over the four bells on the side of the building: "Koetz, #1...Barr, #2 ...La Paz, #3 ...Connors, #4"—in the back lower unit.

Beckett knocked on the door. No answer. He called him out by name,

"Frank Connors, open the door."

Silence. He took two steps back, put his gun in his hand, and came crashing through the door. He lay there for a few seconds. Dead silence, but stirring in the apartment next door.

Beckett found and flicked on the light switch inside the front door and was surprised to see how small the apartment was. There was no indication from any of the clothing in the closets that Connors had planned to leave town.

As he began checking dresser drawers, a man's voice at his back caused him to freeze.

"Put your hands in the air or I'll kill you."

Beckett raised his hands as the ominous voice pierced the quiet of the early morning.

"Turn around."

Beckett turned around, slowly. The middle-aged man with the gun had an incredulous look on his face.

"Lieutenant Becker?"

"Beckett," the lieutenant corrected him.

"Yeah, right," the man acknowledged. "Is this a police matter?"

"It is," Beckett affirmed with his hands still raised high above him.

"Geez. I'm sorry. I'm Carlson," the man said. "I own the building, live next door, heard the door coming down. Was that you?"

"Yes," Beckett answered while pulling his hands down at his side.

"You looking for Frank Connors?"

"Yes, I was," Beckett said visibly irritated. "Still am."

Carlson finally realized he was still holding the revolver and he shoved it in the pocket of his night robe.

"Sorry about the gun."

"You got a permit for that?" Beckett snapped, acutely aware of the guns of the laws of the state.

Carlson looked sheepish and couldn't hide the fact that he was. "No."

"Then, it's a good thing I didn't see it."

Beckett continued searching Connors' apartment, but he couldn't find anything significant, as Carlson watched him with mounting curiosity.

"Is Frank Connors in some kind of trouble?"

"No," Beckett said without turning around. "I'm on an Easter egg hunt."

"Oh, sure."

Beckett checked the bathroom, the kitchen, and the bedroom as Carlson kept a close watch on him.

"What did Connors do, shoot someone?"

It was a strange thing for Carlson to ask but Beckett didn't give him the satisfaction of confirming that.

"I can't tell you."

Carlson nervously asked, "You want to know where he's at?"

Beckett whipped himself around and now faced Carlson for the first time since stopping him with a gun pointed at his back.

"I sure do."

"Gee, I'm sorry," Carlson said, squinting to see through his fogged-up bifocals. "I can't help you. I don't know."

"Thanks for asking."

Beckett satisfied himself that the clothes closets were filled to the brim and he checked out two pieces of luggage. Both were empty, but there could have been a third.

"Connors say he was going anywhere?"

"No, sir." Carlson looked a bit cross-eyed as he paused for a moment to wipe his glasses clean with a small handkerchief before putting them back on. "Didn't say anything like that to me."

Beckett used the opportunity to pry deeper and determine if he would want to call on Carlson again.

"You remember anything unusual or different Connors said or did in the last few days, the last few weeks?" he asked.

"Nope."

"I need to call the station. Stay put. I may have other questions."

"Go right ahead, lieutenant."

Beckett pulled out his smartphone and dialed. He got the late-night dispatcher Debra Roberts, a recent new hire who had replaced the retiring Susan Childress, and ordered an all-points bulletin be issued on Connors. He gave the dispatcher a complete description: "The APB should cover seven western states. Understood?"

"Right," Roberts replied.

"I'll be in at the station at six this morning."

Beckett looked at his watch. It was already two o'clock. He needed at least three hours sleep to function.

"Anything I do?" Carlson asked.

"Yes, send me a bill for that door tomorrow," Beckett said realizing he had misspoken. "Well, I guess I mean later today."

"It's on the house, lieutenant."

"No," Beckett insisted, "it's not on the house any more. That's why I want you to send me a bill. Okay?"

"Okay."

Beckett left and drove straight home. It wasn't until he got there that he noticed he had a small cut over his right temple. For a moment, he thought he might have been grazed by a bullet. Then, he examined it more closely and realized he had struck his head on something when he dived for cover in the car. He slapped a small Band-Aid over it and reminded himself how lucky he was.

Beckett remained convinced that it was Frank Connors who was behind the whole thing and that made him in his mind his number-one suspect until proven otherwise.

Predictably, Johnny Robelli was stationed in booth number nine at Enrico's Ristorante that same hour. He nodded as some of his father's associates stumbled their way out the front door after a night of libations with a luscious lady on each arm. Flagging down the hostess, he ordered a double Scotch on the rocks. It arrived at the same time Dalton Spears did. Spears could see Johnny was seething and he guessed why.

Robelli set the tone of the meeting by speaking so low Spears could hardly hear him.

"What the fuck happened to you?" he asked, enraged. "I thought you were the big shot hit man. You were shooting like drunk in a barrel of snakes."

Spears looked at Robelli as if he was crazy.

"Let's have that again?"

"You heard me. What were you trying to kill, Beckett or the car?" Robelli demanded in a thundering voice. "I understand you put a half a dozen bullets into the car and none in Beckett."

Spears leaned forward with a look of astonishment on his hard features.

"Are you out of your fucking mind? I never went through with it. I never shot at Beckett."

Robelli couldn't believe his ears. It was mystifying to him that that Spears hadn't carried out his orders.

"What do you mean you never shot at him? Your tellin' me you hired someone else to do it or what. What you are you saying?"

"I'm saying," Spears said slowly, "I never carried out any hit on anyone."

"But I had a deal with you." The normally tough Robelli looked on the verge of the tears when he said it. "You couldn't go against a deal."

"I had to."

"What does that mean?"

Spears always had been aboveboard in all his dealings. It was one reason why old man Robelli had kept him on the payroll all this time. He wasn't the type of guy to fuss around and gave Johnny the answer he needed to hear.

"I don't know if I can tell you. What I can tell you is that I've already mailed your money to you. I was planning to go back east and then I got your call to come here. I knew you'd beef about it but I figured I ought to give you the courtesy of listening to the beef."

Robelli shook his head as if to clear the cobwebs out. It wasn't what he was expecting Spears to say, especially from someone so feared whom his father had entrusted for so many years.

"Let's, let's take this from the top. I pay you to hit this guy. You agree to do it. I give you half now, half later. Someone ambushes him and they bungle the job. Now you tell me it wasn't you. Why wasn't it you?"

Spears sighed in resignation. He knew with young Robelli he wasn't dealing with a guy who understood how things worked.

"When was the last time you talked to your old man?"

"My old man," Robelli said with a surprised look on his face. "What the fuck's he got to do with this?"

"Everything," Spears said.

"Why everything?"

"Look, first I work for him, remember," Spears put it bluntly. "I'm not just a piecework guy, I'm on retainer. I'm the house's man. I'm family."

"So?"

"Your old man, he has to know whatever's goin' on."

Robelli sat back. He felt like the kid with his hand in the cookie jar but it was empty.

"Jesus!" he exploded. "You mean to tell me that you ran to my old man and told him my business...our business?"

Spears was beginning to lose patience. He was twenty years Robelli's senior and old school mafia. He identified with Carlo Robelli, not this young wet-behind-the-ears punk who never did the organization any service in his life. He gave him some respect because he was the old man's kid. But there was nothing in the book that said he had to take any crap from an inexperienced bastard like him.

"I work for Carlo Robelli, not Johnny Robelli," Spears said with certainty. "Sure, I was willing to do a little side job for you, but only after I checked with your old man first."

"Jesus!" Robelli billowed in a seething and boiling rage. "A fuckin' conspiracy...that's what it is."

"Whatever you want to call it, I check with the old man first. That's the way it is. That's the way it's always been. If you worked in the organization, Johnny, you'd know that."

Robelli could feel his face flush red with anger. It was bad enough to even be seen talking to this neanderthal, now he was being criticized by him and it wasn't his style to just shake it off.

"Spears," he said, each word rolling off his tongue like tiny explosions, "I ought to break your head."

Spears looked at Robelli for a long minute and then broke out laughing.

"You...break my head?"

Spears leaned forward, his eyes suddenly shiny, within an eyelash of Johnny's face and set him straight.

"You little shit, I'm old enough to be your father. But I could break you in half with one arm. After this, you stay in your goddamned playpen where you belong. Go play with the girls and drive your cars and sniff that shit that you sniff. Come near me again and I'll hand you your ears."

With that, Spears slowly removed himself from the booth and walked straight out the front door.

Robelli watched Spears go, the whole time thinking of his father. Who did he think he was, God? Then another thought crept in Robelli's well-coiffed head, which was already buzzing with the double Scotch he had ordered: If Spears didn't shoot at Beckett, then who did? Then the final, most jarring thought of all: What if Beckett thought Johnny had shot him? That maniac would be coming for him guns blazing.

The last thought chilled Robelli and suddenly he felt an urgent need to be anywhere else but at Enrico's in downtown Palm Springs. He put down twenty bucks, the smallest he had, and split as fast as he could without drawing undue attention to himself.

The waiter saw Robelli leave in a rush and went over to the booth to pick up the glass. He spotted the twenty, picked it up, and nodded to another waiter who came over.

"Look at this," the young waiter said. "Twenty bucks, and all he had was a double Scotch. And they want you to believe these mafia guys are no good. You know what I mean?"

13

Late Monday morning, just on the off chance that Frank
Connors might still be in town, which was doubtful,
Beckett decided to drive to the Van Ander home and check
to see if Connors might have stopped there to pick up something
he may have overlooked when he left for good. Charles met
Beckett at the door, showed him in and invited him to look
around.

Beckett caught Charles as he was preparing to end his employ
with the Van Ander estate to join the Fieldings in service the
following week. Meanwhile, the house was being sold by the
estate while Dolores, the housemaid, would go to work for the
Emerson family in Indian Wells in the east valley. Charles was
looking forward to taking Beckett up on an invitation to have
dinner with him some time soon.

Beckett didn't stick around for long. He went through
Connors' personal quarters, examining every nook and cranny,
and Van Ander's former handyman and groundskeeper seemed to
be gone for good. He had left nothing behind but a faded
restaurant receipt in the bottom drawer of his dresser that was
immaterial to Beckett's investigation.

Beckett quickly left the premises. He had planned to lunch at Old World when he suddenly realized he was in Katie Cahill's neighborhood. With some amusement, he thought about the spunky little old lady who had engineered her own kidnapping to recharge her boring existence. Why not stop by and say hello, show the old girl someone cares about her? Probably break the monotony, something she would greatly appreciate, he thought.

Beckett poised with his knuckles a few inches from the door and wondered why Mrs. Cahill was playing her music on her Dolby stereo system so loud. The din was awful. He knocked but there was no answer. He turned the knob slowly, and the sight that caught his eye chilled him to the bone. There before him were at least thirty ladies, not one of them under sixty-five. They were sitting, standing, dancing, drinking, playing bingo and a round of Nintendo Wii ping pong complete with rubber foamed paddles on the 70-inch 4K high-definition television mounted on the earth tone stone wall in the great room. It was a curious mixture of La Dolce and Leisure World and they were noisy. So noisy that when he raised his voice and called out to Mrs. Cahill, only one of two heads turned to see who was joining the festivities.

One old doll in a beaded dress and a jeweled hat with a pheasant feather sticking out of the top of it waltzed over and pointed her cigarette holder at Beckett.

"Hello, big boy. If you're the Roto-Rooter man, there's an awful lot of girls here who would like to meet you."

"Girls?" Beckett thought, keeping such thoughts to himself. "Some of them were old enough to be his grandmother."

"Is Mrs. Cahill here?" he asked after speaking up. "I'm a friend of hers."

Pheasant Feather, still standing in the doorway and gladdened by the sight of the handsome young police lieutenant, smiled, and winked.

"I'll bet you are," stepping aside so he could enter. "Sit down, handsome, and I'll chase down Katie for you."

Pheasant Feather left and Disco Dolly crept up from the side seemingly out of nowhere.

"Want to dance, blue eyes?"

Blue Eyes declined on the grounds that he suddenly remembered he had two left feet.

"Then, we can sit this one out," Disco Dolly offered, hopefully, pointing to a nearby sofa with the hand with the martini in it. She spilled half of it in anticipation of enjoying his companionship in such tight quarters.

Beckett mumbled, "No thanks."

In the nick of time, Katie Cahill stuck her head around a corner. She smiled broadly when she saw Beckett, leaned over, and whispered something in another's lady's ear, then swept out in a baby blue housecoat trimmed in white fur and gave him a big hello and hug.

Suddenly, she leaned up and he leaned down as she whispered in his ear: "I told the girls you're one of my fellas. Go along with it, will you?"

Beckett grinned, and nodded, and she guided him back to the kitchen. Two much older women were arguing the relative merits of breast enhancements at their age, so they slipped out onto the back patio. It wasn't quiet there either, but at least no one was within ten feet.

Mrs. Cahill plopped in a chair and Beckett followed suit. She sighed and smiled a contented smile seeing him again.

"You look happy," Beckett said.

"God, you know, I really am," she said beaming. "I know what I did was crazy but it worked!"

Beckett agreed that it sure did with one eye on Mrs. Cahill and the other on Pheasant Feather winking at him through the French doors leading out onto the patio.

"It's not like this all the time?"

"Oh, no," Katie said with a shrug. "Maybe four, five days a week. I'm a media celebrity, you know. The media made me famous and suddenly people who used to walk across the street to avoid me are inviting me to parties and fighting to get on my guest list. I'm not just an old dame now, I'm the Auntie Mame of the desert!"

They both laughed at that until Beckett suddenly said he had to split, especially since Pheasant Feather hadn't taken her flirting eyes off him.

"I'll give you a call one of these days and we'll go have a drink or something like that."

Cahill nodded and she looked deep into Beckett's blue eyes while squeezing his right hand gingerly.

"You're a real friend, lieutenant. A real friend. I know the difference between acquaintances and friends. Believe me."

Beckett nodded. He understood. She took mercy on him and showed him a way out of the house and back to Ford Explorer without having to face Pheasant Feather and all those born-again *The Fabulous Palm Springs Follies* flappers who were raising the roof in front of the house. In moments, he was off again, smiling to himself at the transformation in Katie Cahill's lifestyle. She had class, that old lady, and smarts, he thought. She knew exactly what she was doing, having a ball before someone came along and punched her ticket. Why the hell not?

Some people would rather go out to the racetrack and watch the horses run than do anything else. Others can sit for an hour in their living rooms and chronicle the activities of a couple of kittens or a cat playing with a ball of string. With Beckett, it was people watching. He had done it all his life and since he was a kid, he played a game trying to guess people's nationalities and trades or professions. He got pretty good at it after a while, and occasionally it came in handy in police work. He noticed small things—people's hands, the texture of their skin, the cut of their clothes, the style of their shoes. After a while, regional accents stuck out like the glare of the hot morning sun. The way a person crossed a street told him whether he was from the west or east coast or a small town or a big city.

The Palm Springs police station is just a fast tap dance from the Palm Springs International Airport, and Beckett pulled up in the no parking zone and walked inside just to kill a few minutes before heading over to Ruth Hardy Park for a clandestine meeting. He got a friendly wave from the Avis and Budget Rent-a-Car girls. Hertz wasn't talking to him. He broke their last date and she wasn't about to put him in the driver's seat again until she had punished him for a while.

Beckett gave a half salute to his friend, Bernie, at the Visitors and Convention Bureau kiosk, superficially examined a new luxurious, loaded to the max Volkswagen Passat on display from a local car dealer, and sat down on a bench to contemplate his navel.

They saw each other at about the same instant. Beckett was surprised. Dalton Spears was startled.

"Spears?"

"Yeah. You're Beckett."

They didn't really know each other. When Beckett was a legend around Hollywood, Spears had come in town a couple of times. But he didn't operate on the seamy side of Hollywood in those days without hearing about Beckett all the time. He was the terror of the streets and he made it his business to know what he looked like. Beckett knew Spears from a picture in a mug book. He had memorized the faces of about two dozen hit men. That was another hobby, studying wanted posters and mug shots.

A battalion of wrongdoers resided in Beckett's head. Most of them would never materialize and present themselves in real life. But here, right in front of him, was an exception…Dalton Spears. Thought to have assassinated at least two dozen men, maybe more. But when he did a hit man for the mob ever get caught? They were a strange and special breed without conscience, without honor, without sensitivity.

"Coming or going?" Beckett asked innocently.

Spears forced a half smile.

"Going."

"Visiting relatives?"

"Something like that."

Beckett's mind was turning fast. Someone had tried to blow his brains out in the wee hours of the morning but here was a notorious mafia hit man leaving town. Was there a connection?

"How soon you leaving?"

Spears looked at one of those three thousand dollar watches he saw advertised by Van Cleef and Arpels, or was it Donovan's?

"About half an hour."

"Cuppa coffee?"

"Why not?"

They walked in silence to the coffee shop...the Odd Couple. The tough young police lieutenant, the equally tough and ruthless older mafia hitman who made his living making corpses. The coffee shop was nearly deserted, except for a very old couple at the far end with the man sporting an outrageous tam o'shanter. They took an isolated table, almost automatically, and a pretty, red-haired waitress materialized and flashed a toothsome smile at Beckett.

"Two coffees," Beckett ordered. "One black. And the other...?"

"The other tea. No sugar, just lemon," Spears offered.

Beckett smiled ever so slightly. He wondered how this man, who must have been in his mid-fifties, had lasted so long. He measured hitmen's lives like he did those of a dog or elephant. Ten years was about the average work span, if they were lucky, he thought.

How Beckett saw it, hitmen lead a precarious existence for obvious reasons. Few were ever caught by authorities, principally because a professional murder is one lacking the main ingredient to look for: motive. Most hitmen were done by the very same people who hired them. When a professional killing was required, only a seasoned professional could handle it. At first, the client is extremely grateful and generous. But organized crime is a paranoid business. In no time at all, the client begins to worry about such nasty little things as blackmail, or a hitman trading information if he is nailed on another murder or another serious charge. In short, it was the hitman's special knowledge that made him first an asset, and then a liability.

Spears was the first to speak and start the conversation as he ripped open a packet of sugar to add to his hot tea.

"You sort of retired down here among the cactus and the Cadillacs?"

"No, what makes you say that?"

"Well," Spears said pointedly, "it's no Los Angeles, no Hollywood."

"You know about that?"

"Sure. They pointed you out to me once. Like you were a local stop on the Gray Line bus run. 'There's Zorro,' they'd say, 'the fiercest cop. Over there, Grauman's Chinese Theater, and down the street, the Hollywood Roosevelt.'"

Beckett smiled. How could memories of Hollywood be pleasurable and painful at the same time, he thought. They must be the best and the worst days. That's why.

"I looked you up in a picture book the Chief lets me play with if I've been a good boy," Beckett said in jest. "I'm not allowed to color it, but I can look at all the pretty pictures as long as I want to."

Now it was Spears' turn to smile.

"They set you down."

"You heard about that, too?"

"Yeah. Instead of giving you a medal."

Spears wasn't trying to be complimentary. He was expressing his individual feelings about pimps. These guys were funny. They had their own code of who and what was good and bad within the framework of bad. A matter of degrees, so they thought. Bank robbers were admired for their guts, their daring, their willingness to put their lives on the line. But child molesters were despised. They could get one hit inside the joint for a pack of cigarettes and sometimes short eyes, a child molester, took a knife in the gut just because of what he was.

Beckett tested the coffee. It had cooled enough to drink. He watched Spears squeeze some lemon into his tea and sip it quietly between comments.

"Well, things probably turn out for the best," Beckett said. "Down here, I help little old ladies across the street, and make Toll House cookies for sodality bake-offs in my spare time."

"But it's a cool town."

Spears meant that the mafia was not active on the premises.

"That's true. We call it Little Geneva ...King's Ex," Beckett observed. "The only place in the country we know of where all the families come together and instead of shooting each other, they have a picnic in the park on Columbus Day."

Spears smiled wryly. He knew what was exaggeration and what was not. He also knew that what Beckett was saying was largely true, but quickly changed the subject.

"I understand you had a rather jarring experience the other night."

Between sips of his coffee, Beckett suddenly stiffened in his seat.

"How do you know that?"

Spears shook his head, as if admonishing Beckett for his suspicion.

"A man picks up things, anywhere he goes."

"All right," Beckett said. "Someone tried to store a half a pound of lead in my thick Irish skull. But if the Russians ever attack, I hope he's with them. He'll wipe out a whole battalion of his own."

"That's what I heard. Hit everything but you."

Beckett finished his coffee with one more gulp and indicated to the waitress he wanted more. He didn't want any more coffee, it upset his stomach. But he wanted more conversation with Spears while he had him up close and personal.

"More tea?" he suggested to Spears.

"No thanks, I'm catching a plane," Spears said, a reminder to Beckett that the conversation was nearing its end.

Spears may have finished, but Beckett wasn't. He was just warming up.

"Where were you, would you guess, when I was doing a disco dance under the front seat of my car the other night."

"Naturally, I don't know exactly what time that was. But I can tell you where I was. Playing five card studs with a deputy sheriff from Riverside County."

Beckett's eyebrows went up a half an inch.

"Which one?"

"Kelly Pickett."

"A friend of yours, Kelly?" Beckett asked.

"My brother-in-law."

"I see. Nice fella, Kelly."

"The best."

They sat in silence a moment, and then Spears looked at his watch and made motions to leave. Beckett made no effort to interfere with his plans. Spears got up, looked at Beckett, then sat down again.

"Look, ask yourself this: If I wanted to hit you, would you be sitting here now?"

Beckett stared into Spears' face that had acquired a rugged and chiseled look with age. He pursed his lips, as if thinking very hard. Then he said, "No. No, I wouldn't."

Spears shook his head in an "I told you so" gesture.

"Look," he said, "I'll give you one, free. Maybe because I'll be retiring very soon now, okay?"

Spears didn't wait for Beckett to answer.

"Next time you see Carlo Robelli," he continued, "maybe you say, 'Thank you, Uncle Carlo.'"

Spears' comment clearly got under Beckett's skin and Spears saw it had.

"Carlo Robelli?"

"Yes. That's all you get and if you're half the man I think you are, you won't quote me and you know that's the end of this conversation."

Beckett knew exactly what Spears meant. This was a tough old bird, maybe the toughest. Neither Beckett nor the U.S. Army could frighten him, or squeeze one word out of him that he didn't want to give voluntarily.

"Good trip, Spears."

Beckett stuck out a hand. Spears took it.

"Don't take any wooden nickels."

It was an ancient expression. Beckett's father used to use it. It meant good luck and hope you make out okay.

Beckett watched Spears head for the boarding gate and thought, "With that black suit and steel grey hair, now I know who he looks like: Father Mulcahy. Wouldn't the good father say a thousand Our Fathers and Hail Mary's if he heard me say that!"

Beckett walked slowly out to his car, got in, turned on the ignition, and cursed under his breath. There, waving in the breeze, was a ticket for parking in a red zone. He got out and read the ticket. It was signed by Officer O'Brien, a young new officer assigned to the beat. Beckett realized O'Brien had no way of knowing the unmarked black Ford Explorer was owned by a fellow officer, someone so new to the job.

"Goddamned cops," he muttered to himself. Then he shrugged and drove over to the station to see more of them.

The one thing that stuck in Beckett's mind during the drive was that Spears had implied he owed old Carlo Robelli a favor. That would take some figuring, and he was already at it but he was stumped. What had this mafia king pin done for him, and why? That was enough to baffle him for a week, except he didn't have a week to be baffled. There was too much piling up in front of him.

14

Porky Kelp shifted his bulk on the park bench in Ruth Hardy Park, a family-friendly twenty-two acre spread near homes in the historic Movie Colony of Palm Springs, and tried to look casual as the passing parade strolled by, paying absolutely no attention to him. But convince Porky of that. He was certain that people were stealing sidelong glances at him, whispering about him under their breath, avoiding making any eye contact with him, and suspecting him of all sorts of dire deeds.

Paranoia goes with the territory when that person is a snitch and Porky was a good one. He had worked in his erratic way for a half-dozen California police departments. Not for any department, really, and never officially. He would latch on to one investigator who would introduce him to another, and soon he would have a stable of clients. In Palm Springs, Porky reported to Lt. Luke Beckett and Chief Tom Batters. He was passed along to them by a fed, Bill Heenan of the IRS, who found Porky, despite his appearance, to be a reliable source of information when needed.

Beckett was amused as he caught sight of Porky, trying to look inconspicuous. Porky stood five-foot one-inch tall in his stocking feet and tipped the scales at three hundred pounds.

That's when he was on a diet. He looked like a king-sized Sparky McFarland of The Our Gang movie comedies someone had left out in the rain too long. Porky was at least fifty years old, and it's embarrassing to be fifty years old and still look like an overgrown member of Our Gang.

Porky had called Beckett and offered him some information. Beckett clearly understood that Porky was not about to volunteer his information as a good citizen. That's why Beckett had signed a voucher and taken seventy dollars from petty cash.

Beckett knew how Porky liked to operate, so instead of walking up to him and saying good morning, Beckett did it, Porky's way, which was twice as suspicious. Beckett walked past Porky, and Porky looked around and then began walking behind Beckett. The two-man parade continued until Beckett turned a corner in the footpath and stopped, shielded from the street by a large blooming Bougainvillea bush. Porky joined him.

Beckett smiled to himself. He always maintained that Porky didn't do it for the money, that he really loved this cloak-and-dagger stuff. It made a short, fat man who couldn't hold any other kind of job feel important.

"Yeah, Pork," Beckett asked, "what's up?"

Porky looked around, as Beckett knew he would, to make sure the coast was clear.

"You're looking for somebody, right?" Porky said gnashing his teeth and flashing a phony smile.

"I'm always looking for somebody."

Porky whispered, "I mean this Frank Connors guy."

Suddenly, Beckett was interested.

"Go."

Porky stammered and stalled. He always did anytime he got nervous creating an unnecessary fuss that only made him more nervous and fidgety.

"I, uh, geez, this inflation is really fierce, ain't it?"

Beckett handed him a twenty. It was a single bill but Beckett swore Porky was trying to count it, probably out of habit.

"Thanks, lieutenant," he said as beads of perspiration dripped from his brow. "I can give you this Connors guy."

"Well," Beckett said impatiently, "that's what I thought you said. Give!"

"Right," Porky paused, looking wilted under the hot baking sun. "Is it hot in here or what?"

"We're *outside*, Porky, and yes, it's hot," Beckett said. "You were saying?"

'Okay, okay. Here's the goods: This guy Connors has been staying with a friend in a place where you'd never look for him."

Porky looked fifty pounds lighter after getting the load of his mind. Beckett ran with it.

"Church?"

"Nah," Porky noted, shaking his head for no other reason than it created an instant breeze that cooled off the top half of his body. "In the Palm Springs Canyon Sunrise Mobile Home Park."

"No shit!" Beckett was surprised. That was the mobile home complex where he lived. It was the last place in the world he would look—on his own doorstep.

"Got an address?"

"Space number four. That's all."

Now Beckett shook his head but for a far different reason. That was only four doors from him and one street over. But Connors couldn't know Beckett lived there. Probably thought cops lived in big houses. Even Beckett had to admit to himself, most of them did; he was the only outlier who didn't.

Pleased by the inside information Porky gave him, Beckett started to pat Porky on the shoulder but thought twice about it since Porky was still carrying on his inconspicuous covert spy act to the hilt and Beckett didn't want to ruin it for him.

"Thanks, Porky. We all right?"

Beckett knew Porky knew he meant the twenty dollars he had given him.

"Sure, lieutenant," Porky said with a pause. Beckett knew Porky only paused for an effect before turning the cheek and play on the good lieutenant's sympathies and he was right. "But the wife's got this awful cold. Can't seem to shake it. I really wish I could afford to take her to a doctor. But you know how expensive them bastards is."

Beckett knew. He gave him the remaining fifty dollars he had drawn out of petty cash.

"God bless ya, lieutenant," Porky said gratefully. "That's from the misses, too."

Porky looked around trying again not to look suspicious, then waddled off, as Beckett watched him. He wasn't going to worry too much about Mrs. Porky, especially since Porky was a bachelor.

Beckett drove straight to the station and inquired after Lt. Garcia, next in line to become the new Chief of police after Batters retired. He was stuck in Indio serving a warrant on a con man who had convinced sixteen Palm Springs millionaires to invest in an oil well. He had promised the investors that there would be plenty of oil there, and even had a geologist's report to prove everything he said. There was only one hitch: The oil and the land belonged to Shell Oil Corporation.

"It's the old Shell game," Garcia told Beckett on the phone, and had to congratulate himself for the great pun, even though Beckett wasn't laughing.

Beckett instead moved on to Mike Farnsworth, who was on duty at the time. Farnsworth was a sergeant in his mid-thirties, medium build, dark hair and blue-eyed who hated work. He had devised thousands of complex plans to avoid it whenever possible. Beckett took Farnsworth with him when there was no one else and there was no one else.

On the way to Palm Springs Canyon Sunrise Mobile Home Park, Beckett filled Farnsworth in on everything he needed to know.

"Connors is wanted for questioning in the Van Ander slaying. He had skipped, now he has been located."

Beckett had no idea if Connors was dangerous, frightened, or confused, but told Farnsworth in passing to "prepare for possible resistance, even a gun, even though he has no history of menacing anyone with a service revolver."

Technically, Connors was not guilty of any crime. He had simply not kept himself available as the investigating officer had ordered him to do. Farnsworth understood.

"No worries, lieutenant," he said glancing over at Beckett. "I'm prepared for anything."

Beckett knew the man at his shoulder wasn't about to win the Nobel prize for the smarts, but he was a careful, if plodding, officer. If he made a mistake, it would on the side of caution, and that was good enough in this case.

It seemed odd, planning to make an arrest in his own mobile home park. Beckett's neighbors were mostly retirees—people who had worked hard all their lives and some of whom had very little to show for their efforts. Most of his neighbors had paid cash for their modest mobile homes while some had difficulty meeting the high space rent payments of $700 a month, relying on Social Security checks and part-time jobs to supplement their income. The more fortunate old people were living out their lives in comfort and luxury in Rancho Mirage and other exclusive gated communities. Their less fortunate peers were enjoying the same sun, but little else, in mobile home parks like this one. Still, Beckett liked the environment. At the end of a day of police work, he found this unofficial over fifty-five compound an ideal place to escape the reality of the outside world.

Beckett had frequently left the confines of his mobile home at sundown and walked to the tiny park in the center of the community. In the sales brochure, the park looked like Yellowstone. Truthfully, it wasn't much bigger than a large welcome mat. Seven weather-beaten benches, and four to six seniors on each one of them.

While the old folks in Rancho Mirage sipped their very dry martinis before dinner, their counterparts in the Palm Springs Canyon Sunrise Mobile Home Park split a can of Coors or poured Thunderbird or Ripple into paper cups. The talk was always pretty much the same from whomever had gathered to chit-chat or blow off some steam on any given day. What their children and grandchildren were doing, and it was always something magnificent, who was ill with what, which restaurant was having a special this week, and what businesses were featuring discounts for seniors.

Beckett hoped none of the old folks would be nearby if his encounter with Connors took a violent turn. He found himself almost wishing Connors would not be there. Better to take him in a safer place where there was no fear of someone getting hurt.

Beckett saw his turn coming up, wheeled left, and drove into the compound and up to the manager's mobile home and office. It was a little larger and older than the others, and so was the manager. Beckett guessed Sam Swanson to be almost eighty years old. Yet, he stood remarkably straight and his voice was still strong.

"That mobile home," Swanson said in answer to Beckett's inquiry, "is the residence of William Beam."

"What do you know about Beam?" Beckett asked further.

Swanson knew all the residents by name and almost everything about them to the point of ad nauseum but to a police lieutenant all of it vital when investigating a murder case.

"Used to be a postman in Chicago. Lived here, oh, maybe the last six years. A widower," Swanson happily explained. "Loves to go fishing at Hidden Lake but he's got arthritis now, mostly in his left leg, and can't get around too much anymore. Had a dog, Obie, it got killed last summer on South Palm Canyon Drive. Hit by a beer truck."

There was still more—more than Beckett needed to know. Finally, he cut Swanson off as time was the essence

"Thanks, Mr. Swanson, you've been quite helpful."

Beckett and Farnsworth left as Swanson kept an eagle-eye watch on them jumping into Beckett's sport utility vehicle and heading down the street to Beam's court street, Outer Drive. Oddly named since it was not an outer street but an inner street but that's another story.

Beckett wanted no trouble, no excitement and especially, he didn't want anyone want to get hurt. He expected Beam probably was home. He watched television morning until late at night, and in between, made his own flies for fishing, although he rarely got to use any of them. Swanson indicated that he knew someone was staying with Beam for a few days, but didn't know who. He hadn't met him, but had seen the man several times. He fit Connors' description, exactly.

It was easy to locate space number four. Beckett told Farnsworth to look as inconspicuous as he could while he walked to the back of the mobile home. Farnsworth had instructions to apprehend anyone trying to escape out the back way, but to draw his gun only if his own life depended on it.

Farnsworth went around the back while Beckett walked up to the front door and knocked. He heard the television blaring loudly. The door opened squeakily and a man's face appeared behind the screen door.

"Yes?"

"Hello, my name is Lt. Beckett. I'm a detective with the Palm Springs police department. I wonder if I might talk to you for a moment?"

"You sure you want to talk to me?" the shadowy figure asked. "My name is Beam."

"Yes, Mr. Beam," Beckett assured him. "Are you alone?"

Before Beam could answer, suddenly Beckett heard a tremendous crash inside and the sound of somebody running. Noises inside a mobile home sound much louder than in a house or apartment. The paper-thin walls amplify the sound tenfold.

Beckett tore open the screen door, brushed Beam aside, and burst into the mobile home just in time to see what looked like Frank Connors tear open the back door and disappear. Connors had panicked, leaped up, tripped over the cord connecting the pole lamp, and tried to escape out the back. Beckett ran through the mobile home and outside. There was Connors, wild-eyed and panic-stricken, standing like a trapped animal with Farnsworth holding a gun on him.

Beckett approached Connors and did a quick body search. Then he turned to Farnsworth.

"Put that goddamned piece away!" Beckett shouted as he gave Farnsworth a cold, hard glare. "You want to give someone around here a heart attack?"

Beckett then turned his attention to Connors and immediately tried to put him at his ease.

"Don't get so excited. No one is going to hurt you," he said in a measured tone that was neither threatening nor reassuring. "I told you to keep yourself available to me for the investigation. I've been looking for you for several days. I just want to talk to you, that's all."

Connors had fixed a frightened stare on Beckett, and it was as if he had heard nothing Beckett had said. Behind them, Beam walked up, huffing, and puffing more from excitement than the short run he had made to catch up to them.

"What the hell is going on here?" Beam demanded.

"Not much, not much at all," Beckett said. "Frank and I and Officer Farnsworth are going to have a visit and there's nothing for you to be concerned about."

But Beam was concerned—concerned about not only his safety and that of every resident in the tiny mobile home community but also Frank Connors, even though he was only a guest.

"Frank, did you do something?" Beam asked plainly. "Should I call a lawyer?"

Connors was so scared he didn't respond. He kept looking at Beckett as if he were confronting a wild animal.

"Mr. Connors will probably be back here within an hour or two," Beckett patiently explained. "There's nothing to be concerned about. He's helping us in an ongoing investigation."

Beam wasn't too sure about any of that, but he didn't argue with Beckett this time.

The three men walked back to Beckett's Ford Explorer. Beckett opened the back door and Connors got in without assistance. Beckett indicated to Farnsworth that he wanted him to drive and Beckett got in with Connors.

"Where to?" Farnsworth asked.

"Let's not go to the station. Find an open space somewhere where Mr. Connors and I can talk in private."

"Right."

Connors' nerves were on edge and it was evident by his trembling voice. "Where are you taking me?"

"Like I told the man, somewhere we can talk in private."

"I want to go to the police station."

"Why?" Beckett asked.

"I want to go to the station. I got a right to be taken there."

Farnsworth caught Beckett's eye in the rear-view mirror of the car. Beckett nodded to Farnsworth.

"All right, whatever you say. But we've got to talk."

Nothing more was said between them as Farnsworth drove off. Beckett was seeing it again, the raw panic in Connors' face, and his utter terror seemed to be caused by Beckett. But why? Connors obviously wanted to go to the police station because he was afraid of being alone with Beckett. He didn't want to go to "a private place" with the police lieutenant. It didn't make any sense. He would hardly be a decent suspect at all if it were not for his own bizarre behavior. That was what kept directing Beckett's attention to him.

At the station, Beckett thanked Farnsworth for coming along and ushered Connors into his office. Connors sat down, facing the open door. Ordinarily, Beckett would have closed the door, but he was dealing with a paranoia he didn't understand and so he left it wide open, so Connors could see and hear the human traffic just a few feet away.

Beckett sat behind his desk, pretended to be looking for a

paper, got up and sharpened a pencil, sat down again, this time putting his feet up on his desk. He was trying to appear as casual as possible in order to put this kook Connors at ease. He knew he couldn't get anything out of a panicked man.

"Frank, you worry me. You behave like you're guilty of something very heavy and the odds are, you're not. You're technically a suspect in a murder case, but there is nothing that links you to the crime. Yet, you panic every time you see me and you deliberately didn't keep in touch with me as I asked you to do. You made me find you, and when I did, you panicked and ran. If I hadn't given Officer Farnsworth instructions not to hurt you, if he had been a younger and less experienced man, you could have been shot, fleeing a police officer like that."

Connors still looked wild-eyed, but he nodded. He understood what Beckett was saying, but his level of fear hadn't retreated very much.

Beckett waited a long moment, and Connors dropped his gaze and looked at his shoes. He didn't like locking eyes with the lieutenant. Beckett was becoming impatient and finally exploded.

"Connors, for Christ's sake, say something?"

Connors finally did and it wasn't exactly the eye-opening confession Beckett was hoping for.

"I have nothing to say."

Beckett began pacing to burn off the rage building inside of him while still speaking.

"Your behavior makes you look guilty of something."

"You know I'm not," Connors responded coolly.

The whole time Connors kept his head down and still never made eyed contact only to provoke the ire of the good lieutenant even more.

"I know you're not? I don't know any such thing. How could I know you're not guilty of something?"

"I'm not going to say anything else," Connors said crossing his arms in defiance.

"Christ, you haven't said anything yet."

Beckett quit pacing by now and he thought he gave Connors a start. What was it with this man? He looked as tough as a ten-dollar steak but he reacted like a rabbit when he was around Beckett. Beckett didn't have a thing on him. Not a thing. Why wasn't he smart enough to know that?

"Look, Frank, I'm going to drive you home and this time you don't leave this area unless you tell me where you're going and when you're coming," Beckett said. "You have to understand that. If you take off without telling me, you're going to be arrested. Now is that clear?"

Connors didn't look at him but eked out, "Okay."

Then Connors added, "I don't want you to drive me home. Let me use the phone outside and I'll have someone come and pick me up."

Beckett misunderstood him and his one-track mind got the best of him.

"It's no trouble, I'm going out that..."

"I don't want you to drive me home," Connors said so loudly that an officer passing by the door stopped and stared before Beckett waved him on.

"Okay," Beckett relented. "Just remember what I said. Don't make a small thing into a big thing. Don't hurt yourself."

Beckett walked out and Connors followed him. Beckett indicated a phone he could use and Connors went over to it and started dialing. Beckett poked his head in Chief Batters' office and he signaled him to come in.

"What the hell was that all about?" Batters asked agitated.

Beckett quickly ticked off the facts as he knew them to the Chief to bring him up to speed.

"I honest to God can't figure it out. That guy is either as guilty as sin or I'm losing my mind. I guess he thinks I'm the Big Bad Wolf. He shakes when he sees me. If I come within two feet of him, he shakes and quakes."

Batters fixed a suspicious stare on Beckett continuously for at least five seconds.

"You punched him around at all?" he asked, expecting Beckett had.

"Christ, no."

"You sure of that?"

Batters knew Beckett's temper. It was his business to know about it and it often worried him.

"I swear to God, Tom, I've never laid a glove on the guy. Never threatened him, nothing. No reason to," Beckett said. "He was Van Ander's handyman. He was there the night of Marcia's murder. That's the only reason he's a suspect. But he's hiding something and I can't figure out what."

"How good a suspect?" Batters asked.

"Not all that good."

"Well, keep an eye on him," Batters said incredulously. "Frightened men are capable of doing desperate things."

"Thanks, Chief. Great advice," Beckett responded with a smile. "I can see why you made chief."

"It wasn't for my good looks and charm.

15

Midtown at his palatial desert estate, Carlo Robelli had sent for him. His son Johnny needed no more clues than that to convince himself that he was in big trouble when his father called and arranged a private one-on-one Tuesday afternoon meeting with him. On the infrequent occasions he saw his son it was social or some personal family business, usually involving finances but never the mafia business. Old Carlo always waited for Johnny to come to him. A son went to his father, a father never went to his son. Johnny understood it better than anyone it wasn't the other way around as a member of a mafia family.

Johnny could count on the fingers of one hand the few times Carlo called on him. When he got the Ambrose girl pregnant and his father had to pay heavily because she was Catholic and insisted on having the baby. When Johnny got a little too drunk at the Zambruski wedding and then got in his car and struck and seriously injured a fourteen-year-old girl with his Porsche convertible. She was left permanently crippled. Those misdeeds had cost the old man plenty. Another time, Johnny tried to scare off a minor lieutenant in the organization by warning him that if he didn't stay away from the girl Johnny wanted, he would call on his father. The implication was clear, but that one backfired on him badly. The mobster went straight to Carlo and Carlo backed him up, effectively breaking up Johnny's budding romance with that beautiful young actress who just landed her own starring dramatic television series on CBS.

Johnny knew why he was there. But he had no choice but to sit in the massive living room and wait for the old wolf to make up his mind when he was going to see him. Johnny had no job, in or out of the organization, and he wanted none. He lived off the income his father provided. The senior Robelli cleaned up after Johnny because he was the only family he had left.

The uncles, Tommaso ("Thomas" in Italian) and Alessandro (an Italian name for Alexander—as in Alexander the Great), were dead. Tommaso was killed in Cleveland by a bank guard during a robbery; Alessandro was dispatched with a shotgun by the organization after a skimming scandal in Las Vergas. Carlo's wife, Theresa, had died of cancer nine years ago. Johnny had always related to his mother better than his father.

Theresa Robelli was a gentle and loving woman, a very devout Catholic who had once studied to be a nun, and never approved of her husband's business dealings. She knew what Carlo did for a living, but tried not to think about it. She never wanted her handsome young son to join the organization, but that wasn't the reason Johnny had been kept outside of it. Carlo decreed that Johnny wasn't qualified to belong. His peers agreed. Behind his back, they sneered and said the old wolf had spawned a rabbit.

Johnny had always been a disappointment to his father. Carlo was an old bull who had hoped to sire a dozen strong young sons. But Theresa could have only one and the one she had turned out to be, in Carlo's eyes, a weakling. The boy didn't fight, there was nothing he could do well. A man must be proud of his son; Carlo wasn't. Carlo loved Theresa deeply, and Theresa protected the boy from this man she both loved and feared at the same time.

Father and son had never been close. An invisible barrier stood between them, and neither made any attempt to break it down. Each considered it more of a shield than a barrier. Their father-son relationship was a biological accident, one they could not ignore, but one which neither felt obligated to celebrate.

Carlo Robelli knew that Johnny was downstairs waiting for him. He had combed his grey hair into place and moved closer to the mirror, noting the wrinkles around his eyes and the droop to his cheeks.

"You are drying up, old man," he told himself. "One day soon, your time will come and it will all be over."

Carlo was certain nobody would weep his passing—certainly not that misguided pup downstairs, but would be the first to ask how much was left to him instead whether the old man suffered in his demise.

Something had happened to the world that Carlo Robelli did not understand. It had changed. The young ones, once the backbone of the family and its future, were now weak and dependent and yet self-indulgent and thirsty for material things and power. But they didn't want to earn anything. They were takers, not givers. They didn't like the old rules. They didn't like *any* rules.

Carlo had worked his way up from the gutter to a position of power and authority and respect. He had paid his dues, a thousand times over. He had won his place through extortion and labor racketeering and before that an illegal gambling operation that had earned him millions. But those were acceptable crimes. Robelli had not touched drugs or pornography. They were for the depraved. A man does not make his living off sick children. But men more powerful than Robelli had told him he was old-fashioned, outdated, not moving with the times, and out of step.

So, Carlo Robelli, a don of one of the most respected Cosa Nostra families in America, was diplomatically pushed aside, told to go to the desert and soak his aging bones in the sun and not worry about business and day-to-day operations any longer. He had made his contribution. That was in the past. Now he had earned the right to relax, except that Carlo didn't want to relax. Even the oldest of tigers doesn't want to lay down with the lambs. He would be better off dead than to be no further use to the organization.

Carlo looked at the beautifully framed picture of Theresa on the vanity. He thought how strange blood can be. If he applied a different yardstick to Johnny, if he said, "All right, if he is not my son, what would I think of him?"

Carlo knew the answer as he looked away from his beloved Theresa smiling up at him. He would not have given Johnny the time of day if they were not blood. There was nothing in the boy to admire. He was weak, selfish, vain. He had no sense of honor. Perhaps that was his greatest sin, one for which there was no absolution.

Moments later, Johnny rose respectfully as the old man entered the room, clutching a Cuban cigar in his right hand and tying his black velvet robe with his left hand. He waved Johnny to sit down and then took a seat in the high-backed chair by the window. He studied Johnny for a full minute before he spoke. When he did, it was from behind a screen as blue smoke illuminated by sunlight streamed through the window.

"Your mother always said, be patient with the boy," he said staring off into space and blowing smoke rings in front of him. "I have been patient."

Johnny didn't like the sound of it and immediately pleaded for mercy.

"Poppa, I..."

Carlo raised his hand to stop him from speaking further.

"I will talk, you will listen."

It wasn't a suggestion; it was an order. Johnny recognized the tone of voice. He had witnessed it before. There was no emotion to it. Carlo, someone once said, was "a block of ice." Johnny could feel the ice in his words. This was the tone of voice his father used when he talked to someone in trouble and this time it was him.

"Times change. People are not the same," he continued. "I came to this country, I was dirt. I couldn't even speak the language."

Johnny had heard it all before. The poor boy from Italy makes good story. Every mafioso who made it in America had his own version of it. The story was designed to make anyone much younger feel inadequate. There was nothing to do but listen.

"I went to night school. The first thing I learned was how to speak the language of my new country. I got a job helping a man with a clothing business. Soon I owned that business, then ten, twenty, thirty, and then more. By the time I was thirty, I branched out to owning my own factories that made clothes."

Carlo's energy and passion for what he was saying started to wane. Even he was beginning to tire of rehashing ancient history.

"Enough of that. All in the past. I did what I had to do to get what I had to get. It's all behind me," he said between puffs of smoke from his cigar that drifted over and encircled Johnny like blood-thirsty buzzards ready to pick his bones bare. "Now let us talk about Johnny Robelli. Your mother told me to be patient. I have been patient. But my patience is gone. You have made a lot of mistakes, Johnny. Now you have made a mistake that is too big."

Johnny knew what he meant. Spears had warned him he would rue the day after trying to pull a fast one over his father but Johnny refused to listen.

"Poppa, let me explain. This Beckett…"

"This Beckett," Carlo interrupted. "Ah, what a one he is."

Johnny thought he detected admiration in the old man's voice, but he must have been mistaken.

"I have heard about this tribe in Africa that hunts lions," Carlo continued, the ringlets of smoke from his cigar now growing smaller with each short puff. "They think that if they eat the heart of a lion, they will become strong and fierce like the lion. I don't know but I think maybe the lions think that is very funny."

Johnny wasn't sure he got the analogy, but the old man now fixed his coldest glare on him and laid it all out the facts as he saw them for his heir-apparent-son to absorb.

"There are rules, Johnny. I thought you had enough brains to know them. Listen to me very closely. We do not kill policemen. It is not a practical thing to do. If you a kill a policeman, more come at you and more after them. The one thing a policeman cannot forgive is killing another policeman."

Carlo paused puffing long and hard on his smoldering cigar before resuming.

"This is a nice warm place, this desert. It is not by accident that so many mafioso are here. It is a good place to soak the cold of the east out of your bones. It is a good place to talk things out. The organization likes this place because it is quiet. If it no longer is quiet, it no longer is a good place."

Growing more impatient, Johnny was beginning to tire of his father's mob boss act.

"Poppa," he pleaded, "this Beckett was going to frame me and…"

Old Man Carlo sneered and, as he did, Johnny immediately stopped.

"A man frames someone only when there is no other way to handle him. I know this man." Carlo spoke like someone who had examined the soul of his opponent, the good lieutenant, and liked what he found. "He fears nothing, he feels nothing, he owes no one. He does not need to frame anyone."

"But, Poppa, he put his arm on me at the top of the tram," Johnny stated nervously. "He made it very clear that he was going to do something to me."

Carlo laughed in his son's face but there was no mirth in his laughter.

"A man like that does not give warning. He strikes by instinct.

I know how he thinks. He would squash you like a bug if he thought you were worth the trouble."

Johnny realized he was fighting a losing battle. He could throw himself on the mercy of the court, but his father was no court. He was judge and jury rolled into one.

"Okay, Poppa. Okay," Johnny relented. "I know what you're saying and I know I made a mistake. I'm really sorry but at the time…"

Carlo waved the rest of his words away with a sweep of his hand.

"You know nothing. The families are all here. They live in peace. This is like a truce territory. It is understood by everybody that nothing must happen here or we no longer will be welcome," he explained. "The police here understand these rules. We do not bother them or anyone else, and we remain welcome. Someone kills someone, and it is all over. Do you understand?"

"I do, Poppa, that's why I say…"

Carlo again waved off his son silencing him. He was not through with what he had to say.

"Did you imagine for even one minute that this man Spears would not report to me?" he asked coldly. "He is a soldier. You tried to hire a soldier and you are not even…"

For the first during their discussion, old man Carlo found it difficult to finish the sentence. He looked out the window for a moment, then returned his attention to Johnny.

"If this man Beckett had been killed," he said, "it would have been the worst thing that could have happened."

Johnny sighed in frustration. "Where was all this leading?" he wondered. Had the old wolf figured out a fitting punishment for him? Maybe temporary exile like sending him to Acapulco. He had done it on two previous occasions.

Carlo had other ideas. He already had cast his decision before sitting down to talk to his son and the penalty, as severe as it seemed, fit the crime as far as he was concerned.

"You will take the money you have in your bank account and

your clothes from your luxury condo, and your car, and you will drive away from this place and never come back. I do not wish to see you again."

Johnny's jaw almost fell open with surprise. He knew there was no appeal. The old man had talked to him like he was one of the hoodlums rather than his flesh-and-blood son. He had seen his father operate too long to think his mind could be changed. He was intractable and there was no point in trying.

Johnny rose slowly. One day, he would get even with that son-of-a-bitch Spears for ratting on him, but now was clearly not the time.

"Goodbye, Poppa."

It was all Johnny said as he turned and walked out the door while his father looked away from him, staring out the window with shame in his heart.

Carlo kept listening for the front door to close behind Johnny. After an eternity, it did and Carlo sighed deeply and inaudibly. With that, he got up and pulled his robe around his once-strong body and a hacking cough nearly gagged him. His son had failed him for the last time. Theresa was gone, Johnny was gone. Soon, he would be, too.

Carlo walked upstairs very slowly and sat on the edge of the bed. Never had he felt so old. Slowly, he removed his robe and crawled into bed. He reached over and turned out the light. In the darkness, where no one could see or hear him, he cried. The tears Carlo shed were heartfelt and sincere. They were not because he was left with no other choice but to excommunicate Johnny after disparaging the good family name. They were because he knew he should have done what many had suggested sooner—send the lion out to slay the lamb and spare him the indignation he was feeling at this very moment.

***

Crosstown at the Palm Springs Police Department, Luke Beckett couldn't believe what was happening. Here he was, standing in the Chief's office, knee deep in a murder case that seemed to be going nowhere, and watching Batters' lips which seemed to be saying, "This is Charles LeBaron, the famous psychic, and Betty Michelson, Senator Helleck Michelson's daughter, and they'd appreciate it if you would take them over to the Van Ander's house and around town because Mr. LeBaron is going to see what his psychic powers tell him. What do you think of that, lieutenant?"

What did he think of that? He would like to tell the Chief what he thought but instead gave the best answer he could in this case.

"Right, Chief. Of course."

Beckett knew he had no choice but to do what Batters had asked. Batters was a master at playing politics. It's how he survived so many years on the job. He pulled the right strings at the right time and this was one of those times. He knew very well who Betty Michelson was. She was the darling daughter of the high-ranking U.S. Senator who chaired two powerful Senate committees. Betty was two years out of Northwestern University and built like a brick house, a little too ample here and there to become the model she had hoped to become. She decided instead to become a feature writer for the national weekly tabloid magazine, *Happening Now.* Daddy made a couple of phone calls and here she was with this phony psychic, prepared to write one of those idiotic stories people read in idiotic magazines like hers.

Beckett smiled sweetly at Batters and the Chief read the smile and smiled back. Beckett's smile said, "Don't expect me to bail your ass out next time you come crying to me about the air conditioning," and Batters' smile said, "This is for all the headaches you've caused me, smart ass. Now we're even."

Michelson said they would ride in her car if that was alright with the Beckett and it was. Naturally, this underprivileged child drove a press car that was just a touch above average: a 2021 Audi A6 fully equipped all-wheel drive sedan that had earned the top spot on many *Editors' Choice* lists for mid-size luxury car of the year. She suggested it would be nice if Beckett drove and he drove slowly so she could sit in the back with LeBaron and record comments from him on her iPhone's voice recorder app. Beckett was as amicable as a saint mostly so he could get it over with as fast as possible.

Beckett started her Audi, marveling at the quiet sound of the V-6 turbocharged engine, and guided it over to Palm Canyon Drive and headed for the Van Ander home. Right away, Betty eagerly asked LeBaron, "Getting any vibes yet?"

The flamboyant and fastidious psychic glibly responded, "No."

Beckett thought they were getting warm because LeBaron kept touching the tips of his index fingers to his temples and nodded his head in communication no doubt with the spirts from another world. It was the first time either of them had been to Palm Springs, so Beckett pointed out sights along the way. LeBaron didn't seem to hear anything Beckett was saying, immersed as he was in his own thoughts, but Betty seemed fascinated.

"Beautiful…Just beautiful," she declared with jaw-dropping amazement. "The palm trees are so close you feel like you can touch them."

Beckett wanted to comply and give her to chance to get an up close and in person view, but thought otherwise. He knew he would never hear the end of it from Chief Batters if he veered off course just to "sightsee."

As they pulled near the Van Ander home in the exclusive, guard gated compound of Mar Vista, one of five-million-dollar-plus residences in what *Living Magazine* called "the platinum subdivision," LeBaron let out a shout.

"Stop! Stop the car!"

Beckett wasn't going fast but hit the brakes so swiftly that everybody's head bobbed back and forth like a trio of baseball bobbleheads but without the interminable frozen smiles on their faces.

Of five mansions on the expansive street, all of them flanked the back nine of a private eighteen-hole golf course shared by a neighboring gated community. The fourth house was the Van Ander residence where the street dead ended and LeBaron sensed they had to be near the scene of the murder unless Beckett had deliberately taken them to the wrong street. None of the homes had names in front of them—a security precaution no doubt—besides a massive wall and gated entrance that required permission from the guard on duty, Sam Court, to enter.

"We are near the scene of the murder," LeBaron insisted with his eyes shut tight he was feeling some otherworldly spirit connection close by.

"Wow!" Betty said, her bright green eyes flashing with excitement.

Beckett wasn't a believer. "Bullshit," he thought.

LeBaron's forefingers went up to his temples again, and Betty was delighted as Beckett turned around in the driver's seat and watched with detached amusement. Betty remained fascinated.

"It's all happening right in front of me!"

"You, uh, got a lock on the house?" Beckett asked.

"I have to get out of the car!" LeBaron demanded. He said it like a Shakespearean actor flinging his hand above his head for dramatic effect and impressed everyone but Beckett.

Finally, LeBaron scrambled out of the sedan and held his right hand over his head, placing his left hand on his hip. Beckett thought, "The son-of-a-bitch is going to do a ballet step."

LeBaron turned his body so that he now faced the homes on that side of the street. He moved his unraised hand as if it were a periscope on a Navy submarine, finally pointing it directly at the Van Ander house.

"It's the large white house with custom desert art landscaping in the front yard," he asserted with his usual grandiose flair.

As soon as LeBaron hopped back inside, Beckett pulled up to the guard shack and through the half-rolled down car window briefly exchanged pleasantries with Sam, who promptly opened the gate and waved him through.

Betty oohed and ahhed and snapped half-a-dozen pictures with her iPhone after jumping out of the parked Audi sedan and walking up with Beckett and LeBaron to the front of the Van Ander residence. Beckett didn't understand her over-the-top reaction. Since the murder, the exterior of the house had been photographed and shown in newspapers and magazines and television news broadcasts a hundred times. It would have been easy for LeBaron to look up the story and study the pictures online.

"Isn't he marvelous?" Betty whispered in Beckett's ear as they reached the huge exquisite hand-carved front door built to perfection.

"Yes, marvelous," Beckett said with a hint of sarcasm in his voice.

A Mr. Maritime came to the door. He was with the Van Ander estate and had been informed they were coming. He hoped they didn't have anything sensational in mind, that Betty's article would be in good taste. The estate had agreed to cooperate only because of Senator Michelson's intervention. They could use an influential U.S. Senator like him in its corporate corner.

After the amenities, LeBaron asked if he might go into the lush garden opposite the opulent swimming pool and contemplate in private for a few moments. He knew, as anyone who had followed the case at all had known, that Marcia's body had been discovered there.

"Can I go with him?" Betty asked Mr. Maritime politely.

"No," he said firmly. "No photographs of any kind."

Betty had to have at least one picture of LeBaron in the garden to go with her story.

"Just one picture, please, of Mr. LeBaron in the garden," she pleaded. "That's all I need."

"One picture and then you must vacate the garden and join us back here."

"Okay. Thank you."

Beckett watched her and LeBaron step into the garden and turned to Maritime circling his right index finger around his temple several times.

"Cuckoos," he said.

"I read you," Maritime said, dropping his corporate demeanor for a second.

Two minutes later, Betty emerged, flushed with excitement. Five minutes later, LeBaron emerged with a spot of bird dung on the left shoulder of his tan cashmere jacket that hung there like a wet noodle that dried so fast in the hot sun it looked baked on. Beckett decided not to tell him what a little birdie had done to him. Who in their right mind wears a cashmere jacket in the desert in the summer anyway? he thought.

Betty, who was quick to notice, finally spilled the beans.

"Check out your left shoulder. Looks like you've been slimed."

The good psychic peered over and immediately lost his cool.

"Oh, hell. Damn!" he shouted and ripped the jacket off fast like it was some of kind of contagious disease. "Pardon me. But I just got this jacket out of the cleaners."

LeBaron whipped a cloth handkerchief out of his pants pocket and feverishly tried wiping the bird doo off. The more he wiped, the more it spread and widened across on the shoulder like a smear of melted chunky-style peanut butter. He concluded it was a total loss and gave up, much to his chagrin.

Beckett wisely changed the subject.

"Did you discover something, Mr. LeBaron?" he asked.

"Yes," he said half-heartedly, still clinging to his lost-cause cashmere jacket in one hand and soiled hanky in the other.

"What would that be?"

"I detect a note of sarcasm in your voice, lieutenant. But that's alright. I deal with cynics all the time," he said smugly. "Mine is a *rare* gift. Not easily understood. I'm not sure I completely understand it myself."

Betty interjected, "What did you find out there?"

LeBaron held up his hand with the bird-splattered handkerchief dangling from it to Betty, as if to say, "Wait a minute, I'm listening to an inner voice." Then he broke his silence.

"I'm not sure what it means, but I can tell you what the feeling is."

Beckett looked at his watch. Betty held her breath.

"The feeling was unmistakably clear. Whoever perpetrated this murder has returned to this house many times," he stated emphatically. "I feel the presence. It is here even as I speak."

"Man or woman?" Beckett, always the cop, asked.

"Just a presence," LeBaron said. "I can't tell you no more than that."

"Swell!" Beckett responded, throwing his hands up in the air.

LeBaron didn't appreciate the lieutenant's cheap theatrics and gave him a cold, hard glare while pointing the finger at him with his ruined cashmere jacket clinging to life in his hand.

"I don't say I'm right or wrong. I don't know," he explained. "All I can tell you, and I tell you most sincerely, is that I really do get these, uh, sensations, feelings, and thoughts that I haven't thought come into my head."

"Your thought is that whoever did the murder returned to the scene of the crime?" Beckett asked.

"Yes."

Beckett kept his response to himself. He thought there was no way someone had returned to the crime scene, except, yes, Frank Connors. He left, came back for his clothes, left again, and came back again for some personal effects he had forgotten. Charles and Dolores had finished up their services, so it couldn't have been them. Frank Connors—it always, no matter how he saw it, came back to him.

The good lieutenant suddenly changed tactics and employed some good humor to win LeBaron over.

"Are you going to buy the chauffeur a drink?" Beckett asked, "Or can he buy you one?"

LeBaron smiled broadly for the first time since meeting him while Betty, against the wishes of Mr. Maritime, snapped another picture of the immaculately kept grounds with her iPhone.

"Lieutenant, if I were in your shoes, I'd probably think what you're thinking, too," LeBaron declared while gingerly folding the bird soiled cashmere jacket across his arms when he said it.

"What am I thinking?"

Beckett asked the question placing his index fingers to his temples mockingly and LeBaron reacted in a way he didn't expect.

"That I'm a phony son-of-a-bitch!"

Beckett laughed long and hard before collecting himself.

"Now I know I'll buy you a drink."

LeBaron threw a playful punch at Beckett's stomach as Betty pleaded, "Just one more picture."

"Stuff it!" the great and powerful LeBaron said.

Instead, the normally persnickety psychic went out and got that drink with Beckett—with Betty tagging along since after all it was her sedan Beckett was driving—and turned the day into something special they would always remember.

16

The morning after, Jo Ann Tracey never felt more like a woman than when she was lying close to the rock-hard body of Luke Beckett and were both still naked after enjoying the pleasure of each other's company the night before. Her head was nestled under his left arm and her groin was pushed up against the curve of his buttocks. She thought he was asleep when she gently passed a hand over the flat, hard stomach, propped her head under her arm and looked into his face to find his eyes were wide open.

"You're not asleep?" she asked, wiping the sleep from her eyes.

"No."

"What are you thinking about?"

"Nothing." Beckett said it in a way that he meant it.

"You can't think about nothing."

"Sure, you can, but it takes a lot of concentration."

"No, really," Jo Ann continued, "what are you thinking about?"

"Okay, if you must know…Batteries."

"Batteries?" she laughed.

Jo Ann laughed easily and musically, with a little gurgle in her long white throat. It was one of those things Beckett liked about her, not that there wasn't a whole lot more to like. She had the body of one of those women they put in a centerfold, only hers was a smidge more ample where it ought to be. Her long blonde hair was natural, the deep-set grey-green eyes almost luminescent in the early morning light.

"There's nothing wrong with your battery, Lukey," she purred affectionately.

Suddenly, Beckett frowned and said, "Don't call me that."

The anger in him never developed slowly, like a tide building. It always came without warning. Like a volcano that engulfed him, smothered him, and naturally the person on the opposite end.

"Okay. I never called you that before," Jo Ann responded defensively. "It's just that you look like a little boy in the morning."

Beckett squeezed her gently. Even at that, she winced a little.

"Tell me about…what did you say…batteries?"

"Some other time."

Jo Ann knew he wouldn't. He never let her close to him. That was a funny thing to say after a night of the most satisfying lovemaking she had ever consummated. But that was body stuff. She was thinking about head stuff. She knew every inch of his body like the back of her head, touched it, tasted it, caressed every curve and flat of it. He was generous and patient and kind in the way he made love to her. She had never experienced anything like it before, and she knew there would never be anything to approach it again. But Beckett's mind, that was something else.

Beckett looked at the clock on the wall of her apartment. Instead of numbers, it had little figures of animals. It was fifteen lions to polar bear. He gave her a reassuring hug.

"Sleep a little more. It's early."

Jo Ann squinched her lovely head back into the security of the crook of his arm and sighed. In a few moments, she had drifted off to sleep again, more exhausted than she had realized.

Beckett closed his eyes but he knew there would be no more sleep. He never required more than four or five hours. Like a farmer, he always awoke at first light. But back then there were no cows to milk at 65th and Morgan on the south side of Chicago where he grew up.

Waking up at dawn was a pattern set it seemed a thousand years ago when he was little Luke Beckett, the youngest of the three Beckett boys. If it was winter, the old brick-and-mortar five-room house his father had updated and renovated would be groaning in the cold. The furnace always went out and didn't last through the night. When his feet hit the linoleum floor, Luke would automatically recoil from the chill.

Terrence Beckett would already be up, shaved, and fixing breakfast for himself and his sons while their mother slept in, and when Luke came around the kitchen door in his cut down pajamas, he would always be greeted warmly by the giant of a man he called father.

"Good morning, commissioner!"

Beckett's father had been a cop nearly eighteen years. He was still a patrolman. He would always be a patrolman. Not that he wasn't a good cop. He had more than a dozen citations. But his personnel record said he was an alcoholic, given to fits of temper that his wife and children never saw. He had been suspended many times for punishing prisoners on the street because he had seen too many rapists and child molesters and pimps and thieves wiggle out of the arms of justice because they paid off the right cops or judges or could hire lawyers smarter than anyone in the prosecutor's office.

The big hands would swoop down and grab Luke and he would feel like he was in a vice. But they would gently place him in a chair next to his brothers Timothy and Anthony and would begin the very special kind of breakfast they had. While most people had bacon and eggs or pancakes or cinnamon buns, they would eat warmed over stew with huge chunks of homemade bread heated in the oven. When they finished, Luke would watch his father strap on his uniform and his gun and he would walk him to the front door and be kissed and hugged goodbye. Then his father would drive off on Halsted Street and Luke would have his face pressed hard against the window with the bitter cold seeping through the pane, trying to see him until he was out of sight. But the angle of the window never let him watch his dad beyond Green Street, a half block away. By that point, Luke would go back to bed and dream of the day he would be a policeman.

Childhood memories kept flooding back to Beckett as lay there next to Jo Ann until suddenly startling himself with the realization of saying aloud, "Batteries not included."

He glanced at Jo Ann, still asleep, lying on his shoulder with her eyes closed tight. She never awakened to wonder what it meant after resolving to herself she would not ask him again. Not ever.

It wasn't because Beckett had said something about batteries and she didn't understand it that she was upset. He had said something else, in his sleep, and she did understand it.

He had said – Marcia.

***

Every city in the world has a place like Turkey Keeler's They can be found in New York, Boston, Chicago, Philadelphia, and San Francisco. Cop hangouts—taverns that cater to cops because the owner is an ex-cop or a badge-fan. They are offbeat watering holes where an off-duty cop feels safe, and sometimes even wanted and understood. A place where a guy with a badge can come and talk to guys like himself, talk shop, talk sex, talk anything. It was the middle-class man's version of the gentleman's club.

It could be said that a joint that panders almost exclusively to cops would be one of the safest places in the world. Most people think that and believe that, but they'd be wrong. Cops are people, too. They do equally silly and even dangerous things when they drink too much. Consider that at any given time, in a place like Turkey Keeler's, there are anywhere from three to twenty armed men drinking at the same time. It's a potentially explosive situation and, at times, the potential is realized.

Last February, when Ace Hartigan had succumbed to a compulsion to prove his storied marksmanship and tried to shoot out the bullseye on the dart board above the electronic juke box, Ace missed but assassinated a toaster in the upstairs apartment before he was jolted back to the real world.

Two weeks later, Sam Lieberman shot off the toe of his right boot while trying to demonstrate his fast draw. Then, last April, Hal Kibbe took his turn. Hal had been drinking most of the night with some poker pals, went home to sleep for a few hours, and woke up sick. He headed right for Turkey Keeler's for a bit of the dog that bit him. Kibbe's fatal mistake, according to experts in such things, was that he decided to switch from Jameson's Irish Whiskey to Harvey's Bristol Cream, which is sweet sherry with a kick. Kibbe downed three fancy little glasses of Harvey's and suddenly realized Harvey's had little therapeutic value. He ran to the men's restroom and heaved and when he came back, there was much fire in his eye as there was in his gut.

The bottle of Harvey's Bristol Cream on the back bar suddenly turned into Ike Clanton, and Kibbe became Wyatt Earp and announced to the throng he was going to "wipe out the whole Clanton Gang." Botchie, the bartender, begged Kibbe to wait for his brother Virgil "Doc" Holliday, but Kibbe wasn't having any of that.

He went for his gun and it was at that point that Luke Beckett stepped in and put him mercifully to sleep with a well-aimed beer bottle. Kibbe collapsed like a sack of dirty laundry and his partner, Dan Krebs, recruited two volunteers and they took Kibbe home.

"I owe you," Botchie told Beckett.

Beckett promptly forgot it, but not Botchie. That's why he was on the phone with him now.

"Right away, lieutenant," Botchie said. "If you can get away now, all the better."

Beckett could get away and, ten minutes later, he was sitting at the end of the bar and Botchie was telling him an interesting story.

Jill Jenkins had shown up there not more than twenty minutes earlier and was anxious to find Beckett. She didn't have his cellphone number, so early Wednesday morning she called his home, the station, Bob's Big Boy, and a couple of other places she knew he frequented, but couldn't find him anywhere.

"Tell him I got to talk to him right way. It's very important," she told Botchie, and now Botchie was telling Beckett.

"Thanks, Botchie, but where is she now?"

"Here's her number," Botchie said handing it to him on a bar napkin with her number scrawled on it next to a pair of hand-drawn hearts. "She left it for you in case I saw you."

When Beckett called from his cellphone, Jill's roommate, Sandy, was disappointed when she found out Beckett wasn't a customer.

"You can find her over at the Art Museum," she said tersely.

"I didn't know Jill was interested in art," Beckett said.

Sandy misunderstood what Beckett meant.

"His name isn't Art. It's Herman and he's just another trick."

Beckett caught Jill coming out of a back exit to the Palm Springs Art Museum's Annenberg Theater with a big, red-faced off-duty security guard artfully disguised in huge, oval sunglasses, bright red-and-white plaid stretch knit pants and white shoes. She told him to wait in his car and she would be right along and then told Beckett what was bothering her:

"I got a call from the north end of town two hours ago and while I always checked out tricks ahead of time—God knows if my mother were alive today, she would have been as cautious—I was so desperate for cash that I decided to take a chance and just service the call without checking it out."

After a slight pause, Jill continued with her voice wavering a bit as she spoke.

"I get to this motel, the Brewster, the kind I wouldn't take a fifty-dollar trick to. It's that rundown, and I ring Room 29 and this big black dude answers."

Right away, Jill said she became frightened. He looked like trouble in waiting and he could read it in her face that she was turned off by him, got mad as hell, and violently yanked her by the hair into his rathole of a motel room.

"Give me trouble," he said forcefully, "and I'll cut you a new slit you won't be able to rent."

Jill took him at his word and, while she was undressing, a white man came out of the bathroom and it turns out they were going to take turns doing tricks with her.

Beckett was sympathetic about her plight but started losing his patience with her.

"What the hell does this have to do with me?" he bluntly asked. "Do you want to file an assault complaint and have the two guys arrested or what?"

"Hell, no," Jill said adamantly. "I don't give a shit about those two. I took eighty-five bucks from them and I only have one small bruise to show for it, so what the hell."

Jill blabbered on until finally she said, "The point is while I'm getting undressed, I happen to glance at an open suitcase on the bed and I see two cut-out newspaper pictures on the top of the folded clothes and who do you think is in the pictures but my old friend Luke Beckett. Now that is strange or ain't it?"

Shocked and surprised by her revelation, Beckett agreed it was.

"It sure is."

His mind immediately began racing to the evening someone tried to turn his car into a shooting gallery.

"Did you see a gun anywhere around?" he asked.

"No, I did not."

"The suitcase? Were they packing to leave?"

"I think so."

Beckett glanced at his watch—it was a knee-jerk reaction he had done countless times before but this time seemed more important than the rest.

"How long ago was that?"

"About an hour ago."

As he began reaching for his cellphone, Beckett asked, "Did they have a car? Did you a see one—a make and model?"

"I don't know," Jill responded nervously. "But people who stay at motels usually have a car, don't they?"

Beckett called the office and asked Lt. Garcia to run over to the Palm Springs International Airport and delay any black man in the company of a white man. He gave Garcia the description Jill provided. Beckett ended the call, retrieved the phone number of the motel, and called it. He got the manager Hal Green. Beckett explained who he was and asked about the two men.

"The party in room twenty-nine? They checked out."

"How long ago?" Beckett asked.

"Half an hour, forty-five minutes maybe. I'm not sure but I can tell you one thing, lieutenant."

"What's that?"

Green paused letting out an audible sigh and his answer came out in a rush.

"They sure left place looking like a pig pen. People like that..."

Beckett didn't have time to listen. Thanked Green and hung up. Then he thanked Jill and ran to his Ford Explorer. His only hope was the airport. If they had their own car, there was no way of finding them. He had no description of the car, if there was a car, and they would have given phony names to the motel manager.

Then, Beckett remembered that most motels require guests to write down the license numbers of their cars when they register. Damn. Routine piece of information he should have remembered. Why hadn't he thought of that immediately?

He dialed the airport, where half-a-dozen car rental companies do business. Hertz said no, Avis couldn't remember, but Budget did remember. The reservation agent Rebecca Ramirez recalled, "Yes, the pair had rented a black Chrysler 300 luxury sedan and they had turned in it."

"When was that?" Beckett inquired further.

"Fifteen, twenty minutes ago."

Beckett sped to the airport. He didn't even pull his keys from the ignition as he leaped out and rushed through the door. There, behind the counter of the Visitors and Convention Bureau kiosk was Lt. Garcia with the two men being held for questioning. Both had their arms on the counter, as he had instructed them to do, and Garcia, not knowing how serious the chore he was doing, had his gun trained on them but wasn't visible from the other side of the counter. Both men were hopping mad, complaining, "This is a violation of our civil rights," and threatening, "Wait until the top brass hears about this!"

When Beckett walked up, the men froze as if they had seen a ghost.

"Did you frisk them?" Beckett asked Garcia.

"Yes, they're clean."

Beckett went behind the counter and they herded the two men into a frosted glass wall office hidden from the ground entrance traffic of the airport. Garcia watched them closely as Beckett took their tickets for their outbound flights to Los Angeles and grabbed the airport manager, mid-forties with dark hair and a cherub face, Luis Mendoza. He was able to intercept their bags just before they were loaded on the Los Angeles flight. Beckett carried them back to the office and opened them. He stared down at the brown bag and then looked up at the two men.

"Fans of mine?"

Beckett didn't mean the question the way it sounded. He wasn't jesting, he was dead serious when he asked it.

Both had grown sullen and neither would respond or look at Beckett.

"Look at this," Beckett said to Garcia, indicating for him to come over.

Garcia walked over and squatted, picking up two newspaper clippings, each with a photo of Beckett. They were stamp-dated and the source said: "Hollywood Branch Public Library."

"I didn't know you were famous," Garcia mused.

"Used to be," Beckett said. "Used to be."

"What the fuck you think you got on us?" the surly white man asked.

"Are you kidding?" Beckett questioned back. "An 807 in the California penal code"

"What the hell is that?" the black man asked.

"Stealing newspaper clippings from a public library for starters."

Less than half an hour later, the pair was sitting in the Palm Spring Police Department lockup and a fingerprint check was underway. They were booked on suspicion of murder and it looked the charges would stick. An Army Colt .45 was stuffed in a denim blue shirt in the white man Bill Wickup's bag and the black man, who went by the name of Randy Miller, had been carrying the newspaper clippings in his bag. Beckett had dug two .45 caliber bullets out of his car and ballistics would match them with bullets they would fire from the Colt .45 found in Wickup's bag.

Both men, of course, denied any knowledge of the attempt on Beckett's life. But with their fingerprints being checked and their prints and pictures on the way to the Los Angeles Police Department, Beckett felt confident they would soon be identified. Who they were was of less importance to Beckett than why they had tried to kill him? If they were hired killers, good help was sure as hell hard to find these days. He remembered the professional hit man, Spears, saying, "If I wanted to kill you, you wouldn't be here." These guys couldn't hit the side of a Boeing 747.

Beckett walked into Chief Batters' office. The Chief was reading a paperback mystery, *Scared to Death*, about a young twenties woman television news anchor who solves a series of strange deaths of a host of famous celebrities when he looked up.

"Looks like a good collar," he said, flipping the page.

"It could even be the break we need in this case if we could find out who hired him," Beckett said.

"You're not suggesting I take a walk while you..."

"Would you?"

"No, I wouldn't," Chief stated emphatically.

"I didn't think so," Beckett said plainly. "That's why I didn't ask. But how about playing good cop, bad cop with me?"

"Get Garcia to do it."

"Come on, Tom, you know how to do it better than anyone."

Batters stared at his paperback mystery for a moment and then thought, "What the hell!"

"Okay," he said, "you go first."

Beckett got the lockup key from Ramos and let himself into Miller's cell. It is routine for officers to hand their piece to the lockup keeper but Beckett had arranged with Ramos to keep his gun. Ramos, of course, understood what was going down. He knew the gun was empty.

Bad cop Beckett glared at Miller in a manner that normally sent shivers down the spines of those he was interrogating to rattle them into confessing.

"Listen, you rotten son-of-a-bitch," he shouted. "I know you tried to kill me and I know why."

Miller looked at him and then looked away. He didn't take the bait.

Beckett walked over and grabbed him by his short, curly hair, jerking his head back and causing him to wince.

"Look at me when I talk to you, you black ass bastard. You're going to tell me what you know or I'm going to break every one of your fingers one by one and if you still don't talk, I'll cripple you. Believe that!"

Miller immediately cowered and screamed at the top of his lungs, "Hey, somebody! This cop is trying to kill me. Somebody helps me. By Christ, he's trying to kill me."

Good cop Batters came running out of his office and over to the cell.

"What the hell are you trying to do?" he screamed at Beckett. "Open this door!"

Beckett reacted slowly, sullenly. When he finally swung open the door, Batters shoved him through it.

"Get out of here! You're crazy, you know that? Crazy!"

"Chief, let me have five minutes with this bastard," Beckett pleaded, of course, all for show. "Just five minutes."

In doing so, Beckett slammed a fist into a palm and almost sounded like a firecracker going off to further get under the skin of Miller still trembling in the corner.

"Get out of here!" Batters screamed again, then sighed, and sat down on the cot adjoining Miller.

"The man is overworked. Last week, he almost beat a prisoner to death. There's something wrong with him," Batters said tapping his right temple.

"Then why is he a cop?" Miller asked quivering.

"Why? Why? That's what I asked myself. You know how he got here?"

Miller shook his head no.

"Beat some poor son-of-a-bitch to death with his fists up in Hollywood. Some poor guy just tryin' to make a few bucks running a few girls. Is that a capital offense, for Christ's sake? He gets away with it because his family has deep political connections."

"Yeah," Miller said suddenly turning defiant. "That's the way the fuckin' system works, don't it?"

Batters could tell Miller was starting to crack but playing the good cop-bad cop routine might take longer than he expected to get a confession out of him, so he asked Ramos to open the cell door and left. Miller was grateful to be alone again.

Ten minutes later, Beckett was back at Miller's cell. He didn't say a word this time. He just stood outside the door and withdrew his service pistol from his shoulder holster and swung open the cylinder and spun it around like a roulette wheel with the cylinders clicking loudly. Then he put it back in its holster and aimed a forefinger at Miller's head.

"Bang!" Beckett spouted off softly, and then walked off.

Miller took the bait, crying out, "Chief! Chief Batters!"

Batters rounded the corner within seconds, his timing impeccable as always.

"What is it? You want some coffee or a sandwich or something?"

"Chief, that guy Beckett was back here again," Miller said with his voice quavering. "I tell you that mother fucker is going to kill me."

"Oh, I didn't think so," Batters said reassuringly. "Oh, he'd like to get at you all right, but I don't think he'd actually try to kill you. Besides, you don't have that much to worry about. We're going to transfer you to Riverside County overnight and then it's up to Los Angeles."

Miller didn't question any of that, which told Batters he had no idea what was going on. He just wanted to get out of Palm Springs.

Half an hour later, Batters walked past Miller's cell with Beckett at his side. Batters was saying, "Now, when you get to Riverside, I want you to tell Captain Denning that he's to keep the prisoner in isolation until the FBI finishes with him. Then...on the way back..."

The two men had walked out of earshot and Miller couldn't hear the rest of the conversation.

"Oh, my God!" Miller squealed. "Everybody in this mother fuckin' place is crazy!"

Batters came back without Beckett and Miller ran to the bars clawing feverishly at them with his hands like a rat trying to flee a sinking ship.

"Chief! You ain't gonna let that crazy cop deliver me up to Riverside County? You ain't gonna do that, are you?"

Miller looked terrified while Batters reverted to the sympathetic good cop.

"I'm afraid I have no choice. He's the only man I can spare. We've got a night parade downtown and a special event at the mayor's house and a big political rally, and we just don't have enough people. I've got no one else."

Miller shook his head with a look of fear in his eyes.

"That mother is going to kill me. Kill me, you hear me? Can't you do anything?"

Before Batters could answer, Beckett came up, all smiles. Batters glanced over at him.

"Well, you look happy. You win the California lottery or something?"

"Come here," Beckett said, motioning Batters to move out of earshot of Miller.

Then Beckett spoke loudly enough so Miller could hear just about every word he was saying on purpose to get under his skin.

"Wickup says...and the gun. Well, at...kill me...then later...at the motel. Not buying that...a previous rap. So, you can understand why he'd have a change of heart."

Batters nodded his understanding. Then he turned to Miller.

"Uh, there's been an, uh, new development. It changes a lot of things. We'll have to unload you right away. Beckett, get the prisoner ready and you be ready to leave with him in ten minutes."

With that, Batters turned on his heel and walked off dropping out of sight.   Miller jumped to his feet and screamed after him.

"Come back here! I want to talk to you. I don't want go anywhere. Chief! Chief, come back here! Wickup, you bastard. What you have been tellin' them?"

Batters returned and Miller said, "Not while he's here," indicating Beckett. Batters instructed Beckett to wait in his office and he complied.

Five minutes later, Batters had a complete confession from Miller, who was Morris Williams, brother of Candycane, the pimp Beckett had killed in a fit of rage when he worked on the Hollywood vice squad. It wasn't the confession that Beckett wanted. Williams plainly admitted, "It was Wickup. He planned and carried out the whole thing."

Wickup was his real name. He had no previous record like Williams and Wickup confessed his role but said, "Williams did it."

A simple polygraph test or more grilling would clear that up, but Batters and Beckett knew they had all the evidence needed to convict both men. They would do a respectable stretch of time for the attempted murder of police officer either way.

Back in the office, Beckett stuck out his hand and Batters took it.

"That's why I wanted you and not Garcia. I'd like to give you a goddamned Academy Award. You sure were hitting on all eight cylinders in there. You almost had me believing it myself."

"Well, it wasn't all an act," Batters said matter-of-factly.

"Oh? What part wasn't?"

"That part where I told the creep that you were a crazy son-of-a-bitch!"

Beckett walked out of the station higher than a kite and then he remembered something that brought him back to earth. He had thought these men might be a link to Marcia's murder. They were not. It would have been so much better if they were.

17

A loud booming voice thundered after him somewhere outside in the parking lot of the police station, "Yo, Beckett!"

Beckett whipped his whole body around and saw the bulk of Sgt. Robby Waco rippling behind him at a half trot to hook up with him.

"Got to talk to you," he shouted at Beckett with a slight wave of the hand to attract his attention. Of course, with Waco's massive frame—he put the Incredible Hulk to shame, he wasn't hard to miss.

Beckett liked Waco. He was a marshmallow, a guy who should have been a social worker or a priest, he was that soft. Never pushed around a prisoner in his life, never broke a rule. He was married to a younger woman he had picked up on a grand theft auto charge, and he was supporting her mother and her congenitally out-of-work brother. That's the kind of man he was.

"Waco," Beckett said politely. "Don't tell me, you found this stray dog and he had moo-cow eyes and you want to find him a nice home."

"No," Waco insisted. "I'm missing six Mercedes."

"Oh," Beckett said half-smirking and half-serious. "That doesn't sound like too much of a problem. If you were missing, say, ten Mercedes, I'd really be worried for you."

Somehow, Waco never disappointed. Nothing usual ever seemed to happen to him. If there was one offbeat, never-ran-into-one-like-this-before-case, Waco seemed to have it. This one fell right into that category.

"Okay, here's the scam. We get a call from the Sand and Sun Hotel on Tahquitz Canyon Way close to the Convention Center," Waco explained.

"They're having this big bash and they've hired this valet parking service because they're expecting maybe one hundred fifty to one hundred seventy-five guests."

Beckett, not known to indulge in idle chit-chat, suddenly interrupted.

"And six of the valets made off with six Mercedes and haven't been seen since."

"No," Waco continued, "it's not that simple."

With Waco, Beckett remembered, it never was.

"These valet guys are parking the cars and everything goes swell at the bash," Waco related, "and then everyone comes out with their little parking tickets in their hands and what do you think?"

"I think six guys with six Mercedes give their parking chits to the valets and the valets can't find the cars to fit the stubs."

"That's right," Waco noted. "A gang of car thieves has stolen six Mercedes right out of the parking lot."

"Wait a minute!" Beckett said haltingly. "The Sand and Sun Hotel has restricted, behind-gate parking. You can't just come in and steal a car and drive out. You need a ticket to get out of their lot, and each parker has a ticket, right?"

"That's what's got me stumped," Waco said scratching the top of his buzz cut haired head. "The only guys that can get out of that lot with them cars are either the owners with the proper tickets or the uniformed valets themselves. Since the owners didn't steal their own cars, then the valets had to steal them."

"Except that what?" Beckett asked.

"Except that there were only four valets on duty, all regulars with the Curb Service Valet Parking Company, all long-time employees, and they were always in sight of each other and it couldn't be any one of them. It *couldn't* be."

"Then why," Beckett asked, "are you telling me all this?"

"It's my case, Luke, but I need help."

"I don't have much time to spare. But, okay, let's go over to the hotel and look it over and be quick about it," Beckett said, resigned to the fact Waco couldn't solve the case without him.

Waco breathed a sigh of relief and they got into his squad car and drove straight to the hotel, just minutes away from station.

As Beckett entered the long driveway entrance, he remembered it had a public parking on the left and if he drove another fifty feet or so, he would come to the valet parking station and the restricted parking lot in the front of the hotel. Local visitors parked in the public parking lot for nothing and walked. The affluent guests and tourists often used the valet service. It was a luxury that reminded them they were on vacation.

As Beckett pulled up and parked in a red parking zone, much to the dismay of the valet on duty, he caught sight of the hotel's manager Steve Kearney. Steve was a beanpole who stretched somewhere around six foot five inches and his bony frame was unmarred by a single muscle. Steve was shitkicker from Oklahoma whose father had tripped one day and fallen into a natural oil field. Like most devoted fathers, he had lofty ambitions for his son. He started out hoping Steve would become President of the United States. By the time Steve was nine years old, he had modified that ambition slightly and hoped the boy might get a job in the corner drugstore if he equipped him with a college education. Mr. Kearney altered that thought when Steve was unable to stay in high school because of an I.Q. that nearly got him the coveted "Mope of the Year Award" in Tulsa, but the old man eventually found something for the boy to do. He bought him this hotel in Palm Springs. It kept him off the streets and too busy to visit his father and mother, except for a week or two each year.

Now thirty-five years old, Kearney had risen high in his world, but he never forgets his father's good advice: "Change your underwear several times a week (no one else will know you're doing it but *you* will know, that's what's important), and never pass gas in the elevator." Important words to live by.

"Lieutenant Beckett, nice to you see," Kearney said in a welcoming voice.

"Nice to see you, Steve," Beckett said, taking the hotel manager's extended hand and shaking it. "Are you gonna be on this case?"

"No," Beckett explained. "It's Waco's case. I'm just sort of keeping him company for a while."

Steve nodded. Beckett was a hot-shot cop. Steve was hoping he was here to find the missing Mercedes. Kearney's fly-by-night insurance company was having a fit. The claims on the six Mercedes would top three hundred thousand dollars and Kearney was having visions of red ink dancing in his pointed head.

Beckett and Waco followed Kearney into the bar. They had coffee while Kearney downed a Scotch.

"Never touch the stuff before eleven," Kearney explained. He was right. It was already two minutes after eleven.

"What about the valets?" Beckett asked Waco sitting opposite of him.

"I checked them out. They're clean. Three are college kids working their summer vacations. The fourth is Councilman Kepper's nephew, sprung from the family mansion and learning what real life is all about."

"Real life is a missing Mercedes?" Beckett asked in jest.

"Yeah," Kearney said, ignoring Beckett's attempt at humor.

"It couldn't have been them kids. They work here every summer. I figure somehow somebody gets into the parking lot and makes off with them cars."

"But how?" Beckett pondered openly. "How could they have raised that gate without one of those cards the valets carry unless someone stole one of those cards?"

"No way! They're using the same original four cards we've always had," Kearney said emphatically. "Each card is made to fit only one gate. Like, our cards won't work in any other gates in town, anywhere else. That's guaranteed by the company."

Beckett gave Kearney an understanding nod.

"Let's assume the valets didn't do it. What's left?" Kearney asked. "Someone sneaks into the restricted lot but can't get the gate up. Doesn't make sense."

Kearney looked pained and his face showed the tremendous strain he was under. The whole time Waco was studying Beckett's face. He thought he saw something coming. Something was.

"I think I might have it," Beckett said.

Kearney leaned forward and motioned for another Scotch at the same time while Beckett continued.

"Just a possibility. Try this: The valets didn't steal the cars, and no one took them from the lot guarded by the gate. They never got to that lot."

Waco and Kearney looked at each other, then at Beckett.

"I don't get it," Waco said befuddled.

Kearney, the one-time reigning "Mope of the Year Award" champion, didn't get it either.

Beckett offered another possible theory, even better than the first one.

"Okay, picture this: Mr. Big moves up the driveway in his Mercedes. A valet, maybe uniformed, maybe not, steps out, smiles, and motions him to a stop. The valet hands Mr. Big a parking chit. Mr. Big takes it, walks up to the entrance of the hotel, and goes into the affair in the hotel. Follow that?"

They thought they did but they weren't at all sure.

"Don't you see? One or more phony valets have stationed themselves at the lower parking lot and they stop only those drivers who have Mercedes, the kind of cars they're looking to heist," Beckett continued. "The Mercedes owners don't know what's going on, why should they suspect anything at all? They see a valet, he smiles, he takes their car, they get a receipt, and forget about it until...until the ball is over and it's time to claim the car. No car. The valets...long gone."

Waco whistled. "Geez, you're good. That could work. That could explain it."

Kearney nodded in agreement pushing his second Scotch aside on the tabletop and showing signs he had had enough for the day.

"But where would they get those parking tickets?"

"Probably an inside job," Beckett said. "One of the valets figured out this little beauty in those boring hours between parking cars. Those people were in there—how long?"

Kearney waited for Beckett to finish before interjecting an important point he had to make for whatever it was worth.

"Anywhere from one and a half to two hours, if they stayed for the whole
program, which all of them seemed to do."

"Right. So, the car thieves had plenty of time to get away," Beckett concluded. "You put the four valets on the polygraph lie detector and ask each of them about those parking tickets, and I think you'll find one of them was holding out extras from before just so he could mastermind this little business."

Waco made a note of that and Kearney's face brightened immeasurably.

"Let's go down and check that lower lot," Beckett said, "just for laughs."

Kearney excused himself, he had more urgent hotel business to do, and wobbled off while Beckett and Waco walked to the lower lot without him. It was unpaved, partly clay, partly black soil packed tightly from the weight of parked cars, with a sprinkling of gravel.

Waco looked at the lot and saw a parking lot. Beckett looked at the lot and saw something else. He walked over to a portion of the lot where he had noticed deep tire marks. He motioned Waco over.

"What does this look like to you?"

Waco joined Beckett in a crouching position and studied the tracks.

"A truck?"

Beckett began walking alongside the number of steps it took to go from one end of the tire tracks to the other.

"Goddamned long truck, if it was a truck."

"Hell," Waco said, "there are a lot of big trucks."

"Yeah. But why should a truck park in this lot?" Beckett paused and contemplated the reason logically and methodically. "Too far away from hotel deliveries. Truckers don't spend the night in one-hundred-twenty-five-dollar-a-night hotels, do they? I know they make more money than we do."

Waco agreed they did not.

Beckett took out a small notebook and carefully put some figures on it Then he tore out the page and handed it to Waco.

"Is Solly Krebs still the Mercedes dealer in Cathedral City?"

"I think he is," Waco said.

Krebs' old police record was a mile long. He was a Philadelphia boy who was into everything from phony pigeon drop schemes to numbers scams. Sol read the handwriting on the wall, liquified his assets, and bought the Mercedes dealership and was now retired. Maybe. Nobody knew for sure.

"What's this?" Waco wanted to know.

"The approximate dimensions of the vehicle that made those tracks. If it's what I think it is, you might find it over at Solly's lot. I'm guessing it's a car carrier."

"You mean one of those..."

Beckett uncharacteristically broke into wide grin—he knew

instinctively his deduction was on the nose and there wasn't any doubt in his mind—when he answered the young officer.

"Those trucks that transport automobiles. Yeah. I don't know what else it could. See if you can't find one of them over at Sol's dealership. Compare the dimensions and if they're close, you might check to see if any car carriers are anywhere near Sol's. If you're lucky, you might find those six Mercedes all ready to go to parts unknown, probably Tijuana."

Waco was astonished. It was like something he saw in the movies once. He never thought it happened that way in real-life detective work until now.

"I will. Thanks, lieutenant."

Beckett was certain he had figured it right. Some enterprising young men intercepted luxury automobiles while posing as parking valets, and then took the cars and ran them up on the waiting car carrier parked in the lower lot. When they had the cars they wanted, off they went. But did they go down the highway or what? Would Sol be dumb enough to pull a stunt like that? Beckett thought about that one for a moment. He decided, yes, Sol would be dumb enough.

It turned out it wasn't Sol. It was a friend of Sol's, Clarry Getz, the used car salesman who bought the Mercedes dealership from Krebs. Like Sol, Getz's police record back east was extensive. They found the cars and the carrier still intact in Ensenada, Mexico. But that was a week later. Waco was bestowed one of the department's highest commendations for his work, even though he couldn't have solved the case without Beckett.

This day held other diversions for Beckett later that same afternoon. Bob Harris could hardly contain his excitement. He was just two years out of law school and had landed this good job as a special investigator for the state Attorney General's office and here he was, hand-picked by the A.G. himself to go down to Palm Springs and interview more than two dozen reputed organized crime figures who lived there year-round or during the season.

How would Harris be so lucky? What a unique opportunity it would be to talk to the likes of Tony Sirelli, Mack "The Enforcer" De Mayo, Carlo Robelli, and Jerry "The Torch" Cardoni.

Maybe after it was over, Harris would end up becoming a cover story on *Time* or *Newsweek* magazines. His wife Kassandra, who was five years older than him, was worried, of course. Harris had not done a whole lot to allay her fears. Here was her man about to beard the mafioso lions in their sandy dens and he was saying, "If there's trouble, I'll handle it." She knew he would, too. He had given her many thrilling accounts of how he would pick up hardcore criminals and transport them to court. Daring things like that where he was in danger every minute.

Once he arrived in Palm Springs, Harris would touch base with local authorities, and be escorted by them to the homes of the mafioso. He had been well schooled in the exact nature of his mission. It was what the intelligence boys still called "the Welcome Wagon." It was same program dreamed up by the attorney general just coincidentally before his last re-election campaign.

When an organized crime figured moved into the area, an A.G. man or a representative of the county sheriff's office or a local law enforcement officer knocked on his door and said, in effect, "We want you to know that we know who you are and where you are and we strongly suggest that you keep your nose clean while you are on our turf. If you do, you have nothing to worry about. If you don't, if you do anything to embarrass state or county or local law enforcement, we will make life so untenable for you that you will wish you were back in New York or Chicago or New Jersey or Philly to suffer through those cold winters again."

It wasn't a bad program. It worked surprisingly well.

Beckett had drawn the Welcome Wagon assignment for the last couple of years and he had found it rather amusing. He had greeted quite a few of the mafia boys in the time that he was in

Palm Springs, and more were arriving every year after each record cold snap in the east.

It was re-election time again, so the A.G. pushed up his calendar a bit and put out his famous list of organized crime figures in California a little early. It was a good way to pull the voters' chain. Transplants from Iowa opened their newspapers or turned on their television one day and were shocked to discover that so top hoodlums in organized crime were living in California, and many of them were in Palm Springs. But not to worry. The Attorney General was attentively aware of who they were and where they were and was monitoring their comings and goings.

The Attorney General was brave and strong and smart and unafraid of organized crime. He would protect the good citizens from these bad people. He was not afraid of them. He would tell them if they so much as tried to put slugs in a cigarette machine, he would put them under arrest.

Re-elect the Attorney General. That's why Bob Harris was standing in Chief Batters' office and Beckett was responding to a summons to appear. The Chief introduced the attorney general's special investigator and the three of them immediately sat down and got down to business.

Harris started the proceedings, saying, ""I'd like you to look over our list and see if we've got any one on it that you don't have or vice versa."

"Right," Beckett said, "and then do you want to get started on making the rounds?"

"As soon as possible."

"Right."

Eighteen minutes later, Beckett pulled up in front of the Mediterranean style mansion occupied by Jerry "The Torch" Cardoni. Beckett pulled up his left sock, which was sagging, while Harris checked his gun.

"You won't be needing that," Beckett assured him.

"You never know," Harris said ominously. "Where's yours?"

"In the trunk," Beckett said as Harris followed him up to the front door.

A dark-haired young and pretty woman answered and Beckett wasted no time introducing himself.

"Hi, I'm Lt. Beckett. Is your dad home?"

"Sure," she said flashing a beautiful smile, "come on in."

They followed her through the tastefully decorated living room and formal living room and she said over her shoulder, "Daddy's barbecuing out in the back."

Sure enough, he was, doing what he did best, Beckett thought, playing with fire.

"Hey, howsa goin' Beckett?" Cardoni asked a massive man in his early sixties with a stronger than firm handshake. "You met Sissie?"

"Helen," the pretty teenager corrected him.

"Oh, sure. She's too grown up to be called 'Sissie' any more. You know what I mean, Beckett?" Cardoni asked with a laugh. "Hey, you gonna stay for a steak? Stay for a steak. I got cutlets. Only two on a whole cow, ya know?"

Beckett indicated Harris standing next to him.

"This is a friend of mine, Mr. Cardoni. Bob Harris from the A.G.'s office."

Cardoni pumped Harris' hand vigorously, embarrassing the young investigator, and insisted that they all have a drink. Beckett ordered a Scotch and soda tall, no ice, and Harris explained that he never drank on duty.

"That's nice," Cardoni said. "Good policy."

Mrs. Cardoni suddenly came out, looking like the lady on Mama Celeste's frozen pizza, and carrying a plate of snacks and gave Beckett a playful punch on the arm.

"If I knew you were coming, I'd have locked up my daughters," she said with a big toothy grin.

"You're the only one who's not safe when I'm around," Beckett said, and she laughed until every inch of her one hundred and sixty pounds was jiggling.

A look from Cardoni and she excused herself and disappeared in the kitchen leaving the three men alone. Harris cleared his throat nervously before finally speaking.

"Mr. Cardoni, I'm here to inform you that your name appears on the State Attorney General's list. You have been identified by a committee of congress, or a crime commission, or some other official body as a member of organized crime."

Cardoni was half listening, still trying to be a good host, sidestepping everything Harris said.

"Maybe a soft drink?" he offered the special investigator. "I know, one of them diet drinks. Sissie drinks them because she wants to be a model."

Harris continued unabated and unmoved by Cardoni's bloviating.

"We are not here to make any formal charge of any kind but merely to inform you," he explained, "that we know who you are and are aware of your presence here in...uh...Riverside County."

Cardoni, smiling and now humming some obscure Italian opera tune, turned another steak and seasoned it with far too much salt on the natural stone finished, stainless steel grill island behind him.

"Hey, Beckett, you still running around with that nurse? Nice girl. You know, you ought to get married. A man gets an ulcer eating in restaurants."

"I hope you didn't mind the interruption today from your activities," Beckett said in a friendly tone.

"I only wish you'd come around more often," Cardoni said with a wide grin on his face. "Sissie's always looking for someone to play tennis with and an old man gets lonely sitting around listening to his arteries harden."

Beckett turned to Harris as he could tell Cardoni had said all he was going to say. No reason to push it farther.

"Should we be running along?" he asked pointedly.

"Yes," Harris said surprisingly, perhaps sensing the same thing.

Cardoni rubbed his hands on his apron which had a huge heat

pressed-on image of the late great Italian operatic tenor Luciano Pavarotti on the front.

"Drop by soon again, okay? Maybe we'll play a few hands of poker. Bring your young friend."

"Right," Beckett said as he started to make his way back through the house.

He waved at Mrs. Cardoni on the way out and noted that Sissie—or Helen as she preferred to be called—was growing. She had changed into a pair of skin-tight white shorts and was wearing a fire engine red silk blouse tied in front, braless.

"Hey, guy," Sissie said temptingly to Beckett in passing. "When do I get the tennis lessons?"

"Maybe soon," Beckett said with a half-smile. "When Sissie is really Helen."

"Ahhh, gwan," she said smiling.

Back in the car, heading for the next stop, Harris finally broke his silence.

"I don't get it."

"Get what?" Beckett asked.

"You talked to that man like he was a good friend of yours, a solid citizen."

"Well," Beckett said, "he is a friend in a limited way. He's friendly, let's put it that way, and he is a solid citizen…here."

"But he's Jerry Cardoni."

"Yes, that's right. But you saw *The Torch* in action. The biggest fires he builds these days are in that barbecue pit."

Harris found it hard to fathom why Beckett handled such a noted mob figure with kid gloves. It went against the grain of everything he stood for as a special investigator hired by the attorney general's office.

"Do you mean to tell me that all the intelligence on him is wrong, that he hasn't set millions of dollars' worth of fires, that he isn't the top arsonist in the country?"

"I didn't say anything like that," Beckett explained to clear up any misunderstandings Harris had. "Do you think we could go into his house and arrest him for everything he's done in the past?"

"Well, no."

"That's the point." Beckett knew he was right and underscored it all with facts that were irrefutable. "Here, Jerry Cardoni is the owner of a legitimate construction business. He meets a medium-sized payroll each week, pays his taxes, gives money to the church and to all the right charities, and belongs to two of the most exclusive country clubs in town. What do you think I can do about all that?"

Harris sighed. Beckett had him cornered but the young special investigator wasn't about to give up, yet.

"I guess what disturbs me is that you seem to be on such friendly terms with him."

Beckett reasoned with him. "I understand, but remember, I've met Cardoni several times, thanks to the A.G.'s program. I could go in each time and order him to spread 'em and search him and warn him that if he got out of line, I'd come after him but don't you think a man in his upper sixties who's been in organized crime since he was eleven years old understands all that?"

Harris finally figured it out and couldn't believe what he was saying when he said it.

"So, you have an almost social relationship with him?"

Beckett winced at the notion but met Harris halfway to make sure there was no confusion over what his intentions were.

"In a way. He isn't going to reveal anything to me if I come in with a police revolver and a rubber hose. He knows we're playing a game and he knows my role and he knows his role," Beckett explained. "So, we play our parts in a way that makes it easy on both of us. No sweat. I don't embarrass him in front of his family, he doesn't say anything out of line to me."

"But he's mafioso!" Harris said, his voice rising in frustration.

"Right. Mafioso. But he's not shaking his rattle in our playpen. That's the point. He hasn't been indicted and he hasn't done time for any crimes. People like that hire others to do their business for them. You must know that."

Harris just shook his head in disbelief and didn't say another word after that as Beckett motored ahead to the next resident mobster on "The Welcome Wagon" list.

Peter "Parky" Bonnano, a big man in mafioso circles who kept a low-profile these days, was watching a Hispanic gardener mow his front lawn as Beckett drove up. He waved to Beckett and came over to the car before they could get out with his talking African grey parrot "Brando"—famously named after legendary actor Marlon Brando—sitting on his shoulder.

"You Irish bastard, you owe me some money," he shouted.

Harris stiffened at the thought.

"I owe you money, my ass," Beckett chimed in. "Where do you get off saying that? Before I forget, this is Mr. Harris of the A.G.'s office. Meet Peter Bonnano."

"Hello," Bonnano said swiftly before getting back to Beckett and the business at hand. "Listen, Beckett, you bet me five even money the Rams were going to take the Jets in Dewey Kleinemann's. Remember?"

Beckett suddenly did. It had slipped his mind.

"Shit! You're right. How could I forget?"

He took a five-dollar bill out of his wallet and started handing to Bonnano.

"Ah, forget it," Bonnano said waving him off. "You just shake down some poor old tourist lady to make it up."

Brando wasn't about to let Beckett off so easy.

"Five will get you ten! Five will get you ten!" he squawked.

"Don't mind him," Bonnano said with an embarrassing smile. "You know my boy, Brando, he's got a one-track mind like his old man!"

"You and Brando sure got my number," Beckett said as he forced the five in Bonnano's hand over his protestations so he couldn't hold it over him in the future.

Brando immediately snapped it out of Bonnano's hand, holding on to it like it was a king's ransom.

"Give me that!" Bonnano shouted.

Clenching the five-dollar bill between his bill, Brando screeched in a garbled voice a la his namesake Marlon Brando as Don Vito Corleone from *The Godfather*, "It's not personal. It's business!"

Bonnano laughed and so did Beckett before Bonnano finally snatched the five dollars from Brando's beak. The only person who wasn't laughing was Harris, who didn't appreciate any of Brando's funny antics.

Beckett leaned back and looked at Harris whose interest he could see was quickly waning.

"You want to tell Mr. Bonnano anything, Mr. Harris?"

Harris shook his head. It was clear that the special investigator didn't like the game Beckett was playing and chose not to play along.

Brando, on the other hand, wasn't so easily convinced by Harris' silence that he started pacing back and forth on Bonnano's left shoulder and comically combined two famous mobster quotes into a Brando the talking African grey original.

"Never rat on your friends," he squawked, "and smile while you still have your teeth."

Beckett could tell Harris was unamused and knew it was time to move on before Brando ended up serving five-to-ten for embarrassing a public official.

"Listen, we gotta go," Beckett said with a smile. "We're making the milk run."

Bonnano nodded at Beckett that he understood.

"Hey, save you some time, Beckett. Perelli's in Newport Beach. I think he's trying to avoid a process server put on him by that ex-wife of his. Big Tuna went back to Chicago for some meeting. You won't find Pieti here either. He went up to L.A. to get a facelift. Can you imagine that?"

"Don't tell me," Beckett said, "let me tell you. He met a young broad…blonde, blue eyes, tall, athletic build and long-legged."

Bonnano roared with laughter over that one.

"You son-of-a-bitch, you got it. Right on the nose," he gushed enthusiastically and then snickered. "She's a dancer at the strip joint over on Perez Road in Cathedral City. I told him, 'You better get more than your face lifted.' I've seen this broad and she's gonna send him to an early grave!"

Brando, bobbing his head up and down excitedly, chimed in at that exact moment, "Married to the mob! Married to the mob!"

"You'll have to forgive, Brando," Bonnano said with a straight face. "He's a wise guy and knows it."

Beckett smiled and said, "It's okay. Listen, we gotta run. Tell the lady I said hello."

"Hey, yeah," Bonnano replied, tapping the side Beckett's driver side door with his hand, and then stepping back with an uncharacteristically quiet Brando on his shoulder. "Stop by some time, will you? I mean it. I'm going crazy out here!"

Beckett started the engine and they moved off, slowly. Bonnano threw them a casual wave, not before Brando sprung to life and cackled a parting salvo of "Make him an offer he can't refuse," before returning to the post on the front stoop to watch the gardener finish the rest of the lawn mowing.

"That man once ran organized crime in three states," Harris said to Beckett as if he didn't know that already.

"That's right. Now he's in charge of mowing the lawn. The feds are convinced he really is retired—I know they all claim they are—but they keep a close watch on him. I think they're probably right."

The visits got shorter and shorter and Harris became more and more discouraged because the scenario wasn't working out anything like he had expected. He felt like he was visiting a bunch of old Italian friends of this man Beckett. They never talked crime or police work, just food and women and arthritis and the summer heat and the new wing of local hospital and some kid's Holy Communion and someone else's divorce.

Beckett left for the last house that loomed ahead. It was almost Sunday, and he could see the figure of an elderly man leaning on the mailbox in front.

Beckett drove up and got out of the Ford Explorer. Harris followed him and Beckett walked up to the man leaning on the mailbox—Carlo Robelli's groundskeeper, Tony Rosario, and said, "How's it goin', Tony? Is Mr. Robelli home?"

"No, sir. He had business in San Diego."

"Goddamn shame, Tony. Mr. Harris here is with the A.G.'s office and just wanted to say hello."

"You want I tell Mr. Robelli you were here?" Rosario asked, his face shaded by the wide brim of the straw hat he was wearing.

"Sure, Tony. Sure."

"His sister is having members of her club over," Rosario explained. "Nice ladies."

"I know, Tony, I heard. I know a couple of the ladies."

"Mr. Robelli will appreciate you stopping by," Rosario said with a smile. "I know he'd glad to see you any time."

"I'll remember that. Take it easy, Tony."

They got back in the car and Rosario nodded at Beckett as he started the engine and drove off.

Carlo Robelli watched Beckett's black Ford Explorer until it turned a corner and went out of sight.

"Class," he said half-aloud. "A man with class who knew how embarrassed my sister would have been if two cops had come in while she was having her fund-raising luncheon for some of the social elite of Palm Springs."

He would remember the gesture for a long time. Carlo Robelli never forgot small favors.

In the car, Harris was saying he thought he had learned a lot on the trip. Beckett hoped so.

"Just one thing," Harris said. "Take this guy Cardoni, or Bonnano, or any one of them. If you could get the goods on them, what would you do?"

"Throw their mafia asses in jail for a thousand years," Beckett said without flinching and moving a muscle.

"Could you, uh, kill one of them?"

"Easy."

Harris believed him and, to his surprise, he was beginning to understand him.

18

There is such a thing as instinct and it can be trusted when reason fails and logic no longer seems to make sense. Everyone has it but not everyone has learned how to develop it, how to listen to it, how to react to the clues it offers, and how to act upon what it indicates.

Luke Beckett has trusted his instinct all his life and he never remembered it failing him. He had had trusted it that night on the barricaded man stakeout in the Wilshire district in Hollywood. Crazy Kelly Timmons was holed up in the Dharma Inn motel with a double-barreled shotgun and a box of shells and his little five-year-old girl at his side, half-hysterical from the excitement of floodlights and bull horns and a crowd of two or three hundred people who came to see the free show.

After four long, grueling hours, everyone's patience was exhausted and it had been decided to rush in and pray to God that Timmons wouldn't make good on his promise to kill the little girl and then himself. The angle of the motel had made tear gas an impossibility and there was no other choice but to storm the building. If they waited any longer, the girl would die anyway.

She was long overdue for her insulin shot. Timmons had kidnapped her from his wife who had obtained custody a year before, and had hidden her away for nearly a week.

Instinct told Beckett that if there was one thing in the world that Timmons loved it was that little girl of his. Instinct told him that despite Timmons' stubborn silence, he was experiencing pangs of conscience and eventually would give himself up. But no one else believed that.

Beckett asked for permission to lay his gun aside and approach the motel with his hands raised high. Permission denied.

Beckett went anyway before anyone could stop him.

"I'm un-armed, Kelly," he yelled out to Timmons who had suddenly grown silent, "and I'm coming in and taking your little girl where she'll be safe. I don't care if you want to die, they'll accommodate you. But we have to make her safe."

There was an agonizing silence from the motel and then Beckett disappeared into the building and re-emerged twenty-one tension-filled minutes later with the girl in his arms and Timmons at his side, sobbing uncontrollably.

Beckett received one of the severest reprimands of his career with the Los Angeles Police Department for that one. He had disobeyed orders, and risked the lives of a child and a citizen—and his own.

But Beckett knew his instinct was right and he knew it now. His instinct had told him that the key to Marcia's murder was Frank Connors. He went over it again his mind for what seemed like the thousandth time. Connors was the only one at the party who was not visible most of the time. He was the only one who admitted he was in the garden within the hour when Marcia was slain.

But Connors had dropped out of sight in direct violation of the orders Beckett had given him to remain visible and not to leave Palm Springs without notifying the police department where he intended to go and for how long.

Connors had not been seen at his apartment, his daily newspapers were piling up, and he had not visited the mobile home of his friend since they had rousted him out of there. The man had few friends and the few he had sworn they had neither seen him nor heard from him. Frank Connors had dropped off the face of the earth, or so it seemed.

After returning to the station, Beckett put out an APB for him, and alerted every snitch in the county to watch for him and listen for any word about him. He began a tireless search for his number-one suspect, touching base with as many motel and hotel managers as he could and showing Connors' picture to airport employees and bartenders and hookers and ministers and supermarket checkout clerks and parking lot attendants—everyone he could think of.

Nothing happened.

It was while Beckett was making the rounds, still inquiring about Connors, that Connors surfaced in the most unlikely place of all...the Palm Springs police station. He walked into the station as nice as he pleased and asked to see Chief Batters. As he told Batters, "I went to Downey to see my brother, a priest. I needed advice and guidance and now I knew what I needed to do."

Batters had tried to put him at ease. The man was obviously under a massive emotional strain, and Batters excused himself and put out the word for Beckett to report to the station as quickly as he could.

By the time Officer Nelson spotted Beckett at the Agua Caliente Casino on East Amado Road, where he had stopped in to say hello to an old friend, and told him about the latest development, Batters had taken a complete statement from Connors. In the meantime, Beckett broke a few of the speed laws he was sworn to uphold on his way to the station.

This was the break he had been waiting for these many weeks. He knew it would come. His instinct had been right all along. Connors was the key.

When Beckett walked into Batters' office, it looked like a traffic jam. Connors visibly jerked as Beckett entered Batters' office. Lieutenant Garcia was sitting next to Batters, Sgt. Walker was sitting next to Connors, and on the other side of the suspect was Officer Lorton, who ordinarily would be assigned to traffic on the Palm Canyon Drive at this hour. It was obvious Connors had spilled a confession of some kind and Beckett could hardly wait to hear it.

"Luke, I've got a statement from Mr. Connors," Batters said, indicating two typewritten pages in front of him.

"Luke? MISTER Connors?" Beckett thought, shifting his weight from one foot to the other, a gesture of impatience. Something was going on and he was the only person in Batters' overcrowded office who didn't yet know what it was.

"Yeah, okay. May I read it?"

Batters held the pages tightly in his hand and didn't appear he was ready to hand over them to Beckett.

"I'll read it to you," he said firmly.

Beckett's impatience was beginning to grow with the Chief. "He's going to read it to me?" he thought. "What the hell why?"

Beckett leaned on the wall, and looked from Batters to Garcia to Connors to Walker and back to Batters again before uttering his response.

"Fine."

Batters raised the papers in front of him and began reading them verbatim.

"I, Frank Connors, do hereby—well, we'll skip that," Batters paused. "Here's what were interested in..."

Then Batters, without interruption, resumed reading the statement as written:

> I had a couple of drinks in my room at the house and took a nap, but I woke up after only a few minutes and in my half-awaken state suddenly

realized that I had forgotten to turn on the sprinklers in the garden. I went to the garden to turn them on and then went back to my quarters. As my head began to clear of sleep and the drink, I suddenly kicked myself and said, "You jerk, you weren't supposed to turn on those sprinklers," so I went back to the garden to turn them off. By the time I had, it must have been about ten minutes after one o'clock in the morning when I did. No one was in the garden and I went into the kitchen and made myself a cup of instant coffee. I reached into my coveralls for my flashlight and realized I must have dropped it. I figured it probably popped out of my pocket when I reached down to turn on the sprinklers or maybe when I turned them off. I didn't need the flashlight to do that because the moon was full that night.

I took my time drinking the coffee. I could still hear the party behind me and then I finished the coffee and headed back to the garden to look for my flashlight…

Beckett thought, "Where is he going with this? What's he trying to get at?" But his face remained expressionless the whole time as Batters kept reading Connors' prepared statement, unabated:

I was walking along the bushes and they're thick but there are little openings here and there and, as I got closer to the garden, I thought I saw figure in there and as I got to the corner, I stopped dead in my tracks. I saw two people in the garden, standing very close to each other, talking, or maybe whispering is more like it. I couldn't hear what they were saying, but I could see one of the figures was Miss Marcia and the other was a man, a broad-shouldered man, a big man.

Beckett sighed. "Jesus, if what he says is true, he's giving us the murderer. At least, the missing link, the eyewitness, the break we've been looking for."

Batters' voice droned on in the background over Beckett's deep thoughts:

Miss Marcia looked sad and then she looked scared, but I didn't know who she was talking to and I didn't want to walk in there because, Christ, you never know, it could be a lover boy or something like that.

Beckett bristled at Connors and said, "You filthy minded bastard."

"That's enough!" Batters ordered in a commanding voice after the interruption. "You want to hear this or not?"

"I'm sorry, Chief."

Batters picked up reading Connors' statement from where he left off:

The man took her by the shoulders and kissed her, real hard. I don't think she liked it but I figured if this wasn't someone she knew very well, she would have called out, or screamed or something, right? I mean, even a little scream would have brought a half-dozen people running out there, but she didn't scream. I see this man point a finger right in her face, almost touching her nose, and then he suddenly jerks the chain from her neck and shakes it in front of her and she begins shaking her head, but she wasn't making a sound.

Then, the man says something I can't hear and she says something I can't hear and I decide it's time I quit eavesdropping. It ain't none of my business. I'm just a goddamned handyman. What do I know? I was just about to turn and to go back to my quarters when a helicopter whirls overhead and this guy turns his head for a moment to look up at it and I see his face.

Batters glanced up from the papers at Beckett and said, "At this point, the recording secretary noted a pause." He then returned to reading the statement:

I didn't know who it was, but I know who it is now. It was Lt. Beckett.

Beckett's jaw fell open and his mind almost blocked, he was so shocked by the statement. Every pair of eyes in the room, except Connors', suddenly were fixed on him. Then rage blotted out everything else, every thought, every emotion.

"You dirty rotten lying son-of-a-bitch, I'll kill you," Beckett screamed and headed for Connors.

Walker jumped up from the chair instantaneously and blocked Beckett's path, but Beckett swept him aside with one swing of his arm, sending the officer crashing into a wastebasket in the corner. Before Garcia could get his reflexes working, Beckett had the screaming Connors by the throat with both hands and was shaking him like a rag doll.

Garcia threw his right arm around Beckett's neck and tried to tear him off Connors, but he was unable to dislodge him. Batters leaped up, cursing, "Damn you, Beckett!" and reached for the heavy paperweight on his desk.

Connors was turning blue by the time Batters reached Beckett and he swung the heavy paperweight against Beckett's head. The first blow didn't seem to affect him at all. The second loosened his grip and a third sent him crashing to the floor, where Garcia and Walker jumped on him.

Coughing and spitting up phlegm, Connors couldn't find his voice. Beckett was semi-conscious and shaking his head, as if he couldn't grasp what was going on. Garcia and Walker, at Batters' instructions, half dragged, half carried Beckett into his own office and placed him carefully on the couch in the corner. He was mumbling but they couldn't make out what he was saying.

"Stay with him," Batters snapped, and then turned to Connors, now on his feet but holding his reddened neck and still gagging between words.

"See…that's why…couldn't face him," Connors said, clearing his throat and getting voice back. "I wouldn't have talked but he kept hounding me, trying to find out what I knew, what I saw. Why else did he zero in on me? Because I figure he knew I saw him. I knew in my bones as God is my judge that he would try to kill me because he killed her."

Batters said in a fit of rage, "But you didn't actually see him kill her."

"He was the only man I saw in the garden," Connors continued, "and he was the last one who was with her."

"But he wasn't the only man in the garden," Batters noted.

"Who else was there?"

"You."

Connors shook his head violently.

"Oh, no! You don't pull that. I don't get framed on a murder rap just because it was a cop I saw. Oh, no, you don't pull that on me."

Batters said calmly, "No one is trying to frame you. I am merely pointing out that while you saw Lt. Beckett in the garden, or thought you saw him—and we'll check that against the polygraph lie detector—you did not see him murder Marcia Van Ander, unless you want to amend your statement to say that you did."

"No, I didn't actually see him choke her. I didn't see that."

"That's my only point, Mr. Connors," Batters explained patiently. "Wait here, please."

Batters got up and went down the hall to where Garcia was handing Beckett a cup of water and an ice pack for the small welt on his forehead. Beckett looked embarrassed as he took a small sip.

"Jesus, Tom, I'm so sorry. I don't know what came over me," Beckett suddenly blurted. "I must have gone off my rocker. I thought that guy was fingering me to take the heat off himself."

"Sure, Luke," Batters said softly. "We'll give him the polygraph test and see how he makes out on that. Why don't you go home and rest?"

"I'm okay, I'm okay. It's my case," Beckett said, anxiously inching forward in his seat and wincing from the beating he took as he did. "I want to be here for anything else that happens."

"Okay, I'll call the polygraph expert and set up an examination of Connors tomorrow," Batters replied. "We'll charge him with evading police and keep him in a holding cell until we can't straighten this thing out."

Beckett nodded. He knew Connors would fail the polygraph test. Why in the world, he wondered, would Connors have tried to link him to the murder if Connors himself had not done it? It was as plain as the nose on his face. Beckett was still convinced he had his man and knew how to break him and make him tell the rest of the truth.

Beckett apologized to both Walker and Garcia and they both shrugged. Garcia somehow had collected two small cuts on his forehead and Walker had a lump on his head where he had crashed into the wall. But both men respected Beckett. They knew the kind of pressure he had been under ever since Marcia's unexpected murder. They knew, just as Beckett knew, that this Connor was lying. Any suspect like Connors might have done the same thing of trying to pin the murder on Beckett. It was a cop-out, a diversionary tactic. In the end, Beckett was convinced it wouldn't work.

Connors said he had turned on the sprinklers in the garden area and then changed his mind, and went back turned them off and it was then that he first saw Marcia's body. Turning on the sprinklers at that time of morning by mistake? Then going back and turning off and discovering a body? It sounded too suspicious to Beckett.

Then, there was what the colorful psychic Charles LeBaron had said. Right in front of Beckett, he told him the murderer had returned to the scene of the crime *several* times. Only Connors had done that. He had left and returned, and left again, and returned a second time.

Finally, there was Connors' psychotic fear of Beckett himself. He was literally terrified every time he was in Beckett's presence. Why would he experience such extreme paranoia if he were not guilty?

No, Connors was the key. It always came back to that.

Beckett was determined once and for all to get the truth out of Connors if he had to beat it out of him and hang him by the heels off the roof of the Renaissance Palm Springs Hotel with an upside-down view of the San Jacinto Mountains until he decided to talk.

19

Only the largest urban police departments employ the full-time services of a polygraph examiner to administer examinations to police candidates, sworn and civilian employees seeking assignments to specialized units, and suspects or witnesses in criminal investigations. As a result, the Palm Springs police department had to dispatch a request to Riverside for Chris Kooten, who held that position with the Riverside County Sheriff's office and occasionally with the feds, to conduct the test with Connors.

If Kooten was a cynic with very little confidence in human nature, he might be pardoned for his cynicism. He had been lied to more often than a train full of homely wives. Like all polygraph specialists, he had become a keen judge of fine acting. He had seen more than his share of Academy Award performances in the lie detector box theater.

Kooten was professionally skeptical, and discreet, and secretive, like most of his breed, because he had seen and witnessed it all during his career that resulted in hundreds of convictions. The greatest piece of acting he had ever encountered went to Tall Man Hunt, the elongated freak who made a hobby of whittling on young and pretty girls he found hanging around Venice beach. He'd get the girls high on whatever he had in current supply and invite them to his beachfront shack. He had a makeshift operating room in the back, and God only knows how many poor things died in there. He boxed the remains and dropped them off in oil drum-shaped trash cans as far south as Huntington Beach in neighboring Orange County. They nailed him for only one murder, the last...the Dilston girls from Marina del Rey.

When they put Hunt on the lie detector box, he acted and sounded like an acolyte. He loved his mother and petted stray dogs, gave to all the neediest charities, admired children and respected women, and would never, never think of harming a soul, much less an innocent young girl.

As cynical as Kooten was, after analyzing the results, the freaky Hunt had set a Guinness Book of Records high-water mark for lying. Hunt remains on death row where it unlikely he will ever be executed because of California's laws outlawing capital punishment.

Everybody trusted Kooten and his polygraph lie detection box. The guilty screamed bloody murder when Kooten's technology and comprehensive testing pointed the finger at them, and the cops screamed when he cleared an innocent man whom they were convinced was guilty as sin. But, in the end, everybody admitted that Kooten was precise, accurate, and honest. They accepted his judgments, which really were those of the technologically advanced lie detection system.

Kooten was busy Thursday morning but he showed up exactly when he said he would at two o'clock in the afternoon. He was ushered into the small reception room where he was joined by Chief Batters and Lt. Beckett, Frank Connors and a local criminal defense attorney named Fred Wayne whom Connors had hastily hired to defend him, and Lt. Garcia and Caspar Pine, an assistant district attorney who would have a special interest in Connors if he failed the polygraph test.

Connors didn't quite fail the test the first time around. Kooten called the results "inconclusive," not at all an unusual development.

Kooten suggested to Chief Batters after reviewing the results, "I recommend we do the test again tomorrow when Connors' level of tension and anxiety might be somewhere lower."

That seemed fair enough to all concerned, except Connors, who had been through this before. They agreed to reassemble at 10 o'clock Friday morning. In the meantime, Connors agreed to go into protective custody and that afternoon, Kooten conducted a polygraph test of Frank's brother, Charles Connors, for which Beckett was not required to attend. His test also proved "inconclusive," and Kooten scheduled to retest him Friday afternoon following Frank Connors' second polygraph examination.

Immediately following Frank Connors' polygraph examination, Beckett took a drive through that special, remote, and isolated place of his—the sand dunes—to get away from it all. Amid the grandeur of the crested dunes of fine sand and the blooming white-cup shaped desert primrose and purple sand verbena, he saw in his mind's eye the investigation into the murder of his ex-wife Marcia finally coming to an end. In the scenario he envisioned, the following morning, Connors would fail the second polygraph test, and then they would sweat him. He would crack, and they would find the physical evidence that would link him to the murder. Beckett didn't quite know what it would be. Connors had no previous record, and Beckett, without Connors' knowledge, had done an exhaustive check of his movements and habits and lifestyle and background. He had even searched Connors' quarters on two occasions, but came up dry.

But there would be something linking Connors to Marcia's murder. Beckett was sure of that. But what was the motive? It had to be the result of Connors' sexual fantasies and frustrations. He had various pornographic magazines hidden from view in his quarters at the Van Ander home. They didn't indict a man for his fantasies, and sometimes if they acted them out in their heads, they didn't translate them into real-life actions or murder. Or so the psychologists were always saying.

Beckett had nothing concrete on Connors, but he was sure he would find it, one way or another. Whatever it was and wherever it was, he would love the satisfaction of seeing that Marcia's murderer went to prison for the longest possible term. He only wished he could go to the gas chamber if California's laws were different. Even that wasn't enough in his mind.

The next morning, the same cast reassembled and Connors looked and acted like a new man when his attorney Fred Wayne led him into the room. He was clean-shaven and was wearing a clean shirt and even a tie with his hair neatly combed and he looked as relaxed as a man facing a second polygraph test can look. Chief Batters took the first chair down the line from Connors and soon Lt. Garcia and assistant district attorney Caspar Pine joined him. The last one to sit down was Beckett, who positioned his chair on an angle in the sight of Connors' peripheral vision.

The state-of-the-art polygraph system Kooten was using recorded the results on five channels—the subject's respiration (on two channels), Galvanic Skin Resistance, and cardiovascular activity and physical activity—displayed live in a series of graphs on a laptop to which it was connected on the table in front of Kooten unseen by Connors and everyone else. Before commencing, Kooten methodically strapped a blood pressure cuff on Connors' right arm to record his pulse and blood pressure, then a set of rubber tubes over his chest and abdomen to record his breathing, and finally two metal plates to fingers on his left hand to record sweating. Connors was a model citizen throughout the preparation stages for the test.

At long last, Kooten went to work, by asking Connors a series of questions he hadn't covered the day before to measure Connors' responses and find evidence of whether he lied or not.

"Did you know the victim personally?" Kooten asked.

Connors, sitting erect in his chair, didn't waver in answering. "Yes."

As Connors answered, the lines of the five graphs on Kooten's laptop barely moved.

"Did you ever engage in a sexual relationship with her?"

Connors, surprisingly calm, didn't flinch.

"No."

By the lack of movement, the graph confirmed Connors was telling the truth.

"Did you hope for a deeper relationship with the victim that included sex?"

Connors eyes narrowed as he pondered the question. On the surface, it appeared he didn't like Kooten's question and for the first time in the process he acted and sounded evasive.

"Do I have to answer that?"

At that moment, the lines of the graphs on the polygraph jumped erratically indicating a deep unease and questions about Connors' believability as a suspect.

"Just answer the question," Kooten demanded.

Beckett inched forward in his seat in anticipation that this would be the moment when Connors finally cracked. Connors apprehensively peered over his right shoulder at his attorney, who by his nod affirmed what Kooten was asking him to do. Connors shed the façade he had been putting on. Suddenly twitching nervously, he went off the rails and admitted what Beckett had long suspected.

"Yes, yes!" he shouted. "I wanted sex with her, alright, in the worst way. But it never went that far between us."

Kooten watched as the top two lines on the graph recorded a normal response indicating Connors was telling the truth. It was far from the kind of condemning evidence Chief Batters and Beckett needed to convict Connors, but, of course, Kooten wasn't through and pressed Connors further.

"In the heat of the moment, did you ever sexually assault the victim?"

Connors became so incensed he wanted to jump out of his chair but knew if he tried, it was all over him. He would never get another chance again to vindicate himself. This was it. Settling back into his chair, he paused after taking a long deep breath and said with a look of defeat in his eyes, "She didn't even know I existed."

The graphs on the polygraph confirmed Connors was being forthright and gave no indication otherwise that he was lying.

Kooten moved to wrap up the second polygraph with one final make-or-break question—one that Beckett was waiting for Kooten to ask.

"Did you strangle the victim, Marcia Van Ander, that night in the garden after she turned you down to have sex with her?

It was a straight "Yes" or "No" question that Kooten hadn't asked so directly the day before and seemed appropriate in the investigation of murder case where the facts so far pointed to Connors becoming sexually frustrated by her lack of interest in him.

Connors sat there quietly as he thought over the question, and his voice was deliberate and measured when he finally answered.

"I did not strangle or kill Marcia Van Ander...Period. You can ask me the question a thousand times over and my answer will be the same. Like I have said many times, I happened to see her in the garden that night but kill her? Never!"

Kooten concluded, "Thank you, Mr. Connors, for coming here today and agreeing to do the second polygraph test. You are free to leave."

Kooten rose from his chair, walked over, unstrapped the various devices from Connors, who then stood up and started for the door with his attorney at his side. Beckett moved up the line past Chief Batters, Lt. Garcia, and assistant district attorney Caspar Pine to attract Connors' attention and did. Connors glanced over with an unctuous grin on his face as he was halfway through the door. It was the kind of look Beckett had seen hundreds of times before on the faces of known criminals and interpreted it to mean that Connors knowingly got away with murder and knew there was nothing Beckett could do about it, not even with a second polygraph test.

Beckett bolted toward Connors in a fit of rage as Connors turned away and was escorted out the door by his attorney. Chief Batters' immediately grabbed Beckett by the collar and yanked him back before embarrassing himself and the department and putting the entire investigation in jeopardy.

"Settle down. That's not how we do things here," Batters barked as he reeled Beckett in as if he was the big catch of the day.

"He's murdered Marcia, I know it, and he's going to get away with it," Beckett said, incensed.

"Let's not get ahead of ourselves and wait for the results of the second polygraph. Okay?"

Beckett reluctantly nodded as he and Chief Batters took turns leaving the room.

Following the second polygraph, Kooten told Batters he would analyze the results very carefully and would produce them after lunch that afternoon.

Connors ate with his attorney and Kooten had lunch at Dominick's with Beckett, Batters and Garcia. During lunch, Beckett tried hard to be fair-minded in his discussions with Kooten but was too close to the case to be objective. He could have killed Kooten when he absolutely refused to commit himself one way or the other on the second polygraph test when Beckett asked him point-blank about it. Beckett knew, from experience, that Kooten already knew how it came out but wasn't to break protocol a favor to him. Kooten was a perfectionist. They would have to wait. It had to be "official."

They didn't have to wait very long.

At precisely one o'clock Friday afternoon, Kooten emerged from the little side room at the police station they had assigned him as a temporary office off the reception room. With the test results in his hand, he made a short announcement:

"On the basis of this second test, which I have checked and re-checked, there is absolutely no doubt in my mind that Frank Connors is telling the truth. Every word in his statement, as far as I can tell, is the truth."

It was difficult to say who was most astonished, but Beckett seemed to be.

"Christ, are you sure?"

"Of course, I'm sure," Kooten said emphatically. "You know better than to ask me that."

Connors didn't smile, but he did release a sigh of relief that sounded like it had traveled all the way up from his toes.

Beckett grabbed a chair and sat down heavily. He looked at Connors and Connors, for the second time that day, looked him right in the eye, only this time Connors played it cool and wasn't grinning to raise suspicion.

"Well, Mr. Connors, on the basis of this polygraph test, and our own investigation of you, I'm pleased to say you're released," Batters said without a trace of emotion in his voice. "You're a free man, and the city of Palm Springs congratulates you and thanks you for your cooperation."

Connors nodded, pleased, and shook hands with Kooten and then with the Chief. Then he and his lawyer walked out. They listened to the retreating footsteps in silence, except Beckett.

"Jesus Christ!" he exploded.

"You took the words right out of my mouth," Batters said.

Caspar Pine, the assistant district attorney, cleared his throat for attention and got it.

"It occurs to me, Chief, that there's some other business here."

Batters didn't look at him. He knew what was coming. Beckett didn't.

"If this man Connors' charges were all aimed at Lt. Beckett here," Pine resumed speaking in a raspy voice that sounded strained, "and the polygraph test says he was telling the truth, well..."

The full impact of Pine's comment didn't hit Beckett for a few seconds. Then he came charging to his feet and Batters stepped in front of him.

"What the hell are you trying to imply?" Beckett shouted around Batters' head.

"Sit down, Luke!" Batters ordered. "Sit down. No more of that."

Beckett was breathing heavily he was so overwrought. Finally, Batters stood in front of him.

"Get pissed off or not, it doesn't matter. He's right, Luke. If you were conducting this part of it instead of me, and if neither of us had a vested interest in it, would we put the other man on the polygraph box or not? Answer me that, Luke."

Beckett was staring at the floor. Of course, the Chief was right. His gut and the Chief's own words told him so.

"I can't argue with that, I guess. But Jesus, Chief, to even think that any of you would…She was my *wife*. I loved her. You *know* that."

"We know that," Batters said softly. "At this point, the evidence we have is all circumstantial. We can't prosecute Connors without physical evidence linking him to the murder and so far, we have none, if he is the murderer at all."

After a short pause, Batters continued. "We also know—Chris, bear with me on this—we also know that Connors may have passed the polygraph test only because he really thinks it was you that he saw in the garden. Even if it was a hallucination, and he believed it to be true, it would show up as true in the test. Chris?"

Kooten quickly added, "Of course. All we've really established with Connors is that he never had any kind of serious relationship with her, didn't strangle or kill her, and he *thinks* the man he saw that night was you, Lt. Beckett. That doesn't make that man you."

Beckett knew in his heart they were right. It was just the craziness of the thought that he said the unthinkable.

"Give me the polygraph test."

"No way, Luke," Batters said in protest, his friendship for Beckett surfacing again and getting in the way of his thinking. "It's nothing you put into court without the agreement of all parties. I know you didn't do it. Everybody does. You don't need to take it."

"But I want to take it."

"Why?" Garcia asked. "The Chief's right. It's voluntary and sometimes these goddamned things aren't accurate. Isn't that true, Mr. Kooten?"

"Well," Kooten paused, "they aren't perfect, even with the latest technological advancements. Nothing is."

Beckett knew how good they were and wasn't going to back down on going through with it.

"Look, I'm okay. I got shook up for a minute. No, I absolutely want to take the test. I would feel…bad, if I didn't. So, please, let's get on with it."

Kooten relented and agreed to conduct it but not as soon as Beckett was hoping.

"Maybe we ought to do it tomorrow. You're pretty emotionally upset right now."

"No" Beckett insisted. "I'm not as goofy as I've been looking. Really, I'm okay now. Let's get it done."

The same routine took place in doing the test with Beckett, but they had to draw up a specific list of questions for him, not having a statement to play from:

"Were you in the garden the morning between one and one thirty?'"

"Did you argue with Marcia?"

"Did things get heated between you?"

"Did you try and choke her?"

"Did you kill her?"

Those were the keys, surrounded by the control questions and bracketed with other questions that had no special bearing on the murder itself, only on the subject's credibility.

Following its conclusion, Batters, Beckett, and Garcia sat in near silence, except for a few routine phone calls to Batters, while Kooten analyzed the results.

It seemed like days to Beckett before the polygraph expert emerged from the little room.

"Here it is, and I'm pleased to say—which was no surprise to me, let me add—that our Lt. Beckett on the basis of this interrogation, is cleared of any suspicion."

That was not news to Beckett, but somehow, he was finding it difficult to smile. He thought he saw the faintest suggestion of surprise on Batters' face. He hoped and prayed he was mistaken. But Garcia was all smiles. He clapped Beckett on the back.

"Good, good. Now I'm glad you took it," Garcia declared. "What the hell, you know?"

"Yeah, yeah," Beckett said, half-brooding and half-smiling. "Like you, why the hell not."

Assistant district attorney Pine walked over to Beckett as he was preparing to leave the room and said, "Congratulations."

"You know what you can do with that?" Beckett said pulling himself away.

"Just doing my job."

"Sure. Sure."

Pine left and Garcia drifted off and Kooten busied himself collecting his polygraph equipment and records. Batters nodded in the direction of his office and Beckett followed him as he closed the door behind them.

"I want you to take the rest of today off and the weekend."

"I don't want time off."

"It's not a suggestion," Batters said agitated. "It's an order."

"But why?"

"Look," Batters explained, "you've been under God-awful tension for these last few weeks and it's beginning to show. Your nerves are on the raw edge. You're flying off the handle and don't even realize it."

"I'm sorry, Chief, I…"

"Goddamnit, you're always sorry, Beckett. But then, you've always got something to be sorry about," Batters reasoned. "I'm telling you, take the rest of the day and the weekend off and report back here at nine o'clock Monday morning. I'm anxious to finish this investigation, but it can wait until then. Meanwhile, I want you to do a lot of thinking."

"What does that mean?"

"Just what I said," Batters said flatly.

"Think about what, the case? My behavior? What?"

"Think about Luke Beckett."

"What the hell is that supposed to mean?"

"If you'll start thinking, it'll come to you," Batters said, and he wasn't smiling.

Beckett nodded, and walked straight out to his Ford Explorer and drove away. It was if the car knew where he wanted to go, and he didn't. He was almost surprised when he found himself pulling up in front of Jo Ann's apartment. She was a nice woman, someone who always helped him forget his troubles.

"Luke. At this hour?" she asked welcoming him at the door. "You haven't been fired, have you?"

Beckett shook his head no and she let him inside.

They sat in the kitchen. She had on a satin robe and it clung like a body stocking. She wore nothing underneath it. Jo Ann knew she was sexy and she loved being sexy, especially for him.

Jo Ann closely studied Beckett's face. The little boy was back. She could always tell.

"What's the problem?" she asked.

"I'm not even sure. God's honest truth, I'm not."

"Want something to eat?"

"No, thanks."

Jo Ann didn't stop there. She could tell Beckett wasn't himself and wanted to please him.

"How about a drink?"

"No."

"Well, here's what's left."

She stood up and slapped a thigh, smiling, exposing some of her bare skin.

Beckett put up a hand in protest to her surprise.

"Any red-blooded man in America would recommend I see a therapist for this," he said, "but…no thanks. Not now."

Jo Ann wasn't insulted. She didn't think he wanted sex. It was her way of trying to lighten him up. She sat down again, and the robe loosened and allowed her pretty boobs to hang out so they were almost touching the top of the table.

"Want to talk about it, or anything?" she asked in a soothing voice.

"I'll have that drink now. Okay?"

Beckett had the drink and the food she pulled together, and Jo Ann, too.

Afterwards, they were all good—better than good. He kissed her goodbye and went back to his car and drove home.

Jo Ann had watched him walking to his car. "Poor sap," she thought, "I could make him so happy."

If anybody could. No, nobody could…not even her. They made one mistake. When they buried Marcia, they should have buried Beckett with her because he has been dead ever since.

20

Beckett had tried very hard not to think about what might happen Monday morning when he met Chief Batters. Not that it had helped much. The murder case never left his mind. Even when he was making love to Jo Ann, he saw Marcia's face before him.

Since his ex-wife's death, the characteristically short-tempered and volatile police lieutenant had driven himself to the point of exhaustion and breakdown. It was no wonder Batters had complained about his behavior. If he was honest with himself, he had to admit he had come close to the brink several times. But he was a cop—a good, solid, experienced cop. He would endure all this and go on. He only hoped that he could remain on the case. He was certain that Batters planned to take him off. That was what this morning meeting in his office, he was certain, would be all about.

Batters would remind him that he had eliminated one suspect after another, finally concentrating on Connors, until the last polygraph test eliminated him from being a suspect. So, Beckett was left with no suspects. He had checked and re-checked again the stories of everyone at the party that night. If they had eliminated Connors, which the polygraph test had done, then none of the others could possibly have killed Marcia. They either were not in the right place at the right time, or they were in each other's sight during the time she was killed. The autopsy report, as he recalled, was very specific about the time of death.

To be fair about it, Beckett had to admit that Batters would be justified in removing him from the case. No one else could solve it, he was certain of that. But he had had his chance and maybe his conflict of interest was affecting his judgement and impeding its progress.

As a longtime police veteran, Beckett wasn't about to beg or plead for another chance. That wasn't his style. He would not even ask for a few more days. He had failed and that was it. Batters knew it, Beckett knew it. So, what else was new?

Beckett found Chief Batters sitting on the couch in the corner of his office. What he didn't know was that Batters had told the staff to hold all phone calls and had ordered that no one was to interrupt them, not for anything.

Beckett walked in and Batters motioned him over. The two men sat, half turned, facing each other on the couch. A couple of beats and then…

"In the time you've been with me, Luke, I've grown to like you, to trust you, to respect you," Batters said. "You believe that?"

"Sure, Tom, I…"

Batters put up a hand stopping from him saying more.

"Luke, I'm going to ask you not to say a word, okay? Not a word."

Beckett nodded an understanding nod. He hadn't counted on the Chief shutting him down the way he had and went along with it.

What Batters said next rolled off his tongue with ease, unrehearsed but well thought out.

"I've been a police officer for more than twenty years now. I've seen a lot of cops, a lot of cases, good and bad, both. You're just about the best officer I've ever encountered, but with one fatal flaw: Your temper. But even that a commander can overlook because you deliver, so well and so often. This is a tough one, what I'm about to ask you to do."

Beckett knew the verdict that was coming from the Chief's lips: Withdraw from the case, and expected him to say that next.

"I want you to check out a new suspect," Batters said to the surprise of his top investigator. "His name is Luke Beckett."

Beckett was immobile. His brain suddenly froze. The only movement in his whole body came from his eyes, and they blinked twice and then remained fixed on Batters.

Finally, when he spoke, it was with some difficulty.

"You want me to check out...myself?"

Batters nodded and kept silent while Beckett kept on processing it all.

"Which means that you think...You think I'm a suspect after all."

Batters lowered his voice to above a whisper in response.

"Am I talking to Lt. Beckett, my officer, or Luke Beckett, my friend? Because it's the officer I want to talk to. He's the one I need right now."

Beckett got up and walked to the door, stopped, and faced Batters, who didn't move off the couch.

"I could just quit."

Batters said, "But you won't."

"Why won't I?"

"Because you're too good a cop to do that and you've got too much invested in this investigation, both personally and professionally."

"You're counting a helluva lot on what you think I am, aren't you?" Beckett said, taking the Chief's comments head on. "What makes you think you know so goddamned well?"

"I know you, Luke," Batters said reassuringly.

Beckett pursed his lips. He walked over to the window and looked out, but if there had been a major fire and shootout in the parking lot, he would not have seen them. A full minute passed.

The ticking of the tiny desk clock on the Chief's desk wasn't even noticeable before. Now it sounded like Big Ben was in the room. Finally, Beckett turned and faced Batters again.

"I think you're crazy. I *know* you're crazy. But I'll do it. By Christ, I'll do it."

"Thanks, Luke."

"Don't thank me," Beckett said. "It's going to prove you're an asshole."

"Do *that*, then."

Beckett walked out without saying goodbye as Batters sighed and put his head back on the backrest of the couch and stared at the ceiling. At that moment, Garcia walked in and said, "What did you say to Luke? He walked out of here like he was in a trance."

"He's just got lot on his mind, that's all," Batters said. "Go back to those homicide reports."

Did any cop in the history of the world ever receive a more curious, more insane, more impossible assignment than this? How many could handle it if they did? How many would want to? How many would even try?

Perhaps, it couldn't even be done and that was no idle thought. How could Beckett split himself in two, into investigator and into suspect? Can it even be done? Or does it go against the first law of human nature: survival?

Beckett, the cop, started out with the presumption that Beckett, the suspect, was innocent until proven guilty. How could he begin any other way? He knew in his heart he couldn't possible have killed the woman he loved. Hell, had he ever even struck her? He loved her, he was kind to her, he was gentle with her, always. These things he knew about Beckett, the suspect. Was there something else he didn't know?

Beckett found himself thinking like a cop all right. That's what he was, a cop, and that was the trump card Batters was playing in the grand scheme of things. He knew Beckett was more cop than anything else he could ever be. An honest cop, a dedicated cop, a relentless cop. That's what Batters was counting on when he literally told him to investigate himself, prove, if he could, that he didn't kill his own wife.

Beckett, the cop, slammed the door of his Ford Explorer and got behind the wheel. Where to begin? A profile of the suspects, perhaps? What about this man, Beckett? What was his background? What if anything was there in his makeup that might indicate he was even capable of violent behavior?

That answer came almost too quickly for the suspect's comfort. Yes, he had a record of violence, a definite pattern that began in childhood. He had been an angry, frustrated and often violent child who grew up into a no quarter asked, no quarter given police officer.

Ironically, though Beckett, the cop, this suspect was the only one who has ever killed a man. Strike that, stepped on a bug, the bug being Candycane. No, a bug has an ecological purpose in life. Candycane was sub-human lice. Hardly qualified to be called a human being. But in the eyes of the law, yes, a human being he was.

All right, this suspect, Beckett, was a man who could kill. Has killed. But anyone can kill, given the right circumstances. Isn't that what the shrinks and so-called experts say? Isn't that what his own experience and the experiences of all his cop friends indicates? Okay, he could kill, for what that was worth.

"What about opportunity?" Beckett, the cop, asked himself. Where was the suspect Luke Beckett on the fateful Sunday night between the hours of midnight and one-thirty in the morning?

Beckett realized that he was still sitting in the parking lot at the station, and ten minutes had passed. He had been thinking so hard he forgot where he planned to go. Oh, yes, the Van Ander home, the scene of the crime, to revisit perhaps one last time. He wanted to go back there, take his new suspect there, and see if he stood in the environment of the murder, something might come to him. It didn't make much sense, but Beckett didn't know where else to start.

The house was already in the hands of a Sotheby's

International real estate agent specializing in the sale of luxury homes. The agent on duty, Robert Sherman, who hoped to make a whopping commission when it sold, expressed to Beckett when he approached him the hope that no more police or news people would be prowling about the premises.

"That could be very bad for the sale," Sherman nervously confessed. "People have a bad feeling about homes where violence has taken place."

Beckett assured him, "No one will know I am and that I was I here. I won't be here very long."

Beckett walked out to the lush garden and an eerie feeling came over him instantly. Someone was here that night, someone Marcia knew and trusted enough to meet in the dark. God only knows how many people in her life qualified for that kind of trust. Mary Ann Morrison? Johnny Robelli? The recently deceased Lionel Van Ander, of course. Others? What about...Beckett, the suspect. Yes, of course, him, too.

Where was Beckett in those key hours that very morning? The cop nudged the suspect's memory and it all came flooding back to him. He had worked until 6 P.M, had a bite to eat at Old World restaurant, sat at the bar for about an hour or so and talked to a couple of friendly locals, then went straight home. He arrived at his mobile home at about nine o'clock that night. He read a gripping new crime novel, *Right of Passage*, on his Kindle for a while, and then turned on the television. He started to drink about 9:30 P.M., when suddenly he felt restless and bored.

At 10 P.M., Beckett watched the latest episode of his favorite hour-long Sunday night CBS crime drama, *Crime Stoppers*. "Little Clues," that was the name of the episode that night. That took him up to 11 P.M., time for the nightly local news broadcast on KESQ-TV with Brick Morton reporting the latest happenings. By then, his eyelids were heavy and his head was swimming and he felt too lazy, too tired to undress, so he just fell asleep on the couch in a drunken stupor. He rarely drank like that. He couldn't explain to himself now, now that he was reviewing his behavior for the first time, why that night? But he did. He woke up two or three times in the middle of the night. He never could sleep well with too much booze in him. It heated up the blood or something—and he watched television before going back to sleep. As he remembered, he did that several times. Then he woke up, and stayed awake, around seven o'clock the next morning.

That accounted for all his time that night and into the morning. Didn't it?

Beckett, the cop, had more questions for Beckett, the suspect. Would a man with Beckett's personality, admittedly in a drunken stupor, go to Marcia and have a confrontation with her? Beckett, the suspect, seemed to be on solid ground there. He had never done it before. Why should he have done it for the first time on this night?

There's a first time for everything, of course. Beckett, the cop, couldn't discount that. He had to investigate Beckett, the suspect, for patterns of behaviors in crimes as he would any criminal. Beckett had never confronted Marcia before. He had to admit he had driven by her place many times, hoping to catch a glimpse of her shimmering blonde hair in the sun. But he never had anything but the kindest thoughts about her when he saw her, or when he didn't see her.

At that moment, the Sotheby's real estate agent Robert Sherman had surfaced again and he said to Beckett, "There's some people here and I'd like to take them out in the garden area. How do I explain you?"

Beckett was quick to respond.

"You don't have to give them any reason," he said before taking the side path out to the driveway.

As he walked down the path, he suddenly had a strange feeling. What was the French word for the feeling—the feeling that he had been in this place before when his conscious mind told him it was the first time? No, no, that was impossible, he thought. His mind was beginning to play tricks on him. Well, why not. It had been worked to a frazzle, and he rarely gave it a rest. This path, though, this was the way the murderer got in and got out, the only practical way he could have without being seen by someone on the grounds or at the party.

The murderer walked this path for sure. He must have called Marcia and arranged the post-midnight rendezvous in the garden. She would never have walked into that darkened garden at night without a special reason. Now it seemed very doubtful that a would-be burglar or robber would crouch there with the vague hope that someone would fall into his clutches. No, it was an arranged meeting for certain.

Beckett, the cop, asked Beckett, the suspect, "Would she have arranged such a meeting with you if you demanded it?"

Beckett, the suspect, was slow to answer. His answer was, "Yes, I think she would have."

Marcia never said she stopped loving Beckett, the cop and husband, only that she couldn't live with him and share his lifestyle any more. Beckett, the cop, agreed with Beckett, the suspect's conjecture in his mind: Yes, she would have.

Beckett's policeman's mind kept working. Was the suspect capable of strangling someone? Physically capable? Of course, he was. Psychologically capable? No.

Beckett, the cop, reviewed the facts from his findings so far and concluded: "We have a suspect who was physically and psychologically capable of the murder. He also was one of the very people who would have had access to the victim. He says he was asleep during the time of the actual murder. That he cannot remember anything else is not important. That he cannot prove he was asleep and not at the murder scene is significant. Not conclusive by a long shot, but important."

What about physical evidence tying Beckett, the suspect, to Marcia's murder? Beckett, the cop, pondered. The murder took place in a darkened garden after midnight and on freshly watered grass. But since there was no signs of a struggle and Marcia succumbed silently and quickly, there would be no grass stains on the clothing of the murderer. Some grass was found clinging to the blouse, slacks, and shoes of Marcia, because the grass had been cut only the day before and not all the shavings had blown away before the sprinklers were turned on, by mistake, some eight or nine hours later.

Beckett, the cop's mind gravitated back to what Connors had saw. He confessed that he had seen the murderer, the one man who looked like Beckett, rip a small chain from Marcia's neck at the height of their heated argument. The chain wasn't found with the body or on the ground, so it might be assumed the murderer took it and threw it away on the road or, possibly, but highly unlikely, kept it.

What else was there? Was he missing something?

The helicopter—yes, the helicopter that whooshed over the grounds of the Van Ander estate. Connors had said he saw the murderer's face for an instant when he turned to look up at a night flying helicopter. But who flies helicopters at night? The police department's Big Brother Unit, which carried giant floodlights to illuminate a suspicious area, were a possibility. But none of the area police department had a record of one of their choppers in the air that night. Again, there was no record of any area television news station flying a news chopper that night, ruling them out as well.

What was left? The Air Force was the only other possibility. Beckett had called Long Beach air station. The Air Force had a copter in the air that night on a routine training flight—it wasn't uncommon for them to fly out to the desert as part of their training. The captain on the phone was extremely cooperative. He read Beckett the complete flight plan and with his engineer's background figured out just about where the helicopter would have been between 1 A.M. and 1:30 A.M. on the night in question.

"Yes, based on flight records from that night," the captain stated, "it well could have been passing overhead at 1400 hours. Entirely possible, even probable."

That said, it was doubtful the Air Force had any connection to Marcia's murder and it was most likely a coincidence that the training flight took them over the mansion at that precise time.

The weatherman at KPLM confirmed that it was a bright full moon that night. So, Connor's statement about a helicopter passing overheard and the murderer looking up as it went by and making out his face when he did in the moonlight rang true.

The only evidence yet to be found that would eliminate Beckett, the suspect, and connect a different person to the murder of his ex-wife Marcia was the chain she was wearing that was ripped from her neck.

"Look for the chain," Beckett, the cop, thought, "and you will have your murderer—the real one."

But look where? He and a team of investigators had scoured every inch of the Van Ander estate, inside and out, following Marcia's untimely death and came up empty handed. Beckett, the cop, had one place to look—it was a place he hadn't checked out before. It was silly, even a little crazy, of him not to think of it before. He would go through the motions because it sounded ridiculous that it be there. He would search his own closet, just as he had searched Connors' quarters for any clue to his possible involvement in the murder.

Beckett, the cop, kept trying to replay the sequence of events that night—his movements, his drinking, his waking and sleeping. Nowhere in any of it did he remember driving to Van Ander's home, confronting Marcia, and strangling her and killing her. How could he? It didn't happen. It couldn't have, that much, he was sure.

From the Van Ander residence, Beckett went home and surveyed his quarters. They looked just a little different to him and he knew why. He was looking at them, for the very first time, like they were the residence of someone else—a murder suspect—who happened to be him. As Beckett, the cop, he would do due diligence—search the place and search it well for Marcia's little gold chain and any other possible evidence, including checking his shoes to see if any of them showed traces of dried grass on the soles.

Wearing disposable protective gloves, Beckett went into his only closet of his one-bedroom mobile home rummaging through the pockets of slacks, jeans, and dress pants first. They yielded ninety-eight cents in change he didn't know he had, two phone numbers he couldn't identify, and a very stale stick of Wrigley's Juicy Fruit gum.

Next, he carefully sifted through the pockets of his shirts and jackets, including the brown sports jacket he wore that night. He remembered he wore the jacket so seldom any more. He had dropped seven pounds since he wore it regularly. Now the jacket was a little loose around the middle and didn't hang quite right, so he didn't wear it very much, always making a note to have it cut down at the tailor's and always forgetting to have it done. Zippo. Nothing in any of the pockets and no bits of grass struck to them, no marks. Nothing.

Lastly, he tackled examining his shoes for signs of any physical evidence. He even checked his jogging shoes thoroughly for good measure. Nothing in the brown ones he wore that night, but checked them all anyway. Why? He didn't know why. It was just the way he did things as a cop—routine but thorough.

As Beckett put his right hand into one of three pairs of black shoes, he froze. Gingerly, he retrieved what his fingers had discovered: a fourteen-inch, twenty-four carat gold chain. His fingers trembled as he held it up to look more closely at it. Oh, my God, was it Marcia's? Could it be, could it possibly be?

Beckett got off his knees and put the chain in a dry and secure sealable evidence collection bag, the kind he always carried in which to place small items, bits of evidence. He found himself wanting to turn the shoe over to look at the sole. He did and he found what he didn't want to find: tiny bits of dried grass clinging to the bottom of the shoe.

He sighed, audibly, and lay the shoe on the floor, topside up.

Then he picked up its mate and examined it closely. More tiny fragments of dried grass, before placing the second shoe next to the first shoe soles up.

"Dear God!" He said it so softly if someone were at his shoulder, they might not have heard it.

At that very moment, Beckett almost knelt and said a prayer, but forgot that he didn't pray any more. After a long moment, he picked up the shoes and placed them carefully on the kitchen table. Then he called the station.

"Give me Batters. This is Beckett."

After the longest of pauses, Batters finally answered.

Chief Batters."

"Tom? It's Beckett. I've found something. Will you be there?"

Batters confirmed that he would.

"Yes, I will."

The Chief had worked with Beckett long enough to sense something was wrong and sounded disturbed about something. Batters pressed him further.

"What is it?"

Beckett took a deep breath and what he was about the say he never thought he would in a million years.

"I'm bringing in your murderer…me."

21

When he arrived at the Palm Springs police station later that morning, Beckett expected a squadron of police cars would waiting there for him and would be handcuffed and charged. He was surprised to find only Chief Batters standing outside in the parking lot. He thought for sure he would be taken in to custody while they built a case against him for the murder of Marcia Van Ander based on the physical evidence he had uncovered.

Instead, Batters stuck his head in the passenger side window.

"Let's take a drive," he said quietly, and opened the door and got in.

Beckett wasn't sure what this was all about—he suspected the Chief knew something he didn't and played along.

"Where to?" he asked.

"Nowhere...Anywhere. Let's talk."

Beckett turned the ignition key and drove off. An eerie silence pervaded the air around them. They didn't talk, not for about two or three minutes. Batters was waiting for Beckett to begin. Beckett was trying to find a way to start and finally broke the silence as Batters sat and listened.

"I thought you were a little crazy when you told me to investigate myself. But I found some things. Let me tick them off for you."

Beckett then told him how he had confirmed Connors' story about the helicopter passing over around the time of the murder, and that was, indeed, a full moon that night. But the important things he saved for last, for effect, maybe.

Batters' eyes widened as he told hm about the gold chain and the grass clippings dried to the soles of his shoes. He examined the chain carefully, using a ballpoint pen to hold it up in front of himself without physically touching it, as well as the soles of Beckett's shoes. As Batters sat the evidence down, they were passing the Cask and Cleaver restaurant. Batters jerked a thumb at the restaurant indicating for Beckett to pull in and park.

"Let's grab some coffee and talk some more."

Beckett tooled into the driveway and surrendered his sports utility vehicle to the valet after carefully placing the bagged evidence in the truck for safe keeping. He looked at Batters for approval and got a reassuring nod.

They walked in and wondered whose voice it was that was welcoming them, the darkness so engulfing after stepping out of the hot summer sun into restaurant.

"Two for lunch, gentlemen?" the male host to whom the voice belong belonged queried back at them.

They asked for and got the most isolated table in the back. As soon as they were ushered to it and took a seat, Batters said to Beckett, "Interesting. Interesting as hell, all that stuff. You've done a good job, but I think you're a little off track in naming yourself as the murderer. I know you instinctively believe because of the evidence you uncovered you murdered Marcia. You're a good cop. But so am I. Now listen to this, it's the other side of it and there's always another side, right?"

Batters didn't wait for a response. He wasn't through yet.

"You confirmed the helicopter overhead and the full moon above that. That doesn't place you at the scene of the crime at all.

It only places Connors there. He says he saw you. Maybe it wasn't you. We know for certain he was there, he saw the moon, the helicopter and someone threatening Mrs. Van Ander."

Beckett wondered where Batters was going with this. He certainly didn't sound like a man who thought that Beckett was guilty of murder.

"The shoes with the grass clippings on them. Are they clippings from that specific patch of grass in that specific garden? They may not be. It may be a coincidence. We all walk over wet grass, don't we? Sometimes, it's freshly cut. I walked over some to get to the parking lot to meet you. If grass was freshly cut and wet with dew or a sprinkler, some of the grass would be sticking to my shoes right now and be there until I wore that same pair of shoes again, right?"

"Right," Beckett said. His face brightened almost immediately considering the new possibilities the Chief had raised.

"The chain. That's a toughie. No explaining that chain. There are only two logical explanations," Batters offered. "One is that you did yank the chain off the girl's throat and you did kill her. The other is that someone else did that, someone who knew she was wearing a chain at the time of the murder, and that someone planted that chain in your closet in that shoe."

Beckett's head was whirling. The Chief was right on all counts so far.

"But, Tom, aren't we asking for an awful lot of coincidences, and then conspiracy, to eliminate what looks like a pretty good circumstantial case against me?"

Batters, easing back in his seat, nodded in agreement.

"We are. Your goddamned right we are. Because I don't believe you did it, and you didn't want to believe it, and if you're faltering, I'm telling you I wouldn't send you up for ten or twenty years on the kind of evidence that you've just handed me."

"But how much of that is colored by our friendship and the fact that I'm your cop," Beckett asked, "and if I went up for murder it would reflect on you and the department?"

"You dumb Mick," Batters said in a tiny explosion of anger that quickly subsided. "You'll be Irish all your life. Do you think for one minute I'd cover for you if I thought you murdered that girl? Not in a fuckin' world series of Sundays. You don't know me very well or you wouldn't even suggest it."

"I'm sorry, Tom. My head is so clogged…"

"I understand. Now…where in the hell is the coffee we ordered?"

The waiter materialized at that very moment with two cups, sugar, sweet and low, saccharine, and honey.

"No lunch, thanks."

Batters made the comment without considering if Beckett wanted to order something to eat and Beckett never corrected him. It didn't seem important at the time—his stomach was too tied up in knots to eat anyway.

Batters prepped his coffee before taking a sip and continuing.

"When I asked you to look at Luke Beckett, the suspect, I had no idea you'd find anything in your closet. But look on this as a plus. Let's both assume that you didn't kill the girl. We've got to start there, Luke. So, assume you didn't kill her, someone else did. Who does that other someone else look like more than anyone else?"

Beckett blurted out the answer without any hesitation in his mind.

"Frank Connors."

"Of course. Why? Because he's the man who sees the full moon and he's the man who hears the helicopter and he's the man who knows about the little gold chain, although some of the other party guests will confirm she wore it if she wore it and he's the man who watered the lawn by mistake and would be painfully aware of those grass clippings. Am I right?"

Beckett shook his head. Suddenly, the knot in his stomach wasn't so strong and the cobwebs were clearing.

"Tom, I swear to God," Beckett declared and he didn't lightly, "I was going to turn myself in when I came to the station."

"I know that. I read it in your voice on your phone and saw it in your face when you drove up," Batters said momentarily pausing before resuming. "There was the same kind of blank it in when I had to tell you that someone had killed your ex-wife. Let's finish the coffee and split. I've got a department to run, you've got a murderer to catch."

Beckett felt so emotional he was having a difficult time speaking. He wanted to thank this man who turned out to be his best friend.

"Tom, I... There isn't anything..."

Batters looked at him and averted his eyes.

"Just get this goddamned case over with," he said feistily. "I've got some really rotten assignments for you after this, and I cannot wait to see your face when I hand them to you."

"Thanks a lot. I can always count on you to screw up my life!"

"You better believe it, turkey," Batters said with a chuckle.

It was the way hard-nosed cops made love to each other. The only way they dared.

Batters went back to his routine and Beckett went into his own office, shut the door, took the phone off the hook, and began pacing up and down. What was there about Connors that he didn't know, hadn't found out yet, hadn't even thought of? He had done a complete check of the man's background all the way back to elementary school. There was nothing distinctive or unusual anywhere in it. He was Mr. Lower Middle Class. The kind that gets lost in the crowd. People who were introduced to his kind forgot about him in half an hour.

Connors was something of a loser. Here, he was in his forties and he was a handyman. No handyman, no matter how handy, could command much of a salary and enjoy much of a lifestyle. But many people are content with very little in their lives. Not everyone aspires to have the big house on the hill, the air-conditioned Cadillac, the private club membership. On the other hand, maybe Connors had been like Charles—living very well in the millionaire's mansion and eating the finest food and drinking the finest booze and maybe bringing a girl over on his day off to impress her with his surroundings.

What was Connors' link to Marcia? Why murder her of all people? What possible motive could he have had for killing her?

That one wasn't too difficult to figure, the oldest story in the world: Marcia, young, beautiful, sensuous; Connors, unattractive, middle-aged, fantasizing about putting that gorgeous young thing in his bed. A man his age, frustrated and unattractive secretly lusting after the beautiful young mistress of the manor. He had admitted as much in his second polygraph test.

It could have happened. Maybe it did.

Those soft-porn magazines Beckett saw in Connors' old quarters at the Van Ander house told him that Connors may have been sexually frustrated. If he was in a serious relationship with another woman, he wouldn't have to drool over pictures of other naked women. What did that well-known, prominent sex therapist on Maury Povich's syndicated tabloid talk show, *Maury*, call them? "Masturbation magazines," he said, adding, "They might even be healthy for single men to get their pleasure off this way instead of letting the lack of sex build up and then they may develop other bad habits."

Beckett called Mary Ann Morrison and was relieved to find her at home. She was as friendly and welcoming as always when Beckett rang the doorbell. He kept their chat strictly professional and on task, explaining his reason for calling her. He asked her several specific questions leading up to what had been rattling around in his mind.

"Was Marcia wearing a plain gold chain that night?"

Mary Ann racked her brain and came up blank.

"Sorry, I can't remember."

Failing to yield anything new and relevant, Beckett thanked her for her time, left, and called some of the others he hadn't spoken to in quite some time and asked them about the chain. None of them could recall what kind of chain Marcia was wearing that evening, if any, and Beckett drew blanks when asking them if they could be more specific.

Just when things looked hopelessly deadlocked, Beckett's cell phone rang. It was Mary Ann. Beckett didn't have to prod her all. She started gabbing and didn't stop.

"Yes, I remember now," she said excitedly. "Marcia did wear a little chain around her neck at the party because she had gone in the swimming pool. I remember her carefully removing it to swim and then asking for help in putting it back on after she got out of the water and dried off."

"So, it was the chain she wore that night?" Beckett asked.

"Absolutely."

"We'll talk again soon, Mary Ann. You've been a big help."

After ending the call, Beckett thought about the shoes and grass clippings. He went out to his car, scraped some of the dried clippings off the soles, and drove to the Green Giant Nursery outside of Palm Springs. If the man who greeted him was the Green Giant himself, Beckett imagined, he's shrunk. The little man with coke bottles for glasses looked like a bug, but he was a gentle little soul and cooperative.

"Could you tell, by looking at these grass clippings, if this was a special kind of grass," Beckett asked while handing the evidence he had collected from the bottom of his shoes.

"Yes, I can. Give a minute."

The man walked off with the grass clippings in the sealed evidence bag Beckett had stored them and returned within minutes.

"No, it isn't very special," he said. "It's annual rye. You see it all over Palm Springs."

"Thank you very much. That's exactly what I was looking for."

As Beckett turned to walk away, the Green Giant-less man took advantage of Beckett trying to sell him some other goods.

"How about some roses to take home with you today?"

Beckett paused and then said, "No. No thanks, the roses sound fine but I live in a mobile home without a yard."

"You could grow them in a window box," the whispery-voiced, balding man said.

"Good idea. But maybe some other time. Thanks anyway."

Beckett turned and walked off giving him a short wave of appreciation for his help as he did and drove off.

Robert Sherman, the Sotheby's International real estate agent at the Van Ander home, wasn't too happy to see Beckett again. He reminded the lieutenant of a no sale so far with his listing because of all the negative publicity surrounding it.

"Yes, of course, you can go back to the garden," Sherman said with a forced smile on his face that looked plastered on. "Every other person who comes to the house pretending they're interested in buying it heads right for the garden. Morbid curiosity, I guess. It's becoming the biggest tourist attraction in Palm Springs."

Beckett bent down and took some cuttings from the grass in the garden. They looked just like the clippings he had shown the tiny Green Giant at the local nursery. He headed back to the nursery and waited for the small man to finish selling a tourist a $12.50 arrangement of mums and vase that was $2.50 extra.

The little man extolled the virtues of the woman's purchase.

"Yes, it would be a perfect as a hello gift to the relatives you have dropping in and that are staying with you."

"Perfect!" the woman said, beaming.

After the woman left, the little Green Giant salesman remembered Beckett right away and greeted him with a warm smile.

"You're back. Changed your mind I bet on buying the roses."

"No. Nothing's changed," Beckett said emphatically. "I have some other grass clippings I'd like you examine. Are they the same as the ones I showed you before?"

Little Green Giant fixed his expert bespectacled eyes on the clippings. He held them up with his fingers, went to the cash register, and returned with a magnifying glass. He studied both sets of clippings closely. Then he smiled.

"These," the nursery man said pointing to the clippings from the shoes, "are as I told you the annual rye variety." He paused and, pointing to the fresh clipped samples Beckett had collected from the garden, then added, "These are from the Bermuda family."

Beckett could have kissed little Green Giant, thought twice about it, and decided he had better not. Instead, he thanked him profusely for his help and in appreciation bought a dozen roses from him before walking back into the burning sunlight to his hotter than Hades Ford Explorer.

Afterward, Beckett stopped off at Jo Ann's apartment, but she wasn't home and Mrs. Carmody on the first floor took the roses from Beckett to give to her later.

"I'll put them in fresh water for her," she said, approving of Beckett's choice of flowers. "They should stay nice and fresh until the young lady gets home from wherever she's gone."

"Thank you, Mrs. Carmody," Beckett said thinking how Jo Ann probably didn't qualify to be called "a young lady," but to someone as old as Mrs. Carmody she would.

When Beckett returned to the station, Chief Batters was out for the rest of the day and evening, so Beckett texted the him a note with important details for him to read at his leisure:

> Tom:
> A Big One! I took the grass clippings from my black shoes and cut some new samples from the grass at the Van Ander home and had the man at Green Giant Nursery compare them. He says they came from two different places entirely, and they're not even the same kind of grass. I'm having the lab double check that, but I think we can safely assume it was a frame. Someone who thought grass was just grass didn't bother to take that shoe all the way back to the Van Ander's garden to stick the grass on it. They probably

went right around the corner from my house. Entry into and out of my place is almost too easy. I checked that, too. A five-year-old kid could pick the lock. You can do it with a common nail. I'm working on something else, too. Be in touch before nightfall.
Luke

Beckett's spirits were higher than at any time since Marcia's murder. He wasn't out of it, not yet, but things were starting to look better. Then it hit him like a jolt. Things weren't all that good, at least as he first thought. There was one thing standing in the way of Connors being the murderer, and it was no small thing. Connors had passed the second polygraph test. How did that square with all the other theories and evidence that seemed to point to him? Something was wrong, somewhere, but Beckett couldn't figure out what it was.

Beckett did what he hadn't done yet. The next morning, he gassed up his Ford Explorer and headed for Downey, a suburb of Los Angeles approximately 91 miles from Palm Springs. For the first time since he was a little boy, he was going to see a priest and not just any priest. This was one special. He was Frank Connors' brother.

22

It was the longest of long shots, but Beckett decided to take it. It cost him nothing to try, except a tank of gas and a two-hour drive each way. He couldn't shake the idea from his head Frank Connors' brother, though he was a priest, was the one man who could help him solve the murder case. He remembered Connors saying that before he came into the police station to tell all he knew about Beckett, he had gone to his brother for advice and counsel.

Beckett had had lots of experience with priests, both personal and professional. As a cop, they frustrated him. They knew everybody's darkest secrets. They heard all and told nothing. He remembered Father Cavanaugh back in Hollywood. Every hustler on the street who thought he was still a Catholic unburdened all his crimes to Father Cavanaugh, and he wouldn't so much as give Beckett the time of day if he asked for a clue as to who had been doing what to whom, including murder. It was all between the doer and Father Cavanaugh and God so to speak.

When Beckett arrived in Downey, he began looking for a tavern. That was like trying to find hay in a haystack and he soon found himself sitting at the bar of Bisby's Tavern, ordering a beer, and trying to convince a buxom blonde bar girl he didn't want lunch at 10:30 in the morning so soon after having a big breakfast at Bob's Big Boy before making the drive from Palm Springs. That tavern was directly across the street from a factory. The night shift had gone off duty three-and-a-half hours before, but most of the hangers-on with no other place to go were still swilling beer and singing Karaoke songs, and doing a terrible job of it.

Beckett almost had to shout into his cell phone to be heard and the voice on the other end was so faint he couldn't make out all the words. Finally, he cursed, ended the call, paid for his beer, and stalked out. Outside, he called the Catholic Archdiocese Chancery office in Los Angeles and lucked out. The lady on the other end was pleasant, cooperative, and bright.

"I'm trying to locate a priest named Connors at a parish in Downey," Beckett explained. "Can you help me?"

"Yes, I can look that up for you. Please hold."

The woman inadvertently forgot to put the call on hold, so Beckett could hear her clicking on a keyboard as she typed in the priest's name. She returned shortly realizing Beckett was on the phone the entire time.

"So sorry, lieutenant," he apologized. "I'm new here and I am still learning how to use their phone system."

"It's okay. I understand."

"I looked up the information you wanted in our computer database. I'm sorry, but there is no Father Connors at any Catholic church in the entire Downey area. There had been a Father Connors at St. Stephen's, but he went back to Ireland about a year ago."

"Are you sure?"

"Yes, lieutenant," she reaffirmed. "Our database covers all churches, monasteries and schools. There isn't a Father Connors at any of them."

"Thanks, I guess. Can I call you again if I need assistance?"

"Anytime, lieutenant."

Beckett couldn't believe it. Another dead end and no Father Connors, of all the luck. Had Frank Connors made him up? Why should he? What end would that serve? He sounded so sincere when he said he had gone to Downey to ask his brother's advice and counsel. No need to say something like that if it wasn't true, knowing full well the police would check out his alibi.

As Beckett was leaving the scene, a beefy-faced cop walked up and stuck out his hand.

"Remember me?"

"Yes," Beckett said, but the tone of his voice said no.

The cop grinned broadly. One tooth was missing near the right corner of his mouth.

"Bullshit. I know you don't. You were a sergeant in Hollywood and we were both sent down about the same time."

That rang a bell. Beckett remembered who the man was and what he had done to deserve being reprimanded. He had been caught shaking down hookers and he beat one up one night. Unfortunately, for Fat Jack Baker, Internal Affairs officers had been following him and they saw the whole thing. Goodbye, Hollywood. Hello, Downey.

"Yeah," Beckett said, "it's all becoming clear to me now."

"Whatcha doin' up here?" Fat Jack asked.

"Oh, it's a real pain in the ass. I'm getting a plaque from the Good Government League and I have to line up one of those places that rents tuxedos."

Fat Jack lost interest and melted into the background. It was at that point Beckett spotted the priest. He was standing outside a Catholic run counseling group, and had accompanied a teenage boy and his parents. They were having some of sort of conversation with a social worker, and Beckett waited until their business had been completed. As the group turned to leave, Beckett walked over, put a hand on the priest's arm, and asked if he could talk to him for a moment. The priest said goodbye to the parents and the young boy, and Beckett asked the priest to sit down.

This guy looked like a priest was supposed to look, Beckett thought. Tall, athletic build, a face that looked too young to be topped by silver white hair. Beckett wasted no time introducing himself.

"Father, I'm Lt. Beckett of the Palm Springs police."

"Father Walsh."

"Glad to know you father. Here's my problem."

The priest listened with apparent great interest. He had been in Downey for eleven years, hinting that he lost his parish in Burbank because of a drinking problem. A very candid fellow this Father Walsh was.

"I think I know every Catholic priest in this town," Father Walsh said, "and probably all of the Episcopalians as well. It's a common Irish name, Connors, but I'd bet there isn't a Connors in town right now, hasn't been for some time."

Father Walsh paused and then added, "Are you sure that it's a priest you're looking for?"

Beckett's face instantly brightened. Father Walsh inadvertently provided the alternative clue Beckett was looking for.

"Bless you, father, you're broke my mental log jam, loosened the block that was hanging me up. Thanks father, I appreciate your help more than you know."

Father Walsh turned and left and Beckett decided his next course of action was to look up all the Connors living in Downey. There couldn't be that many of them. He used the Whitepages app on his smartphone to retrieve the information. There were twenty-three Connors residing in Downey, including their names, addresses, and phone numbers, and he started calling them individually. Seven didn't answer. Those who did were plumbers, barbers, factory workers, a fireman, a jewelry salesman, a woman bartender, a manufacturer of plastic ash trays, a pharmacist, and an unemployed aerospace worker. Not a priest in the lot, and none of them had a relative named Frank Connors who lived in Palm Springs.

Of the seven who didn't answer, Beckett could tell by their Whitepages app listings that three of them were in business and that's why they were not at home when he called. Two of the businesses were listed, so he called them: Pat Connors who had no brothers, and Lawrence Connors who had a brother but was living in Europe and worked in the import-export business.

That left Charles Connors who operated a hardware store. Beckett called the hardware store who informed him that the boss was "out to lunch." Beckett decided to drive there and make an in-person visit.

It was a nice hardware store, too. Not a chain, but a well-stocked and well-lighted independently owned-and-operated one with an ample number of clerks, all of whom wore neat smocks like dentists' wear, except theirs were bright orange with purple letters that said, "Connors Hardware, Depend on Us."

Beckett strolled in, saw no one who looked like the boss and then saw someone who looked like his assistant. He guessed right. He was a brassy, bossy young man named Stephen who told Beckett when asked, "Mr. Connors is due back any moment. He is still at lunch. Is there anything I can do to help you?"

"No. No thanks," Beckett said.

"We have a special on hammers today. Two for the price of one."

"I'll wait. Thanks."

Wait he did. For about forty-five minutes before Mr. Connors returned. As he walked in the door, Beckett blinked, then broke out in a Cheshire Cat-like grin across his face after studying the man closely. When he thought about it, Downey wasn't the grim little town he had thought it would be. No sir, it might even be the prettiest little city in the whole world, and this was one of the happiest days of Luke Beckett's life.

Beckett stepped outside the store momentarily out of the sight of Mr. Connors and his assistant to call the station. He got Lt. Garcia and made an unusual request of him.

"Get hold of Frank Connors and bring him to the station. It's important that you stash him inside without the Chief seeing him. I know that sounds off, but trust me. I'm trying something and if it works, I think I might be able to wrap the Van Ander case. But it's important that you don't tell Connors what we're up to."

"Okay," Garcia said unequivocally. "He was at home last night. But what are you up to?"

Beckett bristled at the question, and felt Garcia should know better than to ask.

"It's a long goddamned story. When I get there, I'll cue you in on it, okay?"

Garcia could tell Beckett had reached his limit and went along with his request.

"Fine," Garcia said. "Where will I find Connors?"

Beckett gave him two addresses he had stored in his smartphone.

"Connors has to be on the premises when I get there," Beckett said and then suddenly looked at his watch. "Within two hours from now. But it's very important that Batters doesn't see him. Understand?"

"Right," Garcia confirmed. "Then you'll owe me one, right?"

Beckett laughed but not so loud anyone could hear him.

"Sure. Do this for me and I'll buy you that tactical military watch that does everything but make coffee that you've had your eyes on."

"An all-expense paid trip to Rosarito Beach to visit my family would be even better."

"Don't push your luck," Beckett chuckled and then hung up.

Beckett went back into the hardware store and took another look at Charles Connors. Then he headed directly for the Downey police department to look up an old friend, Capt. Rudy Trumbull.

Meanwhile, back at the Palm Springs station, Chief Batters was more than a little upset with Beckett. Batters had finally received and read his text message—everything Beckett told him about the grass clippings, which was good news—after a snafu with his phone's text message software had resolved itself the next morning. But Beckett had not said where he was going or what he was doing, and that always made his superior officer nervous. Beckett was a good cop but an unconventional one. The kind of cop who can give his chief an ulcer. Batters couldn't be that sure he didn't already have one, thanks partly to Beckett.

Batters considered calling Beckett, but decided to hold off. He knew if he called him that he would blow his top and might say or do something that would not help solve the murder of Mrs. Van Ander. That doesn't mean he didn't sit there and stew about it.

It was nearly 5 P.M. when Beckett walked through the door to Batters' office.

"Where the hell have you been?" the Chief ranted. "I had a couple of warrants you could have served and that Mrs. Ritchie, who thinks you're Robin Hood, said you promised to speak to that neighbor of hers she thinks is looking at her with high-powered binoculars whenever she takes a shower."

"Chief, Mrs. Ritchie is 79 years old."

"So? Maybe the Peeping Tom is eighty-one."

"Look," Beckett said, "I've got something here I want you to see."

Batters tried to beg off. He was up to his ears in paper work and still mad at Beckett for leaving him in the dark.

"No, Chief, this is important. Believe me."

Batters yielded with an impatient shrug and Beckett disappeared and returned with Charles Connors in tow. Connors looked tired, and more than a little crestfallen.

"Chief, you know this man?" Beckett asked.

Batters stared at Beckett as if he was on some of the nasty stuff that was taken out of the Sanchez boy's pockets the night before and then at Connors standing before him.

"Of course, how are you, Mr. Connors?"

Beckett grinned, enjoying every second of his little dream.

"But you've never met before, Chief."

Batters, impatient, said, "What's the matter with you, Beckett? Have you flipped out?"

"Chef, you're looking at Mr. Connors all right. But not Frank Connors. This is Charles Connors."

Batters turned his head slowly. He fixed his stoniest stare on Charles Connors' face and couldn't believe his eyes.

"My God!" he blurted in disbelief.

"Yeah, that's what I said."

Batters was looking at as perfect a twin as he had ever seen in his life.

Beckett walked to the threshold of the door and yelled, "Lieutenant Garcia!"

Garcia's head popped out the doorway of a small room at the end of the hall.

"Yeah?"

"Bring him in here, will you?

Garcia had kept Frank Connors completely in the dark like Beckett had instructed him. He had been told only that he was being brought in for questioning again, and that didn't make him very happy. When no questions came and he realized Garcia was literally guarding him, Connors had become very nervous and angry. When he walked through the Chief's door, he was ready to threaten "to sue everyone in sight."

Then he saw his brother Charles and all the starch went out of him.

"You!" he said with an accusatory tone. "Tell them nothin'. Nothin', you hear?" He was shouting by this point.

Charles Connors looked down at his own shoes. Batters didn't like being fooled, for effect or otherwise. He then turned to Beckett.

"Okay, what the hell is this all about?"

Beckett motioned everybody to chairs and the Connors brothers made it plain they didn't want to sit anywhere near one another.

"I found Charles here in a hardware store in Downey. He owns it," Beckett explained. "Remember Frank Connors had said in his statement that he had gone to Downey for some advice and counsel from his brother. He said his brother was a priest. Of course, he's not."

Batters was a very sharp cop, at least as sharp as Beckett, if not a whole lot less expressive.

"Are you about to tell me," Batters asked, "what I think you're about to tell me?"

Beckett knew he had guessed the rest, but this was his moment in the limelight and he might as well enjoy it.

"This is what Charles told me, and I've got it all down in a signed statement witnessed by two other officers at the Downey police station. All nice and legal."

Frank Connors glared at his brother Charles, who still refused to look at him.

Summarizing the facts of the case from Charles' signed and sworn statement, Beckett continued without stumbling over his words.

"Frank Connors knew we had next to nothing on him. There was only one thing he feared and that was the possibility we might ask him to take a lie detector test. He could refuse, but that might make us even more suspicious," Beckett explained. "Well, he had an out that few people had: An identical twin brother. It took some convincing to get Charles Connors to do it, but Charles owed Frank a couple of big ones from way back, and Charles eventually and reluctantly agreed to go along with it, although he was scared shitless to do it."

Beckett paused a moment and then added, "That's why Charles' first polygraph test was inconclusive. He was terrified at the thought that he might be exposed. Anyway, he composed himself enough for the second test, and he passed it. No way he couldn't pass it, if you remember the questions. He had never met Marcia, had never even seen her, had no motive for killing her. He knew nothing about the crime, really, because his brother Frank even convinced him it was a frame by the cops, and so he half-believed Frank was innocent. I say half, because Frank's been in trouble before, but nothing this big."

In his frustration, Frank Connors tried to leap out of his chair and attack his brother Charles, but Garcia, alert for just such an eventuality, quickly restrained him.

"Any more of that and I'll put you in restraints," Batters warned Frank Connors.

"That dirty, lying, squealing motherfucker," Frank Connors screamed.

"Goodness," Beckett said, "is that any way to talk to a priest?"

The muscles in Charles Connor's face began twitching uncontrollably. He was a shy man, and abhorred any kind of trouble. The tension was unnerving him and it finally began to show.

Beckett wasn't finished. Piece-by-piece, he methodically laid out the facts he had uncovered that, combined with the physical evidence, would tie Frank Connors to Marcia's senseless murder.

"Charles helped fill in Frank's background. He always like the ladies, but they didn't like him very much. So, when he had a chance to get married, Frank jumped at it. Charles was his best man. What he jumped at was a woman ten years his senior with a face like five miles of bad road and a figure like a blown-up laundry bag," Beckett said. "It wasn't long before Frank was hanging around the high school in his neighborhood and wouldn't you know it, he finally talked a fourteen-year-old girl into looking at his etchings one day when her mother was downtown waiting on tables."

Frank Connors began mumbling incoherently at this point, and Lt. Garcia stuck a long finger in his chest that quieted him again.

"Well, says Charles, Frank got off the hook, paid off the girl's old man, who wasn't much better than Frank himself, and that's why we couldn't find a criminal record on him," Beckett noted.

"He later got a seventeen-year-old girl pregnant, and the same thing happened. Payoff. That one broke up his marriage and that's when he headed for Palm Springs and the anonymity of a handyman's job with Van Ander. The rest is easy."

Batters grunted his approval, Frank Connors cursed audibly, Charles Connors sighed and Lt. Garcia whistled that low whistle he reserved for times when he was impressed. This moment was one of them.

Suddenly, without provocation, Batters turned to Frank Connors and asked, "What do you have to say about this now, Mr. Connors?"

"You can all go fuck yourselves!" he shouted.

The rest was downhill from there. On the advice of his lawyer, Frank Connors pleaded guilty to Marcia Van Ander's murder. A jury trial was held three months later at Superior Court in Indio with Judge Horatio Alvarez presiding. It was one of the most covered murder trials in Palm Springs Police Department history. Mobile television news trucks from all the major broadcast and cable news networks, including all Los Angeles and local news channels, televised live reports from the scene with updates throughout the day and night. Reporters from every major news organization—newspapers, wire services and news syndicates and national radio networks—descended on the perimeter of the courtroom like a pack of locust to report on the latest "Breaking News" every day as the trial proceeded.

During the trial, Frank Connors' lawyer sought to get Connors off with a lighter sentence pleading "diminished capacity" at the time of the murder for his client. He painted a picture of Connors—as a hard luck guy all his life who never got a break—that seemed to move the jury until the evidence presented in court stacked against him. The number of witnesses willing to testify were plentiful and all them came and testified, including Charles, the butler, Dolores Colter, the maid, and Mary Ann Morrison, Marcia's lesbian lover. Each were credible in their testimonies, reciting chapter and verse everything they had told Beckett in previous interviews during the long and laborious murder investigation.

It wasn't until the trial that Beckett under oath remembered why he would not have worn those shoes initially thought to have linked him to the murder of his ex-wife, proving otherwise. As he testified in front of a packed courtroom:

"They were black, and the night of Marcia's murder, I wore my brown sport jack and slacks. I would never wear black shoes with a brown outfit. Besides, the shoes were a little tight and too new to throw away, so they just sat there in the closet, rarely used."

The most damning testimony of all was from Charles Connors, Frank's identical twin brother who testified against him. During cross-examination, Connors, sitting sternly on the witness stand, pushed aside any personal feelings he may have had for his brother and told the judge and jury everything he knew without reservation to the cold, hard stares of Frank looking on.

As revealed in his testimony, Mrs. Van Ander may or may not have tried to frustrate his brother Frank sexually, but the fact she had made a habit of sunning in the nude almost every day around the swimming pool because she liked an all-over tan left her open for trouble. While it was understood that Charles, the butler, and Frank would give the pool area a wide berth at those times, Frank used to watch her through a mail slit in the door of his quarters. He would crouch there, "peering through the horizontal mail slot, frequently fantasizing about having this beautiful, vivacious young woman for his own. That had driven him to the point of distraction and ecstasy and the night of the party, he drank too much and successfully lured Marcia into the darkened garden on the pretense that he would tell her something very important that he had overheard her husband, Lionel Van Ander, say about her that she deserved to know."

Marcia never dreamed that Frank Connors could harm her. She had assumed they always had a good mistress-servant relationship.

When he struck, it was without warning. She had no chance to cry out, he testified.

As Charles added during his emotion-filled testimony: "When Mrs. Van Ander lay at his feet, dead, my brothers' mind began working overtime. At first, he wanted to panic and run. But then he decided on a plan so crazy he thought it might work. He knew about Marcia's previous marriage to the police lieutenant. According to my brother, it was common Palm Springs gossip, and the servants knew more than their masters in the desert did."

Immediately following his brother's testimony, Frank Connors took the stand. He had a look of man who was off the rails mentally and gave every indication he was through his actions and behavior—characteristically muttering one second and shouting wildly the next like a man strung out on drugs.

"I was always somewhere around the Van Ander house, manicuring the grounds," he confessed, "and frequently saw Beckett drive by the house."

Connors froze momentarily and stared daggers at Beckett sitting in the gallery. Antagonizing the good lieutenant gave him great pleasure, even though Beckett appeared unmoved by his attempt to get under his skin, and the assistant district attorney stepped forward and intervened.

"Mr. Connors, answer the question."

Suddenly, Connors body jerked and shuddered wildly without provocation that persisted for a good minute or more. Then, snapping back to reality, he calmly answered the district attorney's question speaking softly as if he had entered a confessional to confess his latest sins.

"On at least two occasions, I saw Mrs. Van Ander catch sight of the lieutenant's Ford Explorer and wave to him. I knew that they· had talked once on the premises and, once in town, when Beckett had taken her to lunch."

Connors suddenly paused and asked for a glass of water, took a long sip, and then stated how he devised his devious plan.

"I knew then they were still in love. They had this special way of looking at each other…"

Connor's voice trailed off for a second. Then, with his nerves on edge, he suddenly pointed his finger agitatedly at Beckett while speaking in a shaky voice.

"He was the perfect patsy. Yes, I planted the gold chain in that creep ass Beckett's shoe, dampened the soles and stuck some grass clippings on them. Why? Because he didn't deserve her and wasn't good enough for her. I was. I loved her and could give her the kind of love no man had before. Do you understand?"

Connors bolted from the stand like a madman and lunged toward Beckett in the front row with outstretched hands to strangle him. The bailiff quickly restrained and tackled him to the floor.

"Mr. Connors, one more outburst like that and I will hold you in contempt of court," Judge Alvarez said in a booming, authoritative voice,

Pulling him to his feet, the bailiff returned Connors to the witness stand where he went off half-cocked when questioning resumed telling the judge, the jury, and anyone listening why he murdered Marcia Van Ander.

"She had it coming to her. Taunting and teasing me every day with her sultry wet naked body and bountiful breasts glistening under the hot sun as I sweated and toiled around her for peanuts, and tempting me to have her above all else." Connors paused and licked his lips like the sick animal he was. "Oh, I gave it to her alright. When she wouldn't give me the time of day, I made her happy like no man ever could and she went out with a beautiful smile on her face."

Judge Alvarez pounded the gavel so hard it sounded like a series of gunshots ringing out in the courtroom as he tried to restore order.

"Mr. Connors, I warned you before, you are in contempt. Bailiff take him away."

Connors wriggled his way out of the bailiff's grip and plunged toward Beckett coming with an inch of striking him. Beckett immediately jerked back in his seat while the bailiff and an extra officer on duty handcuffed and hauled him out of the courtroom kicking and screaming.

"I'll get you for this, Beckett! I'd keep looking over your shoulder if I were you. You haven't heard the last of me."

Frank Connors was never heard from again. They would become the last words ever spoken by him in public or a court of law. By his own admission, he premeditatedly killed Marcia Van Ander that night in the garden of the Van Ander estate and the twelve jurors who sat through the exhausting testimony and deliberations over the evidence showed him no mercy. That afternoon, all participants reconvened in the courtroom for the jury to announce its decision.

After the jurors took their seats in the jury box, Judge Alvarez asked, "Has the jury reach a verdict?"

Jury foreperson Michael P. McGarry, a gray haired and goateed area resident of Irish descent, stepped forward. Clearing his throat, he unfolded a piece of paper in his hand. Then, with the faintest trace of Irish brogue in his speech, he read the verdict aloud as an uncharacteristically sedate and handcuffed and ankle shackled Connors, clad in an orange jumpsuit, stood before them.

"Yes, we have your Honor. We find the defendant guilty of the charge of first-degree murder."

The huddled mass of spectators in the gallery broke into a thunderous applause following the announcement. Chief Batters and Lt. Garcia were all smiles and joyous over the verdict. Beckett resisted joining them. Bowing his head momentarily, he stood there solemnly at first and then appeared more relieved that a huge weight had been lifted off his shoulders. Justice was rendered. It may have not been the kind of justice he had wanted—frying Connors in the electric chair or gassing him to death in the gas chamber wouldn't had been enough for the hideous crime he had committed, but at last the horrific case was over.

As celebrations rang out through the courtroom, Judge Alvarez finally slammed the gavel and ordered, "May I remind everyone this is a court of law and refrain from such demonstrations."

The bailiff moved toward the judge's bench handing Judge Alvarez the jury's verdict. Seconds later, he announced to the courtroom his sentencing, handing out the stiffest sentence allowed under California penal law.

"Mr. Connors, you willfully took the life of another without remorse for your actions and by your behavior here today, it is clear you deserved the stiffest sentence I can render," he said. "It is the decision of the court that you will be incarcerated for life in a state penitentiary without the possibility of parole for the crime committed."

Pounding the gavel one last time, the judge added, "Court dismissed."

Connors' attorney immediately ran out of the courtroom and filed an appeal that same day seeking a reduced sentence because of his client's "Insanity or lack of mental capacity," but was denied.

Meanwhile, all eyes were on Frank Connors while a pair of police officers duly escorted him out of the courtroom and await extradition to a maximum-security prison. On the other side of the room, Chief Batters and Lt. Garcia slowly shuffled their way to the exit with their eyes peeled for Beckett, who was nowhere to be found.

"That's the thanks I get for sticking by him I guess," Batters said with a shrug.

Beckett had inconspicuously snuck out a side door to escape the glare of photographers and television news people ready to pounce outside the courtroom to snag a comment from him on the decision handed down that day. Beckett wasn't so lucky, however. When Jim Conroy, a reporter for Palm Springs' own KESQ-TV, spotted him and shouted after him, "Lieutenant Beckett, a comment please on today's proceedings," the entire entourage of news people scurried over and engulfed him to get a sound bite, anything, from the man most responsible for solving the case.

Beckett, sporting military style sunglasses, halted as reporters bombarded him with a flurry of questions all at once. One reporter in the maddening crowd who won out was Casey Sampson, an overly eager, mid-thirties, blond haired reporter for Fox News Channel, who had pushed and shoved his way to the front of the pack.

"How are you feeling at this very moment?" he asked.

"What kind of question is that?" Beckett snapped.

Sampson quickly rebounded to amend his question.

"I mean, are you happy with the outcome?"

Beckett paused deliberately to collect his thoughts. He had a long time to think about such a question over the weeks in investigating Marcia Van Ander's murder if it were ever raised.

"As many of you know, Marcia Van Ander was my ex-wife. She was many things but, most of all, the most beautiful, caring, and loving person I have ever known. Today's decision will never bring her back. Was the sentencing tough enough? No. That's all I have to say."

Beckett started to briskly walk off but couldn't break through the horde of media encircling him and reporters peppered him with more questions.

"Lieutenant Beckett, Susan Strauss, ABC News. You, more than anyone, had much to lose, notably your job, in your handling of this investigation. What would you like to tell the public that hasn't been reported or written about you?"

Beckett eyed Strauss from behind his sunglasses with a melting glare.

"This investigation was never about me. It was about seeking the truth at all costs. Many of you know of my reputation as a tough-as-nails cop. Well, walk in my shoes for one day and you'll find it isn't as easy you think. I owed it to myself to see the case through to the end but, more importantly, to Marcia."

At the conclusion of his remarks, Beckett bolted through the crowd of reporters knocking down photographers and a television news crew in his path to his car parked on the street. He had said publicly all he was going to say on the matter. Try as they may, they couldn't keep up with him before finally retreating. As soon as Chief Batters and Lt. Garcia emerged, the pack of media ran back en masse to the courthouse steps and fired away with a round of questions at the pair from the Palm Springs Police Department that went on long after Beckett had departed.

For Luke Beckett, solving the murder of Marcia Van Ander would mark the crowning achievement of his long and experienced career in law enforcement. As he jumped into his Ford Explorer, turned the ignition key, and drove off, his mind wandered a bit. Then it was flooded with a single thought of the woman he still loved, Marcia. In his mind's eye, she was smiling radiantly from the heavens above in loving gratitude for a job well done.

For Beckett, he didn't need anything more as the warmth of her love swept over him and he faded from sight with the memories of her living on with him, forever.

Epilogue

Frank Connors is presently serving the first year of his life sentence at California State Prison Centinela, a male-only facility that houses some 3,000 inmates of all security levels, in Imperial, California. He is confined to a maximum-security cell block with what they call, "the worst of the worst" and most dangerous offenders. In a short time following his imprisonment and becoming a model citizen, Connors fittingly works in the prison library dispensing books and magazines to inmates.

For his full cooperation and court testimony, Frank's brother Charles Connors was granted full immunity and all charges against him were dropped. Connors walked scot-free and was allowed to go back to running his independent owned-and-operated hardware store in Downey, which was no small sentence.

At the conclusion of what many called "the greatest murder trial in the history of the department," Tom Batters, the longest serving chieftain in Palm Springs Police Department history, hung up his shield and retired as chief of police. The power elite of Palm Springs gave him a bigger sendoff than the former chief at the luxurious Hilton Hotel downtown. Now Batters spends his mornings playing golf at Bermuda Dunes Country Club and his evenings watching television or playing cards with fellow retirees from local law enforcement.

There's a new name on the door of the chief's office: Chief Robert Garcia. Since his promotion, he has added six new Hispanic officers to the force, and has effectively improved the department's standing with the undeserved Hispanic community in the region.

Charles, the Van Ander's former butler, changed positions again after his employment with the Emerson family didn't work out. He is now employed by that superstar comedian of film and television—his popular catchphrase, "Get Out of Here!" turned him into a worldwide sensation—who lives in the big house high up on the hill and splits his time between his opulent winter home and Bel Air residence in the Los Angeles area.

Dolores Colter quit working as housemaid and married again. She and her husband, Rafael, own and operate that new highly successful Mexican restaurant, Fernando's Hideaway, north of town and right near the Palm Springs tramway. Their specialty includes a "2-for-1 Margarita Special" every Tuesday and Thursday between 4 and 6 P.M. (no coupon needed).

Mary Ann Morrison is now blissfully married to another woman, Sheila Johnson, tall, athletic, and dark-haired, and following the murder trial moved as far from the desert as possible. They live in a three-bedroom oceanfront townhome in the seaside village of La Jolla, known for its seven miles of spectacular and breathtaking coastline along the Pacific Ocean, and run a small boutique there selling "Hers and Hers" items and accessories.

Carlo Robelli still gets his name and picture in newspapers and magazines whenever some feature writer decides to re-do the story of the "Mob in Palm Springs," and it happens at least twice a year. Arthritis has seriously crippled old Carlo, so he doesn't get around as much he once did but still rattles around in that big mansion of his and makes life miserable for underlings in the organization who unseated him.

Johnny Robelli sends Papa Carlo a Christmas card each year—the extent of his communication with his father these days, who has never reciprocated, since excommunicating him from the family. It's always postmarked Quito, Ecuador. Johnny put his good looks to work and married a South American oilman's beautiful vixen daughter, Carlotta Vargas. She's got a violent temper, and one day, she'll probably confirm her suspicions that he's dipping his pen in other inkwells, and he'll wake up one morning minus some key anatomical equipment.

His Honor, the bean-headed Mayor Parker, was re-elected to a third term by a wide margin in Palm Springs, largely due to his successful campaign to embrace a pro-gay agenda and proclaiming the city a sanctuary for the LBTQ+ community. For good measure, he has since erected a permanent statue in the heart of downtown honoring gays of all persuasions. So far, it has attracted more visitors annually than the towering statue of Marilyn Monroe with her upswept skirt.

Timmy Farrell, the notorious all-time confessor of crimes he didn't commit, finally hit pay dirt. The local Palm Springs *Desert Sun* newspaper ran a lengthy feature story telling about his proclivity for confessing, and a producer at Universal Studios saw it and now plans to make a movie about his life. It's tentatively titled, *The Compulsive Confessor*, and they're trying to get Tom Hanks to play the lead. Timmy wants to hold out for Matt Damon, but, then, he always was a dreamer.

Porky Kelp, poor devil, met a slim, attractive widow from Burbank who moved down to Palm Springs and put Porky on a strict diet and forced him into a regimen of aerobics and jogging to melt the pounds away. An outpouring of police officers, some as far away as Sacramento, California, came down for Porky's funeral. They figured they owed him that much.

Big-man mobster-turned grill master Jerry "The Torch" Cardoni finally put pen to paper and authored the cookbook of his dreams, *100 Recipes I Love and Better Buy or I'll Crown You*, with a foreword by an old family friend, actor Leonardo DiCaprio, after Cardoni made him an offer he just couldn't refuse. The book is selling so well, he is already planning a sequel, *100 More Recipes I Love and Buy This Book or Else!*

Peter "Parky" Bonnano's talking African grey Brando became such a huge hit with friends and neighbors and anyone who met him that Bonnano signed him up for exclusive representation with a Hollywood agent. Brando is busy trying out for character roles in major motion pictures and television shows, developing a stand-up comedy act to take to Las Vegas and beyond, and recently signed a recording contract with MCA Records to produce a solo album of him crooning all his favorite movie gangster songs, called *Rappin' to the Mob.*

Beckett's girlfriend Jo Ann Tracey met and married a *Chicago Tribune* reporter, Joseph Klimowski, who came to Palm Springs for a three weeks' vacation last December during that terrible cold snap in the Midwest. Jo Ann told her best friend she still loves someone else, but, "What the hell, I'm not getting any younger and he's a damned decent guy, even if he is a Polish."

Like all good reformed criminals, the infamous Ramirez brothers found Jesus. Amazingly, it was a triple conversation. All three "saw the light and heard the call" at the same time after that celebrated televangelist, Kenneth Jaffa, was quoted as saying during that now-famous *60 Minutes* interview how many American television ministers had become "instant multimillionaires." Now the Ramirez brothers have turned their natural talents to extorting souls for God.

And Luke Beckett?

Three months after Frank Connors was incarcerated for the murder of his ex-wife, Luke Beckett chose to go to an even worse place, New York City, where he's now a deputy police commissioner and forced by custom to lecture regularly before classes on criminology at a top criminal justice university downtown. In his spare time, he makes law and order noises before do-gooder civic luncheons. But about once a month, Beckett parks his braid in the closet, pulls on some well-worn old jeans and a plaid shirt, and goes stalking the predators on Seventh Avenue.

Once a cop, always a cop.

ABOUT THE AUTHOR

 JEFF LENBURG is a prolific, award-winning author of 35 books, both fiction and non-fiction, among them two bestsellers. His works include 18 acclaimed celebrity memoirs and biographies and more than a half-dozen entertainment histories and popular references that have been nominated for numerous awards, including the American Book Fest Best Book Awards for "Best Biography," the American Library Association's (ALA) "Best Non-Fiction Award," the Evangelical Christian Publisher Association's (ECPA) Gold Medallion Award for "Best Autobiography/Biography," the Foreword INDIES Book of the Year Award for "Best Biography," the Theatre Library Association (TLA) Award for "Best Performing Arts Book," and the annual International Book Awards for "Best Biography."

Jeff has interviewed and written about Hollywood legends and cinematic lore since he was 15. This is his second novel following his first cozy mystery, *Scared to Death: A Lori Matrix Hollywood Mystery*. He makes his home near Phoenix, Arizona, with his wife Debby.

For more information about Jeff's upcoming books and the latest news, visit www.jefflenburg.com.

Made in the USA
Middletown, DE
22 October 2022

13287876R00182